Also by J. M. M. Butterfield

Bastion: Holy City

J. M. M. BUTTERFIELD

THE GODS WHO FELL

CHRONICLES OF A STAR-BORN KING
BOOK TWO

First published in Australia in 2023 by J. M. M. Butterfield
Copyright © 2023 by J. M. M. Butterfield
www.jmmbutterfield.com

A catalogue record for this book is available from the National
Library of Australia.
ISBN 978 0 6483943 2 7 (paperback)
ISBN 978 0 6483943 3 4 (ebook)

Printed in Australia, United States or United Kingdom by
Ingramspark, Lightning Source Inc

Cover by Lara Hardy from Billie Hardy Creative
Images on license from Shutterstock

ACKNOWLEDGEMENTS

An enormous thank you to those individuals who have helped during the writing of book two. As always, thank you to my wife, Kelly Butterfield, for her enthusiasm and the occasional prod when I veer off track. Thanks to my children, Keira and Angus, for their love and support. To my test readers: Carol and Greg Butterfield, Jemima Hoult, Colin Smith, Gary Matthews and Gabrielle Cooper, your words of support after reading the first draft was incredibly encouraging and thoughtful. To Lara Hardy from Billie Hardy Creative, thank you for helping organise the cover. It looks amazing. And finally, to Paul Willmot and Elizabeth O'Brien, who both read book two and offered their expertise in regard to editing and structure. It takes time to write a book this size, and time enough to edit. Thank you for adding your time into its creation.

THE GODS WHO FELL

PROLOGUE

It was the sweet smell of wood-smoke that roused him.

Ra'tor rolled to his side and pushed heavy arms beneath him, sitting with some discomfit on cold stone beneath a pre-dawn sky. He rubbed his shoulder with a clawed hand, cursed under his tongue at the lack of heat to begin the day. On his home world, the sun - known as the Eye of Bhral - provided the Deios with warmth to fire the blood. Only here, in the dwelling place of the Lesser Beasts, the sun took until midday before it blazed hot enough to truly rouse him.

He repositioned his considerable bulk closer to the fire, let his eyes gaze into hypnotic flames licking dry timber. His brood had decided to collect the broken wood found scattered throughout the ruins. It was plentiful, burned easily, and added comfort during cool nights under unknown stars.

'In the name of the Blood-God, where are we?' Ra'tor lifted heavy eyes away from the fire, hoping first light would be soon. He could see a handful of his scouts standing near the shining blue walls of the temple, pacing quietly, their task to watch pathways leading away from the monstrosity. They'd defeated the Lesser Beasts ten days earlier in a battle of epic proportions, yet it would be folly to believe they were the only ones capable of fighting for this dwelling place. Since the defeated had fled, several others, of differing size and shape, had caught their eye, shifting on the fringes of their newly claimed territory. Despite some close encounters, they had failed to hunt the newcomers down.

The situation kept him on edge.

'Ra'tor!' the voice was deep, cut through the morning air like a clap of thunder. Ra'tor took his time to stand, shifted to see Rax't walking towards him. The tall Deiosian had a sparkle in his eyes, and he was not alone. Three similar sized Deios walked behind him, their kilts stained green. It appeared another brood had crossed the door-between-worlds during the night.

'Greetings,' Ra'tor rumbled in reply, casting his eye over the newcomers.

Rax't came to a stop, offered a slight bow. 'Ra'tor,' he began, his hands opening at his side, palms face up, 'I've returned from our home world, once again, and this time I return with a brood belonging to Fass'it.' He nodded in the direction of the largest Deiosian standing beside him. He was impressively built, broad and thick of arm, his scales an impressive hue of crimson gold. Ra'tor stood straight, flexed his shoulders. He was a foot taller than Fass'it, a fact evoking a minor twinge from his mouth, the slightest hint of a smile.

Fass'it stepped forward, and like Rax't, offered a bow, only this one was lower. As he returned to his full height, he spoke. 'I pledge my brood to yours, Ra'tor,' there was excitement in his gravelly voice, matching the lust in his eyes. 'Rax't has shown me the wonders here, and I would be honoured to share the hunt with you.' He stepped back with another bow, his fangs snapping shut. He shared a subtle look with Rax't.

Ra'tor's eyes narrowed. 'It would be an honour to lead your brood,' he almost snarled, his right fist clenching tight. 'How many hunters do you bring?'

'Three score.'

Ra'tor knew his brood now approached one thousand hunters. In all his life, never had a brood been so large. 'And the breed-partners?' he asked.

'Two score.'

It was adequate. They were here to help discover whatever wonders might be forthcoming. They were also here to help defend certain wonders once found. 'Your brood shall be mine to command, Fass'it,' Ra'tor moved back to the fire and held out his hands. 'Rax't will show you where to camp. Come midday, you may hunt.'

The Deiosian smiled, a baring of sharp teeth, vicious.

'Ra'tor,' Rax't waved the three Deios away, moved to stand before him again. 'Have you decided?'

He looked his second in the eye, knew what he wished for. They had spoken on numerous occasions over the past ten days, ever since they chased the Lesser Beasts into the blue temple. Hunting had been prolific, especially in the beginning, only with the added number of Deios now crowding the surrounding temples, meat from the Lesser Beasts was becoming hard to find. Yet they both knew there were thousands to be found within the pyramid. They had seen the crossing into the golden light. He had balked at following initially, now he was beginning to believe it was his destiny.

And the Patriarchs were here, in the new world, and they believed the same.

Ra'tor spat to the side. The Patriarchs had arrived with Rax't once the door-between-worlds reopened, eager to see the glowing blue pyramid, the one he wrongly believed held Bhral: their Blood-God. And ever since their arrival, they had spoken of sending Deios hunters through to see what lay within the golden sphere.

'You are the obvious choice to lead, Ra'tor,' Rax't prompted him, looking for a response. 'You said yourself that Bhral was missing, held captive someplace. We need to find him. We are destined to follow him to the promised land: a land of eternal hunting.'

Ra'tor closed his eyes. He'd heard enough talk from Rax't. He was sounding very much like the Patriarchs, dithering with their painted bones and carved rocks. 'I've not yet decided,' he refused to give his thoughts away, 'but I'll answer the Patriarchs soon. Meet me at the temple with the tall pillars, on the banks of the river an hour after sunrise.' He pointed a clawed finger in a vague direction towards the ruined structure. 'I'll speak to the elders then.' He noticed Rax't bow his head slightly, a glint in his eye. Then he was gone.

'There is an eagerness about you, Rax't,' he whispered as he knelt to pick up a piece of timber before throwing it into the fire. A hundred sparks leapt into cold air, reminding him of the desert fireflies back home.

He breathed deep, smelling the wood smoke, so foreign to his senses. It was thick and pungent, smelt of fragrant oil. A stark contrast to the wood burnt in the sacrificial fires back home; dry and brittle, snapping like bird bones between broad fingers. Yet it was also a reminder; a reminder of how unfamiliar this place was. He already felt a desire to return home. The dwelling place here, on this cold world, was beginning to lose appeal. His initial thoughts of claiming this land, of hunting its beasts, now seemed irrational. They didn't belong here. He doubted they could survive here indefinitely. Something was bound to go wrong.

Yet the Patriarchs insisted he travel further, to go beyond this world and discover other oddities unfamiliar to their kind. "There is much to learn," they would say, rubbing soft palms together whilst they sat on woven mats and fiddled with their bright-coloured trinkets.

He sat back down, felt the warmth from the flames as they danced higher. He would answer them soon, although he was still unsure. And yet one fact remained true. There was much to learn.

*

He walked with heavy steps towards the ruined temple.

Cracked and broken, it still evoked a sense of awe in the Deios leader. Tall pillars of marble ranged along a promenade, facing a wide river that ambled slowly to the sea. Beyond stood a towering entrance, arched and columned, inviting by its magnificent size and grandeur. His brood made it their unofficial abode, a place of comfort in a labyrinth of stone. Now it was home to the Patriarchs: those Deios vested with knowledge from the *Beyond.*

A curse rolled from Ra'tor's tongue as he walked up the first set of steps.

He didn't care for the Patriarchs and their maligned ways, felt them more burden than help to any brood they attached themselves to. They sat and reflected on sights and sounds, sought to sway leaders with ideas of their own.

And they did not hunt.

14

How could Deios live such a life?

The question had plagued him for many cycles, yet he never found an answer. They were weak and unskilled, yet incredibly manipulative.

He reached the highest step, paused to let the sun warm his back before heading to the shadowed hall beyond. He knew what he was walking towards, knew what the Patriarchs expected of him. Ever since they saw the blue pyramid, they'd spoken of being reunited with their Blood-God. Apparently, markings in their oldest caves back home suggested such an eventuality. The markings were ambiguous ten days ago, now they spoke volumes. To the Patriarchs, everything made sense.

And yet the old hunter knew what game they were playing, knew how dangerous the next few days would become. He'd baulked at stepping into the golden light at first, not because he was afraid, but because of all he could potentially lose. This dwelling place was incredibly vast and wonderfully detailed. Everywhere they looked rose marvels of creation unseen by any Deiosian. The enormity of the structures, the planning involved, all revealed an intellect far greater than they possessed. And it was now his. He owned it all by right of conquest. He was the victor; for it was he and his brood that found the path.

Now the Patriarchs had settled in his space. And they would ask of him a boon.

He could smell their weakness the moment he stepped into the hall. Twenty-six scrawny Deios, draped in scarlet cloth to their bony knees. They stood in a semi-circle at the centre of the hall, bathed in light from a vacant ceiling. Beyond sat almost a hundred observers, lesser Deios with little influence, often solitary hunters without a brood.

More weaklings.

Long strides took him to where they sat. He rolled his impressive shoulders back, rested one large hand on the pommel of his great cleaver strapped to his belt. He snarled with obvious disdain, revealing contempt for those before him.

A Patriarch with mottled scales rose and stepped forward, a metal chime in one hand, a small metal rod in the other. He struck the chime, waited for silence to fall.

'Ra'tor,' he said, his voice carrying easily, 'you come before us, as we knew you would come.'

'I come of my own free will, Patriarch,' there was venom in his tone.

'And so you do,' small, beady eyes flickered. 'Be that as it may, will you do as we have requested, Ra'tor, and lead a contingent of Deios into the golden sphere? Will you search for our Blood-God, so that he may return to guide us?'

There was a murmur from the Deios now standing behind the Patriarch. Few knew of the Patriarch's initial request, and only those belonging to his inner circle were privy to his thoughts.

'I will do as you ask,' he snarled, drawing his cleaver so that it swung above his shoulder. The blade was heavy, yet his enormously muscled arm held it aloft with ease. He held it there for a dozen heartbeats, then lowered it to the sound of footsteps marching into the hall. He looked over his shoulder and gave a slight nod.

The Patriarch craned his head to see a group of Deios enter the hall. 'How many of our brethren will you take on your journey, Ra'tor?'

He waved those Deios standing behind him to step closer, shared a grin with Rax't as he took his place by his side. 'I'll take those who are strongest,' he said. 'Along with Rax't, I'll take the leader of each brood to have stepped through the door-between-worlds.'

'Good,' the Patriarch waved his chime in the air. 'We commend your commitment, Ra'tor. We have suffered far too long without our Blood-God to guide us. With the loss of our god came a loss in creativity. We have dreamt little during the past ten generations.' He gazed at the hall he stood in, the twinkle in his eyes revealing his desire to emulate the construction. A moment passed before he pulled a small clay vessel from beneath the folds of his robe. 'Come, Ra'tor, allow me to share the blood, so that your journey may be blessed.'

A brief smile touched Ra'tor's lips. He motioned towards Rax't, encouraged him to step forward. The Patriarch offered a bow, then placed a clawed finger in the vessel.

'Will you accept the blood, Ra'tor?'

A dry tongue raced over his pointed teeth. He knew the ritual was nothing more than subservience disguised as a blessing. He cared little for their mind games. But he'd counted on their predictability.

'I'll accept the blood, Patriarch. Mark me. Smear the blood of the chosen on my cranium, so that I may fulfil my destiny.'

'Let it be so.' The Patriarch lowered his claw-like nail deeper into the vessel.

'No!' Ra'tor snarled, his hand lashing out to grasp the Patriarch's feeble wrist. 'Not that blood.'

There was confusion in the Patriarch's eyes, darkened with fear. 'I have no other blood at hand, Ra'tor.'

The smile on Ra'tor's face broadened into a vicious grin as he lifted his heavy blade of steel. An audible inhale of breath sounded in the hall . . . then held.

His blade swung in a terrible arc of power, chopping through scaled flesh with ease. The thud of a body hitting the tiled floor arrived next, followed immediately by the wet slap of a severed head.

'Here,' he kicked the severed head across the floor so that it rolled before the Patriarch. 'Use the blood of Rax't.

'It was worthy once.'

CHAPTER ONE

The darkness was growing.

Will Tolsten took the brass looking glass from his eye, twisted its length and snapped it shut. The light was fading fast, and despite his vantage within the ruined Belfry of Eli, he could see little to inspire optimism.

He shifted his shoulders, sought to ease the burden that settled so effortlessly upon him. Ever since he saw his father, Derrick Tolsten, fall under the demon onslaught, he'd vowed to take his place and lead what remained of the Nocturnals. Only leading such a crew was becoming increasingly difficult due to frightening circumstances. He scratched his bearded chin, knew he hadn't shaved since the Fall, then raised his hand to probe the bandage wrapped about his scalp. The wound beneath no longer felt tender, although he'd been told not to tamper with the dressing for another day. The blow to his head when he fought beside his father had been a glancing one, but the power from the beast was enough to knock him out cold. A shiver raced up his spine as he recalled the brief skirmish, and once again he let out a sigh of gratitude to still be alive. The thankfulness turned sour a second later as he recalled the broken body of his father, his head crushed like a melon.

'Twelve days,' he whispered to the approaching night. Twelve days since the Fall; twelve days living on instinct alone. He remembered regaining consciousness after the first attack, remembered gathering as many men as he could find before heading for the streets of Bastion. They numbered forty at best, but they were determined to exact a toll on those who killed the Shadow Brethren. He led the way, blood seeping from his hastily bandaged skull, his eyes squinting as they adjusted to the light of day. As they reached the tortured streets, they sought higher ground, hoping to find those responsible amongst the broken shell that was Holy City. Their search led them to Aston's Tear, where he and his crew watched the battle before the pyramid. Too far away to help, they watched as the men and women of Bastion fled into the pyramid whilst a select few held firm. Amongst them he saw Tarsin Va, the swordsman who killed three demons in Undercity, wearing the King's crown. With tear-rimmed eyes he watched his last stand, wished he could have lent his sword. But before he could muster his men the battle was over. Like those before, Tarsin had fled into the pyramid. He was yet to return.

Now, twelve days had passed, and the demons still patrolled the pyramid, guarding its only entrance. Not a soul knew if the survivors of Bastion were within, or if they had miraculously escaped. Since the Fall his scouts had stumbled across several portals within Undercity, shining with multicoloured light for some time, before vanishing in a heartbeat. There was a connection between the radiant swirling pillars and the demons now running through the streets. There was also a chance the men and women of Bastion were still alive.

If only Derrick Tolsten survived.

His father had been well versed in the occult and the unknown laws. A respected member of the Brotherhood of One, he'd delved into tomes for decades, searching and learning from a past few recognised. His insights would have been welcome, his knowledge a candle to the approaching darkness.

Will scraped a booted foot across the timber floor, touched the cracked bronze bell lying against a partially fallen wall. In the fading light he saw a young man stare back at him, blonde hair dust-stained and unruly, the white bandage wrapped around his forehead blood encrusted and dirty. His beard was patchy and spiked, his face long with worry. But his eyes, despite the sadness within, were baleful. Granite-blue and focused, intent on revenge. And though his father was gone and the link to the Brotherhood of One severed, there was another versed in their law and familiar to their ways. A captain of a ship, a man found floundering in the sewers a day after the earthquake, clinging to life by the barest of threads.

The looking glass in his hand was thrust into a deep pocket as he made for the stairwell. There was nothing more he could see from his vantage, and the forces of men he knew to be on the outskirts of Bastion still refused to enter the city. With tired legs he traversed the stairs, his mind working furiously for answers to their predicament. What remained of the Nocturnals was dwindling. It seemed every day a small group would head for either Eastgate or Southgate, hoping to reach the fields beyond. And every day those who remained would listen as screams rent the air minutes after their departure. The demons had neither fled nor dwindled in number. In fact, if anything, their numbers had increased in the days since the Fall. At some point they would turn their attention to the western side of the city; the region once home to Highcastle and the King's Plaza. When they did, it would be a slaughter, for the Nocturnals were poorly equipped for such an encounter.

He reached ground level, placed a hand on an oak door and pushed. A set of eyes lifted to meet his own. 'Anything?' asked a heavy-set man with close-cropped brown hair and a scruffy beard peppered grey.

'No,' Will answered, brow knotted, 'there is little movement from those placed outside the Southern Wall.'

'What are they waiting for, do you think?'

'I've no idea, Col,' he spread his hands out to either side. Like everyone else who remained, he'd hoped reinforcements would have entered the city by now. The danger of being in Bastion was escalating by the hour, and food was becoming scarce. Scouts already refused to patrol east of the river Atvia, the proximity of Aston's Tear a deterrent.

'They'll sniff us out soon enough, you know,' Col said, his demeanour grim. He stroked the hilt of his sword as he spoke, an action that did little to ease his thoughts. One of only a dozen-or-so Shadow Brethren to remain, Col Farren had taken it upon himself to become his right-hand man. 'We can hold them for some time if we hole-up near Thieves' Retreat, but there won't be any escapin' if it comes to that.'

'Then we'll not let it come to that,' Will's heart felt heavy. 'We'll find a way.' He tilted his head to the left and led Col down a small lane, skirting bricks and broken timber, a reminder of the destructive earthquake: the precursor to all their woes. As they moved out of the cloying shadow of Eli's Tower the two men strode with purpose towards an old tavern named the Bloated Swan, a half-timbered establishment, remarkably, left unscathed when the earthquake struck. Such a fact did little to enhance its reputation, for it was a despicably unsavoury destination at the best of times. Now, with its owner fled and its patrons dispersed, it provided his inner circle a place to strategize.

An aging red-haired man holding a crossbow opened the door as they arrived. His leather shirt was criss-crossed with a bandolier, holding several throwing knives. A toothless smile greeted them. 'Underlord,' he said, bowing his head.

Will placed a hand on the man's shoulder. 'Thank you, Patrick.'

'Anything?' he asked, repeating the same question Col asked earlier.

A shake of the head stalled further questions as he moved into the room. Col followed, and together they entered the tavern's main hall. It was long and narrow, unlit hearths at either end, trestle tables flanking either side. At the rear ran a lengthy bar, its wooden top stained black. The shelves behind were already bare, and no sound came from the kitchen out back. A staircase led upstairs to the right, another led downstairs to a cellar on the left. Three men sat in a far corner, whilst a young boy slid his whetstone across a steel blade.

'Is Tessa within?' Will asked, catching the eye of the young boy.

'She's upstairs with the patient,' came the reply. 'His fever has broken.'

Will shared a sigh of relief with Col, then made for the stairs. As they reached the hallway on the first floor a string of curses sounded from behind the second door. He took quick steps and let himself in, only to see the captain lying in his bed, propped atop a pillow. A young woman with curly brown hair wrung a cloth in her pale hands, the sleeves of her blue shirt rolled to her elbows. She spun about on hearing footsteps, presented a tired smile.

'How are you, Tessa?' Will moved to take her hands in his, then leant forward to place a gentle kiss on her cheek.

'I'm well, thank you,' she wiped a hand across her brow. 'The captain appears to have recovered from his fever,' she gestured to the black-bearded man, 'although his leg is far from healed.'

'I'm fine,' the captain growled, shifting his weight, yet Will noticed a tightening of his jaw as he did so. He couldn't blame him. When they found him the day after the earthquake, he was grasping a stone wall with bloodied fingers in the sewers, filthy water sloshing to his neck. As they pulled him clear they discovered a splintered piece of timber stuck in his thigh, its length the size of a short sword.

'Leave us, Tessa,' another kiss, this time on her brow. 'The captain and I need to talk.'

She obliged, throwing the cloth into a small bucket of water as she left. Will took the opportunity to move further into the room, slid a chair to the bedside so he could take a seat. Col took his place on a three-legged stool, next to a side table with a single lit candle.

'How are you feeling?' Will asked with concern.

'Better, lad, now the fever has broken. I can think clearly for a change.'

The seat felt comfortable as Will settled, as comfortable as the night falling outside. But he felt anything but settled on the inside. An assortment of questions plagued his waking thoughts, and the captain, now that he was coherent, was the only man he knew who had ties with the Brotherhood.

'Do you have any idea what is happening out there,' Will waved a hand towards the shuttered window, hoping he would understand his vague gesture.

'I do, lad,' his voice was a low rumble. 'I've been a Seeker of the Brotherhood for more years than you've seen. Although my ship, the *Lioness*, now lies broken in the Bay of

Pennants, I am still a captain. I can still read the signs in the night sky.'

'Good,' Will clapped his hands together, startling Col on his stool. 'I believe you may be of help, which we desperately need. Do you mind if I ask you some questions, Captain Jarvis Vasco?'

*

Jarvis Vasco, formerly captain of the *Lioness,* stirred on his bed.

He felt pain in his left thigh, understandable given the severity of his wound. He'd almost passed out when they dragged him out of the sewer, exhausted and bloodied, his body bruised in a hundred places. His entire left leg was blood-stained, a cause for shouts and curses to fly as men screamed for bandages and clean water. His vision faded between darkness and yellow torch light until an older man with missing teeth and flaming hair splashed the remnants of his spirit flask on his wounded leg. Fire raced through his veins as he screamed from bottomless depths, frothing at the mouth as he curled his hammer fists to pound the stones beneath him. It had been a harrowing journey of pain and delirium ever since, with only short moments of clarity. It was during those times he managed to recall the tumultuous events that led to his current predicament.

Hot winds blew across the Bay of Pennants, rocking the *Lioness,* causing a gentle pendulum motion that almost went unnoticed by the sailors still aboard. Nearly all Ruvin Ciricello's curios were now in port, ready to be transported to various locations, and Jarvis was merely overseeing the last tasks to be completed before he, too, made his way to shore. With the sun inching past its zenith, he felt content and happy to be home.

Until a thousand sea birds took flight, screeching as they left their perch on ship or post.

Several sailors, both aboard the *Lioness* and those nearby on ships at anchor, stopped their tasks to point and remark on the oddity. Having been a sailor and a captain for three decades and more, he took hurried steps to the rail and scanned the water below. It was as he feared, a criss-cross of waves, like patchwork on a winter quilt. He chanced a glance at the city, held a hand to shade his squinting eyes, then watched the first stone blocks shake free from the Southern Dock Tower.

'Earthquake!' he yelled to whoever cared to listen, running towards the anchor. 'Lads, help me weigh anchor.'

Only by the time he reached aft of the ship, the Bay of Pennants was beginning to empty, as if one of the gods themselves had descended to devour the sea with a single swallow. There was a moment of calm as he and his men watched in terrified awe, before the sea, now released with a vengeance, came rushing back in. Two sailors ran the length of the *Lioness* and leaped into what was left of the bay, their arms frantically swirling as they sought to reach land. He remembered cursing under his breath, then spun to observe the wall of water sweeping towards him. There was nowhere to flee. Like any serviceable captain, he'd remain on his ship. To the last.

The water picked up the rear of the *Lioness* and tilted her with brutal force, causing him to lose his footing. A moment later he was submerged, inwardly screaming as waves and timber pummelled his body.

In the blink of an eye he was cresting a wall of water, gasping for air as he was swept with terrifying speed towards the Southern Docks, its curved retaining wall directly ahead. Pain lanced his thigh as he spun upside down and hit the wall with a thud before he found himself tossed into the air. Seconds later he was pulled back into the frothing wash, a mass of splintered planks and canvas sails coupled with the gurgled screams of drowning men. He spun in rapid circles, hands searching for purchase, before being carried into the city proper.

His torment became a blur thereafter. Darkness engulfed him. When he finally regained his senses, he realised he'd been sucked into the sewers, a hundred scrapes and bruises across his body, a skewered leg burning like wildfire.

But he survived, somehow, only to be consumed by fever.

He blinked tired eyes, sought those of the man sitting before him. Will Tolsten, son of the late Derrick Tolsten, so they told him. 'What would you ask of me, lad?'

Will sighed, gathered his thoughts, and it was at that moment Vasco realised his own turmoil during the earthquake was equally shared by the citizens of Bastion.

'I need your advice, on a great many things,' Will began, 'only it's your knowledge concerning the occult I would first venture. Something has happened since the earthquake, Jarvis, and the city is now plagued by demons. Do any of your teachings in Irongate speak of such horrors?'

Vasco eased into his pillows. He'd been told of the beasts roaming the streets only the day before. Young Tessa, after changing his dressings, spoke of their scaled hides and gleaming teeth. He was wise enough to listen without assumption.

'I was a Seeker for the Brotherhood, Will, and taught at a young age to read signs in the night sky. But I've never heard of any creatures such as those described to me. There are murals, faded and chipped, beneath the city as you're no doubt aware. But beyond such similarities, I have no evidence of who they are or why they are here.'

'We believe they may have arrived through a portal situated near Highcastle. Several other portals have been found to the north and south, only our connection to them has been lost by the demon's proximity. They've spread from the west to the pyramid, both above and below ground. And their number continues to grow.'

Vasco scratched his cheek before twirling a thick finger in his curly beard. 'What you describe is magic beyond my expertise. Portals are the domain of Elder Cappitus. If he was here, you'd have answers of some sort.'

'We don't have the luxury, Jarvis, of calling on his wisdom. The Nocturnals: the thieves of Undercity, are almost all that remain of Holy City. We need help.'

'To fight the creatures?' Vasco prodded.

'No, to escape the city. We're too few, now. Nearly all the Shadow Brethren fell in the first skirmish. At best we number two score, with a dozen more worthy of holding a blade. Only there are nearly two hundred women and children we need to protect. We cannot fight the beasts on their terms. Nor can we hide for much longer. We were hoping for reinforcements from outside the city, only our hope has been in vain.'

'So, what's stopping you from leaving?'

'Many things,' Will fished a hand into the deep pocket of his jacket, pulled forth the looking glass. 'I believe this is yours, captain,' he said.

'Aye, it is. Where did you find it?'

'I didn't. It was in your pocket when we found you. I hope you don't mind, but it's been an asset this past week.'

Vasco held out his hand, felt the cool brass touch his skin as Will passed it over. 'I'm surprised it's not banged and bruised like its owner.'

'It was wet, granted, but we've a tinker or two in Undercity who appreciate valuable items. It took only a moment to realise she was in working order. With you feverish and in pain, I thought it prudent to put it to good use.'

A faint smile touched his lips. 'So, what have you seen?'

Will was silent for a moment as he gathered his thoughts, allowing Col to speak on his behalf. 'Nothing good, Jarvis,' his deep voice reverberated about the small room. 'A small force of men has set up camp in the fields to the east and south. We can see their banners with the aid of your looking glass, but we cannot send word to them. We've no idea if they even know we exist. Now our supplies are low and we're skulking about, fearful of being hunted. Practically every day a group of men and women seek to reach the Eastern Gate. Not a single soul has made the journey to its end. The beasts lie in wait, lurking in the shadows. And they're fast.'

'Then choose another gate,' Vasco suggested, 'or leave by the Bay of Pennants.'

'The bay has been destroyed, along with the ships,' Will replied. 'Northgate has fallen, baring the way, and Southgate is likewise destroyed. The only chance we may have is the small Farmer's Gate to the south-east, although the street leading to freedom is narrow and cluttered. It's also on the other side of the river Atvia. We'd take the underground route any other day, but the risk is too high now.'

Vasco could see the frustration on Will's face. The young man was trying to be a leader, a man of wisdom in a time of peril. It was taking its toll. 'What do you want from me, then?'

'Your counsel if you'll oblige. I'm of a mind to attempt Farmer's Gate. We are sorely pressed and almost without food, and I'm running out of able men. So, my question, Jarvis Vasco, is this. Should I attempt the run myself?'

Vasco wiped the back of his hand across his forehead, aware beads of sweat were beginning to form. His fever had broken, he was certain, only the lethargy of more than a week in the care of others wasn't easily forgotten. His leg continued to ache, a fact he'd declined to mention since he woke, and he'd placed a gentle hand on his thigh some time ago, only the experience wasn't pleasant. 'There's no-one else?'

'No-one better suited to the task.'

'When will you leave?'

Will lowered his eyes to the floor. 'Before first light,' he said. 'If I delay any longer, I fear we'll have lost our chance. We need aid, and the men in the field need to know what's occurring within Bastion. The demons keep guard about Aston's Tear. I dare say for a good reason. We need to know what's inside the pyramid. We need to know if our people are still alive.'

'You'll need help to make it through, use every man you have available. I'd help if I could, but I cannot even stand, Will.' A heavy sigh escaped Vasco's lips as he leant back, his face pale. He was done, spent, lost in a sea of pain. If Will made it to the fields and the waiting men, he wouldn't see it. 'Here,' he raised one of his massive fists, the looking glass gripped loosely, 'take it, lad. Put it to good use.'

Will lifted the piece and placed it in his jacket pocket. 'Is there anything else you can tell me, Jarvis? Anything I should be aware of?'

Vasco closed his eyes, searched for words of inspiration, a verse, even, to fill the young man with hope. But all he saw was darkness, a maelstrom of swirling streams eager to pull him under. He forced his eyes open, aware Will was waiting for an answer. 'I think it best to keep it simple, lad. Stay alive.'

*

Dawn was only an hour away when Will lifted the latch on the rear door of the old tavern and slipped into the common room. Three candle stubs, sitting in a congealed mass of wax, continued to flutter on the stained bar. Beyond their feeble light, almost hidden in the shadows, sat several men, heads resting on folded arms as they waited for the call.

'It's time,' Will said, placing a hand on the first man's shoulder. Col raised tired eyes, then inhaled deeply.

'You all set?' Col asked whilst nudging the man next to him.

'I'm ready, and so are the marksmen.' The men rose to form a semi-circle about the bar. Including himself there were twenty-five men in the common room, all wearing leather armour over padded gambeson. A selection of sharp knives and stabbing weapons sat at hip and thigh, and several belts held an assortment of throwing daggers. Behind them, resting on the table, sat a dozen crossbows.

'How far in?' Col tightened his belt as he asked the question.

'We have position almost to the north of Aston's Tear, just behind the King's Library on the promenade.' Col nodded in approval; setting the crossbowmen during the night was an integral part of the operation. If he was to make his way to Farmer's Gate, he'd need protection. For the better part of five hours, twenty men armed with regulation crossbows had been ordered to sites of advantage. When the first rays of sunshine bathed the shattered streets of Bastion in an hour, he hoped to be running past their location. If he was fortunate, the demons would have retired for the night. On the other hand, if Anok and Eli sought amusement, then he hoped his marksmen could clear a path for him to send him on his way.

He raised a hand to catch the attention of his men. 'Listen, we move now. In silence. The night has remained uneventful, but we'd be fools to believe the streets are empty. I want single file as we walk, every second man with a crossbow. We do not talk. We do not run. Whilst the sun rests below the horizon, we keep to the shadows.' He met their eyes, held them for several seconds. 'Do I make myself clear?'

The men nodded in return. It was enough for him to share a smile.

'Then follow and be diligent. If all goes well, I'll reach the fields beyond Bastion and have reinforcements here within a day.' He was about to move towards the rear door when he spied Tessa standing at the foot of the stairs. He caught her eye, wished he could take quick strides to stand before her and place his palms about her face. The thought of her soft lips pressed against his had his heart racing, and realization that he might never experience such pleasure again tightened his chest. Only his men parted to allow her to cross the floor instead. She reached for his hands and held them. 'Jarvis is gone,' she spoke quietly, although he was certain every man in the room heard her words.

'What do you mean, he couldn't even walk,' Will's words came out in a rush, but he saw the truth in her tear-rimmed eyes. 'He's dead, isn't he?'

She replied with a single nod. 'An hour earlier. He was breathing fine, his rhythm steady. Then he stopped.'

'Was it the fever?'

'I don't believe so. He appeared happy. There was a smile on his face at the end.' She wiped a tear from her cheek. 'But his leg was a mess. I believe the infection was deeper than we thought. I fear we didn't retrieve all the shards of timber from his wound.'

He placed his arms about her shoulders and kissed her brow. 'You did all you could, you know. He was lucky to have survived this long.' She sunk further into his arms.

'I don't want you to go,' she raised her eyes. 'What if I lose you too?'

Will could see his men shifting in the background, eager to be on their way. Dawn was approaching. He shared a single, last embrace, before stepping back a pace. 'I'll make it, Tessa, and I'll return within a day.'

Her sad look suggested otherwise, only he was already leading his men into the rear courtyard. As they filed behind him, a guttural roar sounded from several streets away, followed seconds later by a high-pitched scream.

'Alright,' he spun to his left, slipped past a side gate and onto the cobblestoned street. A hand instinctively drew a dagger. As he reached the corner of the old tavern he peered onto the main thoroughfare, seeking movement. Seeing only a quiet, darkened street, he motioned his men to step behind him. They did so as one, their hands holding either blade or crossbow. 'Single file,' he whispered, stepping forward. Col fell in behind, followed by Patrick with a toothless smile. Both held a crossbow, bolts nocked.

He gave each a brief glance, his eyes devoid of emotion. This was real. There was no returning from this venture. They would either live to see a new dawn, or they would die on the broken streets of Bastion.

With a heavy heart he led the men onto the street, his footfalls no louder than those of a mouse, his breathing shallow. Both his hands now gripped daggers, for he knew if the demons chanced upon his crew, it would be a fight to the death. With two blades in hand, he would have double the chance of killing his foe. Only he prayed it wouldn't come to such a bloody end. If they could reach the King's Library without incident, he would be halfway to his destination. Then it would be a matter of running as fast as he was able, knowing his only defence lay in the hands of his marksmen hiding amongst the ruins. It was a gamble, but it was all he had.

Several minutes passed before he noticed his vision of the road ahead improve. Night's mantle was slipping to the west, allowing the first rays of sunshine to lighten the sky. His men remained on edge, more so now, he believed, although they were making progress. Within moments they'd be able to skirt a toppled cathedral, and beyond, slip along a lane that would eventually lead them to the banks of the river Atvia. He knew once they reached the river it would be a short distance to the Karson Bridge. Of the sixteen bridges spanning the river within Bastion, only six survived the earthquake, three of those six only partially. Karson Bridge was still intact, and it led directly to the promenade and the King's Library. Then it was a matter of turning left, then right to reach Queen's Avenue which ran for three miles between three and four-story apartments, shop fronts, taverns and inns before the narrow Farmer's Gate materialized.

The noise of falling masonry stopped him in his tracks. It came from ahead, a loud clap of stone to herald the arrival of daylight. Col and Patrick both raised their crossbows, seeking movement. For a minute it felt as if every man held his breath, waiting for the screaming charge. It never came, so with tentative steps, he led the men onwards.

'We're almost there,' Col whispered in his ear, his arm pointing ahead. For almost half-an-hour they'd sifted through the streets, pausing when necessary, scampering on light feet when the need arose. Now, as Col pointed out, the Karson Bridge was in sight from the lane they traversed. It was a broad avenue spanning two hundred feet of water, with three spans of bluestone holding its mass across the river. With hurried steps they raced to the bridge itself, climbing a set of stone stairs to place feet on solid timber fifty feet above the water's level.

Yet as they began to move across the expanse, the sound of heavy footsteps caused all eyes to look ahead.

Five demons, seven feet tall and broad of arm, slunk from behind pylons to bar the way. Their hands held heavy blades; their kilts hid thick thighs of corded muscle. They began to run, and within seconds they'd covered a quarter of the distance.

Several men moved to stand alongside him, then bent to the knee.

The voice of Col sounded next. 'What are your orders, Will?'

Will looked to the advancing demons. He knew this was the only plan they had. They were desperate and alone in a city gone mad. They couldn't afford any more delays. 'I only have one goal, my friend,' he spoke so all his men could hear. 'I need to reach the fields beyond Farmer's Gate.

'Take them down!'

CHAPTER TWO

The half-a-dozen men who knelt by Will's side raised their crossbows. Within seconds heavy bolts were flying, followed quickly by another half-a-dozen from the men standing at the rear. The thud of bolts striking flesh sounded a second later. A screech rent the air, blades of steel fell from nerveless hands, and before he could say a word the beasts were lying prone.

Will began to run. The sound of death: guttural calls from demon mouths, would alert others to the confrontation. With his men beside him they reached the fallen and set too with dagger and knife. Throats were slit with emotionless precision, the men moved on.

Within moments they'd crossed the remainder of the bridge and stood at the beginning of an avenue, its length twinning between half-toppled temples and great halls once occupied by numerous guilds. Aston's Tear sat some distance to their right. She was the colossus they'd all come to know, immense and immovable, her lightning-blue walls shimmering as the first light of day brightened the sky with hues of pink.

Will gave his men a moment to reload their crossbows and then waved them forward, stepping into the shadow of a ruined temple.

'The noise we made will have alerted others,' Col whispered as he stepped to his side, crossbow held with tightly clenched hands.

'I know, Col, but once we reach Queen's Avenue, we'll have marksmen hidden in the ruins, flanking us for nearly a mile. My orders were simple. I sincerely hope they've remained quiet and out of sight.'

'I pray you're right because things are likely to turn ugly otherwise.'

A sigh slipped past his lips, yet the two men knew there was no turning back. They were committed, intent on seeing their gamble through. Too many lives depended on their courage and fortitude. Too many lives could be lost if they didn't hold their nerve. With the men taking deep breaths to slow their breathing and calm quickened heartbeats, he knew it was time. He met the eyes of his men, one-by-one, saw grim determination in return.

'It's time to move,' he spoke with a hushed voice, eyes scanning the abandoned street. It was eerily quiet. Since the earthquake and the rise of the demon hunters, the sounds of commerce, the rattle of harness and the creak of wagons were non-existent. So too was the absence of chiming bells and the call of town criers perched on street corners. Only the sweep of rattling leaves caused by the occasional gust of wind broke the silence.

And the random screams.

Keeping to the shadows, Will moved along the temple wall, his men strung out behind him in one long line. His plans were simple from here on. If they were confronted at any stage, his men would distract the beasts and then flee. They were with him to provide a diversion, nothing more. And they certainly weren't here to die. He had every intention of coming back into the city with a host of armed men later in the day to rescue those left behind. Picking up the dead was not on his agenda.

'We've reached Queen's Avenue,' Col whispered into his ear.

A solitary nod was his reply. This was the street that would lead him to Farmer's Gate and the fields beyond. It was broken like every other, closely hemmed-in buildings having lost roof tiles and windows, enormous cracks streaking plastered walls. Overturned barrels and empty hessian sacks lay discarded on fractured cobblestones, along with an assortment of rotting produce adding a ripeness to the air.

And death. He could smell its sickly scent. It clung to the buildings and street alike, a heavy ripeness, strongest amongst the many shadows created by the overhanging buildings.

'Are you sure you wish to do this?' Col asked, looking over his shoulder. 'I've seen paths into Hell's Domain that looked more promising than this.'

'Aye,' Will shook his head. There were too many areas hidden from view. 'The potential for ambush is high,' he returned, 'but I've enough marksmen positioned to help cover my passage.'

'You hope you've enough marksman,' Col fired back, looking down at his crossbow.

'For a mile, perhaps. I doubt they moved any further during the early hours. It would have taken all their nerve to come this far.' He pointed to a building barely seen in the distance, a solid square establishment of stone, four stories tall at the corner of an intersection. 'I know Marcos and three others set out to take position on the second floor of the Stonemason's Guild Hall. Beyond,' he shrugged his shoulders, 'I'm only guessing.'

Col shifted his feet, pushed himself closer to the wall as Patrick stepped close. 'We'll take you that far, then,' Patrick smiled a toothless smile.

'Aye, you will, then I travel alone.' He swung his attention back to the street, peered with narrowed eyes, looking for anything out of place. On a whim he placed a hand into his jacket pocket and pulled forth the looking glass gifted to him from Jarvis Vasco. He lengthened the piece and placed his eye to the small end, focused on the distant gate. It was shrouded in shadow, as much of the street was at this early time of day. The large wooden doors were open, yet an assortment of irregular bluestone blocks sat barring the path, large and immovable. Fallen masonry from the walls above, perhaps.

He snapped the eyepiece shut and placed it back in his pocket, then took his first tentative step along the Queen's Avenue. His men followed, and within moments he quickened his pace, his heart racing, sweat already beginning to bead on his forehead. There was no visible danger to be seen, yet his senses told him there was more than the smell of death and decay lurking in the shadows.

A puff of wind blew coarse sand across the cobblestoned street, accompanied by the clap of a broken shutter banging against a wooden frame. He halted their advance, held his breath as he tilted his head to one side, listening for any other sounds. Out of the corner of his eye he saw his men squat with crossbows propped, their aim ranging the street, seeking any movement.

He breathed again, took another step, moved past an empty barrel.

They were halfway to the Stonemason's Guild Hall when the first scream sounded.

Like his men he spun to peer behind him, saw several demons tearing flesh from those at the rear of the line. The loud twang of crossbow bolts being loosed came next, accompanied by sickening thuds. He knotted his brow, felt fear rise like bile in his throat. He hadn't expected a rear attack, thought the danger would manifest ahead.

Then the realization of his predicament sank home. He turned around, cursed as he saw a handful of demons' charge from a laneway across the street. They were ambushed, as every instinct told him they would be. He knew from experience he faced a canny foe, felt dread settle on his shoulders like a reaper's heavy cloak. The screams of his men were already echoing through the broken city, alerting all to the bloody commotion.

He thought of drawing his sword from its sheath, then realised he was grossly outnumbered. He couldn't possibly defeat them all, but then his plan was never to confront the enemy. All he needed was to slip past and run.

The buzz of crossbow bolts sounded close to his ear, screeching thirty feet to hit a target. He paused, looked behind to see his men reloading. Col and Patrick both stood with fierce intent, the arms of their own crossbows bent as they positioned new bolts. They wouldn't have much time, but their first volley took two of the beasts to the ground. The remaining were wounded, their momentum gone. Will gave a curt nod to his two aides, shared the briefest of smiles. Then he ran.

The street became a blur. He kept his eyes peeled as he raced ahead, his arms swinging with ease. He knew to lose focus and panic now would be his undoing. A wild dash to the gate, arms flailing, would see him falter at some point. Like his men behind him, he needed to have faith in their plan. Despite the ambush, his men would retaliate quickly and then flee. As remnants of the Nocturnals, they would find their hideaway holes, sliding doors and secret chambers to elude the larger creatures. And when the simmering confrontation eased, they would make their way back across the river and return to the Bloated Swan.

And if all went well, he would find them later this evening at Thieves' Retreat, when he returned with a force of men to clear the streets.

He ducked under the overhang of a building, its structure leaning alarmingly since the earthquake. A quick look behind showed a bloodied scene, yet it appeared most of his men had already fled. He eased out from under the overhang, took long strides, and found himself passing the Stonemason's Guild Hall on his right a moment later. From here it would be two miles of straight road to the Farmer's Gate.

Yet as he made to cross the intersection a flurry of bright-coloured scales caught his eye. He saw half-a-dozen demons standing over a prone body. They looked up as he passed, and he saw a glimpse of a black cloak and close-cropped blonde hair. It was Marcos, one of his marksmen. How he ended up on the street he would never know.

The beasts issued a deep chortle and sprang forward with a burst of pace. Will swung his arms harder, head down, hoping he could outrun his pursuers. His confidence was dwindling until he heard the twang of crossbows from above.

He saw three of his men on the balcony to his left. A second later he spied another, leaning out a broken window on the third floor of a tavern, a board swinging on an oiled chain claiming it to be The Flaming Spit. He saw the tension in the man's face ease as he pressed the lever, heard a grunt from behind as a bolt found its mark.

He continued to run.

He slipped past another intersection, then twisted away from the building to his left when a steel hatchet smashed into its timber wall. Shards of plaster and slivers of wood exploded outward, alerting him to the prospect of certain death should one strike him from behind. He chanced a look over his shoulder, saw five in pursuit, two with shiny hatchets held firm.

And they were gaining.

He leapt over a discarded crate, almost lost his footing as his boot slid atop a smooth stone. An internal scream raged within his head, forced him to regain his feet. Sweat beaded atop his lip, spit flew from his mouth. His breathing was ragged, fear clutched his chest.

He kept moving, tired now, his legs burning with every step, his breath coming in short gasps. The prospect of any help was now forgotten. His marksmen would not have travelled this far down Queen's Avenue. His only course of action was to keep a straight line for the gate. He'd be there in minutes.

He ran across a stone landing of an apothecary, leapt over the wooden railing at the end. A moment later the sound of a body crashing through timber told him how close the beasts were. He swivelled, more on instinct than any true belief he knew what was to come, flinched as another hatchet swept past his shoulder to plunge into a window. The ring of broken glass drowned out his shout of alarm, and with aching thighs and tortured lungs, he pushed on.

The last intersection before the gate passed without a thought. He flipped a barrel over as he ran, pulled an awning from a wall. Anything he could find to halt those in pursuit. But as he raced towards Farmer's Gate, clearly visible now, no more than two hundred feet away, his dream of making it out of Bastion alive faded. Another three beasts, six-and-a-half feet tall and heavily muscled, stood braced in the middle of the street. They held wide blades of steel, wore kilts of leather and shared vicious grins full of sharp teeth. Will came to a halt, his objective so close he could almost touch it. The beasts behind him slowed to a walk, aware their quarry had nowhere to flee.

Will breathed deep to ease his hammering heart, then drew his short sword. It would be of little use in the fight to come.

He was about to charge with a blood-curdling cry when a black feather, a foot long if he was any judge, sifted past his nose to land on the cobblestoned street. He looked up, saw a figure perched atop the belfry of The Chosen Few: a temple devoted to Frey: Goddess of Fate and the Four Winds.

A terrible silence encroached on those below as the being above cast a baleful glare. Fear caught in Will's throat. He felt his heart race faster than ever before. The creature above was heavily cloaked, but he could feel its gaze judging him, feel its eyes boring into his soul. It was a hunter, much like the beasts standing before him, only this hunter had the eyes of an eagle and a head to match.

A moment passed before the demons surrounding him dispersed.

Will ran.

He ran as fast as able, lifting legs high, striding with every fibre of his being. Whatever the creature above represented; he wanted no part in any introduction.

He rushed towards the gate, leapt the fallen masonry, could see the splintered stonework he was so close. The dirt road beyond called him.

And then strong hands gripped him around the chest, halting his flight as the air escaped his lungs. Heavy hands pressed over his mouth, and words were whispered into his ear. He went blank for a moment, felt himself begin to suffocate. The pressure on his body eased seconds later, his vision swam, then came into focus.

'Easy, lad,' the voice was hushed, yet commanding. There was sudden movement as he was dragged into the shadows beneath the outer gate, under the overhang and out of sight from above.

The hand over his mouth came away, allowed him to take a deep breath. 'Gods above!' Will wheezed, fear in his voice. 'Who are you?' He could make out the shape of four men, heavily cloaked.

'I was about to ask you the same question, lad,' an older man's face looked at his own, framed with long white hair and a bristling moustache.

'I am Will Tolsten,' he began, 'current Underlord of the Nocturnals. And with my father, Sir Derrick Tolsten, now counted among the dead, I'm also the newly appointed Baron of Deepwell.'

The older man shook his head, then offered his hand so he could sit up. 'Well met, Will,' he said. 'I'm Lloyd Henrickson, Swordmaster to the king. I hope you have some information for us, because we'd love to know what's going on inside our beloved city.'

He returned a nod, keen to explain all he knew, eager to regale all the horrors he and his Nocturnals had experienced in the past twelve days. For a moment he wondered where to begin, felt his head swim with countless information. Then he felt the need to ask why there had been no help from the soldiers in the field.

He was about to voice his first question when a terrible buzzing sound drowned his thoughts, clouding his focus, adding confusion to his clarity.

A moment later he passed out.

*

It was the sound of raised voices that dragged Will out of slumber.

He opened heavy eyes, saw the inside of a tent, grey canvas stretched taut. A small wooden table, cluttered with scrolls and pewter tankards, nestled on the far side. A light blanket looped about his feet, likewise grey, and he found his clothes piled neatly at the foot of the cot he'd been sleeping upon. He unlooped his feet and spun his legs to the side, then stood on parched soil, noting the thin white shirt of cotton he was wearing. It was a long shirt, falling to his knees.

He was about to dress and make his way out of the tent when he heard the approach of booted feet. He fumbled through his clothes, looked for his short sword, then noticed his belt and blade hanging over the back of a chair at the rear. A single step was all he managed before a canvas sheet was pulled to the side, allowing two men to enter.

They were of differing height, he noticed. The first to enter was Lloyd Henrickson, the man who rescued him at Farmer's Gate. The other man was shorter by a foot, his body heavy and thick. A man of comfort if he were to judge.

'You're awake, then,' Henrickson's voice was deep. It was not a question. Will watched as they took another step inside, crowding the small area. There was nowhere for him to move.

'Where am I?' he asked, hoping to stall their approach.

'You're outside Bastion, for the moment,' Henrickson waved a hand to his left. 'Allow me to introduce Lord Beaumont of Rochdale.'

Will offered a brief smile at the introduction. He'd heard of Lord Beaumont before; in fact, he recalled his father having spoken highly of the man.

'You claim to be Will Tolsten,' Lord Beaumont cast his gaze over his features.

'I am, and currently Lord of Deepwell.'

'Can you prove it?'

Will narrowed his eyes. He hadn't thought any further than reaching the gate in the past days. Nor did he believe his authority would be questioned, let alone his identity. It was only now, as he stood half dressed in a tent on the outskirts of Bastion, did he realize the enormity of his task.

'You knew my father,' he met Lord Beaumont's gaze, 'surely we share some resemblance?'

'Perhaps,' he replied, looking him up and down, 'perhaps you look more like your mother.'

'My mother is dead, my lord.'

'Truly! And your brother and sister, what has become of them?'

The fists at his side clenched tight. 'My elder brother died five years earlier, on the streets of Bastion, no less. My sister . . . is still alive, I believe.'

Lloyd Henrickson held up a hand. 'You believe your sister is alive?'

'Aye. The last I saw Kayla; she was fleeing Undercity for the surface. I have not seen her since, although I have a feeling she headed for Aston's Tear.'

The two older men shared a glance before Henrickson spoke. 'Greetings, then, Will Tolsten.'

'Aye,' Beaumont clapped a large hand to his shoulder. 'Sorry about the questions, lad, but we had to know for certain.'

Will kept his opinion to himself, although his eyes simmered. 'I've questions of my own,' he began. 'How many men do you command, and how many can you spare? I've men, women and children trapped within the city. We need to rescue them as soon as possible.'

A moment of silence greeted him. He checked their stance, studied their features. Neither lord seemed prepared to speak.

'So,' he continued, hands out wide, 'how many can you spare?'

Henrickson shook his head, then took a step towards the entrance. He moved aside the canvas. 'Dress yourself,' he said, glancing towards the chair where his clothes sat, 'and meet me outside.'

Lord Beaumont followed Henrickson. Will shifted his feet as the canvas fell back in place, leaving him alone and confused. He stood silently for a minute before reaching for his garments, his mind racing as he pondered the lord's lack of response. Perhaps, he thought, they have few men to spare. Perhaps there are no men at all.

He realised he knew little about the situation they'd been dealt.

He forced his mind to focus, dressed with care, became aware his body still ached from his mad dash through Bastion's streets. He noticed a bandage wrapped about his upper left arm, a small red stain marking the white cloth, and his jaw felt bruised, just below his chin. As he buckled his sword to his belt, though, he realised he couldn't remember taking his clothes off in the first place. Nor could he remember arriving inside the tent.

He pushed the canvas aside and stepped into daylight.

'How did I arrive here?' he yelled at the two lords waiting for him. 'And how long have I been here?'

'You passed out,' Henrickson said with a shrug, as if such an answer explained everything.

'And we carried you here,' Beaumont added, 'and put you to bed. You were exhausted. You've slept an entire day and a night. It's early morning, a day since you reached the gate.'

His jaw dropped an inch. He'd promised his people he'd return later that evening, with an army behind him, ready to cut down the enemy. Instead, he'd fallen asleep on a bed, safe whilst others lived in fear.

'I need to return to the city,' he gasped, eyes wide with intent.

'We heard you,' Henrickson said, 'but we cannot spare you the men you require. We've troubles of our own, right now. Look around you.'

Will cast his gaze beyond the two old men, taking his first look at the result of Bastion's fall. An ordered row of grey canvas tents sat to his right and left, men in uniform: soldiers, moving solemnly along their length. In the distance he could see crowds of men and women standing together, milling on the grass whilst others moved with pace along paved roads. Far to his left sat a small mound, known as The Hillock by the locals, where a sturdy tavern of stone and timber perched. It's surrounding yards were now dotted with canvas sheets and blankets strung between fence palings, makeshift shelters for people now homeless. Everywhere he looked, as far as he could see, men and women gathered, often with children holding outstretched hands.

'As you can see, Will Tolsten, we are in the midst of a catastrophe,' Henrickson stepped to his side, placed a hand on his shoulder. 'Close to a hundred thousand people now seek shelter and food. Not only are we required to provide for the citizens, we are also required to keep the peace.' He scratched his chin, cast his gaze towards The Hillock and the mass of people surrounding the tavern. 'When the people become desperate, Will, they lose all sense of order.'

Will returned a knowing look. He understood Henrickson's words, saw the enormity of the task before him. But despite the difficulties, he doubted the man would forsake those left behind. 'Surely there are some men you can spare to organise a rescue,' he began. 'I can lead the sortie into Bastion, for I know the streets better than any. But I need men. As many as you can spare.'

'We have none to spare, Will,' Henrickson held out his hands.

'We can't leave them to die! I've friends inside; friends and family.'

Lord Beaumont grabbed one of his flailing hands. 'Listen, there is a great deal you are unaware of, lad.' There was strength in the old man's grip, truth in his tired eyes. 'Perhaps you should accompany us to the wall and see for yourself.'

Henrickson consented with a grunt, then began to walk towards the Southern Wall of Bastion. Lord Beaumont and he followed, and within half-an-hour all three men were walking towards the remains of the Southern Gate House. As they reached the wooden doors with their reinforced steel, he saw close to a score of men, soldiers all, pacing a small section of the ramparts. Another dozen manned the gate.

'An enormous section of the Southern Wall is broken,' explained Henrickson, 'and even the Gate House is compromised. But we've repaired what we could in the short amount of time afforded us.'

Soldiers pushed past them as he stepped back into Bastion proper. To his left and right, just inside the gate itself, he noticed an assortment of hastily made barricades fashioned from salvaged bricks and timber. Squatting behind were thirty crossbowmen. The road leading into the city was bare, the street buckled in places, but eerily quiet for this time of day. And yet he could feel the tension in the air, felt the nervousness in the men crouched behind their barriers.

Realization came quickly. 'You're keeping the demons inside the city,' he looked at the taller man, an emptiness creeping into his heart.

'Aye, Will, but they're not the demons you think. Come, follow me.'

He watched the Swordmaster spin to his right and begin to climb a set of stairs to the ramparts above. He traced the older man's footsteps, Lord Beaumont behind him. Once at the top they enjoyed a greater view of the inner city, but he noticed at least another fifty men were stationed along this section of the wall. Nearly all held longbows, quivers brimming with brightly fletched arrows resting at their hip.

'This way,' Henrickson kept walking, headed towards a sergeant positioned a hundred feet away. Three men crouched together, peering through a looking glass much like the one Jarvis Vasco gifted him. 'Anything?' he heard Henrickson ask as they approached.

The sergeant tapped the man closest to him on the shoulder with his short sword. He slipped back a pace, allowed the Swordmaster to kneel and peer through the eyepiece. A moment passed before he offered him the same position. 'Here, Will, take a look.'

Will did as bid. At first, he saw only a shadowed street, but as his eyes became accustomed to the darkness, he noticed a subtle movement. He focused, moved the eyepiece a fraction, caught sight of a heavily cloaked creature. Its features were far removed from the scaled demons he'd encountered in the past twelve days. It was feathered black and smaller in stature.

'What is it?'

'We've no idea,' Henrickosn replied. 'It's canny, though, and not without skills. We fear it employs a form of witchcraft.'

A chill raced down his spine, tightened his stomach.

'We currently speculate they may be demonic minions of Avra the Witch,' continued Henrickson. 'If such knowledge is justified, we'll enter Bastion only when reinforcements arrive.'

Will regained his feet and stood before the two lords. They were right, he knew little of what was occurring in Bastion. But he still had a burning desire to rescue his people. Only his doubts about succeeding were growing.

'Who is Avra the Witch?' he asked, having never heard the name before.

Henrickson reached for an amulet hanging about his neck. He looked troubled, fearful, even. 'If the ravings of a king are to be taken at face value, she is the cause of all we see before us,' he lifted a hand and pointed to the crumbled buildings lining the streets. 'We need to find her. Then we need to destroy her,' he said with conviction.

'And she is somewhere inside Bastion?'

'We believe so. Only it won't be easy. As you can see, there are obstacles standing in our way. It's rather peaceful now, but come nightfall, the action truly begins.'

'What would you like me to do?'

Henrickson shaded his eyes with a hand. 'Grab your sword and find as many men amongst the thousands without Bastion as you can. Equip them, armour them - if you can - and add your number to the ranks lining the walls. There is a fight coming to the people of Dervae. If we do not prepare, it will be over before reinforcements arrive.'

'And if we kill the witch, will all be well?'

'I hope so, Will,' Henrickson's tone was lacking conviction, but there was a glint in his eyes. 'I truly hope so.'

CHAPTER THREE

Night had fallen.

Avra placed a frail hand on the rock before her, pausing to catch her breath as she climbed the steep incline. Ahead, hidden amongst shrubs and ferns and concealed in constant shadow, sat a handful of caves carved by the winds of time.

She craned her neck to the side and felt bones crack, the noise momentarily masking her heavy breathing. She was old, older than any mortal had a right to be, yet she continued to adhere to the whim of her lord. Now she returned from the camp site below, forty men trailing behind her. They walked further back, a dozen flaming brands held high to light their path through the night forest.

She took a deep breath and continued her climb, grasped a slender branch for leverage as she practically felt her way through the encroaching darkness. The night sky was clouded tonight, her unknown constellations hidden from sight. And whilst her vision was impaired, Avra was thankful for the clouds kept the cold air at bay. For five months the survivors of Bastion were fortunate enough to have clement weather, but the days were progressively becoming shorter, the nights cool. Autumn had arrived; she could feel it in her aching bones, and winter was not far away.

She curled her lip into a half-smile, despite the labour of her climb. Once winter arrived the survivors of Bastion would suffer, regardless of their efforts to erect a small town below. They were a lost people now, vagrants on a foreign world. Even Archbishop Treventos, appointed leader and spokesman, struggled before his newly formed flock. His stooped shoulders were a sign of his disposition, a reflection of his people's morale. They were alone, without guidance and terribly desperate.

They were nothing more than fodder for her Dark Lord.

She knew this because there would be no rescue. The portal between the two worlds, the connection they once crossed, had been severed. How and why, she was not sure, although she felt Neema and the tall one, Kian, were privy to the answer. Yet they had fled the moment they locked eyes on each other and hadn't been seen since. It was a frustration, and one that caused unnecessary turmoil between her and the Dark Lord. Like the survivors from Bastion, she also spent considerable time during the past five months watching for the swirling light of the portal to reappear.

They still waited.

She paused to take a deep breath, noticed the men ambling behind her were slowing their pace. It had taken the better part of an hour to reach their current position. An hour since they'd left the relative safety of their camp.

She stifled a laugh, aware the survivors, even under the guidance of Archbishop Treventos, were doomed to fall at some point. Ahriman had spoken of his desire to consume them all, one-by-one, as he fed his ravenous appetite. But the people below knew nothing of Ahriman. They'd been promised a place to escape the demons running through Bastion, a place of safety where they could recoup their losses and plan for their future return. The camp site called Sanctuary was their first accomplishment. Unnoticed she had watched the people construct their rudimentary abodes, knew the collection of shelters desperately trying to house over three thousand survivors was poor at best. Unforgiving weather took its toll in the first weeks, adding doubts and testing their faith. Yet as the second month passed half-a-dozen long halls were near completion, and an assortment of smaller shelters were finished shortly after. Now, with the fifth month coming to an end, the number of long halls capable of sleeping over a hundred men, women, and children numbered twenty. It had been Treventos himself who drove the survivors to such heights, working tirelessly, eager to see every soul under his care with a roof over their head.

He'd given them purpose, taught them to strive forever forward.

As she pushed a branch to the side, she knew it would be to no avail. When Ahriman decided to come for them, they would not be able to resist his call. Whatever hope they harboured; it would all be for naught. She knew this from experience, felt she knew it better than any other soul alive.

Darkness comes on wings of hate, she thought, as measured steps brought her to a small clearing. Its boundary consisted of blackened shrubs to one side, the other pockmarked sandstone walls. At the centre was a circular fire pit, smouldering embers glimpsed red under a mass of twigs and broken branches. A single trail of smoke wound sinuously high, disappearing into the black sky above. A dark mass sat opposite the witch on the far side of the fire pit. It was Ahriman, cloaked in shadow, his form a manifestation of hatred and malice. She looked towards him and felt the rest of her world fall away, as if she'd plunged into a bottomless pit where she knew escape was but a dream.

'You've returned,' he said, his voice a dread whisper.

'I have, my lord,' she panted before walking with slow steps into the clearing. Ahriman remained silent until she reached the smouldering fire. There was little warmth to be felt so she pulled tattered rags close about her shoulders. Within seconds her legs cramped and her twisted back became a discomfit. She briefly wondered if Ahriman felt similar pangs.

'And the men I asked for?'

'They are here, my lord,' she risked a glance over her shoulder, saw the first of the men step from between waist high shrubs to enter the clearing.

There was no response from her Dark Lord. Nor did she expect one. Ahriman had become a patient beast since their crossing to the New World, in direct contrast to the hungering god she first awakened. Not for the first time she wondered if it had anything to do with the fifty corpses of ash and bone lying discarded in the gully behind their cave. They had been a philosophical bunch, the Brotherhood of One, yet strangely not quite as discerning as she'd been led to believe. It had taken less than a month for her to discover each member, and twice that time to convince them to climb the hill to speak to their rightful leader. She wondered, and not for the first time, if Ahriman's consumption of the Order had instilled a like-minded approach to his actions. He seemed unusually cautious of late.

'How is Archbishop Treventos?' he eventually asked.

She sighed, then flicked a hand in the air. 'He's relentless,' Avra replied, 'and their progress is considerable. Most are now housed within some form of shelter, and those on the fringes will be cared for soon enough.' She paused, uncertain if she should probe deeper, then decided she had little to lose. 'Their achievement is remarkable and their resilience doubly so, but for all their labour they resemble a wretched horde on the brink of disaster. I wonder why you allow them to live at all when annihilation is your goal?'

'Time will tell, witch. If I were you, I would not concern yourself. I suggest you merely do as you're asked and nothing more.'

She nodded her head ever so slightly in deference, acutely aware of her place in the scheme of things. She'd asked questions in the past and been rebuked on more than one occasion. 'Yes, my lord,' she stuttered and then fell silent.

'Did you see any sign of the Celestial Sisters within Sanctuary?'

She shook her head. 'No, they remain absent. Not even Treventos has received any word or sign. They simply vanished into the forest during the first day we arrived and have not been seen since. From those I have questioned, it is feasible a number of the Brotherhood may have escaped with them.' She knew Ahriman would not be pleased with her words. His first wish upon settling amongst the caves atop the hill was to have every member of the Brotherhood and the Celestial Sisters brought before him for consumption. The quicker those with power were destroyed, the better. Yet it was apparent some escaped during those first, tumultuous days. It was why she trod with care every time she visited Sanctuary.

The sound of heavy feet sounded behind her. Out of the corner of her eye she saw several men enter the clearing. They moved amongst those who first arrived, jostled for position around the fire pit. Ahriman raised his voice. 'Has there been any word concerning Neema and her small party?'

'No,' her response was always the same, yet she was acutely aware her negative answers were fast altering her Dark Lord's mood. She let her mind recall the names of all those who accompanied the mystic. Once Ahriman had coerced and then disposed of those surviving members of the Brotherhood, it was a simple task for him to delve into their memories and discover relevant information. As far as they knew, Neema fled in the company of Kian, an ancient Nepharii, along with Ruvin Ciricello, Reefe O'Bannon and two boys named Donal and Jarred. But the prize Ahriman sought was the woman named Kayla Tolsten, the woman who shone sun-bright, the one Ahriman craved more than any other.

A shudder, barely glimpsed, raced through Ahriman's form. She diverted her eyes at the last instant, mindful of her lord's ailments and continual pain. He would need to feed again, and soon. Since their arrival, he'd consumed numerous souls besides those of the Brotherhood, for the journey had most certainly not been without loss. The first was a young girl, six years of age, as innocent as dew drops on grass. She had the misfortune to slip on a moss-covered stone and dash her head hard, splitting her skull. The accident was swift but deadly, and Ahriman, even from a distance, was able to summon her soul to join with his. Several altercations between men had resulted in deaths since then, likewise accidents in the forest when cutting for timber or hunting game, but they were few and far between. They weren't enough to help her Dark Lord recover his true form. Only Kayla Tolsten, she'd been told, could offer such sustenance. Apparently, somehow, she was host to thousands of souls, possibly tens-of-thousands.

She glimpsed her Dark Lord from lowered eyes. He was physically stronger since their crossing, although on the few occasions she'd seen the bare skin of his arms, she'd noticed red blotches and pus-filled welts in increasing number. It was not wise to question his health, for the repercussions were bound to be painful. But she feared he needed Kayla Tolsten sooner rather than later. Several men had been propositioned to scout their surrounds on a frequent basis, only they'd found nothing of interest. It was why she'd been tasked with gathering as many hands from Sanctuary as possible without being noticed.

She saw his gloved hand drift from the shadows of his cloak to point at the glowing fire. A word was softly spoken, igniting embers to produce dancing flames. A wave of heat caused her to shift back a foot, but she was grateful for the warmth. She was about to offer her thanks when the Dark Lord questioned her again. 'What of the Others?' he asked, and she instinctively knew he referred to those who dwelt in the forest. Again, she could offer little to appease her lord, for the creatures of the New World were sensed but rarely seen.

'There has still been no contact,' she began. 'Treventos believes they are shy creatures, most likely confused with our appearance. I heard him talking to a dozen women by the stream only yesterday. They continue to leave items of clothing and blankets during the night, along with tools, food and woven baskets, but there has been no physical contact, nor has anyone caught more than a glimpse of flaxen hair and dappled hides.'

Ahriman lowered his head, his thoughts his own for now as the last of the men stepped forward. They came singularly and in pairs, quiet men with dazed expressions. Some were tall and lean, others solid, their slow movements underlying their cautious nature. Yet she saw furtive glances as their number expanded, realised many would share concerns about the coming events. She marked them silently, told herself she would see to them if, and when, it was required. But for now, she held her nerve, for what was about to transpire was no longer her domain.

The last of the men filtered in from the night and bustled into a semi-circle about the fire. Avra's ragged cloak billowed as she stood before them, her shock of white hair wild like the night. Dressed in a conglomeration of tattered rags she smiled, revealing speckled brown teeth as she greeted the men.

52

'Welcome, gentlemen,' she rasped, for her throat was parched from having stood close to the fire.

A murmur escaped the assembled men, a few at the rear pushed closer as they cramped together for comfort. Their reason for being here was not known. All they could recall was an agreement made, a pledge fashioned with an old woman who spoke with a candied tongue.

But they were here now, nervous, and suddenly very afraid.

A slight shift in the night air caused her to look behind. Ahriman had crept forward to stand directly opposite her on the other side of the fire pit. His movement was slow and disturbingly noiseless. She hadn't even heard the scrape of his foot across the earth, or his usual laboured breathing.

'These are the men?' he asked, a shadowed hand sweeping to encompass those standing before him.

'Yes, my lord, as you requested,' she looked up, hoping to see his face, only it remained hidden by the cowl of his hooded cloak. Yet his eyes reflected the small flames before him, creating two orbs of fiery light burning with intent.

'Is there a leader amongst them?' his voice was loud and powerful, rolling through the men like a summer storm.

There was silence for several heartbeats before a solidly built man stepped forward. 'I will lead,' he said, doing his best to control the fear gripping his soul. She cast her eye over the man, noting his bald head and strong shoulders. He wasn't overly tall, but he exuded strength, evident in his manner and speech.

Ahriman held his gaze. 'And you are?'

'Jed Ironmonger,' the name was said with pride, as if the man defied anyone to say he was otherwise.

'Well, Ironmonger,' was there a hint of a smile in Ahriman's words? 'Do you know who I am?'

'I do not,' Ironmonger replied, his eyes darting to the side to see if any of those gathered knew the man cloaked in darkness.

'I am your Lord and Saviour, Ironmonger. I am He whom you will follow. I am Ahriman.'

'What do you require of me, my lord?' he asked, brows knotting, eyes uncertain.

Ahriman paused, allowed the hiss of flames and the crackle of burning wood to fill the silence, for the usual night noises had become eerily absent. He took a slow step forward, stood mere inches from the fire pit. The flames danced at his approach, as if they'd been enticed higher by a subtle twist of his hand. 'Devotion!' he finally said, this time with unbridled force. Every man, all forty of them, felt the ground shake beneath their feet.

Jed Ironmonger lowered his gaze and knelt, digging his fingers into the dirt. He remained there, head down, whilst Ahriman walked through fire to stand before him. Avra watched the procession, saw the flames move hypnotically about her Dark Lord, hissing and spitting as they flickered about his blackened form. 'You are the first, Jed Ironmonger,' Ahriman touched the man's bald head with a clawed hand as he cleared the pit and its flames. 'The men here will answer to you, and you will answer to me. Do you understand?'

'Yes, my lord,' his voice quavered.

'And because you're the first, Ironmonger, it's only fitting I bestow you a gift.'

The bald man lifted his head, eyes startlingly wide. Then he convulsed as purple-black strands of dark energy seeped from Ahriman's outstretched fingers and onto the exposed skin of his face. The man's eyes rolled back in their sockets; his teeth clenched hard. Glossy tendrils snaked into his ears, pushed past his lips and slipped up his nose. His strong hands balled into heavy fists. He struck the ground once, then twice, before a primal scream flew forth, the tortured sound accompanied by long strands of black-stained spittle.

And then he relaxed.

A tear slid down his cheek. Ironmonger wiped it away with the back of his hand and stood. Avra looked to her left, where several trees cloaked in shadow huddled near the pockmarked cave wall. Hanging from their low branches was an assortment of animal carcasses. A number were wolf-like in appearance, only their skin was toughened leather, not fur, whilst three wildcats also joined them in death. They were emaciated, maggot infested and bound with dark energy. Even from where she stood, she could see the ground below covered in filth. It had become apparent to her early on that human souls were not the only source of sustenance available to Ahriman.

'Good,' Ahriman coerced him to stand with a finger. 'Now you are more than a man, Ironmonger.' Ahriman breathed deep, then leant forward, his hand resting on Ironmonger's shoulder. 'Now you share the reflexes, stamina, and cunning of this world's native animals. They are hunters. And now, so are you.'

There was an understanding in Ironmonger's eyes. His body convulsed, and realization came swiftly as raw power surged through his veins. 'What of my men?' There was a smile on his lips and a hunger in his eyes.

'They will bend the knee and receive, as you did.'

Avra watched the men step forward to receive Ahriman's foul blessing. They did so with trepidation at first, and rightly so, for she knew they were about to become lost to the race of man. Ironmonger may have been enhanced with dark energy, fuelled with strength and power beyond the capabilities of man, but the others were about to become little more than vacant vessels imbued with an animal's savage hunger. It took time, but eventually the last man rose to his feet, his eyes glazed and unknowing.

Jed Ironmonger pushed his way through the crowd of silent men. 'What do you require of us, my lord?'

'To adhere to my every whim.'

Ironmonger looked to his men, saw only blank stares in return. 'They will follow my orders?'

'They will. Your voice will be my voice, Ironmonger. They will run for you; they will hunt for you.'

Ironmonger flexed his right hand, felt the muscles in his bicep tighten and bulge. 'What are we hunting?'

'There is a woman, Kayla Tolsten by name, who has fled into the forest. With her travels a tall man named Kian.' Avra heard her Dark Lord's voice rise ever-so-slightly. He was excited, she realised, and hid it poorly. Perhaps now, after so many months scouting, a lead could be found from Ahriman's new hunters.

'There is also an old woman, a mystic,' he continued, 'and a handful of men running with them. I want them found, Ironmonger.' Ahriman's height rose several inches as he swept those gathered with a withering gaze. 'Find Kayla Tolsten and the ancient known as Kian for me. Bring them back alive.' There was a uniform nod from the gathering. She wondered if the men could speak, or if their minds were completely void of human thought.

'And those who remain?' Ironmonger asked.

'Kill them,' her Dark Lord's eyes blazed with fury, 'and let your men feed!'

CHAPTER FOUR

It was the screams that woke him.

Tarsin Va lifted a hand to rub at tired eyes, cursed under his breath as the reality of his situation became apparent. Blood and death consumed his sleeping hours, the high-pitched screams of his fallen men a constant reminder of the final battle before Aston's Tear. No matter how exhausted he felt, the dreams were always there, waiting to engulf him in despair and anger. Waiting to remind him of all he'd lost.

He sat up in silence, aware his men were still asleep. He could barely see them in the pre-dawn light, for even during the height of day, only a narrow beam of sunlight would shine from above, slipping through a crevice in the cave ceiling. Yet his eyes were now accustomed to the gloom. Thirty-six days in confinement would see to that.

He shifted his body, kept his movement as quiet as possible, aware the woven mat beneath him tended to scrape loudly upon the rock and shale of the cave floor. Repositioned, he cast his eyes over the shapes of his men. Twelve remained. Four had died within the first few days, their wounds too great to heal. Several others were lucky to still be alive, yet despite their imprisonment, their captors had provided clean water, linen, and a foul-smelling salve to administer amongst the men. The four who perished were removed, taken by clawed hands into the light of day. He often wondered if his only chance to feel the sun on his face was to die.

He cast his mind back to the fateful day before the pyramid. He could almost smell the blood on his hands, could certainly hear the groans and curses. Yet it was the battle itself that intrigued him: the idea he could have acted differently, the notion that his actions were directly responsible for their current imprisonment. What if he were to change his tactics? What if he sent men running to the streets instead of into the pyramid?

The ideas clouded his thoughts; distracted him.

A gentle sigh eased past his lips. He knew his men required more from their king. An escape from the cave would be a start.

He looked towards the entrance. It was large enough for three men to walk abreast, yet a circular stone was positioned on the outside, polished smooth and weighing a tonne. Griffith and Jaegar had tried on numerous occasions to shift the monstrosity, yet neither could grip the stone tight nor find adequate purchase. The only other exit was a narrow fissure at the rear of the cave. It allowed water from a small pool to slip outside but was solid stone and could not be widened. They were at the mercy of those who captured them. Unfortunately, the men who shared features with those of predatory cats appeared to show little interest in their quarry. Apart from a sack of food being lowered from the crevice above each day, contact had been minimal.

And the men were restless.

On three separate occasions the men had voiced their displeasure, roused into action by a survivor named Bardell. He was an angry man, tall and slender with a quick wit and a quicker hand. Dishevelled black hair, a wild beard and narrow eyes suggested constant anger, and Tarsin sensed a black heart was caged within his chest. From day one he'd been a voice of concern, testing boundaries and causing dissent. Bardell's desire to return to Bastion was paramount, and Tarsin – their rightful king - was always first to hear of his plight. Thankfully, he only held sway over four men, and thus his calls of justice and action were rebuked and pushed to the side. But they weren't forgotten. Tarsin recalled all their arguments. Remembered every foul word and accusation thrown his way. If it hadn't been for Griffith or Jaegar's steadying hand, he and Bardell would most certainly have traded blows.

And yet the question that vexed him most was not whether he should listen to Bardell and return home to Bastion, but what they could do once they arrived? Could they make a difference in the fight against the Deios? Would there be a city for them to return to? Or had the witch, Avra Creswick, offered her mad God the throne so he could rule over a broken city and the demons who crawled within?

So much speculation. So many variables.

Tarsin knew his decisions were fashioned in the dark. He was not privy to any information concerning his enemies. He couldn't see their movements, couldn't begin to even know their location. Even if he and his men could escape their prison and return to Bastion, the journey would be fraught with peril. He asked himself again, as he'd done countless times since they arrived on this strange world, what help could he and his twelve men bring? What difference would they make?

Was there any hope left for the city they loved?

Not having answers to such questions was tearing his sanity apart. And Bardell was simply voicing his own inner demons, the same demons every man under his care suffered. Thirty-six days contemplating a situation they could do nothing about. And if given the chance to return, he still harboured doubts concerning their course of action. As a king, he was confused, and he felt his men were desperate for someone stronger.

He wasn't sure he was destined to be the king they sought.

Not now. Perhaps not ever.

*

It was almost midday when the stone circle blocking the entrance rolled to the side.

Sunlight bathed the men, most still sitting on their woven mats. Tarsin was leaning against the rock wall to the left, the flame-haired Cale Griffith beside him. They raised their eyes, squinting, to peer at the vacant space before them. A cool breeze hinted at freedom. Before any of the men could voice an opinion or express an exclamation, the silhouette of two cloaked shapes materialized from within the light. They reached the entrance, then beckoned with clawed hands for the men to rise and follow. A moment later they were gone.

Tarsin blinked, as did his men. They stood with mouths open for several heartbeats before he clapped his hands together to rouse them. The sudden noise shifted bodies, and within moments they were standing outside, the glorious sun caressing skin and warming hearts.

Griffith leant over to whisper in his ear. 'What do you think is about to happen?'

Tarsin shrugged his shoulders in reply. For too long he'd mulled over an assortment of scenarios regarding their freedom. Now, with clear passage from the cave confirmed, he was at a loss to explain their next step.

'Do we make a run for it?' It was Jaegar who voiced the next question, the Herkosian with his twin-braided beard stood a foot taller than any of the men. With a hand raised to shield his eyes from the sun, he was already scanning their surroundings for a way clear.

Tarsin looked to those who beckoned, saw them walking away from the cave, heading up a dirt path that wound to their left. To their right sat a mound of knee-high grass swaying to a gentle breeze, beyond spread a turquoise sky.

It took a moment for him to realise they were standing near the edge of a cliff.

Tarsin pointed towards the path. 'Let's move,' he met the eyes of his men. They were sombre, for most felt consigned to a life in the shadows. Yet he knew his own eyes were brimming with a vitality he'd not felt since he first returned to Bastion aboard the *Lioness*.

He took the lead, walked ahead, the eager steps of his booted feet tempered by the soft ground. He felt no need to see if his men followed.

He couldn't tell how long they walked to reach their destination: a circular arena of grey pebbles before a carved temple of sandstone, for his vision was consumed by an incredible view of sky-reaching towers of rock in the distance. For as far as he could see, in every direction, pillars of rock thrust upward from a churning sea. Five hundred feet they soared, steps carved into their sides, twirling their way to hollow doors pockmarked upon their stone flanks. Grass fields adorned the top of each pillar, stunted trees adding volume and vibrant colour, whilst vine-like thick tendrils dangled from sandy perches as they sought the ocean below.

Tarsin had chanced a step closer to the edge to peer at the sea below, saw a collection of wooden shelters on enormous stilts, swaying bridges, and numerous jetties inching into frothing water. The distance was impressive, nerve-racking, even, but before he stepped back from the edge he squinted, noticed dozens of bobbing sea-craft traversing the blue.

'Gods above,' Griffith was by his side, 'where are we?'

Tarsin didn't know. None of them knew. When they first stepped into the light, to cross a vast space through a portal inside Aston's Tear, they arrived under cover of darkness. They saw little in their first moments other than clawed hands reaching for them. Hoods were cast over their heads, further blanketing their senses, whilst strong hands gripped their wrists and deprived them of arms and armour. Since then, the cave was all they had known.

A shuffle of feet subsided behind him as his men arrived and settled, the noise dragging him from his reverie. He took the opportunity to survey their surroundings, noted the temple of stone in the background and the arena they now stood in. It was circled by seats carved from the same stone as the temple, a pale yellow in colour. The temple itself was an impressive structure with arched windows and fluted columns, an assortment of etchings denoting flora bordering the vast entrance.

Yet it was the two figures standing before him that caught his attention and held it.

They were of similar height, robed in grey, their hoods masking their appearance. An outstretched hand motioned for the men to sit. Tarsin could see the creature's claws, noticed skin a darker hue than his own. And he could feel their eyes upon him, studying his movements, his actions.

He sat with his men, heard the scrape of pebbles shifting.

The husky sound of a wind instrument sounded from the temple.

The notes were clear and concise. At their conclusion, a parade of robed figures, all in grey, began to emerge from darkened doorways. They walked silently, each holding a wooden staff bound with coloured feathers and rings of leather. They followed each other into the arena, moved with grace to circle the men sitting on the ground. A moment later they stepped back to stand before stone seats, staffs held firm by their side, straight as a pole.

Tarsin could hear the men muttering behind him. They were frightened, and Bardell was already suggesting they make a run for it. Tarsin's eyes found Jaegar, narrowed slightly. The Herkosian understood and told Bardell to cease his chatter.

Seconds later another burst of notes sounded, higher pitched, but equally compelling.

Tarsin felt his eyes drawn to the temple. This time a single figure stepped into the light of day, dressed in robes, only these were a deep ocean-blue in colour and trimmed at the hem with cloth of gold. Like those before, the creature was hooded, its eyes unseen. Its hands were tucked within its sleeves. The creature stopped as it reached the arena, took a seat. The others followed.

'I don't like what I'm seeing,' Griffith whispered behind a hand. Tarsin shrugged in return, intent on watching the one clothed in blue.

'Are we to be butchered, do you think?'

Another shrug. Tarsin doubted they would be so cold-hearted, but then he knew little other than what he now saw. As he mulled over the question, he wondered why it was only now, on this day, that he and his men were to be offered an audience.

There was a ceremony being played out here. He could see the movements of the grey robes, precise and controlled. And he could feel the stillness in the air, as if those surrounding the arena were holding their breath until called upon. He didn't know what was about to occur, but he felt calm, despite the unusual circumstances. This, as far as he knew, was the first time either species had truly surveyed the other. Unless, he thought, they'd been spied upon whilst in the cave. The idea had merit, but he chose to ignore it. There was more to consider now they were outside and under the sun. Despite his dark thoughts earlier in the day, he was king. It was his duty to observe, and if the situation became ugly, to protect. He would be there for his men.

It was all he had left.

Two figures entered his field of vision, stepping from his left and right, both twirling a staff as they arrived to stand opposite each other. They had dispensed with their grey robes, and now wore loose pants of cloth tied with cord. Their muscular chests were bare, although one carried a set of black stripes, possibly tribal marks, that covered most of his torso. Tarsin narrowed his eyes, focused on their facial appearance. It was as he believed. Both were men, only their faces resembled those of a hunting cat, fierce eyes and sharp teeth, thick manes of hair swept back. Both shared a look with the other, then spun to face the one clothed in blue, offered a bow. For several heartbeats all was quiet.

A word was softly spoken by their leader. The two cat-men swivelled to face each other, then began to move with speed, twirling their wooden weapons and rolling their shoulders. Quick steps in were countered by sliding feet backwards as the two fought an imaginary contest, highlighting their skills and showcasing their agile nature. The pace was frenetic, the timing of their strikes and thrusts precise. Subtle tilting at their hips helped them avoid overhead swings, and the sway of their bodies prevented any unwanted contact. Tarsin watched it all with a hunger in his eyes, saw the movements before they eventuated, anticipated the sweep of the legs and the leap to follow. It was true artistry: a performance of sublime skill tempered with endurance, power, and finesse.

It was everything he had been taught by Du Weng Sai.

A flourish of strikes against their wooden poles provided a cracking finale, before the two combatants spun to bow once more to their leader. Deep breaths expanded burning lungs, sweat glistened on bare skin. As they rose from their bow, all was silent.

Griffith leant in close. 'They're good with sticks,' he said, loud enough to be heard by the men they sat with. A number chuckled, despite the unusual circumstances they found themselves in.

A sharp, short whistle cut the air.

The duelling cat-men retreated from the arena to sit amongst those who formed the circle. Within seconds another cat-man left his seat, grabbed his staff, and walked to stand before them. He stood there a moment, unmoving.

'I think he wants one of us to join him,' it was young Connor, the red-haired lad from Ruvin Ciricello's mercenary band who spoke.

Could such be true? His men could not hope to replicate the duel they just witnessed. But if it was a duel of combat skills they wished to see, then he believed they stood a chance. 'Would you like the privilege?' Tarsin locked eyes with the youngster. The lad was strong and well balanced, could take a hit or two. He doubted he'd be as fast, though. Nor as cunning.

'Why not,' Connor rose to his feet with a cheer from the men. Jaegar slapped him on the back as he passed, before a staff was thrown to him by a cat-man standing on the rim.

For a moment, Tarsin wondered if young Connor could handle the situation with enough poise to not look foolish. Then he remembered all he'd been through before they arrived on this strange world. The lad was capable. And having spent more than a month holed up in a cave, swinging a staff would be a means to release some pent-up aggression.

Mostly, though, he believed it to be nothing more than a chance to compare physical skills against each other.

Perhaps it was also an exercise in trust.

Connor took his time to enter the pebbled arena, twisting his body and stretching his muscles as he walked forward. He twirled the staff, mimicking his adversary, then made his way to stand before his opponent.

Tarsin kept his eyes on the cat-man, watched his subtle movements, noticed his shallow breathing.

Combat began with a flourish.

Connor back-peddled as quickly as able as the cat-man launched an attack. The staff snaked out, quicker than lightning, to crack against his chest. It was followed by a sweep towards the legs. Connor jumped on cue, timing his landing with a sweep of his own. The cat-man ducked, his legs sliding atop the pebbles, stretching outwards until he was barely two inches from the ground. Then he leapt up with a spring, bringing his own staff down in a vicious chop. A loud crack sounded as the two wooden staves met. Connor shifted to his left, dipping his shoulder so he could then push off with his braced left leg. Only his opponent was no longer before him. Instead, he was now twirling and cartwheeling across the ground, putting distance between the two.

They circled for several heartbeats, then rushed towards each other. Connor swerved and swung his staff, hoping to connect as he slid his grip towards one end. Yet the cat-man stepped close, blocked the attempted hit, and twisted his own staff across and then down. A sharp crack knocked Connor atop the head and he was down.

Tarsin sighed, signalled Griffith and Jaegar to gather the lad. It was obvious Connor was dazed, but the blow had been tempered. This was a test of skill, not an act of malice.

A familiar sensation began to flow through his veins. He recalled his fight against the colossal demon before the pyramid, remembered the surge of adrenaline. This was different, though. This was not a duel to the death, merely an introduction to see where each species stood when measured against the other.

Jaegar reached his side and dipped his head. 'May I have the pleasure?' he asked with a smile between his twin braided beard.

Tarsin returned the smile in recognition of his request.

The Herkosian rolled his massive shoulders and stepped into the arena. The men to either side voiced words of encouragement, for he was the tallest, and apart from Griffith, possibly the strongest amongst the survivors. As he reached the centre a staff was passed to him by a nimble cat-man, at least two feet shorter than Jaegar. The staff looked small in his large hands, but he gripped it tight and swung it from side-to-side to gauge its length and weight.

Tarsin clapped Connor on the back as he came to sit by his side. 'You did well, Connor,' he said quietly. 'A count of forty-six. Let us see how long Jaegar can stand for.'

The young man smiled, despite the ringing in his ears.

Silence descended as Jaegar took long strides to stand before his opponent. A mutual nod between the two was quickly followed by a flurry of strikes, expertly timed and equally balanced. The crack of wood was crisp in the midday air, the grind of feet on stone mingled with quickened breaths. Connor counted to fifty-two before the cat-man pivoted on a heel, slammed his staff into the ground so he could use it as leverage, and leapt into the air to kick Jaegar in the chest with both feet.

The Herkosian fell on his back with a thud, the air blasted from his lungs. A moment later he regained his feet to re-join the men, anger brewing behind his eyes. 'He's quick,' he rumbled, pulling at his dishevelled beard. 'But if you hit the bastard, he'll stay down.'

'Any others wish to test their skills?' Tarsin met the eyes of his men, saw interest in Setorious, but was surprised when Bevan held up his hand. The man was a canny swordsman, yet he'd suffered wounds few men could survive during their flight. Like nearly every man present, he carried white scars across his flesh, an incredibly vicious seam running across his forehead and one below his ear. For several days Tarsin thought they were going to lose him, but Bevan rallied like the stout old warrior he was and made a full recovery.

'What was Jaegar's count?' Bevan asked as he walked onto the pebbles with a smile.

'Fifty-two,' Connor shouted, also smiling.

Tarsin hid his emotions as Bevan entered the arena, but inwardly he was pleased his men were accepting of the confrontation. He could already feel the tension ease from weeks of confinement, sensed the men were enjoying the physical challenge. He didn't know if the cat-men were performing a ritual to access their skills, or if they were being judged. They appeared to be as fixated with the contest as he was, for keen eyes followed every move, the occasional twitch in a shoulder or flexing of hands indicating a desire to participate.

'Thirty-three!' Connor shouted as Bevan fell to a sweep of his legs.

The men clapped as he returned, only for Griffith to take his place on the field.

Tarsin's first real interest in the contest narrowed his eyes as his wild, red-haired friend with the barrel chest and thick arms picked up a staff. Like Jaegar, Griffith flexed his considerable bulk, then twirled the staff in a tight circle. Within seconds the two combatants were trading blows, only Griffith, being less nimble, kept his footwork concise, his balance measured. He couldn't afford to overextend, for he lacked the speed to defend the blindingly fast thrusts of his smaller opponent. So he kept as still as able, shifting only to remain face on, his hands working furiously so his staff could knock his opponent's attacks away.

His technique worked. Connor reached one hundred and continued to count, with Griffith moving freely, his rhythm gaining momentum. And then, surprisingly, Griffith charged with a burst of speed, dropping his staff and grabbing his opponent about the throat. A second later the crack of two foreheads meeting sounded within the arena. The cat-man fell to the ground with a flourish of arms and legs.

The men cheered and raised hands to the sky.

Tarsin's smile grew as Griffith stomped over. 'Nice move, Cale Griffith,' he said, gripping the larger man's hand.

'Jaegar was right,' Griffith returned, wiping his brow, 'one hit and they're down.'

Tarsin watched the fallen cat-man regain his feet out of the corner of his eye. He was then helped from the arena by two of his comrades, some curious glances cast their way.

'One hundred and five was your count,' Connor said, smiling at Griffith before turning to ask a question. 'Can you do better, my lord?'

The question was backed by several men, voices rising as the challenge was made. He couldn't refuse, he knew, for he was their leader and king. But more than that, he was their inspiration.

Blue eyes sparkled as Tarsin rose to his feet to cease their chatter, before he walked to meet his opponent. Silence reigned immediately. He reached the centre and picked up Griffith's fallen staff, waited for someone to meet him in the middle. The eyes of the tall leader couldn't be seen beneath his blue hood, but Tarsin felt his piercing gaze, nonetheless. He wondered if he would join him.

He made no move, remained unnervingly still.

A cat-man stepped away from his stone seat and shrugged off his grey robe. He was equally as tall, muscular and broad. A thick mane of golden hair swept down to his shoulders, tinged with streaks of charcoal. A set of swirling black tattoos ringed his forearms. He reached the centre and hefted his staff, then stretched his bunched muscles in a short display of coordination and skilled leaps. As he settled to stand opposite, Tarsin slid his feet into the pebbled ground and stood firm, his staff standing straight beside him.

Their eyes met and held. Tarsin could see flecks of silver twinkling amongst vibrant blue. A deep breath, controlled and precise, allowed Tarsin to relax his body. He knew what to expect.

The cat-man leapt towards him with a burst of speed and frightful power. His wooden staff swept over a shoulder to come arcing from his left, swinging directly for Tarsin's torso. Tarsin let go of his own staff, crouched beneath the strike, then surged forward to rise and slam his right palm into the cat-man's midriff. As the cat-man's breath fled his lungs and his body flailed through the air, Tarsin halted his forward momentum and pushed back, grasping his staff before it fell to the ground.

Silence reigned . . .

. . . for a second until the cat-man struck the pebbles hard and slid three feet. A gasp was heard from his men behind him. Every cat-man surrounding the arena left their seat to stand tall, including their leader in his ocean-blue robes.

'I never even started the count,' Tarsin heard Connor's voice clearly, but further talk stalled as the leader in blue took long strides to stand before him. Tarsin could see little of the creature's face for it was shadowed, yet he believed he saw a sparkle from hidden eyes. He tensed his body, aware of how close the taller creature was. Tarsin realised if he raised his hand, he could place it on the chest of the leader.

Instead, the leader leant forward with a swiftness of his own, placed finger and thumb against Tarsin's temples.

Everything Tarsin knew was swallowed by a wave of darkness. His senses were swamped, his clarity of thought taken from him. He sought to retaliate against the rising tide, found he couldn't breathe to fire his blood. Tendrils snaked into his mind, slipping around past thoughts and actions, sinking to depths he cared not to visit by choice. He felt himself drowning.

He heard voices from far away, opened eyes he didn't realise were closed.

The hand about his forehead fell back. The pressure at his temples eased.

'Your name?' said a voice, its accent thick.

Tears formed in Tarsin's eyes. It took a moment for his senses to realign, to realise the creature before him had spoken. He took a deep breath; aware his heart was beating rapidly. He felt a sudden desire to see the face of the man he was speaking to.

'Tarsin Va,' he replied, hesitation in his voice. He wondered how the creature could speak his language, let alone understand him.

'Tarsin Va,' the words were repeated, slowly, as if pronunciation was important. The leader began to walk away, then looked over his shoulder.

'We will talk.'

CHAPTER FIVE

It was the shrill whistle of a bird that roused Tarsin from his meditation.

He was sitting on a patch of moss beneath an unusual tree, one he'd stumbled across the first day he and his men were released from their cave. The hooded creatures left as one within moments of their leader departing, leaving him and his men to contemplate events, basking in glorious sunshine. It didn't take long for the men to drift away from each other, intent on exploring their surrounds.

Yet Tarsin felt content, remained in the arena for some time, musing over the words spoken to him. Countless questions found their way into his consciousness, screaming for answers. Only the tall leader in his blue cloak was gone. Time passed before Tarsin came to the realization he would not be returning, at least not this day. So, like his men, he took a moment to revel in the feel of the sun and wind on his skin, before deciding to explore the area.

It didn't take long.

The expanse was less than a mile in diameter, situated at the peak of a pillar of rock. Five hundred feet below splashed the sea, churning waves crashing into rocky outcrops. He could only assume the portal they stepped through was here, possibly inside the temple itself. But like his men, he avoided the dark doorways that led within. For now, he'd enjoy the sight of green grass and the wind's loving caress. And, as he soon discovered, the wonderful abundance of unusual trees.

It was the knobby trunks that first caught his eye. Twisted knobs of wood, almost like large bubbles, dotted the squat trunks in a patterned conglomeration. He found the pale skin of the tree to be smooth and blemish free when he ran his hand over its surface. And looking up, he realized the tree stood no larger than fifteen feet in height, yet its branches stretched twice that length to either side, remaining low to provide excellent shade from the midday sun. Broad, flat leaves, three-pronged and emerald green were in abundance, but it was the dark swirls wrapped about the narrow branches that intrigued him, for they looked eerily like the tribal tattoos Jaegar wore on his own head and arms. He wondered if they were natural, or perhaps belonged to a ritual practiced by the locals. It mattered not, for they were pleasing and evoked a sense of calm in the swordsman. And for the last three days he'd spent hours here in quiet contemplation.

He opened his eyes, slowly, hoping to spy the small bird who whistled such a beautiful song.

It sat on the tattooed branch above, a small bird, wren-like, only its feathers were angel-white. So similar to what he'd seen before, back in Bastion, yet so different.

'She is a pretty sight, is she not?'

Tarsin tilted his head, then stood in a fluid motion, spinning about so he could see the one who spoke.

'In a cycle's time you will see the male *chilt,* who is a riot of colour.'

Tarsin saw the creature in the blue robes standing behind him, alone, yet hooded, his gold-trimmed garment swaying gently in the breeze.

'How can you speak my tongue?' Tarsin found his voice, although he was acutely aware he didn't hear the leader's approach, a fact that unnerved him considerably.

'I have studied your thoughts, Tarsin Va, and learnt your tongue in the process.'

Curious eyes narrowed. 'You studied my thoughts?'

'Yes, when our minds connected three days earlier. I'm sorry it has taken this long to reach out to you, but I had other concerns to attend to.'

'You're talking about when you placed your hand about my forehead?'

'Yes. I have the means to look deep into another's mind if I so choose. What I found was of great interest, Tarsin Va.'

'So you know who I am?'

The creature took a step closer and held out a hand. 'Not entirely. I need to listen to your voice and hear the emotion in your words to truly understand who you are.'

Tarsin shook his head, realized he was speaking to someone of vast intellect. 'You learnt my tongue within three days, from reading my thoughts?'

'Half a day, actually. As I said, I had other matters to attend. Your arrival has caused quite a stir amongst the locals, Tarsin Va.' A hand swept back towards the temple. 'They were confused and frightened, so I apologize on their behalf.'

'Apologize?'

'For your imprisonment. Their options were few, and without guidance, felt it best to confine you and your men until I arrived. Unfortunately, I was far away. I am sorry.'

Tarsin relaxed at the words, felt the muscles in his shoulders ease. He lowered his eyes to see his hands uncurl. All the harsh words he'd dreamt of screaming to the night now seemed childish. Like Aston's Tear in Bastion, there was a great deal occurring that he knew so little about.

He levelled his gaze. 'Who are you?'

A moment of silence followed, punctuated seconds later by the beautiful call of the angel-white *chilt*.

'I believe you already know what I am, Tarsin Va,' hands reached for the cowl as he spoke, then slowly pulled back the cloth to reveal a face not unlike those that captured them when they arrived. 'I am Inesco.'

'You appear like the locals, Inesco, but there is a quality about you that suggests you are quite different.' Tarsin shifted his feet and narrowed his eyes. At first glance, Inesco shared features common to those they'd seen when they arrived. Broad, flat noses, puffy cheeks and curious eyes full of mirth. Yet his ears were not as pointed, nor his teeth as sharp. And his skin didn't appear to be as weathered. There was also an aura of superiority surrounding him. Not in a forceful fashion, merely a feeling of complete understanding. Although as he finished his appraisal, Tarsin did note the thick mane of tawny hair that fell to Inesco's shoulders.

'You are correct, Tarsin Va, and very perceptive.'

'You are one of the Nepharii, aren't you?'

Inesco smiled, then waved a hand towards where Tarsin had been meditating when he arrived. 'Perhaps we should sit. I have a feeling we may find ourselves talking for the remainder of the day.'

*

Cale Griffith sat his tired body on a sandstone seat, took a deep breath, then raised his eyes so he could continue to watch the morning ritual performed by those called Panthians.

It was something to behold. Twenty monks leaped and twirled in unison, their staves spinning by their side. This was the fifth day since Griffith joined their routine, and he was lasting longer, his stamina improving.

'You're keeping well, Griffith,' Tarsin sat to his left, a smile on his face.

'Aye, I feel well,' he said, scratching his beard. It was now fifty days since they first arrived, and without the temptation of drink and copious amounts of food, he'd trimmed at the waist. Eating only once a day also helped, for the men were invited to consume their food with the monks before midday and then fast the remaining hours. Having been imprisoned for so long, the adaption hadn't proven to be difficult, and more than one survivor had commented on how energetic and clear-headed they felt.

'The monks are almost finished,' Tarsin nodded towards the arena, 'you almost lasted the entire session.'

'I will tomorrow,' Griffith replied, conviction in his voice. With so few duties to attend to, he'd taken it upon himself to increase his skills. Sitting here, on what Tarsin described as the world known as Aeth, was not going to win the war back home. Griffith needed to be ready for any eventuality. When they returned, blood and death were to be the only certainty. He vowed to be prepared.

'I've spoken to Inesco about our arms and armour,' Tarsin began, 'and he believes they can be returned within days.

The monks are curious about their design and function and have been taking notes. Metal is scarce on this world.'

Griffith took another deep breath, wiped sweat from his forehead and brushed back his curly red hair. He looked to his king, studied his bearded face. Tarsin appeared healthy and strong. 'The men are restless.'

'I know, my friend.'

'You are our king. It's your responsibility to free us from this . . . predicament.'

'I'm working on it.'

'Are you? The men have noted you're spending a great deal of time with your new friend, Inesco.' In truth Griffith was equally concerned, only he'd held his tongue from joining the chorus of voices questioning the king's whereabouts and apparent lack of leadership. Tarsin had shared only a small amount of information with the survivors of Bastion. Apart from knowing Inesco was Nepharii and the race of men at the temple were called Panthians, the men knew very little. Granted, the Panthians here were monks: keepers of knowledge and protectors of the temple, but Griffith heard there were other tribes beyond the temple they knew nothing about.

'I'm sorry, my friend. I'm learning a great deal about our situation, much of which is increasingly difficult to fathom. I've been preoccupied with a great many things. I should have shared what I know.'

'Aye, you should have,' Griffith cast his eyes back to the arena where the monks were finishing their stretching routine. 'Right now, we have people wondering where we are, looking for leaders, searching for those who are lost. We cannot sit and contemplate any longer. We should be fighting to reclaim our city.'

'Inesco says time works differently here, on this world, and that we can plan before we act. Besides, I don't think the thirteen of us will make a difference in the battle to come.'

'We have to at least try, Tarsin. Sitting here wondering what might occur is not enough. We have to do something.'

'And we will, Griffith. Listen,' Griffith watched his king, saw the fire in his eyes. His words had stung his friend, as he hoped they would. It was not like Tarsin to sit and dither. He was a man of action, a quick thinker. There were many reasons why he led the Unseen, many reasons why the men swore an oath to follow his lead.

'I'm listening,' Griffith replied, the beginning of a smile tweaking his lips as the blue fire in Tarsin's eyes shimmered. He remembered Jaegar's words earlier in the day. Remembered the Herkosian telling him to confront Tarsin with disappointment and frustration. Recalled him saying it might be enough to jolt the king into action, to fire his blood once again with passion and responsibility.

'Much of the past few days, I have spent telling Inesco about myself,' Tarsin began. 'He claimed until he knew who I was, he could not help me. So, I spoke of my childhood in the orphanage, spoke about the children and how we spent our days running through the streets of Bastion. I told him about our hardships, but more importantly to him, I think, I spoke about the hardships of the people within the city. I described the incredible stench of the tanneries and the smell of brine from the docks. I spoke of the curses flung with disdain amongst those selling wares and the drunken sailors cavorting through the streets. I told him how a group of us would huddle under an overhang on miserable days, watching to see if we could steal some food from those who sloshed through muddy streets. I explained to him how the groans of men and the moans of women plying their trade could be heard in the alley behind us.

'I told him how the men would leave moments later, relieved but still alone, whilst the women would appear shortly after, their face a mask of pain, their only satisfaction a silver piece to see them through another day.'

'You haven't exactly painted a pretty picture of our home, Tarsin,' Griffith shook his head.

'Aye, but it is the truth, and it was important that I do so,' Tarsin replied. 'I also informed Inesco about King Arkos Vantos and how he protected his people. I spoke of the grand temples and cathedrals lining the city, the colourful ships dotting the Bay of Pennants. And then I explained my arrival at Highcastle and our training regime under Lloyd Henrickson and Du Weng Sai, some of the greatest days I've ever lived.

'In the end, though, I told him about our final days in Bastion, revealed to him the inner workings of the pyramid: Aston's Tear, and the coming of the witch and her summoned God, Ahriman.'

'What of the Deios?'

'I explained their arrival, along with that of Kian, the Nepharii. And I told him of our last days, how we found our king dead, how we fought, and how we lost Kayla Tolsten and thousands of our people.'

Griffith cleared his throat. 'It's still not a pretty picture.'

'I know, my friend. But it does show how dire our situation is. We need help, it is what I've been asking for.'

'And will Inesco help us?'

'He will help. In some fashion. Perhaps his help has already begun.'

'How so?'

His king sighed deeply; and Griffith became aware his voice must be parched from all his talking. 'Because in revealing everything about myself, Cale Griffith, including what I fear, those I admire and cherish, and those I love, I have inadvertently reinforced my beliefs in who I am and what it is I am supposed to accomplish.'

'And what is that, exactly?'

'To be your king, my friend, I must care for our people. When the time is right, we will return and rescue those who need rescuing. Then we'll fight for our city and reclaim that which is ours.'

'Aye, that's more like it. When can I tell the others?'

'Soon, Cale Griffith. Perhaps sooner than you think.'

*

Tarsin had watched the single moon arc across the night sky for several hours. He'd been unable to sleep, for his mind was crowded, so he'd left the cave where his men still slept and made his way to the knotted tree. Here he felt something akin to peace, although his mind continued to swirl with ideas. He let go of his thoughts, focused on the stars shining from an unknown mantle as he fashioned his own constellations. The exercise eased his troubles for a time, long enough for him to realize the sun would soon rise.

'Are you troubled, Tarsin Va?'

Tarsin shared a smile with the pre-dawn light. He'd heard the faintest crunch of a dry leaf underfoot as Inesco approached.

'Not as much as I feared,' he spun to look the Nepharii in the eye. He was attired in his usual sea-blue robes, although his cowl was thrown back, his leopard-like face visible.

'I can see a number of burning questions in your eyes, Tarsin. What would you ask?'

'So many things,' Tarsin began. 'I have explained much of my life and the world where I live. I would have you do the same.'

'This world is called Aeth, its people are Panthians. I am Nepharii, a Guardian for this world and the portal that sits behind the temple, much like Kian is a Guardian for the world called Vidae.'

'That much I already knew, Inesco. What of you? How do you share a visage like that of the Panthians?'

'I have been here many years, Tarsin Va, for time here moves differently when compared to your world. I have seen the rise and fall of two ages of Panthians, observed the destructive cycle of life and the wonderful rebirth to follow. After so much time, inevitably, you become that which the eyes see.'

Tarsin nodded his head, still not certain he'd learnt anything new. 'And what of the Panthians? Who are they? Surely there are more than a small group of monks sitting atop a pillar of rock?'

Inesco shared a laugh. 'Certainly, Tarsin Va, they are widespread and varied.' The Nepharii swept a hand to the sea beyond. 'Yet they are mostly tribal in nature, hunting and gathering as they follow the seasons. Like your own people, they occasionally fight, usually over trivial matters, although it is rare for two tribes to be in proximity. This world is large. So, too, are its resources.'

'There are no soldiers to call upon, then?'

'No. There are hunters, though. But asking them to leave their tribe to fight a battle they know nothing about will be difficult.'

'And the monks?' Tarsin asked. 'They seem capable of fighting if pressed.'

'Perhaps,' Inesco ran a hand through his thick mane, 'yet what you see is merely practised harmony. A dance of rhythm for the soul. The thought of killing another creature in combat is abhorrent to the monks.'

'I need warriors if I am to win back my city. The Deios are formidable. I fear I cannot do it alone.'

The Nepharii nodded confirmation, but still refused to commit. Regardless of Inesco's belief that time differed between the two worlds, there was a growing concern building deep within Tarsin's heart. Like Griffith and his men in the cave, he wished to return, despite the danger.

'I fear you may face more than Deios when you return, Tarsin Va. As you're aware, there are many worlds within the pyramid. You have the unfortunate circumstance of ruling a city harbouring the first of our *Kardiversum:* our portal to other worlds.'

'Are you telling me that while we're sitting here talking my city is being overrun by more than Deios?'

'No, it is doubtful. At least not yet. Not all worlds are brimming with bloodthirsty savages. And most should retain a Nepharii Guardian to observe any portal activity. It will take time before ventures are made to establish contact. It has been thousands of years since this gateway was last opened. It will be the same for every other world.'

Tarsin scratched his chin. 'The longer we talk, Inesco, the more I feel hope dwindling. How am I to return to Bastion with only a dozen men and expect to reclaim the city?'

'You cannot.'

'Then what are we doing here?'

Eyes narrowed as Inesco cast his gaze towards the twilit sky. 'We are waiting, Tarsin Va. I told you when we first conversed that your arrival caused confusion and fear amongst the monks.'

'I remember.'

'It was because of what you represent. Your armour, in particular your breast plate, shares the embossed visage of what you call a jaguar.'

'Is that important?'

'To the monks it is, for it was foretold a warrior would arrive who was not a Panthian, but who would be masked like a Panthian. Their order is called *Seb-nii-un*. It translates as "Those who wait for the One".'

Tarsin continued to scratch at his chin. 'And I guess I'm the One?'

'You fulfill such a role at this point in time,' Inesco replied, shifting his gaze away from the fading stars. 'It is why the monks are concerned and frightened, it is why we wait. For although you appear to be their saviour as spoken of in prophecy, your arrival suggests dark times are ahead. I have lived through two ages with the Panthians on this world, Tarsin Va. Each age follows a pattern of survival, followed by prosperity, before ending with destruction.'

'We are due for destruction.'

Tarsin felt his shoulders slump, his heartbeat quicken. Sweat began to bead on his forehead, despite the cool breeze. 'I didn't ask for any of this. You cannot place such a burden on me,' anger brewed beneath the surface, evident in his raised voice. 'I'm not responsible for the Panthians. I hardly know who they are!'

'Curb your anger,' Inesco raised a hand. 'There is much to learn and more to discuss. Like I said, the monks debate even as we speak. They will soon decide upon a course of action.'

'Curb my anger,' Tarsin shook his head. After all the talks they shared, he now felt further from any truth and further still from making progress. 'I need to save my people, Inesco. I need to defeat the Deios. I don't belong here, nor should I be of relevance to a people I know nothing about.'

'How little you know, swordsman.'

Tarsin blinked, aware Inesco hadn't called him such before.

'I have seen you move, and I have heard you speak. I know who you are, Tarsin Va. Despite what you believe, you are more important than you realize.' Inesco swept a hand towards the east, where the last of the night's twinkling stars shimmered before the rising sun. 'Tell me, man-who-knows-nothing, what do you see?'

A deep breath followed as Tarsin watched the sun's first golden rays bathe the underbelly of scattered clouds with a scarlet blush. 'I see a new dawn rising.'

'And how does such a sight make you feel?'

Tarsin calmed his breathing further. 'It is warming. It eases my mind. I feel content, at peace.' He continued to watch as the sun breached the horizon, pushing the last vestiges of darkness from the sky.

'And what, do you believe, does such a feeling represent?'

'Life,' Tarsin said with conviction. 'The rising sun embodies the birthing of a new day. I can feel its warmth. It is love. It is hope.'

'Good,' Inesco approached, held out both hands. Tarsin raised his own, grasped Inesco's firmly and stood before him. 'That is why you have been chosen, Tarsin Va. This is what you represent.'

'The sun?'

'No,' Inesco offered a smile. 'You represent life, love and hope. Do you know why, Tarsin Va?'

Tarsin shook his head.

'Because the world reflects who you are. It knows you, can sense your feelings. And you, Tarsin, will always be what your eyes see.'

CHAPTER SIX

He had never felt so cold.

Ra'tor squinted against the icy wind, looked in vain, he knew, for the last of his hunters to leave the cave. Seven Deios from his expedition had thought to seek game in the wild lands, but after two days he'd neither seen nor heard any sign. It was as he feared. This world, vastly different from anything he'd ever seen before, was proving to be a danger greater than he cared for.

He took a step away from the cave mouth and peered at those who remained. Five Deios - leaders in their own right - squatted about a feeble fire with their hands held out for warmth. Behind them sat the pedestal, a circular platform ten feet in diameter, marked with swirling symbols and intricate lines. It was here they entered the world of cold, stepping onto carved stones from within a pulsing magenta light source.

That was five days earlier.

In the time since, not a single member had seen the pulsing magenta light to herald a reopening of the door-between-worlds.

Ra'tor picked up a branch and threw it on the fire, noted the dwindling pile in the process. Within the hour he'd need to send a couple of hunters to forage for more, only the white powder falling from the sky was increasing. He didn't know what to make of it. It was cold to touch, but soon became water if he held it in his hand for too long. It also made the task of finding dry wood difficult, but their choices were few. If they couldn't maintain their fire, they would die.

'Are we trapped here, Ra'tor?'

The question was voiced by Fass'it, but he knew they all thought the same.

'No, the door-between-worlds will reopen,' he replied. 'It just needs time.'

Fass'it gave a solitary nod, although his eyes betrayed his true feelings about the situation. 'We don't have much time left.'

A low, deep sounding growl issued from Ra'tor's throat. He'd already staved off one bout of dissent with a clenched fist and the brandishing of his cleaver, now he feared he'd be at it again. 'What would you have me do, Fass'it?' he asked, his clawed hand drifting to touch the pommel of his weapon.

The smaller Deiosian shook his head and peered back at the fire. Ra'tor thought it a wise move.

Still, Ra'tor offered a snort to show his contempt, then moved to stand at the cave mouth. He held hope for his seven hunters. Hoped they'd travelled far in search of sustenance. Hoped they'd found some. The pouch of meat strips he bought with him was a distant memory. Placing a hand on cold stone, he knew Fass'it was right. Another day, maybe two, and they would begin to fall. It wasn't just the hunger; it was the cold air. He could feel his body trying to warm itself, sending minute shudders through his arms and legs, yet it was taking its toll. He changed his mind. They would have one more night on this horrid world. They would not survive another.

He sent a deep sigh into the chill air, watched a puff of mist form before his eyes. A haunting wail sounded from beyond the cave. He clenched a fist, wondered if the sound was carried by the wind, or caused by the wind. He couldn't tell. His senses were confused, his surroundings too unusual. He took a step away from the cave, braced himself against the biting wind.

All he could see was the outline of enormous trees cloaked in white powder and an uneven ground equally covered. Visibility didn't reach much further than the first stand of trees, and they stood barely sixty feet away.

He took another step, clenched his sharp teeth together. Instinct told him something wasn't right.

'Ra'tor,' shouted Fass'it from the cave, 'you'll die out there!'

He ignored him and took another step.

'Ra'tor!'

'Quiet,' he waved a hand behind him. 'I can taste blood on the wind.'

He heard the scrape of leather and ring of steel as his hunters gathered themselves. Of the five, three made their way to the cave mouth. He heard them inhale, knew they would taste the blood, just as he did.

'You're right,' said a copper scaled Deiosian named Ess'ik. 'It is fresh.'

Ra'tor nodded in confirmation, held up his clawed hand. A moment passed before he drew his blade.

'What do you sense?' hissed Ess'ik.

He refused to answer. All his senses were tuned towards the tree line. Something was there, he could feel it in his aching bones, smell it, even.

He saw it out of the corner of his eye, arcing through grey sky to land with a wet slap on the ground not ten feet from where he stood. He stifled a shout, for it was the severed head of one of his hunters, hot blood even now melting the white powder below.

'By the blood of Bhral!' Ess'ik growled.

Ra'tor agreed, only he couldn't turn his back and run away. He needed to stand and face whatever it was he sensed out there. He couldn't show any sign of weakness. If he did run, he'd find a blade in his back within moments. Most probably from his own hunters.

He took another step into the cold and bent a knee, enabling him to take a closer look at the severed head. It belonged to Sasa: an aging Deiosian with a dwindling brood. He could tell due to the darkening of his scales and the chipped front tooth. He placed two fingers against Sasa's neck, then lifted his hand to wipe hot blood across his brow.

'What are we hunting?' Ess'ik joined him, also placing his fingers against Sasa's neck. Ra'tor shared a quick look, saw Ess'ik trail two lines across his brow to mimic his own. He was a fighter, this one. Eager.

'I do not know,' Ra'tor kept his voice to a low rumble, 'but they are close.' He stood to his full height of seven feet, felt his blood surge through his veins. He twirled the cleaver beside him, heard the blade add its song to the wailing wind.

'There!' Ess'ik pointed towards the trees.

Narrowed eyes saw the shape materialize from grey surroundings. It was tall and broad, but little else could be seen from this distance.

'There's another!'

Ess'ik was right. Another joined the first, followed quickly by a handful more. They were sleek of movement, appeared to be undaunted by the cold air. As one they took a step forward. Then another.

'Do we fight?' Ess'ik twirled his blade in anticipation.

Ra'tor was about to concede to the blood lust, despite the disadvantage. Besides, he'd last only one more night in any case.

'Ra'tor!'

It was Fass'it, this time, calling from the cave. Ra'tor looked over his shoulder, hoping Fass'it and his remaining hunters would join the fight, only to see the magenta energy swirling above the pedestal.

'The door-between-worlds has reopened!' Fass'it shouted, pointing his shaking hand. 'Come,' he beckoned, 'come, Ra'tor!'

Ra'tor looked back towards the shapes approaching from the trees. They were crossing the uneven ground with loping strides, covering the distance quickly. He could see blades in their hands, knew they would be wickedly sharp.

'Back to the door-between-worlds,' he snarled, grabbing Ess'ik by the shoulder. 'We'll hunt another day.'

He thought the smaller Deiosian would argue, only he moved just as fast to reach the pedestal inside the cave. There were no words spoken as they arrived, only an understanding. Without delay he ushered his five hunters into the light, then followed a moment later.

*

The magenta glow swirled, caused strange shadows to appear on damp walls of stone.

Ra'tor stood motionless as a bout of vertigo swamped his senses. He steadied his body, and his thoughts, before casting narrowed eyes over their surroundings.

Ra'tor and his hunters were in a circular chamber, paved stones beneath their feet, a domed ceiling above their heads. A circular pedestal, twin to the one they just stepped upon, sat at the centre of the room. Magenta light allowed them to see.

'Are we all here?' he took steps to count his Deios. He counted five beside himself. They were all that remained from the expedition.

'Where to now?' asked Ess'ik, his copper scales glistening in the unusual light.

Ra'tor waved a clawed hand in an arc. 'Search for a doorway out of here,' he growled. 'The rest of you, stand with me.' He moved to face the door-between-worlds. If the creatures from the cold world stepped through, he would cut them down before they could gather their senses. Like his Deios, he gripped his blade tight in anticipation as they made room to swing their heavy weapons.

'There is a path!' yelled Ess'ik. Ra'tor peered over his shoulder, saw the smaller Deios standing before an empty space of darkness. 'I cannot see where it leads,' he reported, 'but the stones are wet, and the air is ripe.'

Several of his Deios made a move towards the exit whilst he held his place for several heartbeats, then he, too, moved away from the swirling light to be engulfed by the black.

It took half a day before they found a passage of stone that lead upwards. Close to exhaustion, Ra'tor led the procession with eyes accustomed to the gloom, although he could see shapes only, and barely a few feet ahead. With hands outstretched he walked forward, using his sense of smell to follow the hint of fresh air. It was close.

He paused, for what felt like the hundredth time, and listened for any signs of pursuit. There was no sound, nor could he smell any other creatures. They'd been fortunate not to have been followed, yet he didn't feel at ease. The encounter before they fled still swam through his mind. And the thought of having lost seven Deios leaders did not sit well. The Patriarchs would be most concerned.

As they should be, he thought.

Whoever they were, they were bound to be a problem. And the potential for more to arrive in the coming days was high. If he learnt anything from their foray to the cold world, it was to expect the unexpected.

A draft of warm air drifted past Ra'tor's nose. A faint scent of ash and dust passed with it. He moved to his right, his hand resting against a wall, before he realized he'd found another passage. 'Here,' he called over his shoulder, 'I've found a way to the surface.'

Heavy feet followed, and within moments his large hands were pounding against a wooden door that barred their way. After several hits with clenched fists the door splintered. A moment later he felt the midday sun caress his body.

'By the blood of Bhral!' Ess'ik moved to his side. 'We're back where we began.'

Ra'tor squinted as his eyes adjusted to the light. Ess'ik was right, they'd arrived back in the dwelling place of the Lesser Beasts, with their stone enclosures and paved walkways. It took only a moment for his eyes to adjust and spy the shining blue pyramid in the distance.

'This way,' he moved to his right, heading towards the slow, winding river that cut through the conglomeration of stone buildings. The ruined temple of pillars sat on the banks of the river, the one claimed by the Patriarchs. He needed to speak to them, needed to tell them what he'd discovered.

And he needed to find food. Bordering on exhaustion, he and his Deios were desperate for sustenance.

He continued to walk, aware of the smell of decay wafting on the breeze, accompanied by ash and blood. He followed the scent, found a trio of hunters with their kill in an abandoned shelter moments later. They bowed heads and backed away as he and his companions arrived, offered their kill with hands raised and palms up.

The flesh tasted greater than anything he'd eaten before.

Satisfied, he moved on, leaving enough flesh for those hunters who chased down the unfortunate to begin with.

The sun remained high as he arrived at the Patriarch's temple. He climbed the marble steps, moved past the cracked columns flanking the open doorway. Inside, basking beneath the heat of the glorious sun, sat a score of red-robed Patriarchs in a wide circle. Further back, behind the circle, bunched broodless Deios, also sitting in contemplation, faces raised to the sky.

A gentle murmur sounded throughout the hall as the Patriarchs became aware of his return. Several took their leave from the circle and hobbled towards the entrance, their eyes sparkling in anticipation.

'Ra'tor,' began a Patriarch named Sav'ak, his voice softly spoken. 'You have returned, and sooner than we anticipated.'

'Sooner?' Ra'tor queried, brows coming together. 'We've been absent for six nights, Sav'ak. How long did you expect us to be gone?'

Another murmur sounded from those still seated, whilst the Patriarchs standing before him shared a quizzical look.

'You left us yesterday, Ra'tor. Only a single night has passed since you last stood in this chamber.'

'A single night?' he repeated the words slowly, confusion clouding his thoughts. 'How can this be? We almost starved on the cold world we discovered, having been there so long.'

'It is true, Ra'tor,' Sav'ak placed a clawed hand about his chin, stroked emerald scales with a sharp nail. 'A single night, no more. I believe there is much to ponder in the coming days. We shall know more when our other hunters return.'

He wondered how Sav'ak could know of the hunters he'd lost, or how he could know they would return.

'The absent hunters will not return from the cold world, Sav'ak. They are finished, their blood now with Bhral. They will not be coming back.' He paused, noticed the confusion marring the Patriarch's weathered face. 'We barely made it back alive ourselves.'

'I'm not talking about those absent from your gathering, Ra'tor,' he said in return. 'After you stepped into the light yesterday, to begin your journey of discovery, another group of hunters, twelve in number, also stepped into the light.'

'They did not follow us onto the cold world,' he replied.

'No, they left later in the day, after you'd been gone for some time.'

Ra'tor clenched a fist. 'And who comprised this hunting group? Who gave the order for them to step into the light?' He knew the answer, only he needed to hear it from the smaller Deios before him.

'I thought it prudent we learn as much as we could as quickly as possible. Our search for our Blood-God is paramount, Ra'tor. We need to find Him.'

Ra'tor swung his clenched fist, felt his knuckles smash into the side of Sav'ak's soft head. Bones cracked and teeth splintered as Sav'ak crumbled to the stones at his feet. Blood began to flow. Ra'tor breathed deep, allowed the sweet scent to fill his flared nostrils. Then he lowered a knee and placed his hand about Sav'ak's throat, lifted him three inches off the ground and began to squeeze.

'I give the orders here, Sav'ak!' he snarled. 'Now tell me, who hunts without my permission on another world?'

Another Patriarch, this one scaled bronze and slender, stepped forward and placed a hand on his forearm. 'Ra'tor,' he pleaded, 'let him down. He only thought to help in our search for our lord.'

Fingers eased their pressure around Sav'ak's throat. 'Tell me who hunts?'

The remaining Patriarchs shared troubled glances. 'One of our own,' replied the bronze scaled elder. 'A lone hunter, without a brood. He is under our command, so too the hunters he leads.'

'Weaklings!' Ra'tor felt his fury escalate. His fist clenched tight until he heard the snap of bone. It was pleasing to his ears. He dropped Sav'ak to the ground, took a quick look at his lifeless eyes.

'And where did they go?' He spun his attention to the now cowering Patriarch. He could see fear manifest in his eyes. He could taste it.

'I can show you,' he muttered. Several of the Patriarchs standing by his side began to retreat, moving to stand with their brethren in the circle. 'We did not mean to cause you alarm or disappointment. We are here to guide. We are here to help.'

Ra'tor revealed his large teeth. 'Show me where they have gone, and I will decide whether or not to rescue them from whatever horror they may have discovered.'

'Rescue them?' a fearful whisper was the response.

'Aye. We are not alone in this world, nor are we the only hunters. You were right in the beginning. There is much we do not know. But sending the unskilled will not provide the answers we seek.'

'I can show you where they have gone,' the Patriarch stammered. 'They left late in the afternoon, the plaque they stepped across will be moving into place within hours.'

'I can only guess,' somehow Ra'tor knew Bhral was guiding his hand. It couldn't be any other world but the one the creature with the silver blade fled to, striking like lightning, killing so many of his brood.

It wouldn't take long for him to find out if his instinct was right. But deep inside, he already knew.

*

Unusual constellations lit up the night sky.

Tarsin shared a look with his men. They were behind the Panthian temple, which Inesco said housed the *Seb-nii-un* monks. Like himself, his men were armed and armoured, ready to step back into the city of Bastion. It had taken some convincing, not least within his own mind, but eventually he came to realize the importance of returning home.

Now they were here, sharing the night with countless stars, standing before a circular dais hidden beneath a wave-like rock formation.

'It is almost time,' Inesco broke the silence as he came to stand by Tarsin's side.

'Thank you,' Tarsin forced a smile. The two had continued to share knowledge during the last ten days, enabling both to understand the other, and to also learn some of what the Panthians believed. 'Are you sure you don't wish to join us?'

'I am sorry, Tarsin Va,' Inesco smiled back. 'I am required here, for now. Once you and your men step through the portal, I will disengage its power. It will then be closed to your world, and the Panthians will be safe.'

'But we will not be,' Tarsin lowered his eyes. He'd pleaded for reinforcements on several occasions, yet Inesco would not be swayed. Apparently, it was too complicated, the logistics - let alone the convincing - difficult to comprehend.

'Not initially,' Inesco replied. 'But I will seek aid in the coming days. When I return, I shall power the portal back to life and join you. I can do no more, nor can I persuade the monks further. They have conferred and believe they should remain at the temple. That is their duty. They will not forsake it.'

Tarsin was disappointed, obviously, but his options were few. As he and Inesco discussed, if he and his men wished to return, then it would be fraught with peril.

There was no other way.

'Listen,' Inesco placed a hand on Tarsin's shoulder. 'When you step out of the light, you'll be within a small circular temple, one of twelve surrounding what you refer to as Aston's Tear.' Tarsin nodded his head in understanding. 'Find an exit and make for safety, any way you can. You must remain alive, Tarsin Va.'

'I have no desire to die, Inesco, at least not yet.'

'Your humour escapes me,' the smile on Inesco's face suggested otherwise.

'And you'll seek aid in the coming days?'

'I will, but I hold no promises. The Panthians are accomplished hunters, but they are rarely killers. There is a difference.'

'I know,' Tarsin softly replied.

'Come,' Inesco grabbed his elbow. 'The portal is about to awaken.'

They moved together to stand before the dais. A score of Panthian monks sat cross-legged on the stone ground before them, waiting, it seemed, for the portal to flare into life. Tarsin didn't know how long it would take, but he sensed an energy building in their vicinity, for the hairs on his arms were standing on end.

'There are two things you should be aware of, Tarsin Va,' continued Inesco. 'Firstly, the time you experience here, on Aeth, will be different to what you experience on your world. And the same applies to any other world you venture. Some will be longer, others shorter. For sixty days you and your men have been our guests. In Bastion, time will not have travelled as quickly.'

Tarsin met the Nepharii's eyes, wondered at the wisdom they contained.

'Such an outcome will favour us greatly,' Tarsin replied, his own mind racing with new thoughts. 'Do you know how many days will have passed in Bastion?'

'Fifteen,' Inesco said with conviction.

'A great deal can occur in fifteen days,' Tarsin mused, 'but considerably less than sixty. They may not have consolidated their position within Bastion entirely, perhaps. It is a hope I harbour, but one based on an assumption.'

'Assumptions are dangerous, especially for a king.'

'I know, which is why I have contingency plans for the plans I've already made.' Tarsin locked eyes with the Nepharii, prayed he'd thought of everything. 'What else should I be aware of?'

Inesco moved a hand beneath his ocean-blue robes. 'The second thing of importance, Tarsin Va, is for you alone.' Inesco bowed his head slightly as he revealed the object. It was Tarsin's crown, the golden circlet with its jade stone: the Eye of the Jaguar. 'I believe this is yours, by birth and by deed.'

Tarsin reached for the cold metal with nervous hands. He thought he'd lost the crown when he first crossed over to Aeth, forgot he'd carried the symbol of his kingdom with him through the portal.

'The monks took it along with your armour and weapons on the night you arrived,' Inesco explained. 'They did not realize the importance of the object, nor its significance. Now,' Inesco spread his hands wide, 'you will be everything you're supposed to be.'

'Thank you,' Tarsin placed the crown on his head, felt it settle across his brow. It didn't feel quite as heavy as the first time. Perhaps the responsibility was not as daunting.

A shaft of orange light bloomed from the dais, a slender thread, twirling as it expanded. It caught the eye of the monks and men alike, drew their focus, enticing them to step closer. Flickers of gold and silver sparkled within as they approached, shining bright.

'It has opened,' Inesco said, moving a step forward. 'You may cross back to your world, Tarsin Va.' Inesco placed his hands on Tarsin's shoulders. 'Be vigilant, my friend, and stay alive.'

'Hopefully, we'll meet again, Inesco.'

Tarsin stepped to the side, taking the opportunity to cast an eye over his men. They were eager to return, if a little anxious. Most had drawn their weapons, for they knew the possibility of a fight was high.

The monks sitting about the portal rose to their feet and backed away, allowing his men to file towards the orange radiance.

Tarsin was ten feet away when the first shape materialized within and stepped onto the stone ground before him. It was quickly followed by several others.

'Gods above!' he heard Griffith's voice cut through the night air. 'It's the Deios!'

CHAPTER SEVEN

The carnage was absolute.

Tarsin lifted his gaze to see Griffith swing his hammer in a vicious arc, smashing the red-stained metal head into a demon skull. The beast fell like a stone. 'Are they done?' Griffith yelled as he swivelled his torso to either side, looking for more.

'They are finished,' Tarsin yelled back, appraising the battlefield. He counted the beasts. Twelve had crossed from the portal, armed with heavy cleavers. All were dead.

A keening sounded from his left. He looked to the source, saw three monks holding a brother in their arms. He was about to step forward when Jaegar's heavy hand grasped his shoulder. 'We lost two of our own, my king,' Jeagar pointed to where the fallen lay. The first he saw was Bevan, the old swordsman who fought so hard to stay alive when they arrived on the strange world. For more than three years Bevan had been his aide and second in command when leading Ciricello's Swords. He'd been cut down the middle, from shoulder to waist.

'Who's the other?' Tarsin wiped a single tear, seeking to hold onto the image of the grey-haired man as he was before the attack.

'One of Bardell's cronies,' Jaegar pointed with his axe. 'Bardell won't be happy.'

Tarsin moved to the fallen, stepping over the butchered corpses of three Deios in the process. It was a young man, Heka, by name. Like Bardell, he'd questioned their time spent here; was eager to return to Bastion. He took a moment to appraise the body. He couldn't believe the Deios had crossed and attacked. For a time, he'd hoped everything he'd experienced was nothing more than a tormented dream.

Tarsin took a last look at Heka. He'd lost an arm in the fight, and a portion of his face. It was not a pretty sight.

'What do we do now?' Griffith moved to stand with him, also looking down at the young man.

A calloused hand rubbed his newly shaved chin before he looked for Inesco. The Nepharii was helping monks to their feet and ushering them towards the temple, away from the glowing portal. He was disturbed by events; Tarsin could see it in his eyes even from a distance.

'Inesco!' Tarsin's voice was deep, hoping to catch his attention. The Nepharii heard his call and approached, moving with ease, much as he did when the battle before the portal began. Tarsin recalled seeing the Nepharii step into the charging Deios, his arms striking as his body swayed, avoiding the aggressive chops of heavy blades. Even without a sword of his own, Inesco fought with confidence, his hands hitting like hammer blows to crush his enemies. By the time Tarsin reached his side with blade drawn and bloodied, three Deios were already lying prone. It wasn't enough, though. Half-a-dozen Deios had spread from the initial charge, flanking the monks who gaped in fear. If it wasn't for Jaegar crashing into the fray with his twin-bladed axe, the number of fallen monks would be higher.

'Four Panthians lie dead,' Inesco said, clenching his teeth in agitation.

'I'm sorry for your loss, Inesco. We lost two of our own,' the swirl of orange with its flickering golden sparks caught Tarsin's eye. No further shapes appeared within its depths. 'Should we stay and help,' he asked, 'or would you have us return to Bastion?'

Inesco looked troubled but shook his head. 'No, Tarsin Va, you need to return. The quicker you cross, the sooner I can disengage the portal's power. It will allow me time to find allies for your cause.'

There was steel in Inesco's voice, he knew the words meant something more.

'We'll do our best,' Tarsin looked to his men, 'although we now number eleven. Our odds of surviving continue to dwindle.'

The men gathered about their king as Tarsin spoke, including Bardell. They were blood-stained, still catching their breath as the fire in their veins subsided.

'But we're still alive, King Tarsin,' Griffith snarled as he patted his hammer. He looked like some crazed, red-bearded bear as he stood there, his chest still heaving.

'Aye, we are still,' Tarsin replied. Behind Griffith, two monks made their way towards his fallen men before approaching the gathering. It took only a moment for him to realise one of the monks was the tiger-looking individual who faced him in the arena.

'It looks as though we have replacements for your fallen,' Inesco said, meeting the eyes of the two monks. Brief words were spoken in the Panthinan tongue, too quick for Tarsin to understand. Although he'd taken time to learn some common words and phrases, the speed of the conversation was beyond him. 'Tahu and Zai will accompany you, Tarsin Va, if you would have them.'

Both monks locked their gaze to his own as they stood before him. There was anger brewing behind their eyes, a stark contrast to their usual calm demeanour. Tahu, with his orange mane and black bands swirling about his arms, gave a solitary nod. Zai, with a leopard's visage and a midnight streak of hair did the same. Tarsin returned their gestures, noticed both Panthians held the discarded swords from his fallen men. They rested easily in their clawed hands.

'They can join us,' Tarsin returned, turning his attention back to Inesco, 'only you must explain to them my position. They follow my orders, not their own. I will not compromise.'

'Agreed,' Inesco spoke with urgency, addressing the monks. They nodded their solemn heads shortly after. 'They will follow your lead, Tarsin Va.'

'Is there anything else you require of us, Inesco?'

'No, you should leave now, before the temptation to send more hunters strikes the Deios. We are fortunate only a dozen stepped through.'

There was truth in the Nepharii's words. The number of Deios, and their size, was small in comparison to those they'd fought against in the past. It was possible the Deios lying at their feet were young and inexperienced. They certainly weren't the ferocious hunters he and his men engaged before Aston's Tear.

'Then I bid you farewell, Inesco. I hope your quest to find allies is fruitful, for our need is great. You can see that now.'

'I can see, Tarsin Va. And I will come to your aid. Perhaps sooner than you think.'

Tarsin sighed, gathered his men. Tahu and Zai walked to stand by his side. As he met their tawny eyes, he thought of Tahu and the day he first sparred against him in the arena. Tahu's face was a mask, yet his eyes simmered. Tarsin could sense purpose coursing through the Panthian's veins. He held out his hand, gripped Tahu's tight when it was offered in return. Then with his heart beating rapidly, Tarsin moved towards the orange light and stepped onto the dais. A moment later, he and his men were gone.

*

Will Tolsten took a deep breath.

It was midday on the fifteenth day since Bastion fell. Three days had passed since he escaped the city. The first he'd spent in slumber, exhausted from his ordeal. The last two days had been a combination of recruiting and convincing as he gathered a force to return to the city. It hadn't been easy. Most were frightened by the unusual events and loath to step back onto broken streets. Others were aware of the demons now circling within.

But after two days of plying survivors with visions of grandeur and reclaimed wealth should they embark on such a venture, he now stood before a horde of two hundred men and women committed to his cause.

They were a collection of misfits, he knew, but what choice did he have? Some he recognized as members of the Nocturnals, and with them he shared a mutual trust, for it was their family they sought to rescue. The others, though, had their own gains in mind. In such desperate times the thought of poaching was rife among those consumed with greed. Will knew it, and he'd acted on it. Whatever it took to increase the number of bodies in his makeshift mercenary band. If greed sent them searching for forgotten treasures once they made their way into the city, then so be it. Perhaps if the Goddess of Fate was amused, they'd become a diversion and mask his true purpose.

He could only hope.

He raised doubtful eyes to Farmer's Gate behind him. It stood there, blue stone walls cracked and splintered, its gatehouse barred with makeshift barricades. Two dozen soldiers were positioned within, crossbows and swords at the ready. When Will gave the word, they would part, allowing his force passage within. He knew they'd close ranks as soon as they were through; and quite possibly never think of Will's mercenaries again.

'Are you ready, lad?' the voice belonged to Lloyd Henrickson. He'd appeared at daylight to help muster the volunteers into an organised force. Most were equipped with an assortment of salvaged weapons, but Henrickson arrived with three carts containing short stabbing swords, a gift from Admiral John Rhys who arrived on foot from Aspenvale the day before. His ship, the *Leviathan*, was lying off the coast, full of supplies for a scattered people and brimming with soldiers eager to reclaim the city. Henrickson had been excited to see the admiral as he led his soldiers onto the surrounding fields, apparently for a number of reasons. Will was yet to discover what those reasons were.

'I'm ready,' Will's voice rasped, although he wondered if he truly was. The thought of returning was not fearful itself; it was the fear of not finding Tessa alive that caused the most angst. 'We should move now if we're any chance of returning before nightfall.'

'I agree,' Henrickson clapped him on the back. It almost took his breath away. 'And I'll be coming with you.'

'You're coming with us?'

'Aye, I need to see firsthand what we're up against,' he shared a smile, barely seen beneath his bristling white moustache. 'Besides, since Admiral John Rhys arrived yesterday with his thousand soldiers, I can afford to hand over some of my responsibilities. He can add his expertise to the situation, whilst I gather important intelligence concerning our foes.'

'I'm not here to protect you should danger find us, my lord. I have my mission.'

Henrickson smiled. 'I know, lad. And I'll support you. I'll merely be an advisor. And perhaps my presence may deter a number from fleeing recklessly into the ruins for personal gain.'

'I wouldn't count on it,' Will shook his head.

'Besides,' Henrickson continued, 'I'll have thirty of my finest soldiers accompany us inside. Their fortitude will be most welcome, will it not?'

'Agreed,' Will knew every sword would count, especially those held by professionals. He'd spoken of tactics for several hours during the night, and it was thought a long line, five abreast, would be best as they walked into the city. Every man or women on the outside would hold a polearm or crossbow, whilst those on the inside would grip the hilt of a short stabbing sword. It was hoped such a large force entering the city would cause their foes to reconsider any foolish attack. If they were lucky, they would reach the river Atvia without incident.

If luck failed them, it would be every man and women for themselves.

Will walked towards one of the empty four-wheeled carts Henrickson arrived with. He stepped onto the rear board, made his way to the front so he could address those who would join him.

'It is time,' he said, raising his voice so everyone could hear. Silence fell across the group as faces rose to meet his gaze. 'For those who don't know me, I am Will Tolsten, Baron of Deepwell, Underlord of the Nocturnals. I know many of you have varied reasons for being here, but I thank you all the same, for without such a force, our goals would remain out of reach.' He held up a hand to shield his eyes from the sun as it escaped the confines of scattered clouds. 'When I escaped Bastion three days ago, I left two hundred women and children hiding in a chamber below the streets, hungry and afraid. I vowed to return and provide safe passage out of the city. With your aid, I do so now.

'Only our journey within will not be without incident. There are many dangers lurking in the shadows, some we may not be aware of. If we stick to the plan and keep together, we may find ourselves standing here, in this very spot, come nightfall. If the gods are on our side, two hundred women and children will be standing with us.

'So, my friends and allies, it is time. Henceforth, we are to be known as the Knights of Salvation!'

A roar of approval sounded from the newly anointed knights, accompanied by slaps on the back and cheers for the Underlord.

'Well said,' Henrickson offered his hand as he stepped off the cart, 'but I thought we were supposed to sneak into the city unannounced? You've riled them up.'

'I have,' Will returned, his eyes ablaze. 'Let's see how long it lasts once we walk the broken streets.' He waved a hand in the air, waited for his knights to fall in.

'Come,' he said to Henrickson, his mouth a narrow slit. 'Let's do this.'

*

Lloyd Henrickson watched as the last of Will Tolsten's knights entered the city.

He wasn't overly impressed. Most, he assumed, would flee at the first sign of danger. The remainder were little more than cut throats and braggarts. They would fight to survive, but if Will counted on them to help in a time of need, he'd quickly realise his folly. Placing his trust in strangers wasn't going to end well.

Which was why he'd made plans of his own to help Will's cause.

'My lord,' a young red-haired lad raced to his side. He was breathing heavily. 'The men at Southgate have entered the city, as you ordered.'

Henrickson gave the lad a nod, looked to his thirty men. They were ready, knew what was at stake. 'You heard the lad,' he addressed his men. They slung crossbows over their shoulders, then moved towards the gate. It had been Henrickson's plan all along to bring up the rear, for if Will's effort to rescue his people failed, they would need solid men to hold firm in the face of adversity. He also hoped his little diversion at Southgate would lessen the odds. With Admiral John Rhys returning from the *Leviathan* with his thousand men, they finally had the means to delve into Bastion with intent. Three squads were now being led into the city. The first would strike towards the pyramid, heading up Southway, whilst the other two would split left and right along the inner wall. All three were tasked with discovering what sort of resistance they faced. It was the first real foray he and his aides had been able to organize since the Fall. More than anything, they were desperate to learn who they were fighting, and what sort of numbers they faced. Once they discovered such intelligence, they were to retreat to the gate.

The plan was to attract the attention of whoever resided within the city, enough so that Will could find his people and return without incident.

Henrickson knew such an eventuality was doubtful, but he'd be prepared, nonetheless.

He gave the red-haired lad a pat on the shoulder, then walked to join his men as they passed under the gatehouse. It was quiet, he noted, as he walked around the fallen stone blocks barring his way. He took a moment to peer up at the battlements, saw half-a-dozen archers crouched in position. They'd been sitting there since dawn, keeping watch, looking for any unusual activity. Like his own thirty men, they were placed to provide cover should things turn ugly.

'The rabble hasn't dispersed,' his second in command was Lieutenant Devin Kayne, a tall man with a shock of blonde hair, visible beneath his steel helmet. Henrickson noticed his keen eyes watching Will's mercenaries as they walked ahead.

'No,' Henrickson returned, 'I am surprised. Maybe they fear to run alone.'

It was possible. The street they traversed smelt of death. And the shadows were deep, despite the early morning sun shining. Although even as he and Lieutenant Devin watched, several men took steps towards a ruined building to peer past shattered windows.

'What are they hoping to find, do you think?' asked Devin, his own eyes narrowed as he began to walk past the ruins.

'Anything of value,' Henrickson sighed. 'Clothing, tools, jewellery still adorning the dead.' He'd seen it before; bodies being picked clean. It was nothing new.

They continued to walk, although the column was beginning to halt on occasion, probably at each intersection Will reached. At this pace, they would reach the river Atvia within an hour.

It was longer than he wished for. Henrickson knew every minute within the city increased their chances of an encounter. He knew it would happen at some point, it was inevitable, only the frequency was what he was truly afraid of. A handful of skirmishes he could stomach. Anything more and they might not make it out alive.

Yet he had to trust Will's instinct. He knew what lurked within better than anyone. If he was overly cautious, well, who could blame him.

'There they go,' there was disappointment in Devin's voice. Henrickson followed his lieutenant's pointing hand, saw three men slink into a side alley. A handful of seconds passed before a group of five men and three women departed on the other side of the street.

'Damn the fools,' Henrickson spat to the ground. They would be lucky to make it out alive.

'Should we do anything?' Devin asked, unslinging his crossbow.

'No, leave them to their fate. They answer to the gods, not us. And they haven't exactly been merciful lately.' And yet he felt troubled at his words. He could already sense the beginning of the end. If Will's knights disbanded in quick fashion, which was a distinct possibility, those who remained would be severely exposed.

And yet an hour later they arrived at the river Atvia with only a dozen others having left the column.

Henrickson made his way to the front, where Will Tolsten stood looking across the Karson Bridge. The demons Will's men killed three days earlier were absent.

'We are more than halfway,' Will greeted him as he approached.

'So, what do you plan now?'

'We'll move with pace. I'll lead the way,' Will pointed a hand into the distance. 'Three streets from here, on the other side of the river, lies an old church. Its steepled roof has fallen in, and the windows are nothing more than gaping holes. But at the rear, behind the dais, is a trap door leading to the sewers. That's where we are headed. Within half-an-hour, we'll be at Thieves' Retreat. The women and children are hiding close to the hall, holed up in a chamber with the doors barred from within.'

'Alright then, Will,' Henrickson cast his eye over the milling crowd, 'let's move and make this quick.'

*

He could hear scuttling feet behind him.

Will Tolsten chanced a quick look over his shoulder. It was difficult to see clearly, for they were deep below the surface, the flickering brand he held casting intermittent flashes of light about a narrow corridor.

'We're almost there,' he said to Lloyd Henrickson. The stout old swordsman had moved to his side as they descended into the depths of Bastion. With him came a dozen of his most trusted soldiers. The rest were standing guard at Thieves'

Retreat, barely a mile behind them, keeping an eye on those he dubbed his Knights of Salvation. He truly hoped they would remain and help in the escape.

'Which way?' Henrickson peered over his shoulder. He followed his gaze, saw the corridor branch in two.

'This way,' Will replied, moving to his left. Henrickson and his men kept pace, swords held loosely in sweaty palms. It was stifling down here. Hard to breath let alone think. And yet the thoughts he did have were composed of frightful questions. Questions he feared to learn the answer to.

Will rounded a bend in the corridor, walked into an open space forty feet in width and twice that in length. A dozen men stood braced; crossbows held at shoulder height. Behind them sat an enormous set of bronze doors. It took a moment for his eyes to adjust, but he soon saw the smiling faces of Col Farren and the red-haired Patrick standing in the centre.

'Will,' they both said, lowering their crossbows. Those to either side did the same, relief in their eyes to mimic his own.

He rushed the last few steps to embrace his friends. 'You're alive, thank the gods!'

'Aye, and so are you,' Col pushed him back a pace. 'When you didn't come back for us, we thought you dead.'

'Aye,' chimed Patrick, placing his crossbow on the floor.

Will felt a tear slide down his cheek. 'I almost was,' he spoke quickly. 'It's dangerous out there. More so than I could have imagined. I'm sorry I took so long.'

'Don't be sorry,' Col clapped a hand to his shoulder, then motioned him towards the bronze doors. 'Come, the women and children await,' he looked him in the eyes. 'You *are* here to rescue us?'

'We are,' Will smiled for the first time in what felt like an age. 'Forgive me,' he turned to Henrickson, 'this is Lloyd Henrickson, Swordmaster to the king. Lloyd Henrickson, Col Farren, my second in command, and Patrick, a canny fighter and friend.'

'Well met, gentlemen,' Henrickson replied. 'Will,' he continued, 'it's best we don't loiter.'

Will gave a cursory nod, then watched as Col tapped on the bronze doors. They opened seconds later.

Muffled shouts echoed within, accompanied by cries of joy and the occasional sob. Yet Will barely heard the sounds, for he had eyes only for Tessa, standing at the forefront of the mass of women and children, her lips trembling with poorly supressed emotion.

He raced forward to hold her tight, his heart beating powerfully within his chest. 'I love you,' Will whispered the words in her ear. 'I'm sorry I took so long.'

'I forgive you,' Tessa raised her hands, gripped his face, placed her lips against his.

Henrickson allowed them a moment, then spoke with authority. 'We need to move, Will,' he said, looking over his shoulder. 'The longer we stay, the greater the danger.'

'I know,' Will returned, his hand holding Tessa's. 'Come, my friends,' he looked to his people with a smile, 'carry only that which is light . . . and let us leave this place.'

CHAPTER EIGHT

Lloyd Henrickson took a moment to ponder the significance of life, casting his gaze to the late afternoon sky as he did so.

He was on his knees in the street, barely a mile from Farmer's Gate. Shouts of anger assailed his hearing, mingled with roars of pure aggression and sickening thuds of steel biting into flesh.

He lifted a tired hand to wipe blood from his brow.

It had all been too easy, in retrospect. The path into the city had been uneventful. At first, Henrickson thought it was due to his three squads filing through Southgate, posing as a distraction amongst other things. Yet after Will found his survivors and hurried them across Karson Bridge, a feeling of dread crept into Henrickson's soul. There had been no sightings during the entire journey, nor any sounds to suggest any beast dwelt within the city. It had been too quiet, he finally realised. Only by then, it was too late.

They'd travelled down the same street Will used when he escaped. It was narrow and long, crowded by leaning buildings and shadowed from the sun. It was a great place to lie in ambush, Henrickson thought, for a single look made you feel claustrophobic. With the survivors hemmed in by those knights who remained – and he knew their number had dwindled considerably over the last half-an-hour – they'd moved with as much pace as they could muster. Swords were held in tightly gripped fists, and those holding crossbows kept an eye on each laneway they passed.

But it was as they crossed a broad intersection that he saw with his own eyes how complacent they'd become.

They came in groups of five; large, demonic beasts with sharp claws and sharper fangs. They gripped wide blades of steel, swinging them back and forth through the air, creating a whistling sound that chilled Henrickson to the bone. Down every laneway, out of every vacant doorway and darkened alley they came, to stand and watch the procession.

And they brought fear with them.

It was the screams of the innocent that sparked the frenzy.

Henrickson drew his sword, shouted orders to his men as the first victim fell. The beasts attacked with intent, smashing their blades into the weak and then dragging them from the column to disappear with their prey. Within seconds a dozen of Will's knights vanished, their terrible screams the only reminder they existed at all. Henrickson raised his voice in an effort to rally a defence with loyal soldiers, sent a soldier running to the gate for aid. Only panic erupted a moment later as everyone ran for whatever safety they could find.

The beasts moved in as people scattered, choosing easy targets, slapping the feeble defence aside with disdain.

Another order was yelled to instil courage in his men. Then Henrickson charged.

His men charged with him.

They hit the beasts with a roar, smashing blades into thick hides, loosing bolts from crossbows at close range. For a moment, they managed to push the larger beasts back into a side street. It was enough to allow the survivors a chance to stream past.

Then the counter charge arrived.

Feet locked against cobblestones so Henrickson could hold his own against the tide of burnished scales, his sword thrusting at every opportunity. And then Will Tolsten joined him with the remnants of his Shadow Brethren. They fought with courage, but they were outmuscled, and as he predicted, the trust Will placed in his knights evaporated as quickly as their number. It would only be a matter of time before they were overrun.

Yet he fought so others could escape and live.

Now Henrickson knelt on the cobblestones, exhausted, bleeding, waiting for death to claim him.

He looked to his left, saw a dead beast, its tongue lolling between sharp fangs. At some point he'd fallen hard onto the ground, grappling with the demon. Somehow, he managed to draw his dagger from his belt and stab its scaled neck. It's blood still stained his hands, mingled with his own, he knew.

A dark shape moved to stand before him, blocking the sun, obscuring his vision.

Henrickson tried in vain to lift his sword, but it felt heavy in his hand and his strength failed him. Perhaps he was too old to be fighting. Perhaps he should have let Lieutenant Devin lead the sortie into the city. Only he'd hoped to see the demons up close to discover their manner and learn of any weaknesses. He'd certainly seen them up close.

And he wasn't sure he'd discovered any weakness.

A high-pitched scream sounded down the street, back the way they'd travelled.

'Are you alive?' the voice was deep, yet unusually inquisitive.

'I'm alive,' Henrickson dropped his sword and raised his hand, shading his eyes so he could see who stood before him.

'Good, because I'm in need of a Swordmaster, my friend. More than ever, actually.' A hand reached for his, gripping tight as the newcomer helped him to his feet. The screams were dwindling.

With aching body, Henrickson swivelled away from the sunlight, gazed at the man who grinned back at him.

'By all that is holy!' Henrickson's voice was thick with emotion. 'Tarsin Va!'

*

Somehow, at some point in time, he knew it would descend into . . . this.

Tarsin took a moment from the heated debate raging within the command tent, decided to silently judge the demeanour of those present. It wasn't the first time he'd done so since escaping the city. He was certain it wouldn't be the last.

He caught the eye of Lloyd Henrickson, his head bandaged, his eyes weary. He was tired, needed to rest his aging body. In truth, he was lucky to be alive. If Tarsin and his men hadn't heard the commotion as they climbed from the sewers, the number attempting to escape the city may have been significantly less. As it was, they'd arrived to lend aid to a group of soldiers who were sorely pressed.

It made a difference.

Now the old Swordmaster sat at table, listening to men vaunting their own ideas on how best to reclaim their city. He didn't look amused.

Tarsin shifted his gaze to Will Tolsten, who once again raised his voice to be heard. He was eager to avenge the fallen, Tarsin could see it in his eyes. They were red-rimmed and out for blood. Tarsin recalled the stricken look on his face when they were introduced, just before they passed under Farmer's Gate and into the surrounding fields. Will wasn't pleased to have been rescued, especially by a stranger wearing the king's crown. The fact he was alive seemed to have been forgotten altogether.

Yet Tarsin could see the resemblance; the way his eyes narrowed when challenged, the excitement in his words. So like his sister, Kayla Tolsten.

The thought left Tarsin short of breath. He'd promised to find her, to come after her, to save her. He'd promised.

Yet Kayla was lost, wandering some unknown world, for all he knew alone and in desperate need of help.

Tarsin shook his head. There was nothing he could do about the situation at present. He needed information more than anything else. He needed order for a world gone mad.

'I don't care if you wish to fight, Will,' Admiral John Rhys slammed his fist onto the wooden table, ceasing the chatter. 'Until we have an idea as to how many lurk within our city, I'll not commit to an attack.'

Tarsin knew he was right, especially since news arrived shortly after dark that one of the three squads had failed to return from within. One hundred men - soldiers, archers - lost amongst a horde of demons. They were to gather information, ordered not to engage the enemy. And yet not a word of their whereabouts could be found.

Such a loss dampened spirits, caused grown men to become afraid.

And men who were frightened generally made bad decisions.

Which made the presence of Admiral John Rhys in Bastion all the more important.

Tarsin and the admiral's eyes met across the table, shared an understanding. John Rhys still wore his tricorn hat atop his blonde hair, and his swooping moustache rivalled Henrickson's for size. It was good to see the admiral, despite the circumstances. The man was experienced and a leader, and as such, greatly respected. He was also a former member of the Unseen and could be trusted, despite the harsh words Tarsin and John Rhys shared aboard the *Leviathan*. In fact, he felt an eagerness about the situation that he was certain John Rhys reciprocated.

Tarsin took a moment to reflect on Bastion's destruction since he last saw the admiral, allowed the bickering about the table to linger for several more minutes. He heard nothing to suggest any of those vying for attention knew what they were talking about. The city had fallen; had been overrun. The people needed shelter and aid.

And Tarsin knew several thousand still needed to be rescued from another world, Will Tolsten's sister amongst them.

Tarsin took one last look around the table. Jaegar sat at the far end, Lord Beaumont and Cale Griffith to either side. Beside Griffith rested Setorious, another who'd survived Bastion's darkest days. Closer to his end of the table sat Will Tolsten and his aides, Col Farren and Patrick. Admiral John Rhys and Lloyd Henrickson sat mid table to his right, with Lieutenant Devin Kayne also in attendance. And then at the rear of the tent, cloaked and standing silent, stood Tahu and Zai. Neither had spoken a word since the debate began, and few knew they were even present. Which was just as well, Tarsin thought, for few knew who they were.

The raised voices continued. At some point Tarsin would have to speak and offer his opinion. He was their leader and commander, by birth and by right. It was his duty. And no matter what anyone thought about the matter, he'd been there during the darkest of days. He'd fought the Deios and survived. He'd travelled to another world and returned.

And he hoped, beyond anything else, that aid would be forthcoming.

Because the battle wasn't finished. It had barely begun. And somewhere out there walked Avra the witch and her summoned God.

'Are you going to add your voice to the debate, my king?' asked Will Tolsten, rising from his chair with a hand sweeping before him. 'Or are you tired of our scheming? You seem to be disinterested.'

'Watch your mouth, boy!' Griffith snarled from the far end, obviously not pleased with Will's choice of words. 'If it weren't for our king, you'd not even be here.'

'We would have made it out alive,' Will replied, looking to his aides for confirmation. They gave a solitary nod each, yet both appeared to do so with a lack of conviction.

'Enough!' Tarsin's chair scraped loudly as he pushed it back and stood, stretching his shoulders as he did so. 'There is much to discuss, and the night is young. I agree with the need to reclaim our city. I agree we must wait for better intelligence on our enemy.' Voices rose in anger and support equally. He thought to let them continue, decided to interject instead. 'We also need to rescue several thousand of our citizens who passed through a portal to another world,' his own voice became loud within the tent. 'But right now, it's difficult to act when we don't know exactly who our enemy is, nor do we know how many there are. From what I've already heard since escaping the city earlier this day, there are others within Bastion, others who differ from those we call the Deios.

'Am I right in my surmising, gentlemen?'

Lord Beaumont cleared his throat with a cough. 'It is true, sire. From what we have observed in the past days, there are at least four species of demon now crawling within Bastion.'

'Aye,' John Rhys concurred with a nod. 'I've seen them with my own eyes, and I only arrived in the wee hours of yesterday. You have the Deios: the lizard men you fought today in the streets. There are also eagle men, some who look like crows, and a handful of sightings of bear-like creatures. I have since learnt one of our scouts believes he saw a walking wolf. That makes five.'

'My point, gentlemen,' Tarsin continued, 'is that we need more than mere sightings if we are to step into our city and take back what is rightfully ours. We also need an objective, something to hold and rally from. Something to inspire the men in the battle to come.'

'What do you suggest?' Devin Kayne asked from behind Lloyd Henrickson.

'Many things, Lieutenant,' Tarsin responded. 'But first we need to assemble our soldiers. And I don't mean the ones who are already here. We have thousands of men south in the field, fighting against Prince Rahesh and his southern dogs. We need to finish with this distraction and focus on Bastion.'

'Prince Rahesh's attack on our soil is more than a distraction, sire,' Lord Beaumont suggested. 'And from what I've gleaned through carrier pigeon since the battle commenced, they are pressing harder than ever. I doubt he can be dealt with easily. Nor quickly.'

Tarsin gave a solitary nod. 'Perhaps what you say is true, Lord Beaumont, but if he is pressing hard, it may be because he is desperate.' He looked to those seated about the table. Tarsin would need to send someone to the south. He couldn't risk going himself, not with the city unclaimed. The people would accuse him of abandoning them in their darkest hour.

'Who defends Sovarto?' he asked Lord Beaumont.

'Lord Dominic Gaspar.'

Tarsin knew the man by reputation only. It was said he was of sound judgement, but cautious with his men. He looked to his Swordmaster. 'Henrickson, I'll send you with John Rhys to Sovarto aboard the *Leviathan*. There you'll take command of our southern forces and end this threat.

'Jaegar,' he addressed the Herkosian, 'you'll sail north aboard one of the frigates to Highport. Gather as many soldiers as you can and return. Lord Ottik Fitzman of Highport will oblige, for he was always a friend of Arkos Vantos. Tell him what has occurred here, ask for his help. Then advise him to send word to your people at Haldenborg and Jorgunberg. If the Herkosians can send aid, it would be greatly appreciated.'

'It will take months for them to organise men and sail south,' Jaegar returned.

'I know, Jaegar, but I fear what we are about to face will not be rectified easily. There are too many unknowns at present. The more soldiers I can call upon, the better. In the meantime, we'll do everything in our power to take back our city. If your people arrive via the Bay of Pennants and we greet them from the port, then I'll be happy.'

'Lord Gaspar is not as obliging as Lord Fitzman,' Henrickson added his voice to the discussion. 'He'll not relinquish his forces, nor agree to have his command taken from him.'

'Not even at the behest of his king?'

'I doubt it. Gasper has no love for Bastion, nor did he particularly enjoy your father's company,' Henrickson gingerly wiped his brow, careful not to dislodge his bandages. 'Once he learns of Arkos' death and your rise to the throne, he'll look to usurp your position. He'll not accept you as king, I know that much. In fact, I believe none of the Southern Lords will.'

'I agree,' chimed John Rhys. 'I was born in the south, was raised to believe Bastion cared little for the men and women who lived below her. I also doubt aid will be forthcoming once they learn Arkos Vantos has fallen.'

Tarsin sensed the dark clouds as they began to swarm inside his head. He was aware of the southern lord's angst towards Bastion; had experienced their disdain in court on occasion, if only from a distance. How his father kept his anger in check he would never know.

'Then sail further south, beyond Sovarto, and seek out Prince Rahesh's supply line. Destroy any ships he has lurking in our waters.'

'Aye,' John Rhys said, 'we've a dozen ships in port at Anthos, and a handful at Aspenvale, including the *Leviathan*. There are three warships commissioned by Arkos sailing from Highport even as we speak, ordered by the king before his death, among other things.'

'Then I suggest you gather your forces, Admiral Rhys, and attack Prince Rahesh along the coast. From what I understand, he has fewer ships, and those not as swift,' Tarsin's voice was firm. 'His army cannot survive such a long campaign, especially across such harsh terrain. Take out their supplies and we'll end this ridiculous invasion swiftly. Then I'll have our forces return, with or without aid from the south.'

'Do we have enough manpower to take back our city?' asked Will Tolsten.

'We will because we'll not sit idle. You've already proven you can fashion a force from the survivors. You'll do so again, only this time with the full support of your king. We'll give them purpose, praise them, define them as heroes. Whatever it takes to raise their morale and infuse them with intent.'

'And then what?' Will knotted his brows.

'And then we take back our city, Will Tolsten. One street at a time.'

*

It was late.

Will Tolsten still sat at table, watching as older men gathered themselves, ready to retire for the night. It had been a long day, for he'd risen before dawn as he planned his sortie into Bastion to rescue his people. Now it was after midnight, and he was still awake. But sacrifices had to be made if one was to fight to survive.

He watched Henrickson limp out of the tent. He was sixty years old, looked every bit an old man with his head bandaged and his eyes half closed. Even Cale Griffith appeared tired as he followed him out. All of them, Will surmised, shared the look of defeat already. Where was the spark of anger? Where was the desire for revenge?

It had been absent as they discussed plans to retake the city. So much talk centred around their numbers and supplies. So much talk was wasted on the health and wellbeing of citizens already crowding the countryside. He'd lost count of how many times he'd voiced his displeasure with their train of thought. They needed to act. They should've been formulating strategies to enter Bastion, not ruminating over logistics.

Yet every time he suggested such a course, Tarsin, their newly appointed king, would change tack.

Tarsin Va, bastard son of Arkos Vantos, now King of Dervae.

Unknown to the people, untried as a leader. Yet the men in the command tent appeared to accept his authority without question.

Will wondered why.

The canvas tent flapped as a gust of wind greeted those leaving. Will shifted in his seat, noticed Tarsin hadn't moved from the head of the table. The king's head was bowed in contemplation, oblivious to who sat three feet away.

This was the king who would lead in the coming weeks.

He was only a man, not some powerful figure surrounded by a spiritual aura. He wasn't imposing like his father, either. Yet there was something about him, something almost tangible that spoke of greatness. Perhaps it was his armour. Perhaps it was his sword. Both were striking in appearance, lent an air of invincibility to the man who was king.

Perhaps it was the golden crown that sat comfortably atop his head. He certainly looked the part.

Will leant forward and grasped the tankard that sat on the table, took a swallow of sour-tasting water. 'I beg your pardon, sire,' he spoke softly, 'but I fear your attention to the south is misplaced. We should be focusing our efforts on Bastion.'

The king raised troubled eyes. They were red-rimmed and full of sorrow. When Tarsin and his men first arrived on the street to help in the fight against the Deios, he'd heard talk of another world. For a moment Will wondered what he'd seen.

'There is a great deal occurring that you are unaware of, Will,' the king replied. 'Trust me and my decisions, do only that which I command.'

'We should be taking back our city, sire.'

'I heard you earlier. It's not the time. We lack intelligence on the enemy. I'll not commit our forces on a gamble. We'll consolidate first, then push into Bastion once our supply lines are active.'

'What of those still trapped within? Are we to leave them to die? My sister is still unaccounted for!'

Will had raised his voice, allowing his frustration to manifest. It woke the king from whatever place of contemplation he'd visited. Tarsin's eyes simmered with blue fire.

The king vacated his seat. Two grey cloaked figures came swiftly to his side. 'Would you strike into Bastion and kill all those you come across, Will Tolsten?'

'If they be demon, yes.'

Tarsin looked to either side, motioned to the newcomers. The silent figures raised hands to pull back their cowls, revealing faces like those of a hunting cat.

'Gods above!' Will's chair fell back as he leapt to his feet. Water from his tankard splashed atop the table. 'What are they?'

'Who are they, Will?' Tarsin corrected. 'They are Panthians: people like you and I, only they hail from a different world. I have been to their world, Will. I spent sixty days there.'

'Sixty! What madness do you speak?'

'Time is different between worlds,' the king explained. 'Whilst fifteen days have passed here since the earthquake, I have spent sixty days with the Panthians and a Nepharii known

116

as Inesco. I have discovered much in that time. Learnt a considerable amount about myself and the war to come.'

'And what are they doing here?' Will asked, his hand hovering near the hilt of his sword.

'They are here to help. If we are fortunate, more will come to our aid. You see, Will, not all those who step through the portals harbour a desire for death and destruction. Allies can be found. It is why we need to observe and gather information first.'

'Can they fight?'

'They are capable. And like you, they are willing. They have suffered loss. Now they, too, seek revenge.'

Will took a moment to gather his thoughts. He struggled. So much swirled through his head, and he couldn't peel his eyes away from the visage before him. Men who looked like cats. And their hands were clawed, a fact he'd failed to notice when they stepped to Tarsin's side. The king was right, there was so much he was unaware of. So much he didn't know.

A deep breath calmed his nerves. 'You met my father briefly, in Undercity, right before he died,' he caught Tarsin's eyes with his own. 'All my life I listened to him as he described his exploits and spoke of his victories. I studied his campaigns. If you allow me a group of men, I can lead them inside. I did it today with success. I can do it again.'

'Studying your father's exploits makes you knowledgeable, Will, but it doesn't mean you're capable. You're young and eager, I understand, and you'll have your chance. Just be patient. Everything we see before us is new. Being rash will be our undoing.'

'I cannot sit and wait. My sister is in there somewhere. I mean no disrespect, but I don't need your permission to attempt a rescue.'

'Will, you don't even know where she is, nor what horrors may stand in your way.' The king held up a hand to stall a further outcry. 'Do as I ask. Rebuild your Knights of Salvation. Make them strong. In the meantime, I'll provide an avenue into Bastion, create a stronghold from which to base our sorties. By the time you're ready, we'll have learnt about our enemy.'

'And then we'll rescue my sister?' Will asked, hope in his voice.

'Aye,' Tarsin held Will's gaze. 'Then we'll find Kayla Tolsten.'

CHAPTER NINE

The emerald forest was immense.

At least so it appeared to Jarred as he stood atop a craggy rise of button-grass and held a hand high, shielding his eyes from the morning sun. A verdant sea of rippling leaves and sighing branches sat below him, the colour of jade and unripe apple mingling with the darker shade of fern and purple-black sword-grass. Except to the far north, he mused. It was there, on the horizon, where the dark green forest merged softly beneath pale snow. Winter was here, had been chasing them for weeks. So far, they'd kept their distance.

He let a deep breath whistle past his lips as he placed hands on hips. He'd been running since early morning, his legs pounding the soft turf beneath the tall redwood trees and the crowding ferns. But now he'd reached the highest point in the forest for several leagues, his legs burning from the exertion. Here he could rest a moment to survey his surroundings, realign himself and gather his bearings.

Here he felt . . . what, exactly? The exquisite vista evoked no elation, for he knew its inherent dangers were many, his safety uncertain. The sight was pleasing, though, tranquil. If it weren't for the fear gripping his heart, he dared to believe the forest could be home.

But it wasn't home, that was certain. The forest was enormous, a veritable ocean of ever-swaying life. It harboured creatures both large and small, many familiar in shape and disposition, a few which differed. And the plant life was familiar, redwood and oak, pine, elm and yew. Only some grew taller, others shorter, the size of their leaves sometimes irregular to how he remembered them. A number were textured differently, their bark rough, sometimes spiked, or in the case of the ruby-hued long-berries, their twining stems were surprisingly devoid of thorns and velvet smooth.

A bit like himself, he thought, somehow different.

He flicked his blonde hair over a shoulder. It was long, braided into a single tail at the insistence of Neema. She'd offered to cut it short, but he declined on a whim. He was a young man travelling an uncivilized world. For reasons unknown he'd play the part: untamed, raw, intent on sharing its wonders in an effort to feel welcomed.

Yet the forest, for all its similarities, was no haven. Its immense size provided him and his companions with a means to avoid detection, but it wasn't home. Nor was it permanent.

In the nine months he'd walked across its damp, sodden turf he'd learnt one thing. The forest, despite its timeless appeal, was ever-changing. It changed with the seasons, it changed with the weather. And it most certainly changed between night and day.

And with the changes, crept danger.

Ruvin Ciricello had cautioned him about the dangers inherent with the night. He was a Seeker of the Brotherhood of One, a man versed with knowledge of the wild and its unknown quantities. He'd scoured the deserts of the south back home, climbed peaks from the foothills of the Rykedian Alps and sailed every sea known to man. But even he was cautious concerning the forest on the New World, despite the assurance of Kian that all would be well. There were beasts of the night that were best avoided at all costs. Twice he'd spied forest cats, as he'd come to call them. Although to be honest on both occasions his only glimpse of the large predator had been its sparkling eyes. Kian mentioned they were ferocious hunters and Ruvin agreed, believed they were similar to the panthers found in the eastern jungles of Jenzai back home.

Another deep breath. He knew wild cats were not likely to be hunting this early in the morning. Calm with his knowledge he took a moment to savour the cool, fresh air. The sweet scent of damp earth and wildflower invigorated his aching limbs, as did the cool breeze. With a sigh he swept his gaze to the north and caught a glimpse of a snaking river winding through densely wooded valleys, its sapphire waters reflecting a cloudless blue sky. The sight was untamed perfection: a ferocious, primitive landscape alluring for its wild, yet dangerously savage, existence. For several moments he stood and watched, relishing the opportunity to absorb such a picturesque view. He wondered, as he often did these days, if his interest was due in no small part to the Nepharii memories he harboured before their journey into the New World. Somehow, recollections of past events had seeped into his own mind as he trailed a finger across the diamond pyramid in Bastion, causing confusion and illness. But within a day his body and mind recovered, although he knew . . . things, he should not have been aware of. With Kian's help he was able to understand the Nepharii voices as they whispered ideas into his consciousness, enabling him to derive a purpose to their continued presence.

But the Nepharii voices were no longer in residence, hadn't been felt or heard from since the day he stepped through the portal. Yet he felt a kinship with the memories still and often looked upon the world with a different set of eyes. In the years spent in Ruvin's employ he was an Information Gatherer, only now he did so with knowledge and understanding beyond his shallow years, for the Nepharii, despite their absence, left the young lad with certain gifts. With Kian's aid the comprehension of such gifts was slowly becoming apparent.

He leant over and touched his toes, stretching his hamstrings and calves. Then he adjusted the sword belted at his waist, one of the jaguar blades once belonging to his king, Arkos Vantos, before making his way down the hillside towards the river. He rarely ventured this far north, but the winter day was surprisingly fine, and he'd promised himself he'd make an extensive sweep of their surroundings. Since they fled the portal and the people of Bastion they remained on the move, never occupying a single camp for more than several days, always heading further south. They did so at the insistence of Kian and Neema, both stressing Kayla's safety to be paramount. But there had been no pursuit, nor any sign to suggest someone followed. Now they were holed up in a cave to the south surrounded by tall redwood trees. They'd been there for more than a week, the longest they'd stayed at any one location.

And Neema was nervous.

Jarred pushed fern fronds to the side and stepped over a fallen log draped with grey lichen. As he moved further down the hill he could hear the gushing river splashing over submerged boulders, its resonance soothing, thoughts of its clear waters refreshing. Despite the coolness of the day, he was thirsty. He reached the river in due time and after brushing past several more ferns he stepped gingerly along the bank. The river was fast moving, its sides steep, and a misguided footfall could see him plunge headlong into the torrent never to be seen again. The last thing he needed was Neema fretting over his unexpected absence. She was already highly strung, especially since Kian was no longer with them.

'I wonder where you have gone,' he said as he knelt atop an outcrop and cupped a handful of water to drink. The water was icy cold and caused his eyes to widen. He drank for several minutes before sitting back on the sun dappled rock. Kian had left the day they found the cave, setting out to find help, so he said. No-one at camp knew where help would come from, or who it could be. He'd simply left with a flap of his cloak, disappearing into the forest. Now his absent days were piling up and Neema was beginning to show signs of discomfit. Not because she feared the New World and its endless forest, nor the possibility of them being followed.

She feared for Kayla because her baby was due.

The sharp, splitting sound of a stone striking rock jerked him out of his reverie. He raised wide eyes and pulled his hands protectively before him, slowly rising to his feet as he scanned the opposite bank. Dark ferns and tall trees bathed in shadow stared back at him, crowding the rocks lining the river's edge. And then he saw movement to his left. He lifted a hand to shade his eyes form the sun, saw a man step from behind a thick trunk and onto a granite outcropping. He was dishevelled, his clothes torn and bloodied, his hair a tangled mess. He stood sixty feet away, at least, but even from this distance Jarred could see he was deranged, his faculties absent. There was a wild look in his eyes, a feral gleam that spoke of hunger.

The wild man bent to retrieve another stone with a soiled hand, his fingernails long and stained, almost claw like. Jarred gingerly backed away a step, seeking to put distance between the two of them, but not before a furtive gesture sent the stone slicing through the crisp morning air to strike close to his heel.

'Gods above!' Jarred yelled, stepping back another pace. He didn't know who this creature was, or why he sought confrontation. Was he a native of this world? He wasn't about to stay and find out. Instead, he made to turn back the way he'd come, seeking to flee back to the cave. The wild man was on the other side of the river, with no conceivable way to cross. If Jarred ran now, he'd be hard to find, let alone catch. But as he swung about, he caught sight of another man standing on the opposite bank, further to his right. He was equally foul, his arms grimy, his nails black. But it was his mud-smeared clothing that caused Jarred to pause, for the stained garment was without a doubt the quartered yellow and black of Bastion's City Watch.

Jarred saw the vicious snarl curl the wild man's lips, the sight told him all he needed to know.

After all these months traversing an unknown forest, men of Bastion had finally caught up to them. It took him only a single look to determine their intent. They were hunters, sent on a mission to find those who fled. Whatever Ahriman did to the poor souls Jarred would never know, but from their deranged countenance, he knew it wasn't favourable.

Jarred finished his about turn and began to run, his legs stretching high as he leapt fallen logs and ducked heavy fronds. He needed to return as quickly as possible to the cave. He needed to warn his companions of this new threat.

Behind him, out of sight for now, stepped seven more wild men.

*

Jarred ran without caution, his feet churning the damp earth beneath as large tufts of moss went sailing into the air. His breathing was ragged, his arms flailing wide as he pushed ahead. For over an hour he'd kept moving, ever since spying the wild men across the river. But guttural calls in the forest unnerved him now. He could hear them close by, sense he was not alone. How they crossed the river so quickly he'd never know. Perhaps there were others taking up the chase. A foul curse sputtered from his mouth, accompanied by a wad of phlegm to slide down his chin. He was parched, his thighs and calves aflame. His chest hurt every time he took a breath.

He reached a slight rise, paused, his hand pressed hard against a redwood tree. The trunk was thick and strong, its height stretching over two hundred feet into an azure sky. He looked up, pain masking his boyish face, his blonde hair plastered to his skin. There was no solace to be found here, not amongst its strong branches. They were too far from the ground, and the trunks width was too great for his arms to embrace. He would have to continue his flight; continue to run from those who did not tire. The cave was not far from where he stood, not far at all. He could reach it in time.

But should he lead the wild men to his friends?

The thought left him with mouth agape. If he led them to the cave, they would find Kayla. It was she they were after, he was certain. It was Kian and Neema's greatest fear.

Jarred returned his eyes to the sky; saw only a glimpse of blue above, sneaking through a heavy canopy of green foliage. He sucked in a lungful of precious, dank air. He knew he was at a crossroads, a place of choice. Whatever he decided here and now would sway the events to come. A year ago, he would have balked at such knowledge, doubted he'd even recognize the situation for what it was. But he learnt so much in the briefest of times, thanks in no small part to the pyramid: Aston's Tear.

With a grunt he pushed away from the tall tree and headed to his left, hoping to skirt the cave and continue east. He would plunge ahead for as long as he was able; lead the wild men far from here. If he was lucky - if Frey, Goddess of Fate - smiled kindly down upon him, he would lose them.

But then he remembered Frey wasn't present. This was not her world, nor was it his. He was all alone.

The heavy snap of a branch cracked behind him. Jarred risked a glance, saw movement between the trees. Several figures flitted in and out of sight, their dark forms blending eerily with their surroundings. A surge of adrenalin lent strength to his aching muscles, he pushed on, striding over sodden ground as he rushed towards a cluster of densely packed trees. But before he reached the thicket, he had to cross an expanse of waist-high ferns and sword-grass, gently swaying to a sighing breeze. He stepped within, felt his heart drop as three wild men rose from the undergrowth to bare his way.

They were as he feared; eyes wild and baleful, their hands curled and their nails wickedly sharp. Jarred placed a hand on the pommel of his sword and drew it forth with a hiss. It was one of the king's swords, a jaguar blade. Tarsin had placed both in Ruvin's care before they fled through the portal. On that very first day Ruvin had placed one in his hand. It was for his own protection, he knew, but also a responsibility. Should they be accosted by Ahriman or his lackeys, he was to defend with his life.

Jarred swung the blade high and pointed its tip towards the wild men. His time had come, it seemed, and much sooner than he envisaged. But his options were few and he was out on his feet. And he had nowhere else to flee.

'Tarsin,' he said, almost out of breath as he watched the three men creep close, 'wherever you are, I need your help.'

He felt a tingle race up his arms as both hands held tightly onto the hilt of his blade. He blew a lock of hair from his face; saw the man in the centre grin wolfishly then lunge forward with intent. Jarred swung his blade in an arc, amazed at how cleanly it cut through the air. It hummed, almost sang as he whipped it back and forth to keep the wild man at bay. But then he felt the sharp sting of a heavy blow to his upper arm, followed quickly by the rake of clawed fingers tearing flesh.

Jarred screamed and swung again, this time with deadly force. The blade sank deep into the man's neck, releasing a fountain of blood to pump into the air. Hurried steps put distance between he and the corpse, a frown upon his brow, for he'd killed a man.

A growl to his left alerted him to the presence of the remaining two wild men. He swivelled to keep his adversaries within sight, then blanched as five more entered the clearing. He was grossly outnumbered, his thoughts of survival no more than a passing memory. He lifted his sword one final time, in salute to life and all its foibles, and prayed his lessons aboard the *Lioness* with Tarsin Va would hold him in good stead. Then he waited for the rush.

It was sudden and primal; a roar of frightful rage accompanied by flaying arms and clawed hands. Their eyes were crazed, their mouths lathered. Jarred knew he stood little chance. As wild men crossed towards him, their verbal assault deafening, he thought to close his eyes.

But the twang of a bow sounded from behind, close to his ear.

Jarred gaped as an arrow streamed across the short distance to thud into a forehead, sending a wild man somersaulting onto his back. A second later a dozen more arrows followed the first, striking flesh and bone as wild men fell under the sudden barrage. Jarred watched the carnage unfold; saw blood run thick and fast. The smell of death was pervasive, cloying. He wished he could walk back to the river and fall into its cleansing embrace, wash away the stain of battle.

'Jarred,' the voice was deep and familiar.

Jarred wiped his eyes with the back of his hand and spun about, only to see Kian standing tall behind him, a longbow in his hand. Jarred stepped forward a pace and buried his head against the tall man's chest, felt Kian's hand ruffle his long hair before resting on his shoulder.

'Are you alright, lad, are you hurt?'

126

Jarred looked up into curious eyes. 'I'm alive, thanks to you.' He sniffed as tears slid down his cheeks.

'Come, we must be away,' Kian replied. 'It was only chance we crossed your path this morning and those who followed. There may be more.'

Jarred's eyes tightened. 'Are you not alone?'

Kian nodded once, then with a gentle hand spun him about so he could view the clearing in its entirety. To either side of the thicket drifted men dressed in skins and patchwork cloth died in nature's earthy tones. Cloaks the colour of rich soil dusted with flecks of sun dappled foliage were draped over broad shoulders, whilst strong hands gripped highly strung recurved bows. Jarred could see tension in their muscular arms as fingers held knocked arrows firm. But despite their sudden appearance and silent approach, it was their features that caused him to step back a pace, halted only by Kian's body directly behind him.

'Who are they?' Jarred finally asked, a quiver in his voice.

'They are Cerven, Jarred, although they call themselves Ven.' Kian beckoned them forth with a gesture. 'These particular Ven belong to the *Ildraek* tribe.'

Jarred felt his head nod, yet his eyes remained fixed. They were tall and rangy, similar to Kian in many respects, and like Kian their eyes were almond-shaped, their cheek bones prominent and chins narrow. But it was not their similarities that startled him so. 'Are . . . they real?' he stammered.

'They are real, Jarred.' Kian's voice was soft and reassuring.

Jarred scanned the Ven equally, his eyes not meeting their own, but alighting on a region a couple of inches above, somewhere between their temple and forehead. For it was here that antlers grew, like those found on a deer, covered in soft velvet and many pronged. He knew he stared with an open mouth, noting the branched antlers reaching more than a foot in height as they escaped long manes of chestnut and flaxen hair.

'Come, Jarred, they will not harm you,' Kian guided him back the way he'd come, stepping quietly between sky-reaching trees. The Ven followed, equally silent, hazel eyes watching his every move.

'I'm not sure how the wild men crossed the river so quickly to give chase,' Jarred said, stepping over a fallen branch sprouting thin-stemmed fungi the colour of puce.

'The wild men we killed crossed no river, Jarred,' answered Kian. 'Their clothes were dry.'

'But I saw two men across the river, as wild as the ones in the clearing.'

Kian frowned; eyes heavy with concentration. Their cave was nearby, he knew Kayla and Neema would need assistance should the wild men find them. Ruvin and Reefe were able swordsmen, but as he'd witnessed already this morning, the wild men hunted in number. For all he knew, there could be a score or more traversing the forest in search of their group.

Kian pursed his lips then blew a shrill whistle, summoning Ven to his side. He spoke rapidly in a foreign tongue, his words rolling one after the other, cascading like water over polished rocks, until the Ven replied with curt nods. Seconds later they drifted wraith-like into the forest surrounds, disappearing in an instant, as silent as when they first arrived.

'Can you run?' Kian asked, looking down at Jarred's arm where the torn sleeve of his shirt revealed three bloody scratches.

'Aye, I can run,' thoughts of his earlier flight and the burning in his calves and thighs pressed inside his skull.

'Good,' Kian looked ahead as he peered past the green foliage, 'then I suggest you sheath your sword. We need to reach the cave.'

*

The run through the forest was longer than Jarred cared for. He laboured; his breathing ragged as his chest heaved with every tortured step. The cave was further placed than he remembered, his immediate knowledge of his surrounds sparse.

But he continued to put one foot in front of the other to keep pace with the tall Nepharii who journeyed by his side.

He chanced a glance at his saviour. The man, if he could call him such, was an enigma. He'd appeared from nowhere to help rescue them from the bloody streets of Bastion, only for his supposed sanctuary to become yet another feeding ground for the dark entity known as Ahriman. They'd fled at first sight of the cloaked figure, streaming into the forest with the last vestiges of adrenalin coursing through their veins. It was a mad rush fuelled by fear and loathing and an encompassing need to survive. But furthermore, it was a flight to protect the one element Kian and Neema pinned all their hopes on.

Kayla's unborn child.

What hope a child newly born could fashion, Jarred did not know? Even with his newly found intellect and mysterious understandings, the scope of their situation continued to baffle his teenage mind. Here he was, traversing another world where vibrant life, despite its subtle differences, prevailed upon him the necessity to live. And yet the threat of death haunted their every step, hounding their course, relentless in its perceived pressure.

For nine months they'd travelled south, putting ever-increasing distance between the portal and themselves.

But the darkness had caught up to them, as they knew one day it would.

He staggered to a halt, rested a hand against a damp slab of rock protruding from the ground. It was cold to touch, its minute crevices thick with trailing lichen and cushioned by emerald-green moss. Small mushrooms scattered its surface, orange topped with elegant salmon-tinged fins protruding from beneath their hoods. Before him, though, with his head tilted to one side, stood Kian with hand raised denoting silence. He gingerly stepped the last three paces to reach his side, then looked down upon an open expanse ringed by redwood. Beyond lay the cave, its entrance concealed by broken branches, its depths screened from the light of day. Not a soul was to be seen. All was silent.

And then a scream rent the air.

It was high-pitched, a noise of pure agony, a screech to wake the dead. Its shrill volume chilled Jarred to the bone. Kian moved without apparent thought, lunging down an incline and across the clearing in a heartbeat. Somehow, Jarred found the energy to follow, his legs cramping, his breathing still laboured. Out of the corner of his eye he spied the Ven, likewise on the move, their forms appearing and disappearing with the blink of an eye. He wondered if they'd mimicked their return, running alongside he and Kian in silence.

Jarred reached the cave mouth, stepped past branches dragged to the side by Kian. Another scream sounded, echoing from within, a wail of grief. He pushed on, his sword rasping from its sheath, gripped tightly in a fist shaking with fear. The flickering glow of firelight greeted him as he turned a corner, numerous shadows dancing upon the far wall. Another groan, uttered through clenched teeth. Dark figures spun as Kian and he made strides across the floor.

'Kian,' the voice was Neema's, 'thank the gods you're here.'

He saw Kayla beyond the fire with her back against the wall, several cloaks about her straining form, her legs bent high. Sweat glistened from her brow as Donal pressed a strip of cloth to her forehead.

'She's having the baby,' Neema beckoned them over with a hastily raised hand as Kayla groaned once more.

'How far has she come?' Kian strode to Kayla's side and placed his hand about her clenched fist. Neema repositioned herself between Kayla's legs as he watched, unsure what role to play. As Kian spoke soothing words to the young mother-to-be, Donal rose and joined him.

'Far enough,' was the curt reply. 'It shan't be long now.'

'Jarred,' Kian caught his eye, 'I need you here, beside Kayla, whilst I step outside.' He shared a look with Neema. 'I shall return in a moment.'

Kian rose and left with a bound; and for the first time he noticed Ruvin and Reefe's absence. He was about to ask Neema where they were when she spoke, reading his mind, by all accounts. 'The men went looking for you,' she said, 'and for any sign of Kian. I have delivered babes before, but I fear I'll need help with this one. The babe hasn't turned.'

Neema said no more, and for that he was thankful. He didn't understand what she meant in any case and felt out of his depth. He risked a glance at Kayla and saw her strain, her quick breaths escaping swollen lips with a whistle. He lifted his eyes as a sudden rustle sounded from the cave's entrance. Kian had returned, and with him were two Ven, although unlike those he saw earlier, they sported no antlers from their brow. As they stepped past the light of the fire, he noticed they were female, their leather clothes stained green, their long, unkempt hair a fiery gold. Without a word they sat before Kayla and plunged delicate hands into leather satchels to reveal several items fashioned from bone, including a bowl which was passed hurriedly to young Donal.

'Go fetch some water,' Kian said quietly as the bowl passed to the young boys outstretched hands.

Jarred breathed deep, synchronizing with Kayla as she struggled to maintain control. Her terrible screams had abated, but she appeared to be losing her focus, and with such a loss, her stamina for the journey. Foreign words passed between Kian and the two women, and Neema seemed to understand for she kept her vigil, her hands reaching towards Kayla's loins. For several minutes she probed, offering words of comfort and encouragement, whilst Kian hastily unstoppered a vial handed to him from one of the women and tilted the contents down Kayla's parched throat.

A spluttered cough was the result, although her eyes opened wider, enabling her to focus on the task at hand. Another groan escaped her lips.

Jarred was mesmerized, his own skin hot and flushed, his mind reeling from the intensity of the situation. He had no recollection of time passed, nor could he comprehend how dire a predicament Kayla found herself. Her distended belly was huge, rounded like the largest melon he'd ever seen, and right now she was doing everything in her power to push her babe into the world.

'The babe has turned,' Neema sat back up, a brief smile flashing across her aged face. Kian relayed the news to the womenfolk as Donal arrived, water sloshing within the bowl he carried with uncertain hands. 'Can you hear me, Kayla,' Neema prodded.

Kayla nodded once and let out a heavy sigh, her teeth firmly clenched a second later as a shudder rippled through her body.

'I need you to push on my command,' Neema met her frightened gaze, and Jarred felt his hand squeezed so tight he thought it would break. For several minutes Kayla pushed at the behest of Neema, straining in vain, it seemed, for he saw no babe. Then he saw the flash of golden firelight reflected by a silver blade as one of the foreign women lent in close. A final scream of outrage issued from Kayla as she was cut, but with gritted teeth she pushed once more.

Then there was silence.

Kayla sank back into her gathered cloaks, eyes closed, whilst Neema raised a blood-soaked babe from between her legs. There was no noise, no piping cry from infant lungs.

'It's a boy,' Neema whispered, holding the infant high for all to see. A bloody cord still attached the babe to his mother.

'Rastan,' Kayla opened her eyes to see the child for the first time. 'His name shall be Rastan.'

Kian handed a blanket from the leather satchel to one of the women. She reached for it, then said words in a foreign tongue, swiftly and with a sense of urgency.

'What did she say?' Jarred heard his voice croak, for he was parched from the ordeal as much as any other.

'She said he is Star-Born,' Kian replied with a knowing look in his eyes.

'Star-Born?' Jarred queried, his hand still holding Kayla's. 'What in Frey's name does that mean?'

'It means he is born with many souls.'

132

Jarred was about to reply when he heard a sharp inhale of air from the babe. It was Rastan taking his first breath, the son of Kayla and Tarsin Va.

The Star-Born son of a king.

CHAPTER TEN

The clearing was quiet.

Jarred shifted his feet from underneath him to stretch his legs. Beside him sat Kayla, perched with her back to a log, the babe Rastan feeding at her breast whilst the gentle rays of a winter sun warmed her skin. He could see bruised halos crowding her emerald eyes, knew months had passed since a twinkle sparkled from their depths. Now she sat quietly, exhausted and withdrawn, her black hair a dishevelled mess. Few words had passed her tight lips the past three days, not since the birth of Rastan into the New World. Jarred kept her company out of respect for all she endured, and because Neema suggested an eye be kept upon her. Rastan may have been born without harm, but the threat of Ahriman still lingered. Jarred swept his gaze away from Kayla towards the redwood trees, remembering the sight that greeted him when he first vacated the cave. He'd already felt ill thanks to the enormous amount of blood seeping from Kayla's body, was horrified she'd been cut with a knife at the end. But he was unwise to the trials associated with labour and kept his silence, albeit with a stern look directed towards the Ven women. Then with little else to offer he sought Neema's blessing and rose on tired legs to walk away, seeking the cool winter air outside the cave. His sweaty skin was clammy to touch, his arms and hands dirt stained. He needed to bathe, to dunk his head in the cool water of the nearby stream. Instead, he stepped out of the cave and into the dappled light of afternoon to count eleven wild men lying prone on bloodied ground.

He gasped, noted the wooden shafts of the Ven imbedded deep in the chests of the fallen. Beyond the carnage they stood, silent, their re-curved bows still gripped tight. He'd taken a moment to lift his face to meet their almond shaped eyes. They were cold.

But that was three days past. He'd been surprised and fearful at first, for he couldn't recall hearing anything other than

Kayla's screams that day. But not a hundred feet from where Rastan fought to enter the realm of the living eleven men, formerly of Bastion, crept noiselessly towards the mouth of the cave. And moments later, without so much as a cry of anguish, they were dead.

Kayla shifted next to him as she moved Rastan to her shoulder and began to gently pat his back. Seconds later he offered a burp. Jarred smiled before shifting to watch the babe's eyes close as he fell asleep.

'Will you hold him for me?' Kayla met his gaze.

His mouth opened, then realised he had nothing to say.

'It will not be for long, Jarred. I need to stretch my legs.'

He nodded and held out his arms. Kayla passed the small bundle wrapped in animal skins and fur, Rastan's body neatly cocooned. Once nestled in the crook of his arm Jarred lifted a finger to wipe a trickle of milk from the corner of Rastan's mouth.

'Do not wake him, Jarred.' Kayla said over her shoulder as she walked timidly towards the line of redwood and the stream beyond.

'I won't,' he replied, looking down at Rastan's angelic face. He was a beautiful babe: his cheeks already chubby, his hair soot-black and thick. Neema told him he was perfectly healthy and destined to be robust. And now that help had arrived in the form of the Ven, food would no longer be an ongoing issue. So long as they kept their distance from Ahriman and those tasked with finding them, he would grow vigorously in the coming years.

The sound of booted feet approached from behind. He dared not move lest he wake the babe, so he waited until the shadows drifted over his form before lifting his head.

'Is he asleep?' asked Ruvin Ciricello, his voice a mere whisper.

'Aye, he sleeps with a full stomach, and soundly, too,' Jarred watched as the old man took a seat beside him, closely followed by Kian.

'Where is Kayla?' Kian asked as he crossed his legs and sat on the ground.

'She has gone down to the stream, I think,' Jarred lifted his chin to point in the direction she left. Kian nodded, apparently satisfied. Since the birth and silent approach of the wild men, they'd been on edge. But with a score of Ven patrolling the outer perimeter, along with Reefe and Donal, chances of any sneaking through were minor. And from what he heard discussed the night before, Neema had somehow managed to put a mystical screen about their encampment. He didn't know how it was fashioned, but Neema suggested any breech by the wild men would be felt by her.

'Neema and the female Ven are also by the stream,' Kian said, peering between the redwood trees. 'She will be safe.'

Jarred could see the look of consternation upon his chiselled face. Despite two foiled attacks by the wild men, there was an air of unrest about the camp. There was already talk of leaving within a day or two, depending entirely upon Kayla's mobility and constitution. And yet even if Kayla felt up to the task, it was doubtful they would cover much ground. At least not whilst confined to the winter forest.

'When we leave here,' Jarred spoke in a hushed voice as Rastan stirred within his arms, 'where are we likely to go?'

Ruvin shared his look with the Nepharii. Since they crossed from Bastion to the New World, they'd trusted Kian implicitly. But for nine months now they'd toiled through a forest of encroaching darkness. Winter was here and the daylight hours were brief. To the east and west ranged tall mountains with snow-capped peaks, whilst to the north lay the ever-present threat of Ahriman and the witch, Avra.

'We'll continue to head south, avoid the snow for as long as possible,' Kian spoke quietly, his almond-shaped eyes glazed as he sought some mysterious destination. 'But at some point, we'll need to deviate to the west.'

'Why?'

Kian flexed his fingers against each other. 'We need to put as much distance between ourselves and Ahriman as possible. The Dark Lord is powerful and will become more so if he were to find our group. We cannot allow such an occurrence.'

He'd heard Kian share such talk with Ruvin and Neema during their flight through the forest. 'Are you afraid he will kill us should he find us?'

'He will, Jarred, of that I have no doubt. But it is young Rastan I am afraid for. He is Star-Born, Jarred, which means he will be a powerful man someday. It is our belief he will be able to stand his ground against the Dark Lord.'

'But he is a babe,' Jarred whispered back, careful not to wake him. 'It will be years before he is old enough to stand against him.'

'It is true what you say, Jarred, hence why we must continue to flee in the opposite direction.'

The snap of a twig underfoot alerted them to the approach of Kayla. 'I do not wish to flee any longer,' she said, hands on her hips. 'I wish to return home, to Bastion.'

'We cannot,' Kian was quick to respond.

'This is not our world, Kian,' Kayla pressed, 'nor is it a haven. You promised much and have delivered little.'

'I did not expect the Dark Lord to follow. It was my hope Elder Cappitus and Tarsin Va would win through. With their expertise, I thought we might stand a chance.'

A flash of pain swept across Kayla's face at the mention of Tarsin Va. That the child she bore was his there was no doubt, much to Reefe's annoyance. But with the Dark Lord here in the flesh, his survival back in Bastion had been questioned more than once. Kayla vehemently denied any talk of his demise but Jarred knew Kian and Neema doubted he was alive.

'If we cannot return to the portal and our home, then what life should we expect to lead? Are we to crawl through the forest for the rest of our days?' There was anger in her words. Without a thought Jarred lifted young Rastan, offering her babe to stem the tirade he felt was coming. 'At some point we need confront the monster you failed to keep at bay.'

Kian nodded in reply, hurt in his eyes. Even his shoulders slumped in recognition of Kayla's words. As he took a deep breath to calm his emotions, Neema, Donal and Reefe O'Bannon walked into the clearing. Behind them stood three male Ven with pointed antlers, hands holding re-curved bows.

'Is everything alright?' Neema was the first to speak, her discerning look taking in Kayla's wide stance and glaring eyes before settling on Kian.

'I wish to go home, Neema,' Kayla explained. 'I want to find Tarsin. I *need* to find Tarsin.'

The old matron walked a couple of steps to place a hand on Kayla's shoulder, then gently lifted Rastan and nestled him within her arms. 'There is no guarantee he is alive, my dear,' she said, genuine sadness in her voice. 'I have not said so before because I feared for your safety, but with the Dark Lord here in the flesh, the chances of Tarsin surviving are slim at best. It does not bode well. I am sorry.'

'But you don't know for certain. How could you possibly know?' Tears rimmed Kayla's emerald eyes. 'He may have escaped the demon horde with his men. Perhaps they fought free. And for nine months he's been wondering where I am and when I'll return.'

'No, he will not have,' Kian lifted his head.

All eyes spun to focus on the Nepharii.

'And why would he not?' Kayla raised her voice, daring Kian to deny her thoughts.

'Because the portal you stepped through transcends time and space.'

Jarred shared a blank look with Ruvin. The old man shook his head, unsure of Kian's words as much as he.

Young Donal stepped forward. 'Are you saying the time spent here on the New World differs from time spent in Bastion?'

'I'm saying exactly that, Donal. Nine months may have passed here, but in Bastion, on your home world, barely half-a-month will have passed. The portal is complicated, but it is ever regimented.'

'So, what does it mean for us?' Jarred voiced what he believed they were all thinking.

'It means we have time to find allies, to find a sanctuary and prepare ourselves for the confrontation to come. The Dark Lord will not sit idle for ever, at some point he will actively seek us out.' Kian glanced over his shoulder to look between the redwood trees, towards the hastily dug grave and the eleven corpses piled within. 'In fact, he's already begun.'

'And where are we to find these "allies" you speak of?' The venom in Kayla's voice had eased, but her eyes still simmered. 'Surely a score of Ven is not enough to thwart his designs?'

'They are not,' Kian stood to his feet and brushed his hands against his cloak. 'There is a city to the south, one I hoped to reach before you gave birth. Now, three weeks travel will see us at her gates. It is a city of gold. Ayoshos, she is called, but to the Ven she is known as the City of Angels. Five kings' rule over Ayoshos and her surrounding lands. They are powerful. They are immortal.'

'And the immortal kings will help us, will they?' asked Kayla.

'They will help us.'

'Why? We do not even belong on this world. Why would they do such a thing?'

'Because they are Nepharii, my dear. They are my brothers.'

*

Donal shivered before the feeble fire.

He lifted the collar of his cloak higher, attempting to retain some of his body heat. Wispy clouds had drifted across the blue sky in the early afternoon, causing a sudden drop in temperature. Now it was night, the stars absent and the ground cold underfoot. And he was tired.

He shifted an inch closer to the fire, mindful of his toes protruding through the holes of his boots. It wouldn't do to have them catch on fire, nor his boots for that matter. As worn as they were, they were all he had.

Actually, he thought, they were not all he had. He still carried the silver box he'd taken from Arkos Vantos' study. And he'd kept the maps of Bastion he'd found. On more than one occasion he'd been tempted to part ways with the burdensome scrolls, especially when the rain fell. It was difficult enough trudging through a damp forest as it was without harbouring several scrolls under his cloak. Thankfully they were prepared on vellum and thus able to withstand a little moisture. But the thought of parting with something from home sent shivers racing down his spine. He didn't need material objects to remind him of what he lost, but if he abandoned them, he feared his link to Bastion would be severed.

The crackle of flame snapped him out of his reverie, along with the voices of his elders. Reefe still argued with Kian and Ruvin concerning their new plan of action. Like Kayla, he wished to return to the portal, despite the inherent danger. As he explained countless times before, he was born and bred in the city. Life in an endless forest was not to his liking, nor was it accommodating. Donal felt likewise. He could see more clearly than most the difference in their appearance. They were wasting away. Food had been scarce before the arrival of the Ven, and rarely palatable. Neema alone had shrunk in size since they first arrived. Gone were her many chins and her pudgy fingers resting on a wide girth. Now she was a grey-haired old woman with improved vitality and mobility. But the rest of them, except for Kayla, had lost weight, and with such a loss came a decline in strength and stamina. They could continue to run, as suggested by Kian, but how long could they truly run for?

And now they had a babe to look after.

A shrill whistle sounded from beyond the redwoods. Donal swung his head about as Kian, sitting to his left with Ruvin and Reefe, echoed the same shrill sound. Out of the darkness stepped half-a-dozen Ven, their leathers and cloaks rippling like leaves touched by a capricious zephyr. As they filed into the clearing with their intimidating antlers and strangely hypnotic eyes, he noticed the carcass of some wild beast slung between two poles resting on their shoulders. Its pelt was shaggy grey, its size that of small cow. Without a word they set it down and began skinning the beast whilst two others walked forward to prepare the fire. Words were finally spoken in their sing-song tongue to call forth the women, who with pouches of herbs and wild vegetables began to prepare a broth in clay pots.

'Where did they all come from?' Jarred asked from his left.

'They have been with us since Rastan's birth,' Kian replied.

'How many are there?'

Kian leant back and spoke to the closest, a Ven whose antlers were four pronged and flanked by auburn hair to his shoulders. He was heavily muscled; the breadth of his chest impressive, and his long delicate fingers clasped his skinning blade with consummate ease. The reply was brief, a short statement and no more.

'There are close to sixty Ven in our vicinity,' Kian answered, turning his attention back to those sitting about the fire, 'mostly male, although some females travel with them.'

'Where have they been?' Donal asked, suddenly excited by the activity.

'Close by,' Kian narrowed his eyes as if deep in thought. He believed the expression peculiar until he motioned Jarred forward with a wave. 'Come, Jarred,' he heard Kian say, 'there is something I must do that should have been done earlier.'

Donal watched his friend push himself to his feet and walk towards Kian. The Nepharii bade him sit before him, then once seated, placed his fingers against Jarred's temple. 'What are you doing?' Donal found himself leaning closer; his curiosity piqued.

'Close your eyes, Jarred,' Kian said, before meeting Donal's gaze. 'I'm teaching Jarred how to confer with the Ven.'

'So he can talk with them?'

'No, so he can understand them. It will take time to learn their language, but with my help, and the memories Jarred harbours from Aston's Tear, he will learn their tongue swiftly.'

Donal's eyes widened at the revelation before he sat back to watch the process involved. Kian sat perfectly still; his eyes likewise closed as his fingers gently brushed against Jarred's skin. There was no sound made by either party, nor was there any sudden movement or flourish to suggest the deed was complete. One moment they were sitting in silence, the next Jarred was rising to his feet.

Donal stood and moved three steps towards his friend, placed a soft hand upon his elbow. 'How do you feel?'

Jarred ignored the touch and looked about the clearing, his eyes searching for Ven currently in conversation. Once he found two male Ven exchanging words, he cocked his head to the side, intent on listening. Several moments elapsed before Jarred greeted him with a wide smile. 'Their words are unfamiliar,' he said, 'but I believe they are discussing where their next kill will be made. There is a small pond a day's march from here, fed by the very stream beyond the redwoods. The *callask*,' he looked towards Kian who nodded in confirmation, 'apparently congregate nearby in number this time of year.'

'Very good,' Kian clapped his hands together, an act mimicked by the others now standing about the fire. 'Now, can you recall the technique I utilized, Jarred, and provide Donal with the same ability to understand?'

Jarred shrugged, then as instructed, he motioned his friend to sit. Donal did so and closed his eyes, waited for Jarred to touch his temples. He flinched at the touch of his cold hands, but then settled. All was quiet as they sat there, the flickering flames distant, the voices of the Ven heard from far away. Then a flood of images swamped his thoughts, images of Ven doing menial tasks, of hunting and gathering, of teaching children the rigours of life. Donal followed as best he could as he looked for patterns, discovered similarities in movement and gesture. Sounds trickled into his consciousness, sounds associated with

142

particular motions and activities. He tried to grasp their meaning but there were so many, and the flood was thicker now, the wave of images relentless. He gasped; frightened he would drown; fearful he would suffocate.

The pressure at his temples eased and he opened his eyes.

'Dae na ulla tee?' Kian smiled as he stepped towards him.

'You are asking me if I feel well, yes?'

'I am,' Kian replied.

He shared the Nepharii's smile and looked towards the now prepared carcass. Two Ven bent to lift the pole now skewering the beast, moving to place it upon forked branches either side of the fire. They muttered words as they did so, words Donal listened to with interest. 'They say the beast is plump, and that the meat should be . . . satisfying?' He looked to Kian.

'You are almost correct. The meat will be beneficial. They can see you lack vigour and need sustenance. They will provide for you . . . for all of us, as we journey south.'

Like Jarred, Donal smiled at his newfound ability.

'Come, Jarred,' Kian beckoned the lad once more, 'help me teach Ruvin and Reefe, then Neema and Kayla. With each of us comprehending the words spoken by our new companions, life will be much less complicated.'

Donal sat back down as they continued the procedure, but his mind was already elsewhere, scouting over a multitude of conversations between the male and female Ven. He caught glimpses of what they were discussing and could determine simple sentences when accompanied by certain gestures. But they spoke far too quickly for him to fully comprehend their speech. But it was a start, at least.

As Jarred finished his task and returned to his side, he finally caught the heady scent of roasting meat rubbed with spice and herb. The mere thought of placing succulent fare in his mouth had him salivating, even if it was an animal he'd never laid eyes on before.

'For the first time since our arrival, I feel content,' Jarred spoke with a hushed voice.

Donal agreed, although he was finding it difficult to concentrate. The meat sizzling before him was distracting and his stomach was already growling. And it would be some time before it was cooked well enough to consume.

'Have you taken any notice of the female Ven?' Jarred leant in close to whisper the question.

'What do you mean?' Donal lifted curious eyes to seek out a couple several feet away. They were stirring the broth in its clay pot, adding sprinkles of herbs and spice for flavour as it began to simmer on hot coals.

'I mean, do you not think they are beautiful?'

Donal's brow furrowed as he attempted to look past the preparation of food. The two Ven females were young and lithe. And like the other females, they lacked the intimidating antlers protruding from their foreheads. Their hair was long, the colour of autumn with a hint of sunshine, and their features were as refined as any young girl he'd previously seen. 'I guess so,' he said matter-of-factly.

'You guess so!' Jarred slapped a hand to his thigh.

'What do you think?' Donal asked his friend.

Jarred's smirk was infectious, 'I think they are beautiful.'

Two hands suddenly fell upon their shoulders, fingers digging through their tattered cloaks to squeeze hard. 'Up, lads,' Neema's weathered face peered down at them. 'I'll not have some Ven father concerned about his daughter's welfare this early in the piece.'

'We meant no disrespect,' Jarred spluttered.

'I know, but you need to learn not to stare so obviously.' Neema glared at them both, then pushed them towards where Kayla and Ruvin sat with Reefe. The three were quiet, their thoughts their own for now.

'What will you have us do?' Donal asked as he sat next to Kayla and her babe.

'Wait and listen,' she replied. 'Kian has something he wishes to say.'

The Nepharii soon made his way to where they all sat together, accompanied by several Ven of both sexes. They wore robes of many colours, decorated with feathers of strange birds and pelts of unusual texture. Once they were arranged before the seated group, Kian spoke. 'Today is the third day since the birth of your babe, Kayla Tolsten. It is customary in this land to name your child on its third day, during the Feast of Arrival, of which the Ven have kindly prepared.' He moved back a step, allowing a Ven elder to step forward to offer a woven blanket of intricate design. Kayla accepted the gift with a smile. A female Ven followed, her chestnut hair highlighted with copper and gold that hung to her waist. She swayed forward on balanced feet, a lilting song escaping her full lips. As she reached Kayla she poised above the babe, then planted a single kiss upon his brow. Rastan scrunched his nose then closed his eyes, obviously content with the attention.

'Come, Kayla Tolsten,' Kian gestured she should rise. 'The babe has been blessed; it is time to offer his name so all can hear. Shout his name, Kayla Tolsten, so your friends and comrades may hear it, so those in attendance may speak it, and so the Great Spirit may know of whom you speak. Do so now, Kayla Tolsten, and let the world hear the name of your son.'

Kayla stood with her back straight, her chin held high. Tears pooled in her eyes, causing the fire's flame to sparkle within their depths. She took a deep breath and settled her nerves, then spoke in a loud, clear voice as she lifted the babe above her head. 'Here me,' she began, 'and hear me well. The babe I hold is mine, a son conceived on one world, but born on another. In his veins flows the blood of his father, the king of Dervae and son to Arkos Vantos. But it is his father's name he shall carry, until the day he is reunited. Hear me, and hear me well, as I present to you my child, my son, a boy to be known as Rastan Va.'

The sudden intake of breath was heard to his right, namely from Ruvin and Jarred. Donal looked their way only to see them compose themselves in quick fashion.

'It is done,' Kian moved towards Kayla and kissed her brow. The congregation parted in silence on behalf of the Ven, whilst Donal noticed there was little talk amongst those who remained.

'What just happened?' he prodded Jarred in the ribs.

'Kayla called her son Rastan Va. She called him a bastard,' he whispered back.

'A bastard?'

'Aye, just like his father, Tarsin Va.' The two moved towards the fire pit where the first strips of meat were being expertly cut from the carcass.

'Is calling him such a name a bad thing?' Donal held out his hand for a piece of meat. He pinched it between two fingers and blew on it to cool it down.

'I don't know,' Jarred looked concerned, a look shared by Ruvin as he stepped alongside them. 'What do you think?' Jarred directed the question to his mentor.

'She appears troubled,' was all he offered. 'We must do our utmost to help her in the weeks ahead. Childbirth can be taxing, not just on the body but the mind as well. With Tarsin absent and feared dead, her mental state is now questionable.'

'Raising a child out here will not be easy,' Donal offered.

'I know,' Ruvin scratched his bearded chin, 'but Bastion is far behind us now. If we are to survive, we need to look ahead.'

'What of the golden city, Ayoshos? Do you believe we can find sanctuary there?' Donal asked his questions then ate his morsel of meat. It tasted of smoke and earth, which was strange, but it was tender. As Ruvin cleared his throat to reply, he reached for another slice.

'For a time, perhaps, but we still need to return to Bastion at some point. That is the goal, make no mistake.'

'How long do you think it will be - months, perhaps a year?'

Ruvin closed his eyes and took a deep breath. His lined face looked considerably older than when they first crossed the portal. The nine months had not been kind. And when he finally reached a conclusion, the look in his eyes spoke of further hardship to come. 'Your guess is as good as mine, young Donal, but to be truthful, I doubt any of us will see the streets of Bastion for many years to come.'

'That long,' Donal replied, the reality of their predicament suddenly becoming all too clear. Up until now they'd had a plan of sorts: to protect Kayla from the Dark Lord. Now, their course seemed infinitely more difficult. As he moved away from the fire with another morsel of meat, he wondered if fleeing to the world of the Ven had been the right choice. He missed the Undercity and its countless passages; he missed the camaraderie with those who peddled the streets. But then he remembered the scaled demons Kian called Deios, wondered if they continued to sift through Bastion's streets with blood staining their clawed hands.

As much as he loved his city of birth, until Bastion was free of the demon horde, he was quite content to remain where he was.

CHAPTER ELEVEN

Fear perpetuates fear.

Kayla knew it. For more than nine months she'd lived with it. Fear. Fear of the New World; fear of the unknown. Fear of the Dark Lord known as Ahriman.

Neema said he was the embodiment of Chaos. A creature twisted in mind and body, a creature hellbent on destruction.

And she was his focus.

So, for nine months their small group of survivors had scrambled through an immense forest on a foreign world, doing everything in their power to remain clear of his influence and as far as possible from his clutching hands.

There were tears aplenty. In fact, she struggled to remember a day when her eyes remained dry. The thought of death was forever a companion, and it was not just her own life she was concerned with. Young Donal was in her care, so, too, Jarred. They were children still, no matter the experiences they shared. And she continuously wondered how Reefe and Ruvin fared as they traversed the wilds. Reefe was sour in disposition, every day, it seemed. And Ruvin was an old man. The toll on their bodies: the lack of sleep, food and respite, was noticeable. Constant reminders from Kian and Neema kept them moving, because if they did not, she doubted they'd have survived. Their continual support and encouragement, along with staying alive, was the only motivation they needed.

Except, of course, the health of her child.

Rastan Va. Conceived on one world, born on another. A healthy babe. Robust.

She lowered her eyes from the horizon to check on the sleeping child cocooned about her torso. He was wrapped in woven blankets gifted from the Ven, his tiny fingers visible as they curled above his lips. Gorgeous.

'He sleeps well,' Reefe walked to her side and shared a look, his voice a whisper.

Kayla nodded, not daring to respond lest she wake him from slumber.

They shared the silence for several minutes before Reefe moved on, walking in the footsteps of Kian. Kayla watched him, saw him lift tired legs. He looked as thrilled about their predicament as she, although she feared that was all they shared. She'd seen the way he looked at her since the birth of her child. The lust still shining in his eyes, even when clouded with anger and frustration. She preferred not to talk to him if she could help it, for it was difficult to keep her disgust in check. As his steps took him further away, she remained where she was, glad to shift her eyes to the view she'd been admiring.

Fields of tall grass. A glistening lake of sapphire. A city of gold in the distance.

For more than nine months they'd walked a torturous path through an untamed forest. Incredibly tall trees reached for the heavens, consuming the sky with their ever-reaching limbs. It left them to scamper in the shade, fumbling over damp earth and moss-covered stones. Lichen and fungus gripped any surface not already blanketed with rotten foliage and detritus. They were constantly covered in grime and dirt; shared a pungent scent with the forest as it sought to engulf them. If it weren't for Kian's expertise, she feared they'd wander aimlessly for the rest of their lives.

Only now they were free of its constricting grip.

It had been a single day since they stepped out from beneath the claustrophobic confines of what Kian named the Great Forest. Sunshine, in all its glory, bathed their bodies with a gentle heat to invigorate the soul. Once again, she shed tears. And this time, she didn't care. She let them fall, felt them slide across her grimy cheeks.

Now they stood half-a-days travel from a city of gold. A city called Ayoshos.

They'd made good time since leaving the forest, for there was a noticeable bounce in their steps and the terrain eased from rock and bramble to dirt and grass. And for once their sight was not impeded by trees of gigantic girth. It made them feel whole once more, no longer part of a savage, wild entity they struggled to fathom. She could breathe.

Donal fell in beside her. His blonde hair was long and twined, tied at the nape in the same fashion as Ruvin. The two had become fast friends, helping each other, learning together. Both shared an interest in discovering everything they could about their surroundings. And about their new companions.

She looked over her shoulder, hoping to see the Ven in the distance. Only they were no longer there. She knew they'd returned to their home in the forest. For nearly thirty days they'd kept the companion's company, helping with food and providing warmth in the form of clothing and fire as they journeyed towards Kian's golden city. And they provided protection. She couldn't forget that. If it weren't for their skills, she doubted they'd all be here now.

A small part of her wished they were still by their side, for she felt exposed out here in the open. Yet Kian mentioned they were not fond of those who lived in the golden city, nor did they wish to engage in pleasantries with those they deemed lost. The words were peculiar, hidden with meaning, unfamiliar to her. How could they be lost? They were right before them. She'd shrugged her shoulders after giving it some thought, satisfied she knew little about the ways of the Ven. It was a dilemma she could ponder another time. If she remembered at all.

'It looks beautiful,' Donal reached out a hand to grasp hers, twinning his grubby fingers with her own.

She agreed. They were standing on a hillock, overlooking a lake and the city beyond. Vibrant colours shimmering in the midday sun reflected a spectacular view. If everything Kian said was true, it would be a haven for them, a place to rest and recuperate. A place to find allies in a time of need. From the outside, it was everything she hoped it would be.

'Come,' she pulled Donal along as she stepped through the knee-high grass. He followed, a smile on his face, a glint of sunshine in his eyes. By the end of the day, they'd have a place to call home. A place of safety, at least for a while.

They walked hand-in-hand for nearly a mile when Kian held up a fist, signalling them to stop. He stood there in silence, unmoving, his eyes narrowed as he swung his gaze left and right.

Neema moved to stand by his side. They conversed, quietly, before stepping forward, giving each other space.

'What is it?' she felt Donal's grip on her hand tighten as he asked his question.

'I don't know,' she replied, her eyes peeled. 'Maybe they sense a wild cat in the tall grass.'

Donal gave a nod, although she noticed his hand holding hers tightened further. She was about to offer a word of calm, but a sense of dread swept through her body like a thunderbolt. The fear that travelled with her since they crossed to the New World was back. She could feel it crawling up her spine, feel it swarming through her veins.

She looked over her shoulder, but once again, the Ven were nowhere to be seen.

The scrape of steel being drawn from a scabbard sounded next.

'What's going on?' Donal was borderline hysterical; she could hear the fright in his voice.

Kian unshouldered his long bow and notched a red fletched arrow.

Kayla felt her own mouth open, repeated Donal's question. 'What's going on?'

Neema hissed, signalling her to remain quiet. Reefe and Jarred both drew their steel and moved to stand beside Ruvin. A stillness crept over the field of grass they stood in. A silence followed. Apart from her breathing, that is. Her breathing was fast and shallow, her heartbeat escalating. Panic sought to drag her into the ground.

Several shapes emerged to their left from a small stand of willow trees. Kian swivelled, cocked his arrow to his ear.

A bare-chested man walked towards them. He was solidly built, with a glistening bald head and thick shoulders. Behind him, creeping from the shadows, followed more than a dozen others, dishevelled in appearance, their clothes dirt-stained and tattered. It took a moment, but she soon realised they were men from Bastion, not natives of the New World.

The bald man approached to within a hundred feet, cast his gaze over their number. 'I'm looking for one called Kayla Tolsten,' his voice was loud and deep, made the earth beneath her feet tremble.

'And you are?' Kian levelled his arrow at the bald man's forehead.

'Jed Ironmonger,' he returned. 'You must be Kian.'

The stillness returned as both parties eyed each other. She could see clawed fingers twitching from the men behind Jed Ironmonger, a feral glean to their eyes that spoke of hunger.

'What do want with Kayla Tolsten?'

'Nothing. It is my master, Ahriman, who desires her.'

A wobble began in Kayla's knees. Donal gripped her hand tighter still, but it wasn't enough to halt her descent as her knees sank to the grass. She looked at her son, blanketed and asleep, oblivious to the terror coursing through her body.

'You can't have her,' Kian replied. 'Not ever.'

Jed Ironmonger smiled in return, a hideous slash across his face that reminded her of a cat about to play with a mouse.

'Try and stop me.'

He sprang forward, leaping like some wild beast focused on a kill. The twang of a bowstring sounded an instant later.

She saw the arrow screech across the short distance, then screamed as Ironmonger swatted it aside before it could find its mark.

Another followed, but this time he caught it mid-air, snapping it across his knee in an instant.

She let go of Donal's hand and clutched Rastan tight, forced her head to remain up, forced her eyes to focus on those who sought to capture her. Tears welled, but she held on to them like she held her son.

Ironmonger bounded closer; his savage men moved with him. They were fifty feet away when Neema moved to stand before her, legs splayed, hands moving hypnotically in the air. She muttered words laced with arcane intent, sprinkled dust into the air. A thousand reflections of the sun twinkled before her eyes.

It began with the swaying of the grass, a gentle first breath of wind, almost silent. It quickly escalated into a roar. Cloaks flapped and dust stung as the wind intensified, striking like a hammer blow within seconds. Kayla crouched lower, cradling Rastan beneath her, whilst Donal lay flat on the grass with his hands over his head. The roar of the wind continued, sweeping outwards, towards the wild men and their leader who now stood in confused silence. Black clouds swirled into existence, blocking the sun.

Jed Ironmonger stood braced, a snarl on his face, corded veins swarming his flexed arms. He took a hesitant step against the unnatural storm. Then another.

Neema raised a hand, then swung it down with a chop.

Lightning flared bright, striking the ground with an almighty clap.

Wild men fell as if struck by Aston's hammer itself.

Flashing lights danced before Kayla's eyes. She blinked back tears, noticed a ringing in her ears. Wind gusts continued to buffet their bodies. A growl escaped from someone, primal, ventured into a scream.

Kayla raised her head above the windswept grass. Ironmonger remained standing, his body straining. There was no sign of his wild men. He looked over his shoulder, then back at Neema. Another growl, but this time, its volume dissipated with the wind.

The old matron swung her arms out wide, then clapped her hands together. A tremendous gust struck Ironmonger. He staggered back several steps.

'Begone!' this from Kian as he moved to stand beside Neema. 'Tell your master his prey cannot be found. Tell him it remains out of reach.'

A wad of phlegm flew from Ironmonger's mouth, only for the wind to whip it behind him. He yelled back his reply, only it sounded from far away.

'I'll wait,' the hunger in his eyes remained. 'I'll wait for as long as it takes. One day, when you least expect it, I will come for her.'

By the time his words registered, he was gone, leaping towards the stand of trees to disappear. Several of his men stumbled to their feet and followed. Most remained unmoving on the blasted earth. As soon as he left the wind subsided. A moment later it ceased altogether.

The silence was deafening.

*

Reefe was glad to be sitting on a seat of stone, even though it confused him.

A seat of stone. A seat. No longer a damp branch dripping with lichen, or a moss-covered stump that crumbled once touched. There was no grass to be seen, nor a gentle breath of wind blowing autumn leaves before them. There was only stone, lacquered and polished to shine like gold, everywhere he looked.

The fact the city wasn't built from gold had been an incredible disappointment to Reefe O'Bannon when they first arrived. He'd expected a treasure to rival all treasures as they stumbled towards their destination. Instead, he found the city was lacking when compared to his dreams. It was . . . tasteful, to be sure, yet he found it odd from the outset, and several hours later, now deep within its confines, he knew it could never replace the grandeur of Bastion. Nor would it feel like home, despite the obvious comforts it could provide.

He spared the seat he sat upon another moment of quiet contemplation. He needed to check, one final time, to remind himself there was no gold to be found. It was difficult. But apart from the sheen, he could see the seat was merely fashioned from granite. Whatever technique they utilized to bathe it in lacquer, it worked a charm. It was a gilded masterpiece; yet offered nothing to line his pockets with. He knew because he'd checked. Several times.

A strident voice caught his ear as he sat in contemplation. He raised eyes that hurt from staring at oddities, focused on a Ven dressed in fine clothes who swung his arms out wide as he addressed Kian.

Reefe listened, but the talk was rapid, and despite learning many phrases during his time in the forest, the dialect differed.

'I can't make out what they're saying,' Donal sat next to him, his blond hair home to dawn-coloured leaves, twigs and the grime of nature. His blue eyes caught his own.

'Neither can I,' Reefe replied, waving his hand. 'It matters not, so long as we are fed, bathed and offered food. I could eat a horse,' he winked at Donal, 'except I've not seen one since we arrived.'

The lad smiled, which was rare. He knew he carried demons. Hell, they all carried demons since their escape. But the demons clawing inside Donal's head hadn't let go. He knew because he watched him sleep. Watched the frantic twitching and the curses mumbled in the night. Saw with his own eyes the sweat beading on the poor boy's forehead. He'd watched at first, then offered help with a comforting pat on the shoulder to calm him down. It worked, somewhat, enough to ease the fear rising in his own heart. Since the very first night, when they slept exhausted under a damp overhang in an unfamiliar forest, he'd kept an eye on the youngster.

He still did, although tonight he hoped they'd all sleep with a roof over their heads and a pillow beneath them. And perhaps, if he was lucky, Donal would sleep a sleep without demons.

'Come,' the voice belonged to Kian. He beckoned the others, waving them to stand with him. Reefe obliged, reluctantly, leaving the golden-hued seat behind him.

'I apologise for the delay,' Kian began once everyone was within earshot, 'but it has been centuries since I last stepped foot within this city. It was vastly different back then, and half the size. And it appears I am no longer recognised by those who dwell here.'

'Surely the kings you mentioned haven't forgotten you?' the sneer that followed was deliberate. Reefe still couldn't grasp Kian's talk of being immortal as truth. Some things just didn't make sense. So he disregarded such nonsense as the talk of a madman.

'They will not have forgotten me, Reefe. There are simply more channels to navigate before we garner an audience. Everything takes time, unfortunately, and since the kings are immortal, time is at their disposal.'

Reefe chose not to reply. He found out early it wasn't worth it. Neema and Ruvin believed every word he uttered, so too Jarred, for some reason. Kayla, on the other hand, appeared to harbour as many doubts as he, yet she refused to engage in any sort of conversation with him. Granted, she'd been heavily pregnant for most of their venture and angry as a she-bear, but he'd hoped for more from his fellow thief. They'd shared so much in the past; it would be a shame to lose that connection. She needed him like he needed her. They'd been good together, wandering the streets of Bastion, sharing laughs.

It'd been some time since he heard her laugh.

'In any case, Reefe,' Kian narrowed his almond-shaped eyes, 'we can now make our way to the palace. The kings are waiting, and from what I have gleaned, eager to meet the strangers from another world.'

Neema smiled at Kian's words, but everyone else merely cast their gaze to what they assumed was the palace. It had to be, Reefe thought, for its sheer size dwarfed the golden buildings before it. It rose from a conglomeration of stone to reach the heavens, a tall, slender tower rising from its centre. Like the rest of the city, its walls shone like the midday sun, polished brighter, even, and pockmarked with windows of sapphire blue glass.

He had to admit she looked the part. The entire city was beautiful to the eye. From the moment they walked through the gates, their booted feet kissing tiled roads, one could not help but admire the sites. The buildings were clean, the Ven who walked the streets equally so. There was the idle chatter of friends and family at work, the smell of roasting meats mingled with the stench of livestock nearby. Wicker baskets brimming with produce added a splash of vibrancy amongst the gold, and Ven children chased balls made of twine, laughing as they did so. They received their share of stares when they entered, and the feeling of being observed continued the further they travelled. He hadn't thought to see so many almond-shaped sets of eyes glaring his way. They weren't hostile, but neither did they evoke a sense of calm. As the sun began its descent to what he assumed to be west, he wished they could hurry their pace and reach wherever it was Kian sought to take them.

Now his wish was answered. The palace, directly ahead, was guarded by Ven in shirts and leggings of leather, slender blades sheathed at their hips. Their eyes were wide with curiosity, although they remained tight-lipped. Unlike those in the forest, the Ven in the city grew no antlers from their forehead. Maybe it was a civilized novelty, he thought with a curl of his lip. Perhaps it was so they could wear their unusual headpiece.

He almost laughed. The guards wore a conical hat made of leather like the rest of their attire. A gentle sweep at its base flared enough to keep the sun from their eyes, but its height was considerable and finished with a gleaming metal spike.

'They look impressive,' Reefe shared a smirk as he stood alongside Donal.

'Actually, they appear to be quite tall,' came the response. 'I wonder if that was a consideration when designing their helmets?'

Reefe shook his head. He didn't know where such thoughts came from, especially in a young boy. He was, what . . . thirteen years old? Hell, he was pissing and farting and laughing at the same age, and happy to do so.

They approached the guards, only for another Ven, this one dressed in an emerald-green overcoat that fell to his knees, to step from behind a timber gate. Reefe's eyes widened. He hadn't even noticed the timber behind the comical guards. Now he stood open-mouthed, admiring the intricate workmanship, for the gate was fashioned from countless planks, all twisted and bent as they twinned amongst each other, hand-carved with scenes of hunting and feasting, bordered with twirling vines and enveloping flowers.

'That must have taken some time,' he said to no-one in particular. And it must have, for the gate stood fifteen feet high and was twice that in width.

Brief words passed between Kian and the Ven with the green coat. A moment later the gates were opened so they could be ushered through.

The city was remarkable, it had to be said, although Reefe felt he preferred the contrasts associated with Bastion more. Yet as he and his companions passed the gate and stepped into the palace proper, he found himself lost for words. In fact, his entire head felt numb, if truth was told. A bit like after he'd tried a sniff of that Dorsian narcotic. What was it called? Angel's Pollen. Damn near blacked him out. The heady scent had unnerved him, caused him to stagger for longer than he cared for. A little like how he felt right now. Overwhelmed, as if every sense was being assaulted with something he'd never experienced before.

'Welcome,' Kian was beside him, whispering in his ear. Where in Hell's name had he come from. 'It's quite a sight, is it not?'

'It is . . . incredible,' he managed to say. How his mouth worked, he'd never know. Before him was the most wonderful looking grounds he'd ever seen.

Green lawns, trimmed to perfection, blanketed an area as large as the King's Market Square in Bastion. To his right sat a pond, or perhaps a small lake would be more precise, with a rocky outcropping reaching a hundred feet in height. Its flanks were draped with strands of verdant foliage, countless blooms of molten yellow and sunset pink flowers freckled across its breadth. At its peak sat an assortment of bony protrusions, coral-like in appearance, their colour varied with subtle hues of turquoise and ruby, garnet and fiery opal.

A steady stream of tinkling water fell from an unknown source at the peak, cascading to the pool, leaving a sparkling sheen in its wake. Enormous lilies bobbed below.

But it was more than a well-manicured lawn and a pretty waterfall that took his breath away. It was the two red-barked trees that stood as sentinels before the palace, soaring two hundred feet into the clear blue sky. It was the dozens of animals wandering the grounds, unfamiliar in size and shape, unfamiliar in disposition and temperament. Their hides consisted of coarse hair and smooth velvet. They shared pointy ears and broad-reaching antlers. Snake-like tails and scaled wings fluttered in the distance. So many creatures, vibrant with life, calling in strange tones. Amongst them strode the Ven, carers, perhaps, brushing between ears, scratching necks and patting paws.

Reefe didn't know where to look first, couldn't keep his gaze in one place for long. And behind it all, hidden, if he was any judge, although he knew later it was as obvious as the nose on his face, stood the palace of the Five Kings. As grand as any building he'd ever laid eyes on. Vast, it was, a colossal of design. Pyramid-like at its base, it tapered ever upward, stepped levels eventually reaching the tall tower that stretched from its centre.

His mouth was still agape when Neema grabbed his hand and pulled him towards the palace. They walked across the green lawn, their footfalls all but silent. Ven watched their every step, hands continuing to brush and scratch their animal companions. As they walked around the small lake, he saw what could only be described as a wild cat. They'd heard them in the forest, calling in the dead of night. Sometimes they heard the end of a hunt and the wails of the prey. But they'd never seen one in the flesh.

It was huge. Easily the size of a mule yet rusty in colour. All rippling muscle with sparkling teeth and claws.

And by its side stood a Ven, brushing a wooden comb through its verdant mane.

'Gods above!' he almost screamed, but in the end his voice sounded like a squeak.

They moved past, brazenly, considering the danger thirty feet away. By the time Reefe pushed the wild cat out of his mind, he was standing before the steps leading into the palace, two monstrous trees to either side, shading him from the sun.

A voice broke the silence. He looked ahead, saw the green coat vanish, then five Ven stepped forward with a flourish, halting at the top step.

They were tall. And otherworldly. Shared looks similar to Kian, only they wore such finery, expertly stitched and imbued with such depth of colour. Hints of gold twinkled every time one moved, catching sunlight to reflect their power. And their eyes were sharp, piercing with knowledge and intent. He would have believed they could read one's mind if someone told him so. Hell, if they said they could fly he would have asked how far?

Words were spoken, fluidly. He couldn't grasp their meaning, yet Kian responded in turn, speaking on their behalf, he assumed. The exchange was brief.

'Come,' Kian said a moment later. 'The kings have agreed to shelter us for now. They will provide clothes and food. They will provide a place for you all to sleep.'

He felt his head shake from side-to-side, heard Donal ask a question from behind.

'How long will they care for us?'

'I do not know, Donal,' Kian eased his shoulders, let out a sigh. 'They will seek to learn from us, understand who you are and where you come from. Whilst you are here, you will be under their protection, which is what we sought. When the time is right, they may help us. Until then, my friends, I'm afraid we are to be confined to the palace.

'From what I understand, we are now their prisoners.'

CHAPTER TWELVE

Ra'tor lifted a meaty bone and cracked it between sharp teeth.

The noise snapped him out of contemplation as he took a moment to savour the flesh in his mouth before he peered with intent at those sitting about his fire.

He and his Deios were sitting on stone blocks near the ambling river, the shinning blue pyramid behind them. Night had fallen, barely, and yet the heat of the day was rapidly deteriorating. He looked at those who sat with him. They were not the assertive hunters he'd fought with when they first arrived at this dwelling place. Nor were they as eager. The spark they carried had fled. Too many of their brethren were now with Bhral, their blood staining unknown ground. Within a handful of days more than a hundred had fallen. Now they merely survived, which was exactly what they did on their own world. And surviving in this place was becoming problematic.

He swallowed his food, wiped a blood-stained mouth. As always, the flesh was good. Despite the cold days and foul winds, there was something special about the prey. It certainly made a difference to their moods when the melancholy sank in. Gave them purpose.

'The Others crept closer today,' Ess'ik's voice cut through the sound of tearing flesh as the brood ate.

Ra'tor threw his remaining bone into the fire, watched sparks fly. They always seemed to catch his eye, more so of late. Like they were long lost memories he'd somehow forgotten. Memories of things he should know and understand. Memories that could help him in the days to come.

'You saw them?' he asked, his voice deep.

'I did. And the bronze scaled Patriarch, Vis'ak, scouted with me. He saw what I saw.' Ess'ik scratched his chin, then picked a bone shard from between his teeth. 'I believe the Patriarch is beginning to understand the dangers you spoke of. I believe he won't make any rash decisions, unlike his predecessor.'

Ra'tor knew there would be no more rash decisions. Not from the meddling Patriarchs, nor from those brood leaders who remained. He was the one who ruled. His word was now the only word. Less than half the brood leaders returned from the land of coldness, and Sav'ak, once the voice of the Patriarchs, was now just as cold. Snapping his neck had been the best thing Ra'tor had done in days. And Rax't was gone, just like Sav'ak. Traitors and schemers. Dead traitors and schemers.

'He is scared, Ra'tor,' Ess'ik continued. 'He is scared of you, and he is scared of the Others and what they represent.'

'How far did they come?'

'The Others did not reach the temple. But they did stand and watch as a handful of our brethren waited at the end of the stone pathway. There was a great deal of tension between the two gatherings, even though they stood far apart.'

A gentle, thoughtful nod of his head ensued as he listened to Ess'ik's words. A respectful nod was mimicked by Fass'it who sat opposite. Since they had returned from the cold world, both Deios leaders had pledged everything to him and his leadership. Especially after the visit to the temple to see where Sav'ak's hunters had crossed. A small smile twisted the corner of Ra'tor's mouth. He'd been furious when he saw the metal plate with its unusual design. Was close to losing all sense of normality. Blood had surged through his veins like the dust storms back on his home world, fast and all consuming, threatening to engulf him in darkness. He knew the rage was visible in his eyes, knew it almost took him.

Ra'tor had seen the metal plate before. After the fight against the Lesser Creatures. He'd watched them step into the swirling light. He'd almost chased them. Now a dozen Deios had crossed over the very same plate. They hadn't returned. Somehow, he knew he'd not see them again.

'So,' both hands stretched towards the fire for warmth. He studied them a moment, saw the fading scales. They were the hands of an elder. Perhaps the hands of a Deiosian past his prime. 'What did the Others look like?'

162

Ess'ik cleared his throat, spat phlegm to the side. 'Tall,' he began, sharing a nervous glance with Fass'it, 'and strong and capable. They are definitely hunters.'

'And their features?'

'They are like us, two arms, two legs. But they have a beak, sharp and curved, and eyes that see far. We could tell. They looked straight through us.'

The same had been said from countless of his brood in the past three days. Piercing eyes, a sense of dread. It was not like his Deios to feel like prey. But that was exactly how it was.

'Shall we kill them?' Fass'it caught his gaze and held it.

'No,' Ra'tor rumbled. He knew they'd expect more of an answer, but he needed time to think about so many things. This place, their purpose in being here. What in Bhral's name were they going to accomplish? He knew when they arrived they'd been consumed with bloodlust. But he also knew it was fuelled by rage and a desire to seek revenge.

'So, what shall we do?' Fass'it opened his hands, palm up. 'If we do nothing, they'll creep closer each day. They see the blue temple, and like us, they wish to know what lies within.'

Ra'tor couldn't deny the truth in Fass'it's words. He wondered if his duty was to protect the temple from prying eyes. Was that his role and the role of his Deios? Were they nothing more than guardians of something beyond their comprehension?

'What are we?' he finally said, placing his warmed hands in his lap.

'We are Deios,' both Fass'it and Ess'ik said in unison.

'And what do we do?

'We live and we hunt,' Ess'ik was the first to answer.

Ra'tor shook his head. 'We are hunters. We hunt to live. We only take what we need, never more.' He paused for a moment, lifted his eyes to the darkening sky, knew they'd become something far different since their arrival. 'We have entered a new place, an unusual place, and lost our way. We know nothing about where we are. We know nothing about the creatures who dwell here.'

'We know they are Lesser,' said Fass'it.

'Are they? Lesser in stature, perhaps. Look at this place,' He flung his hand to the side. 'Do we have anything so . . . enormous, on our world? You say they are Lesser, but I think they may be greater. And we don't even know what they are called.

'We arrived here with bloodlust and a desire to prove we were strong. And yet in the days since our arrival, we've lost so many of our brood.'

Silence greeted him. Neither of his aides new what to say, he could see it in their eyes. Always surrounded by death, the Deios were. It was their existence. Let the blood flow, so life could flourish. That was who they were. Hunters.

Not the killers they'd become.

'I'm not sure we belong here,' Ra'tor finally voiced his concern. The thought had been simmering beneath his consciousness for days, only he'd refused to acknowledge it. The deaths of his leaders, his own hand about Sav'ak's neck. The death of Rax't. The strength of his brood had dwindled. And despite the number arriving through the door-between-worlds, he knew their true strength was not the same.

'We must be here for a reason,' Fass'it kept his voice low, possibly to ease his fears. 'Bhral guided us here, you said it yourself. The Blood-God's work is mysterious, but all we can do is walk the path he has chosen for us. If that path is here, amongst strange shelters and stranger creatures, then there must be a purpose.'

'Fass'it is right,' Ess'ik joined the conversation. 'Believing we'd discover the way so soon proves we are arrogant, not lost. Perhaps if we ceased with the needless hunting and focused instead on our surroundings, the way will be made clear.'

Their reasoning was sound. Blinded by blood, he'd been, in honour of his god. Or so he believed. But if he was to truly lead his Deios, to protect and nurture them in a world

164

unlike any they'd seen before, he'd need to quash his anger and trust his aides. He'd need to welcome the weaker Deios, those without a brood, and those who called themselves Patriarchs.

He would need to choose a path he'd never trod before.

'You're right,' he said, once again looking to the sky. 'Everything here is different to what we're accustomed to. We need to adapt and be strong. We need to be united. But more than anything else, we need to learn.'

Three bloodlings walked towards his fire, halting their conversation, heads bowed low. They stopped ten feet away. He could see their dark, juvenile scales, highlighted by flames.

'Ra'tor,' said the boldest, taking a small step forward, 'we have seen several Others approaching under the cover of darkness. We fear they seek the temple of blue light.'

A sigh escaped Ra'tor's lips, for although the night was young, his appetite had been sated. He'd been looking forward to losing himself in the flickering firelight, hoping he could close his eyes and forget about his duties.

'By the Blood,' he heaved his considerable mass off the stone tiles. It would take only a moment to reach the pyramid. Perhaps it was time for him to confront the Others. 'How many?' he snarled.

'Two hands worth,' the bloodling was quick to answer.

A snarl sounded as he stretched his shoulders. 'Come,' Ra'tor waved the bloodlings to join him, tilted his head towards Fass'it and Ess'ik. A gathering of a dozen Deios sat about a nearby fire. On seeing him rise, they followed. 'Let us see what we can see,' he raised his voice as his brood surrounded him. 'Let us learn what we can learn.'

A smattering of growls and snorts greeted him. He patted his heavy cleaver, more out of habit, he thought, than with any intent to use it. He vowed to himself he would not seek to kill the Others when he found them. He would study their progress, learn what he could about their manner. He almost issued an order for a bloodling to go find the Patriarch, Vis'ak, and ask him to join them. Then he realised to much trust too soon was bound to be problematic. One step at a time, he mused, for the journey was bound to be long. No need to complicate the current situation. He would investigate the Others as they approached the pyramid held by his Deios. If they crept too close, he would bar the way. If they were less intelligent then he believed, they would seek a confrontation.

If they did so, they would die.

*

They kept to the shadows as they walked, quietly, cautiously, before reaching a wall of debris. On the other side could be heard dissonant voices.

Ra'tor peered over the block of granite he squatted behind, counted ten of the creatures in the darkness. There could be more, he thought to himself, for dark clouds had drifted to blanket the sky, obscuring stars and moon. A stone wall had collapsed nearby, creating cover for those with ill intent. Fass'it moved away from his right side, peered over the stone. 'How many?' he tilted his head to the side as he asked the question.

'Another two hands,' Fass'it replied. 'Do we take them?'

Ra'tor shook his head. He had to believe what he said earlier was true. They needed to learn more about their surroundings and those who wandered close. Hunting and killing to prove one's strength and courage would take them only so far. Perhaps it was time to observe, and perhaps by doing so they could develop a sense of purpose beyond the ordinary.

'We wait,' Ra'tor hissed back. 'If they creep too close, we'll make ourselves visible. Then we'll see what they are made of.'

A low murmur of approval sounded from the Deios. Despite his call for passiveness, they remained hunters and would act accordingly as soon as he gave the word.

A gentle breeze swept coarse sand across the stone pathway. The noise was slight, yet enough to mask the footfalls of the Others as they stepped forward, this time with haste. Ra'tor watched, saw their long, thin legs carry them easily over uneven ground. Despite the dim light, their shape was becoming more pronounced. Cloaks of black cloth helped blend their features with the night, covering neck and shoulders before sweeping low to mask their waist and thighs. He could see the occasional leather belt holding sand-coloured leggings after each step, and an assortment of steel buckles glinted when exposed. If they carried weapons, he was none the wiser. The wind blew once more, a slight moan, and hurried steps followed.

It was time. He stood to his feet, hefted his cleaver, and took three large strides to position himself upon the stone pathway, blocking the advance of the Others.

The noise of his Deios behind him suggested they mimicked his move.

Eyes narrowed as he saw the Others with their beaked mouths and feathered heads hold their ground. The wind, Ra'tor believed, held its breath.

'Do we talk?' whispered Fass'it to his right.

He held up a clawed hand, clenched his fist. The Others stood thirty feet away. Like his Deios, they remained where they were, silent and unmoving. He took a step forward, pushed his shoulders back. 'I am . . . Ra'tor,' he raised his voice, then slapped his clenched fist to his chest for emphasis.

Feathered heads shifted back and forth, large eyes blinking as they listened to his words. If he wasn't mistaken, a series of clicks passed between the Others, softly spoken but heard, nonetheless. It was repeated once more before three of the Others stepped forward.

Their height mimicked Ra'tor's own, yet their breadth of shoulder was considerably less. He doubted they'd weigh half his weight; such was their frame.

'Ra'tor,' he said his name again with another slap to his chest.

'Chiok,' came the reply from the tallest Other.

Ra'tor's eyes opened wide. He hadn't expected a reply, let alone a voice to answer so clearly. The word sounded nothing like the clicks he heard a moment earlier. He wasn't sure what to say next. Neither would be able to understand the other's language. Name and race were about as far as he could think. 'We . . . Deios,' he looked over his shoulder as he swept a hand back, acknowledging those behind him. Somehow, unbeknownst to him, his ranks of Deios had grown. Word must have passed whilst he observed the Others. He was only guessing, but he felt at least a hundred of his brood now crouched close by.

'Aquilan,' came the response, a feathered arm also sweeping back.

Ra'tor offered a nod of understanding. Took another step forward himself. He wasn't quite sure what to say next. As he contemplated the unusual situation, the clouds above drifted to the east, revealing a multitude of stars to lighten the darkness. He chanced a look to the night sky.

And saw a crowd of Aquilans standing on the rooftops to either side.

A curse spat from his snarling mouth as Ra'tor flicked his gaze back to the leader. He breathed deep, flared his nostrils as he sucked in the night air. Blood surged within his veins.

'Shiv ak issik nah!' The words were shouted at him. He couldn't understand them, followed a pointed hand to the blue temple visible behind him.

'Deios,' he snarled back, his teeth snapping shut with force. He clenched his cleaver tight, took another glimpse at the Aquilans standing atop the shelters. There was an unsavoury demeanour in their posture. With starlight shining in the background, he could see their hunched shoulders, feared they were poised to leap into action. He snapped his teeth together, felt the pull of skin as he shared a smile. If the Aquilans wished to see the temple, they would have to fight for it.

He shook his head.

'Shiv ak issik nah!' the Aquilan repeated his words. Ra'tor couldn't tell whether they posed a question or a demand. He decided it didn't really matter. The movements of the Aquilans appeared hostile. They had arrived in force, secretly, intent on reaching the pyramid. There was little he could say to sway them.

He sensed, rather than saw, Fass'it and Ess'ik move to stand by his side.

'Sept! Sept ik aut!'

'Do you have any idea what it is he is saying?' Fass'it shared a look.

'No,' Ra'tor kept his focus. The Aquilan was agitated, his movements tense. Twice he'd gazed to those standing on the shelters. 'Prepare yourselves,' he could sense the tension in the night air, could almost envisage the call to action.

And then a high-pitched call was made, piercing, loud. The call of a hunter as it moved in for a kill.

It was echoed by those on the shelters and those on the path.

The Aquilans charged.

Those standing on the shelters spread their feathered arms wide and leapt. Ra'tor snorted, was shocked to see them leap from so high. Most were at least twenty feet from the pathway, some, standing further back atop marble columns, possibly thirty feet from the ground. Yet they glided, rather than fell, and hit the stone ground to land in a squat.

Taloned hands drew steel knives from hidden sheaths, and before he could call his Deios to surge forward and fight, hands swept and daggers flew, like silver bolts reflecting starlight.

A roar sounded from his own throat as he ducked and swerved. He could hear the click-click of Aquilan feet on stone as they raced towards him. Could hear the high-pitched calls for battle. He lifted his heavy cleaver, breathed deep. Then watched as a dozen hatchets flew from his Deios in retaliation.

Screams sounded as blades struck flesh and feathers puffed into the air. Ra'tor could smell the blood as soon it began to flow, let its scent fire his own. He charged with his brood, swinging with power, snarling as his blade chopped down and thudded into a body. For a moment, the roars drowned out the screams.

A silver blade snaked for his throat, terribly fast. He knew he couldn't defend with his cleaver, stepped back instead. It came again, swift as lightning. But instead of stepping away, he braced himself and kicked, striking his attacker in the groin. The Aquilan bent over, then fell heavily as he smashed his cleaver into the back of its head.

Black feathers flew in the dark, and screams issued from the dying. Ra'tor surged forward, swinging his blade in short, vicious arcs. He could smell blood everywhere, could taste it on his salivating tongue. The roars of his Deios lifted his soul. This was his purpose: to fight and to bleed. To test his power against others. To be the strongest and most feared. He would lead by example for his Deios. He would be the Blood-King spoken of in ancient lore. He would be the Hand of Bhral.

He couldn't recall how long he fought. One moment he was splitting the skull of an Aquilan, the next he was looking in the dark for another foe. He'd charged ahead as the bloodlust took him, crazed and wild as he sought out the enemy. Only now he was alone, the ground about him littered with bodies. There was no sign of the Aquilans, no sign of his Deios. The pathway he stood upon was narrow, closed in by tall pillars and blackened walls. He looked to the sky. Heavy clouds had rolled in to obscure the stars once more. He couldn't see far. Couldn't hear any fighting.

He wiped his nose, smeared blood over the back of his scaled hand. His calmed his breathing, then felt the fire in his blood seep away, only to be replaced by pain. He checked his body, found numerous cuts and a multitude of bruises. But there was a deep pain in the back of his thigh, tracing fire into his hip. He couldn't see what caused the discomfit, though, not without light. Probing fingers recoiled as pain flared.

A sigh eased from his bloodied lips. 'Where am I?'

There was no reply. Disorientated, he took careful steps forward, sought a path in the darkness that would lead him to the shining blue temple. The pyramid would be his marker. It would call him back to his Deios. In the days since his arrival, he'd come to learn many of the paths surrounding the monstrosity.

Only the path he chose led him further into the dark, twisting and twinning down irregular steps, tall walls blocking his view. The wooden doors he found were either bolted from the inside or led into chambers darker still. In some he could smell the ripeness of decay. In others, only ash and dust.

It took him time, but eventually the realization that he was lost settled on his broad shoulders. Exhaustion was creeping into his blood. The surge he felt when he fought was long gone. And one of his legs was numb, was beginning to stiffen as he tried to walk. He needed to rest. Come daylight, he would find his way.

A heavy thud on a wooden door saw it swing open to reveal a chamber. He couldn't see far inside, but it smelt clean. He entered, his nose sniffing the air for any unusual scent. Satisfied it was empty, he stepped further in, his cleaver still held in a bloody hand. As his eyes adjusted, he noticed the outline of wooden benches spread before him. With a hand poised before him, he moved towards a bench and knelt, resting his considerable bulk with a sigh.

He paused for a moment, closed his eyes. He knew sleep would not be far away.

A voice sounded, faint and soft.

Somehow, he found the energy to open his eyes.

For several heartbeats he held his breath, listening. It came again, a lilting voice, singing, perhaps. He rose carefully from his bench with a grimace, cocked his head to the side. His muscles ached, and his leg was a dead weight, but he pushed their discomfit aside and slowly made his way further into the chamber.

He approached a series of wooden steps, paused to scratch dried blood from a cut on his cheek. He slowed his breathing once more, listened.

There it was. A song. A song like nothing he had ever heard before. As he stood there in silence, he felt his soul soar like it did on the hunt. Felt tears form to slide down his cheeks.

He stumbled up the steps, found a door at the rear of the chamber. He pushed it open, found a small room lit by a single candle. A wooden cot sat in a corner; thick blankets bundled on top. A young creature with golden hair to its shoulders sat opposite, a white garment covering a slender body. Even in the dim light, he could see bright blue eyes peering at him from a pale face.

The small creature continued to sing, its voice soft, focused. He wondered why there was no fear in its eyes. Wondered why its voice didn't falter.

He took one last stride, then bent down with an open hand.

And picked the young creature up by the neck.

CHAPTER THIRTEEN

'Gods above! Is this the best we have?'

Tarsin looked at those standing about the table, his hand - clenched tight - poised above the polished wooden surface. Spread before him were assorted maps of the city.

'I'm afraid it is, sire,' Cale Griffith rumbled from the far end of the table. He stood with Lieutenant Setorious and the newly appointed Captain Devin Kayne, both men having sworn to aid their king in any manner possible. Yet the maps of the city they had found amongst those who survived were of poor quality and dubious detail.

'Unfortunately, gentleman, the maps we have here highlight our predicament,' Tarsin waved a hand over the sheets of parchment. To strategize with insufficient information was causing untold stress. He needed a clearer picture. For six days, now, he'd sought to gather anything and everything regarding the city and her layout. If he was to send his men inside, he would do so with intent. But to be absolutely sure of his positioning, he needed charts that showed more than landmarks and market squares.

The flap of the canvas tent was pushed aside, allowing Tahu and Zai to enter, Lord Beaumont a step behind. The older man had shed a few pounds since the earthquake, having spent more than twenty days in the field.

'Lord Beaumont,' Tarsin offered a curt nod.

'My lord,' he replied with a bow. 'I have news.'

He couldn't tell from his tone whether it was news he wished to hear or not.

Lord Beaumont cleared his throat as he stepped to the table. 'The squad of one hundred men we feared lost . . . have returned.'

'What?' Griffith almost shouted.

'More than seventy men retreated through what remains of Southgate less than an hour earlier. There were casualties, of course, and a handful of injuries, but the majority not only survived but are unharmed.'

'How?' both Kayne and Setorious voiced together.

'It appears they were set upon on the day we extracted Will Tolsten's survivors. The quick-thinking captain ordered a retreat, then moved towards the Southern Docks where they managed to barricade themselves inside the barracks situated there. Apparently, there were provisions and arms in the cellar below, as well as access to the sewers. Not only have they returned, but they have also brought much needed supplies with them.'

'Who is the captain?' Tarsin could hear the relief in his own voice.

'Randal Quinn,' Lord Beaumont appeared as pleased with his news as anyone. 'He'll be present shortly. My sons will bring him in once he and his men add their goods to our supplies.'

'Some pleasant news, at last,' Griffith shared a red-bearded smile.

Tarsin could only hope it was the beginning of something more. Three days earlier he'd sent John Rhys and Lloyd Henrickson south. Two days ago, Jeagar sailed north. Ever since he'd been consumed with doubt concerning his plans. Twice he'd moved soldiers into the city to look for the lost squad, but there had been no sign. And twice he'd moved soldiers through Farmer's Gate in a bid to reclaim some territory. Neither had proven successful. At least not to his expectation. With morale amongst the survivors low and uncertainty fluctuating within the ranks of soldiers, he needed to prove he was not only capable of making decisions, but the decisions he did make were the correct ones. He also needed to garner trust amongst his aides, a fact he was acutely aware of. Since he returned from the world he knew as Aeth, not a single councillor had stepped forward to fulfill their role for their king. He'd sent men looking, but as far as he could tell, they'd all fled south when the earthquake struck. Either that, or they had perished during the destruction.

He knew some would have died, but he harboured doubts they all shared the same fate.

'We'll speak with Captain Quinn when he arrives,' he flicked parchment across the table. 'Kayne,' he continued, 'I take it there has been no word concerning our councillors?'

'No, my lord. I have word regarding several who sailed south from Aspenvale, but not all are accounted for. I do have a lady who would like to speak to you, though. She claims she can fulfill the role admirably. She is waiting outside.'

'Bring her in. I'll see what she has to say.'

The captain left immediately. Tarsin took the moment of silence to gather his thoughts, closed his eyes for a second. He hoped he could find someone who could help manage the burden of leadership. Strategizing he could deal with. And logistics were simply another piece to the ever-expanding puzzle. But attempting to keep his people settled and safe when their city was occupied was proving to be a nightmare. So many had fled east and south, seeking relatives. Others had made for the ports to the south-west, looking to board ships that would take them far from Bastion. And yet the majority remained camped on the outskirts, complaining and fighting, demanding action and food. They were unruly at best, and borderline frenzied when the mood took them. If it weren't for the soldiers interspersing the gathered crowds, he felt the situation could escalate into something regrettable.

The canvas tent bristled as a gust of wind struck its flank. He knew it must be midday outside, yet he hadn't seen the sun since early morning. As soon as he spoke to the lady he vowed to breathe in some fresh air. He was due at Farmer's Gate within the hour in any case.

Kayne returned and ushered in a lady wearing a pleated dress dyed blue. She was tall, almost as tall as he, and fine boned. Her long blonde hair was tied back, a sky-blue ribbon keeping it neat. She looked to be thirty years in age, although it was difficult to tell, for although her skin was fair and line free, there was an air of confidence that suggested she was older.

'Allow me to introduce the Lady Jenna, my lord,' said Kayne as he led her to the table.

'Well met, milady,' Tarsin's eyes caught her own. She was a striking individual, her eyes a softer shade of blue compared to her dress, her hands delicate and her composure refined.

'My lord,' she offered a curtsey. 'I believe you are in need of councillors.'

'I am,' he replied. 'The governing of a displaced population is proving rather difficult, especially considering we've multiple battles to occupy our time with. To be honest, I need help. So, if you have any skills you believe to be useful, please, enlighten us.'

She lowered her gaze to the table, took a breath. When she lifted her face, he could see her strength and composure. 'I can read and write in the kingdom tongue, my lord. I can also do the same for Herkos, the Corphym Isles and Rykedia. I know a smattering of the language they employ in the Southern States, although I fear there are too many dialects for one individual to truly know them all.' She took another breath. 'My numbers I learnt at the University of Sorquos, along with the history of our people and that of the Herkosians. I have also acquired clerical skills concerning ledgers for those in business.'

Tarsin felt his eyebrows rise . . . and noticed every other man in the command tent had done the same.

'Oh,' she continued, 'and I am, I believe, good with people.'

He welcomed the smile, which he felt was the first time in days. 'Commendable,' he offered, 'although I fear there is more to the position than intellectual skills and a pleasant smile. I need someone who can delegate duties as well as gather relevant information. I need someone who can think on their feet.'

'I can do whatever it is you require, my lord.'

'Truly? I must confess, I have no love for councillors. Too many have sought their own agenda in the past, thinking only of themselves. What I seek are men and women who wish to nurture and protect. Trustworthy individuals who can look me in the eye and feel inspired. Not by me, but by what I govern. For it will be their helping hands that pave our way forward. We cannot survive on conquest alone. The taking of Bastion will be a time of Chaos. The rebuilding of Bastion will advocate Order.' He paused, looked to see if any doubt had crept into her eyes. There was none. 'So, I ask you, Jenna, can you see yourself working to usher in Bastion's new dawn?'

'If you accept, my lord, I will see it done. I promise to put Bastion and her people first. This I swear on my grandfather's name.'

'And your grandfather . . . who was he?'

'Lord Fenwick of Avenwood, my lord. We can only assume he died with his king when Highcastle was buried. At least, if he has died, we hope such was his fate. I must confess to feeling a little faint when contemplating the alternative, if you take my meaning.'

An uncomfortable silence permeated the tent. Tarsin shifted his gaze to Griffith across the table. 'I understand, Jenna, and I know such news may be troubling, but I'll not lie to you. I'm afraid your grandfather has passed. I . . . we,' he gestured to Griffith, 'saw him with our own eyes. He lay not far from his king. They lie in the throne room together. I pray they are at peace.'

She took a moment, smoothed her dress with trembling hands. 'It was as we suspected, my mother and I.'

'I am sorry.'

The silence returned, only for the canvas to bustle as another wind gust struck the tent.

'So,' Jenna archer her eyebrows, 'do I meet with your approval?'

Tarsin could think of nothing to deter his thoughts on the matter. She appeared capable. She certainly looked the part. 'You do,' he returned, and once again, every man at table gave their own nod to suggest the right decision had been made.

'Good. When do I start?'

*

The wind continued, unabated, well into the night.

Cale Griffith sat with his feet resting on the polished table he'd been staring at for most of the day. It hadn't changed much, he thought. The useless maps they'd found amongst the populace were still there, bundled atop each other. Tarsin had refused to acknowledge them any further. Instead, he'd discovered a cartographer camped not far from their position outside Farmer's Gate. After a brief discussion, it was agreed a sortie into Bastion was in order, for the man's workshop was within a stone's throw of the exit. Better still, it was said he could provide accurate drawings of the immediate area, at least enough to convince the king they would have all avenues guarded.

Tired eyes looked at his half-eaten bowl of stew that rested precariously next to his booted feet. He'd eaten a mouthful, but the boiled carrots remained stringy, and the spices had been added with a liberal hand. What he wouldn't give right now to sink his teeth into a side of roasted joint, juices running freely over his bearded chin.

'You awake?' the question came from Setorious. He'd pushed his chair back so he could fetch a jug of water.

'Aye, barely,' he replied. It had been a long day, and not one he would remember fondly. The constant talking wore him down. And the planning. He didn't have the head for it. At least not for such a sustained period of time. Tarsin did, though. He could recall the days spent twirling swords and axes with a smile, but when Du Weng Sai ushered his students inside with quill and parchment, his interest waned. Yet Tarsin thrived under Du Weng's tutelage, keen to learn and discover about warfare and all it entailed. If he remembered correctly, it was the puzzles Tarsin enjoyed the most.

He looked up as Setorious passed him a tankard. He took a sip, washed the over-spiced stew from his mouth.

'So, tomorrow it is,' Setorious remained before him. 'Before dawn, yes?'

'Aye,' he could see his lieutenant was tired. Hell, they were all tired. 'First thing. We strike hard, we hold. That's our plan. No need to complicate things.'

'And the king? He has other plans, yes?'

'Always, Setorious. You should know him by now,' he scratched his beard. 'He'll be no different to the Tarsin we saw on the other world. He'll keep to himself when he can. Enlighten us when he sees fit. It's his way.' He raised his hand and tapped a finger to his head. 'Always thinking, he is. Hurts my head just thinking about how much thinking he does.'

'You trust him, though?'

'With my life. Hell, I'd trust him with anyone's life, not just my own. Why, are you having doubts about tomorrow?'

Setorious moved back to his chair and sat. 'Not with the planning, or even with our mission. It's just the scope of what's occurring. I wonder how he can assimilate all the information and then make the right call. It's not just here outside Bastion. It's the plague to the north, the war to the south. It's a nightmare. And at the end of it all, he's playing with our lives.'

'Perhaps you're on to something, but I think you underestimate the man he has become. He is our king, albeit newly crowned, but he has the tenacity and the willpower to be so much more. Few men in his position would openly suggest they need help, but that was exactly what happened today when Lady Jenna Fenwick became a councillor.'

'How does admitting you need help make you great?'

'It shows us he has limits, and he knows what they are. And as soon he knows, he acts, and then his limits are no longer a concern because he has someone else at hand. Thus, his power grows, and so too does his influence.'

'And this is a good thing?'

'Aye, it is. It means he can dedicate more of his time to solving the problems that are profoundly important. Like taking back our city.'

He wasn't sure if Setorious fully grasped all he had said, but the worrying frown he'd been holding onto eased.

'I trust him,' Setorious placed his tankard on the table, then pulled the collar of his jacket close about his neck. Summer was waning, and already the nights were becoming cool. 'Like you said, he's never done us wrong. I just hope he's right about tomorrow. Especially now, with so many demons crowding our city.'

There it was. It took him a moment to realise his lieutenant was frightened of tomorrow's mission. Griffith couldn't blame him; the man had survived when most would have fallen. Still, it came as a shock.

'There is no guarantee we'll see any action, you know,' Griffith did his best to sound nonchalant. 'We could quite possibly reach our target and hold our ground within an hour. Then it's only a matter of solidifying our position and expanding our reach in the days to come. Once our supply lines are secure, we hold. It's as simple as that.'

'And what if it's not that simple? We can't possibly expect our plans to be executed without a hitch. Not all of them.'

'Well, that's where you and I come into the equation. If things do go awry, it will be men like you and I who lead the way. That's what we've trained for. It's what we do best.'

'You certain?'

'Aye, of course I am. Stop troubling yourself.'

'What if we die, Griffith? We've been through so much. Surely it can't have been for nothing?'

'I'd suggest you ease your fears on that count. If it's one thing I do know, it's that we're all going to die eventually. You're like everyone else in that regard. Been dying since the day you were born.'

'Your outlook is . . . unusual.'

'Aye, but it works. Just look at me. No matter what comes hunting down the streets tomorrow, I'll be waiting. And I'm not dying yet.' Griffith smiled, showing his pearly white teeth that were usually hidden behind his red beard. 'Besides, you're of a similar age to Lady Jenna Fenwick, I'd suggest you make a habit of learning a little more about her. Such a good-looking sort.' He shared a wink. 'What do you think?'

'Honestly, sir, I think you're crazy.'

'You know what, Setorious, I believe you may be right.'

*

'There they go.'

Will Tolsten lifted his head, watched as armoured soldiers gripping crossbow and steel passed under Farmer's Gate. He counted quickly, reaching fifty as the last man disappeared into the city.

'They were quiet,' offered Col Farren, sitting on a tree stump.

'They were. It appears those in charge know what they're doing, finally.' He shook his head, amazed the king even decided to act. Seven days it had taken for him to make a significant gesture to those still without a roof over their head. Seven days! And from what he heard, the men entering Bastion were supposed to have left before dawn, not after. Now, the sun was already cresting the foothills to the east. Once again, he felt his better judgement would have provided greater results.

'No one knows what they're doing. Not in these times. Anyone tells you different, they're lying.'

He peered over his left shoulder to see Bardell standing ten feet away. His black hair as wild as the look in his eyes, and he couldn't help but notice the slender fingers twitching near the hilt of his sword.

He guessed early on Bardell had a dislike for their newly crowned king. Well, dislike was putting it lightly. The man practically bled hatred whenever Tarsin Va's name was mentioned. How many times had he heard the story of their capture on the world called Aeth and Tarsin's absentmindedness? Enough, he mused. Enough to know Bardell would stick a dagger in his heart if given half the chance.

'You're up early,' Will gave Bardell another glance then returned his attention to the gate.

'Hoping to see Bastion's finest bleed a little. Nothing could be sweeter this time of morning.'

Will understood the angst, possibly even the hatred, but sometimes the words that came out of Bardell's mouth were beyond him.

Col swivelled on his makeshift seat. 'You'll have a better view at the gate. Won't see nothing this far out.'

'Aye, you're right.' Bardell walked past them both, eyes fixed ahead. Within ten heartbeats he was out of earshot.

'Savage, that one is,' Col spoke softly.

Will offered a nod. 'I know, my friend, but he'll have his uses. For now, amuse him and his foul tongue.'

'It's not his tongue that irks me so, it's his whole disposition. The man is vile. If ever there was a blackheart, he'd be the one.'

'Still, with what he knows, and what he has seen, he has value,' Will returned. 'Best we retrieve what we can before we tire of him.'

'He's dangerous, is all I'm saying,' Col shook his head. 'Tread carefully, Will. He's playing a game just like the rest of us.'

Col's words were as thoughtful as ever. It didn't surprise him, for he'd come to expect nothing less from his second. And he was right, it was a dangerous game they were playing. As far as he could see, their world was in turmoil, their leaders disoriented. Some were even disillusioned. There was no better time to right the wrongs of the past and start anew. This was their moment.

At least so he told himself and those he loved.

Will closed his eyes and pictured Tessa's lovely face. So honest. So caring. And yet within days of being rescued and having promised not to leave her side ever again, he'd left her with the remains of his thieving family so he could set to work on his new plan. The plan he'd harboured for several years whilst doing his rounds with the thieves of Bastion. The plan he never told his father about, for fear of being rebuked by the one man he loved above all others. Derrick Tolsten, former general for Arkos Vantos, hero of the kingdom, some would say her saviour.

'Shall we do the rounds?' Col stood and stretched, savouring the sun's warmth on his aching bones.

'Aye,' Will looked to the mass of people to the east, rising as the sun shone down on pitched tents, tarpaulins stretched between posts and blankets held upright by wooden sticks. A literal sea of people without a home, floundering in the fields whilst the king and his aides dithered in comfort. 'How many have joined the Knights of Salvation so far?' he asked.

'Close to a thousand,' Col flexed his shoulders. 'But it will be more when all is said and done. The people want their homes back. And their businesses. Most share a desire to be working their trades . . . whatever they are.'

'And they're hungry,' Will added. 'Few have eaten a proper meal since the upheaval.'

Col patted his stomach, although Will knew neither of them had eaten anything better. Their fate was sealed with those of the people. Even if he wished to return to his family's estate, it was located to the north. The plague in Benwith was close enough to be a deterrent.

'Let's make a move, then,' he gave Col a clap on the shoulder. 'The sooner we can organise our knights into something of a force, the better. The gods alone know how hard a task that will be.'

He heard the short bark of a laugh issue from Col. Both had been surprised by the number of men and women interested in joining their cause, but there were some who lacked the right kind of conditioning, and many who couldn't understand even the simplest of orders. It certainly wasn't going to be a matter of passing a blade and a steel cap to those with an outstretched hand. The process would take, like everything else, considerable time.

And time was the one thing they couldn't afford to waste.

Not now, nor any point in the future.

For Will Tolsten, Lord of Deepwell, Underlord of the Nocturnals, was fast losing his patience with those in command.

And he had a plan.

CHAPTER FOURTEEN

'Isabelle! Oh, Isabelle! My beautiful daughter, do you know what a gift your voice is? Honestly, my dear, you have the voice of an angel.'

Isabelle opened her eyes. She was in her room at the rear of the chapel, bundled with her blankets in the corner of her bed. For a moment she hoped to see her mother standing over her, telling her how wonderful she was, how beautiful. Only she wasn't anywhere to be seen. Even her voice was beginning to fade. And yet she could hear something close by.

Isabelle turned her head to the right.

There he was, the demon from the night before, curled on the floor with his brightly coloured scales, ivory teeth and clawed hands and feet. The demon who grabbed her by the throat.

She shuddered, lifted a small, petite hand to touch her neck. She remembered hearing the door to the chapel open as someone entered. At first, she kept silent, hoping whoever strode within would soon walk away. But they didn't leave. Summoning her courage, she'd crept to the door and peered through the keyhole. Light was dim, for night had fallen, but a sliver of starlight swept through the red-stained windows. It took her a moment, but she eventually saw the frightful creature slumped before a pew.

She remained frozen for some time, too afraid to even take a breath. When she finally gasped, she dived back to her bed, intent on hiding beneath. Only the words of her mother rang clear in her mind as she struggled with her blanket. The same words she heard this morning as she drifted in between sleep and wakefulness.

'You have the voice of an angel.'

How many times had her mother said those very words? Hundreds, she guessed. Every time she sang a song or a lullaby. Maybe thousands of times. The voice of an angel.

And outside her door, right now, sat a demon from the night.

Isabelle was beyond scared. For more days than she cared to remember, she'd been hiding at the chapel, hoping - praying - her mother and father would come back for her. 'Here, my beautiful daughter, stay here, at the Chapel to Eos. She will protect you while we find a way clear. Trust us, lovely daughter.' Her mother had cried as she said the words. So had her father. There were terrible noises in the street. So much shouting and screaming. Yet it was different to the screams she heard when the ground shook. This was strange. It frightened her parents to tears.

'Stay hidden in the rooms to the rear,' her father planted a kiss on her forehead. 'And don't open the door onto the street for anyone. Do you understand, Isabelle?'

She nodded, for she knew that was what her father expected.

'We'll come back for you soon, dearest daughter,' her mother blew a kiss as father dragged her outside.

Then they were gone.

And they hadn't come back for her.

Instead, a demon had entered the chapel. She saw it with her own eyes. Yet she was a six-year-old girl. How could she avoid something so large and powerful? How could she survive an encounter with such a beast?

She heard stories from her father when he performed. He could sing when the mood took him. Not quite like her mother, who often accompanied his playing of the harp, but he sang with a certain purpose when the need arose. There was power in his vocals. And the songs he sang were of heroes and knights fighting demons in the night. And of angels.

She had the voice of an angel. Perhaps if she sang, she thought, the demon would recoil back into the night. Perhaps it would flee from her dulcet tones.

So she sang, softly, as she sat in her bed with her blankets held against her chest. Only the beast didn't flee. It came for her, all scales and teeth, one massive, clawed hand reaching for her throat. She choked as it picked her up, hand squeezing, her voice catching. She looked into yellow eyes, saw only blood and death. Her voice could not sway the demon.

But it placed her down a second later. Sat her on the end of her bed. Then it bent close, sniffed with flared nostrils, licked its lips. A single, clawed finger poked her shoulder.

A tremble raced down her spine. What did it want?

She opened her mouth and began to sing once more, more on instinct, perhaps, or maybe out of fear. She had nothing else to offer. It was her only defence. The voice of an angel to deter the beast.

It sank back on its haunches as she continued her song; watched her with reflecting eyes now content. There was no lust in them, no hunger. Its head tilted to the side and its breathing became calm. She sang some more.

An hour must have passed before she finally had the nerve to stop. The demon beast was asleep on the floor. It didn't wake as she pulled her blanket up to her chin. She rolled to her side, saw her candle flickering as the last of the wax melted away. She closed her eyes; knew she couldn't risk sneaking past. Hopefully, she'd fall asleep before the light was extinguished. Hopefully, when she woke, the beast would be gone.

But he hadn't left. He still lay on the floor, his scaled body rising with each breath. Light shone from a rear window, bathing him in golden sunshine. Only she could see his scales were smeared with blood and feathers, cuts and bruises. A black pool stained the floor beneath his legs. If it wasn't for the gentle rise of his chest as he breathed, she'd have thought him dead.

Only her luck wasn't with her. And she feared to sneak past. How could she? The demon was enormous. Even now, lying on the wooden floorboards, he cramped her room. Even if she stepped with nimble feet and tiptoed past his outstretched arm, she doubted she could do so without touching him. But neither could she sit and wait. He would wake soon enough, and possibly think her no more than a morning feed to greet the day.

She would only be a small meal, being so young, but a meal, nonetheless.

Panic began to settle on her tiny shoulders. She brushed back her blonde hair, tried to smile at the sunlight streaming through the window. It was a good thing to smile at the sun. Her father explained we had much to be thankful for from its warmth and light. It kept the darkness at bay. It made the gardens grow. It melted the snow in winter so the roof wouldn't cave in. It made people smile, so we should always smile back when the opportunity arose. So her father told her.

Would it keep the demon away? Would it frighten it back to wherever it came from? Would the sun protect her, or would she need to sing like an angel to protect herself?

She couldn't know for sure. And she was tired of asking herself so many questions. Perhaps, she thought, as she shifted her blanket towards her ankles, the king himself will come for her. She knew him, had sat at his table one night when father played his harp and mother sang. He was a wonderful old man, with his grey beard and broad shoulders and a golden crown. So wonderful. He'd even told her a rhyme to pass the time.

Only how would he find her? She knew she was at the Chapel to Eos, a sanctuary for the devout, although she had no idea why there was no-one else about. Usually there were half-a-dozen men and women tending the gardens and chickens out back, and always a priestess to talk and offer advice to those seeking answers. But she was the only one here, she knew, because she checked. Every room, every cupboard. Even the chicken coop that ran alongside the brick wall at the rear of the garden. No-one. Not a single person to offer her a hand or a shoulder to lean on. No-one to hold her close when night fell. No-one to comfort her when she felt so terribly alone. No-one to wipe away her tears.

How would the king find her in a city without any people? How would he know where to look if she didn't call his name?

She might only be six years old, but she was clever. She would find a way. She would find a way to sneak past the enormous demon with his blood on the floor. She would find a way to call the king.

'I will call the king,' she whispered the words, convincing herself they were real. 'I will call the king, and he will rescue me. I will call the king and be saved.'

She heard movement, cringed as claws screeched across floorboards. She looked down, wished she hadn't. The demon roused from its slumber. Its yellow eyes looked about the room. She stifled a scream. It was even more terrifying in the daylight. Dried blood blistered its lips, saliva glistened on large teeth. It winced as it moved its leg. She watched it try to rise, then slump back onto the floor. It looked over its shoulder. She saw a clawed hand reach its kilt of leather and pull it back. A knife sat there, imbedded in its leg. He pulled it out.

The scream sounded from her own mouth; she couldn't halt it. Blood gushed from the wound, oozing onto the floor. Thick and red as molten lava, dripping as it slid between the demon's clawed hands. He tried to stop the flow, but his positioning was wrong, his size cumbersome. A snarl issued from its mouth.

She leapt off the bed and knelt beside him, her blanket scrunched in her hands. She offered it but realised he couldn't possibly hold it to his wound for long. So she did it for him, pushed her small hands against his scaled flesh, blanket between them. She did it, and she held, held it there until the bleeding stopped. Held it there until her arms almost dropped to the floor from exhaustion.

And then she knew. She knew where the bandages and cloths for the wounded were kept, had seen them when she searched the cupboards. Hurriedly, she gathered an arm full of bandages and a bowl of water from the well out back. Then she cleaned the wound, and then his arms and legs, for he was bloody all over. Finally, she wrapped a white cloth about his thigh and tied a knot to keep it from sliding.

She sat back and peered out the window. It was after midday.

'Ra'tor,' came a growl from the demon.

She looked him in the eye. Surely he wasn't going to eat her. Not after all she had done.

'Ra'tor,' he repeated, only this time he clapped a hand to his chest.

'Oh,' she replied, understanding. 'Isabelle,' she also held a hand to her chest.

'Isss-a-bell,' he hissed the word, but it sounded almost right. She smiled and gave a nod of approval.

'My name is Isabelle, and I am six years old. And the king will soon come for me. Because I know him, and he knows me. If you wait here, you will see him. Although I'm not sure what he will think of you.'

She saw his eyes narrow, a look of confusion sweeping over his face. She doubted he understood her words, but it didn't matter. The king would come for her, she just knew it. Until he did, she would care for the demon. Because that's what angels did. They cared. And they sang.

A song eased past her lips, a gentle song to ease one's fears.

And the demon closed its eyes and rested.

*

It was a fine day, and for the time being, an uneventful one.

Tarsin cast his gaze over the city, looked to the distant buildings. He was standing atop the flat roof of an abandoned merchant's apartment, four levels from the street below. Here, close to Farmer's Gate, the land was raised and the view unimpeded. For the last hour he'd been marking certain landmarks with the Map Maker, Casian, who sat at a wooden desk behind him with parchment and quill pen. He could see Irongate, raised above its surrounds as it too offered a view of the city, no more than a mile to the west. Beyond its grey walls he could see the cathedrals circling Aston's Tear, torn asunder by the quake, yet stubbornly reaching for the sky still. And the pyramid, so distant, yet so close, a shining beacon for all to see.

His destination, the one place he desired to be.

Thoughts of Kayla still swirled inside his mind. Black-haired, beautiful, a smile highlighting emerald eyes to melt your heart. He thought of her often yet kept such thoughts to himself. As king of Dervae, his role was beyond individual desire. Yet he couldn't shake the regret of not being able to rescue her, of not being able to find her. If he had his own way, he'd lead a charge towards Aston's Tear and fight his way inside today.

Such thoughts gave him a sense of purpose. Despite being hampered by duty; his heart was already set on reclaiming the pyramid. It would take time, he knew, for he needed to be sure of his actions before committing his men, but it would be at the forefront of all his planning. If they held the pyramid, they would control the city. It was that simple, and yet at the same time, so very, very difficult.

'Here, my lord,' Casian had left his stool and now stood by his side. In his outstretched hand was a newly drawn map of their immediate area. 'I have marked every building between the gate and our current position.'

Tarsin gave a solitary nod. The work was clean and concise, the scale appropriate. It also marked every building currently under his control, an area incorporating an entire block. There had been only a single skirmish as his men marched into the city during the morning. Thankfully, it was a brief engagement, almost over before it began. Half-a-dozen Deios were roused from an abandoned bakery. They were set upon with vigour and left to bleed on the street. 'Thank you, Casian. Our next task will be to liberate the establishments behind those across the street. By day's end, we should have full control of both blocks to either side of Farmer's Gate.'

Casian bowed, then moved back to his desk where he unrolled another piece of parchment. He would be busy in the coming days. As busy as he'd ever been.

The clap of steel hitting the floor sounded behind him. Both he and Casian looked to see the two soldiers standing guard at the staircase salute as Cale Griffith and his man Setorious passed. Griffith held his red-tinged warhammer in one hand, Setorious held his steel shod staff.

'My lord,' both men stopped and bowed, although Griffith did so with a smile splitting his crimson beard.

'You have information?' Tarsin asked.

'Aye,' Griffith let his warhammer slide through his fingers to rest with a thud on the rooftop. 'Lord Beaumont and Devin Kayne have secured the Southern Barracks, as you ordered. Like us, they dealt with small resistance. As we speak, Captain Randal Quinn and his men move further still, seeking to claim an area of warehouses bordering the Southern Docks.'

'Good. Any casualties?'

'Four dead, from the latest report,' Griffith spat to the side, 'but they killed three eagle-looking beasts.'

'Eagle-men?'

'Aye, and they've kept the corpses. One of Lord Beaumont's aides is a physician. He's already cutting them open to see what's inside.'

Tarsin shook his head, wondered what they would find. A voice inside his head suggested their insides would mimic their own.

'Send word to the soldiers stationed outside Southgate. Tell them to be vigilant.'

'Consider it done,' Griffith's eyes flared with approval.

'And tell Lord Beaumont's physician to see me as soon as he's finished with the corpses. I'll need to know everything there is to know about such beasts.'

Griffith peered over at Casian as he continued drawing. 'What about our positioning? Are we to advance north-side today?'

'We will. We need to be decisive. Besides, if we take north-side today, we could potentially have Baker's Lane and the Farmer's Market Square under our control. There are food stores at both locations. It will ease the pressure on supplies coming from Aspenvale and abroad.'

'Put a smile on faces, perhaps,' offered Setorious.

'Perhaps,' Tarsin's tone suggested he wasn't so sure. It would take more than a loaf of bread to dim the pain of being homeless. But it was a start, at least. A start to taking back what was rightfully theirs. He shared a look with Griffith. 'We need to be another block further in within days. We need to have men secure the portal leading to Aeth.'

'We'll see it done,' Griffith's hunger mirrored his own. They both knew if they were to succeed in the coming days, they'd need allies. Both knew Inesco promised aid.

'We'll claim north-side first, though,' Tarsin said, confidant their plan of attack, although cautious, was proving to be a wise decision. 'I've shown Casian the location of the portal, and he is currently working on the location of the others. Once we have their whereabouts confirmed, we can act with greater precision.'

'It will be dangerous once underground,' Griffith suggested. 'Especially once we attempt to hold each portal. We've no idea what may walk through.'

'No, we don't. But until we have dominion over Aston's Tear, I'd rather know what to expect from those other worlds. Besides, I'll not move further into Bastion with unclaimed portals lying behind us. The potential for chaos in our ranks will be too high.'

'Agreed. I'll see to the men, then. The quicker we take north-side, the better.'

Tarsin stepped close and placed a hand on Griffith's shoulder. 'Be careful, my friend. I need you more than you know.'

The big man flashed a smile in return, then hefted his warhammer and swung it over his shoulder. Bloodstain, he'd called it. So aptly named. A weapon for the times.

Tarsin watched him turnabout and head for the stairs, Setorious beside him.

For a brief moment, he wished to follow.

*

Night fell quickly due to a vast-reaching cloud bank sweeping in from the west.

Tarsin cursed under his breath as he watched the last vestiges of daylight twinkle out of sight. The clouds seethed and twirled and bubbled in the darkening sky, possibly the last of the summer storms. Perhaps the most violent. It was no mistake

192

their first night inside the walls of Bastion would be memorable.

And here he was, back on the rooftop of some merchant's house.

It was the serenity he craved, the peacefulness of a silent city. Here, alone, he could gaze over Bastion and admire the view. It was all his. All his to govern.

At least it should be.

He noticed Casian's desk and stool had been removed from the rooftop ledge. It was just as well. The storm, when it arrived, would strike with fury. Knowing he could not halt the tempest to come, Tarsin made for the stairwell and descended to the ground floor. A spacious sitting room lay before him, its excessive furniture removed except for the mahogany table and several high-backed chairs. Planks of timber were nailed across the two windows, both inside and out, and a heavier piece now crossed the only door onto the street. Confined within, twenty men and a lady studied charts and maps spread across the polished table by candlelight, most dressed for combat should the need arise. In fact, it was only Casian and Jenna Fenwick who represented the citizens of Bastion.

'My lord,' several voices sounded as one as he stepped into the room.

He gave a curt nod and moved towards Jenna. 'You shouldn't be here,' he began, looking into her blue eyes. 'I thought I told you to return to camp.'

'No, sire, you *asked* if I could return to camp. I decided I could be of better use here.'

'Doing what?'

'Helping with logistics. Offering words of wisdom. You soldiers are a suspicious breed. Someone needs to be a soothing voice in such troubled times.'

He could feel the smiles on the men as they listened to her words. She had fire in the belly, this one. Showed no fear. Tarsin briefly wondered how resourceful and confidant she'd be in the morning. Especially if the Deios decided to attack. Could she honestly say she was needed here when the beasts screamed for blood? He doubted it. Instinctively knew most of the men in the room would be just as frightened.

'I'm here to help in any way I can, your highness. Even if it means keeping an eye on you.' She gave a wink, then moved to the table where a half-eaten wheel of cheese and a loaf of black bread rested. 'Have you eaten anything today, my lord?'

'I . . . no, not really,' he replied, 'I don't think I've had more than an apple, and that at first light.'

'Then here, eat up,' she piled cheese and bread onto a wooden platter and handed it to him.

He took a knife and cut a slice of cheese, placed it in his mouth. It was good, sharp of flavour. Salted herring would have accompanied it well. And the apple. He wished he had another. 'So,' he took another bite of cheese, finished it quickly, 'what information do you have regarding our forces south of the city?'

'All is well for the moment,' she answered without hesitation, before reaching for a slip of parchment. 'Lord Beaumont and his sons hold the Southern Barracks. Captain Randal Quinn holds the Docks. Last we heard; they were setting in for the night.'

'How many men?'

She peered at the flowing script on her parchment. 'Three hundred soldiers at each location, my lord. Do you think they'll be enough?'

He hoped they would be. Heaven knew he had no more to spare. At least not yet. From what was reported to him, three ships had finally docked in Aspenvale from Highport. Each harboured men and supplies, foreseen by his father before the calamity even occurred if what Lloyd Henrickson and John Rhys said was true. Their numbers would help, but they weren't here yet. For tonight, they'd have to hold on their own, same as his force in the north. Hold for one night, then assess in the morning. If they were still alive.

If the storm brewing off the coast arrived soon, he felt they'd have a greater chance. From what he saw on the rooftop, tonight wouldn't be a time for hunting.

He returned his attention to Jenna, tore off a piece of bread. 'They'll be enough for tonight,' he said. 'Cale Griffith will also hold.'

Jenna returned a nod, acknowledging his claim. Cale Griffith had marched north-side after midday with a force of two hundred men, eager to search the buildings on the opposite side of Queens Way. They'd met no resistance as they swept away from the main thoroughfare, although a dozen children and three women were found hiding in a cellar. They were malnourished and dehydrated, but they were alive. For some time after their rescue, he wondered how many others hid in fear beneath the city.

With his bread finished, Tarsin placed the platter on the table and walked to the rear of the room, nodding to those who asked after his health, smiling to those who looked troubled. On the wall was a painting: a landscape of Bastion from her early days. The outer wall was yet to be built, and Irongate soared above a collection of smaller abodes. But in the background the colossal pyramid sat in dominant style. It dwarfed everything around it, exuded god-like qualities. The blue capstone radiated power.

It was a beautiful painting. Timeless in its simplicity.

A roar of aggression sounded on the street, not far from the merchant's house. It was followed a moment later by a long, drawn-out howl. The soldiers stopped what they were doing.

'It's begun, hasn't it?' he heard Jenna speak their thoughts.

Tarsin tore his gaze from the painting as an image of Kayla flashed into his mind. He prayed she was safe. Prayed she wasn't fleeing from beasts hunting in the night.

'It's begun,' Tarsin's voice was low, controlled. He drew his broadsword. 'Those who can, arm yourself. This may be the longest night of your life.'

The men did as he asked. The sound of steel left a ring in his ears.

Then came the screams.

CHAPTER FIFTEEN

He sat there, a naked boy with chubby arms and legs, black-haired and beautiful.

Kayla's eyes saw him but drifted, looked to the plain of grass beyond her son. A flash of lightning caught her attention, sparks of blue light and the roar of thunder. She could hear the wind screeching, smelt the stench of burnt flesh. She sensed others were near, powerful beings wielding God-like abilities. She felt small and insignificant. She felt alone.

'Kayla,' the voice sounded from behind. 'Kayla, are you well?'

She blinked, let her eyes focus on her surroundings, not her imaginings. Baby Rastan still sat in the garden ten feet away. He was happy, his hands pulling slivers of grass from the earth. The smile of discovery shone from his face.

'I am well,' she replied, as Neema moved to sit on the ground beside her. There was a nimbleness to the matron she'd not noticed before. Then again, there was much she did not know concerning the lady. They all knew she was wise. But the power she fashioned that day on the green field still frightened her. The wind, the lightening. The death of men with a snap of her fingers.

'Rastan looks to be the healthy babe we knew he would be,' Neema smiled.

'He is,' she returned the smile. She didn't know what else to say. Neema had been absent for weeks since they arrived at the Palace of the Five Kings. In that time, a sense of abandonment had settled on Kayla's shoulders. And she wasn't alone. Ruvin, Reefe and Donal all felt the same. It was only Jarred who seemed to have moved on with his life, although he appeared stressed at times. And frustrated.

'He is almost six months old,' Neema continued the conversation. 'I can't believe we have been here so long already.'

'When can we leave?' Kayla placed a hand on Neema's arm. 'I do not wish to be here, Neema. None of us do. We don't belong, and I don't feel safe. The kings are not what I expected.'

The smile on Neema's face vanished like early autumn snowfall. It melted away to be replaced by a frown, thought-provoking, if Kayla were to judge.

'I understand, my dear. I see the frustration in your expressions. Confinement, albeit in a palace, is still confinement.'

'It is,' Kayla waved a hand before her. 'The rooms are incredible, and I am grateful for the shelter and food. But the garden is only so big, and I feel the walls creeping closer every day. I need to run. I need to feel the wind through my hair. I need to be able to leave my room when I choose, not at the behest of another.

'I need to be free, Neema. Right now, I am nothing more than an oddity to the Five Kings. Thankfully, I am of little interest, only that may change. And if it does, there will be nothing I can do about it.' She lowered her gaze to the ground, spoke quietly with a hushed voice. 'Unless there is something you can do, Neema? Something to allow us the opportunity to escape and return home? You have power. More than I expected any individual to wield.'

A small laugh escaped the old lady's lips. 'I have power, lovely child,' her eyes flared with mirth, 'yet the power I can summon is nothing when compared to that of the Five Kings. Like you, I feel most insignificant when in their presence. If you wish to return to Bastion, it will not be through force of will. Nor will it be through force of arms.'

'Then how are we to return?'

'That, I do not know. What I do know, my dear, is that our return is out of our control. Kian speaks on our behalf, constantly. Yet the Five Kings feel no desire to act decisively. They listen to his words, but from what Kian has relayed to me, they are angry.'

'Angry?'

'Yes, Kayla. They are angry because Kian has left his post. He was, or is, a Guardian of the Portal. It was his duty to protect and monitor its operation. The fact Ahriman and his witch have passed through has caused angst amongst the kings. Debate still rages concerning their help. Not all the kings agree the problem is worthy of their commitment.'

Kayla could understand their hesitation. The portal was so far away. It had taken them ten months to reach the city called Ayoshos on foot. Kian had stressed a return journey would not take as long, for her pregnancy delayed them considerably, and his path away from the portal was, at first, convoluted to discourage anyone following their tracks. Still, out of sight, out of mind. The kings obviously had better things to occupy their time.

'Do they fear the Dark Lord and his witch?'

Neema shook her head. 'No, they believe he is beneath them, a tyrant, perhaps, but certainly not a physical threat. Kian suggests otherwise, but they refuse to believe there is another being more powerful. The kings have ruled for thousands of years. They imagine they will continue to do so.'

'And what if you and Kian, along with the Five Kings, confront the Dark Lord? Do you believe you can defeat him?'

'I do not know, Kayla, nor, do I suspect, will I be consulted regarding the matter. If the Five Kings decide to pay Ahriman a visit, I doubt I'll be by their side.'

'But Kian will be. He is strong. He said the Five Kings are his brothers. That will make six of them. Six Nepharii against a Dark Lord and his witch.'

'It may be so. I pray it is so. Like you, Kayla, I also wish to return to Bastion. Only sometimes what we wish for and what lands in our laps is quite the opposite.'

Kayla gave a nod in confirmation. If she knew anything about Neema, the old lady spoke the truth. And yet, she needed more than the truth from the matron. She needed comfort. She needed companionship. Baby Rastan, her beautiful boy, kept her busy. He fed well, he appeared content for a six-month-old boy. He certainly slept well. But he didn't cry like she thought

198

he would. Neema said he was fine when she examined him, yet the fear remained. What if her baby - her beautiful boy – had difficulties with his voice? And what about his future? What if he couldn't talk?

Being alone, in a palace on another world, was sapping her of hope. Fears and regrets were clamouring for purchase in her fragile mind. As wild thoughts of never seeing Bastion again whirled within, tears began to flow.

'Here, here,' Neema slid close and wrapped her in her arms. 'My poor girl, you've endured so much, and stoically, it must be said.'

'I've had enough,' Kayla sobbed, moisture on her lips.

'I know, my dear. The others share your concerns and fears. You are not alone. Perhaps, like them, you need to exercise your mind and body more. The boys have been learning swordsmanship with Ruvin and Reefe. And Kian has taught them all the subtleties of Ven language. Jarred and Donal, in particular, can now speak fluently. There is much to learn, many questions that can be answered. You need only ask, Kayla. We may be confined to our rooms, but if we seek permission, we are free to visit one another.'

She wiped a hand across her cheek. Again, Neema spoke the truth. She saw Rastan, now rolling on the ground, chubby hands clenched full of dirt. She could see he was happy. It would be nice to hear that he was happy. Just a single sound, a gurgle, even.

'You are right, as always, Neema. I'll ask permission and seek out the boys. Jarred and Donal will appreciate holding Rastan. It will do us all good.'

'It will. And even Ruvin and Reefe will be glad, my dear. We are all in need of support. Let us help each other until a way forward is found. Let us all share a smile.'

Kayla lifted her chin, reached out and hugged Neema. There was a time when the old lady was a mound of flesh. Now she was toned and strong, she could feel the muscles beneath her skin. So much had changed during their flight from the portal, but Neema had changed the most. One day, she thought, I'll ask about her transformation.

But not today. Today she'd welcome the comfort of arms around her shoulders. Today she'd be grateful for all she had.

Including her silent son. For he was special.

She could tell.

*

A final clap of wooden blades left a ringing in his ears.

Ruvin whistled, signalling the tutorial over. Both Jarred and Donal stepped back from each other, sweat glistening over their bare torsos. They took a moment to catch their breath, chests heaving. For an hour they'd been swinging wooden swords in practised arcs, back and forth as they honed skills and endurance. It passed the time, kept them hungry for knowledge. It also kept their minds focused. Ruvin knew what was at stake here more than any other. He'd been sailing ships for decades, had experienced the loneliness of confinement. So, like the doting father-figure he'd become, he'd organised a schedule for the boys to keep them occupied.

'That will be all for this morning,' he chuckled as he made his way to where the boys stood. He held out his hands, accepted the wooden blades in return. The boys trained using carved branches to represent long swords. The twin blades entrusted to him by Tarsin were hidden for the time being and never talked about, a secret shared with Neema and Kian. Besides, the boys were too raw to be using real steel, and the thought of having their possessions stolen by the Five Kings was not one he cared for. He shook his head as he gathered the wooden blades, placed them in a wooden box. Then he looked to the sky, felt the sun's warmth. Kian had mentioned the hotter, summer months, had now arrived.

'How are we progressing?' Jarred asked with a smile.

'Well, young man,' Ruvin peered into his eyes. Jarred had grown in the last few months, shooting up to be as tall as Reefe and just as broad. He hadn't grown into his frame yet, but that would come. He was already strong and flexible, his coordination not far behind. If he continued his training, and there was no reason to believe he wouldn't, then he would become a fine swordsman. 'You need to remember your feet, though, Jarred. Move them, be nimble. You should be on your toes, like a wildcat ready to pounce. Standing on your heels gives you no leverage. It may work against a smaller, less skilled opponent, but someone like Reefe will make short work of you.'

The smile faded to be replaced by thoughtful contemplation. It was a trait Ruvin was proud of. No matter the instructions, Jarred always looked within to right any faults. He never argued the point, never felt slighted.

'How did I fare, Ruvin?' asked Donal, his breathing settled.

'Your feet are quick, lad, but you need strength in your wrists,' he patted him on the back. 'But that will come. You haven't reached your full growth, unlike Jarred. When you do, you will find the exercises easier.'

Donal shared a smile, then walked towards a golden bench seat where a white towel was passed to him by a Ven servant. He heard him say thank you in the Ven tongue before he began to wipe himself down.

He was a good lad, Donal, although he was small in height. There was only two years between he and Jarred, but the difference between them appeared considerably more. Jarred now stood head and shoulders above his friend, looked to be ten years his senior. Donal was plucky and incredibly bright, but he would never be a swordsman. There was simply too much fear in his eyes.

'Have you exhausted them yet?' the question came from Neema as she walked to his side.

Ruvin turned to greet the matron, his heart skipping a beat. She moved softly when she chose. He was about to reply when he saw Kayla following behind her, baby Rastan in her arms.

'I have,' he said, but he was already moving towards Kayla, arms outstretched. He hugged her, planted a kiss on her forehead. Like everyone else, he'd been concerned for her welfare. For weeks she refused to see anyone, kept herself locked away in her room. 'May I?' he asked, looking to Rastan.

'You may,' her voice was soft, timid, even. She placed Rastan into his arms.

'Hello, little one,' he waved a finger before Rastan's eyes. They were lightning blue in colour, vibrant. So like the eyes of his father.

'Come,' Ruvin said to the ladies, motioning them towards the golden bench with a nod. 'Take a seat. Jarred and Donal have completed their training for this morning, I'm certain they'll be glad to regale you with idle chatter.' He could see the light in their eyes as he mentioned their names. It was good to see them all together again. It had been too long, by his reckoning.

'Where is Reefe?' Kayla looked out into the garden.

Ruvin's gaze followed her own. Like Kayla's quarters, this room on the east flank of the palace opened onto a lush garden of manicured grass, rock pools, shrubs and exotic trees. It provided them all with the opportunity to escape the confines of their rooms and to feel the sun on their skin. The accommodation was remarkable, except for the fifteen feet walls surrounding the garden that hemmed them in.

'He is out there somewhere,' Ruvin waved his hand. 'Probably asleep under a tree if I know Reefe.'

He noticed Kayla spoke no further on his whereabouts. In fact, the light in her eyes brightened, if anything.

'And you, Ruvin,' Kayla asked, placing a hand on his shoulder. 'How are you?'

'I am well, Kayla. I have the boys with me, and I train them constantly.'

'In swordsmanship?'

'In many things, actually,' he replied. 'Both can speak fluent Ven, although I take no credit for such a skill. Kian has provided lessons in that regard. But I train them in the sword, teach them letters and numbers, discuss anything and everything from my own experience. It was only yesterday the boys learnt how a trade ship operates.'

'And what of the Five Kings, Ruvin, have you spoken to them?'

'Alas, no. They appear to have no time for any of us. Kian says they are preoccupied with a great many things, at the forefront of their thoughts and worries are the survivors of Bastion. They are not pleased with our arrival. Less so with the Dark Lord and his witch. Discussion between Kian and his brothers is protracted. And Kian is equally unhappy.'

'And all the while we are confined to our quarters.'

'Aye, we are. There is nothing we can do about the situation. Ven guards patrol the corridors and are stationed outside our rooms. The walls beyond the garden are too tall to scale. And even if we did manage to crest the walls, the creatures lurking in the palace grounds will see us done for.'

He could see the light fading from her eyes, as he feared it would. There was little he could say to lift her mood. Imprisonment had that effect on people. Despite her venture to their quarters, nothing was going to change. All he could offer was his company and that of the boys. Yet no matter their topic of discussion, he knew they would always return to their present predicament.

Ruvin looked down to see baby Rastan close his eyes, the fingers of one hand curled about his thumb. So peaceful and content. So innocent. He wondered if the baby, when it grew to be a man, would ever remember his time here in the palace of the Five Kings.

He was still looking down at Rastan, admiring the full cheeks and long eyelashes, the pouting lips tinged red, when Jarred and Donal reached for Kayla to wrap her in their arms. They had towelled themselves dry and put shirts of linen on. She almost cried, he could see tears well, but she held onto them and hugged them back.

'You both need to cut your hair,' Kayla frowned as she peered at unruly tangles.

They laughed, and he felt the tension and disappointment of the situation leech away for a moment.

But the levity didn't remain. The door to their quarters opened a second later. Kian strode in, half-a-dozen Ven guards behind him. They were dressed in leather and steel, slender blades belted at their hip. With their conical helmets, they were almost as tall as Kian.

The Nepharii's face was carved from stone, his eyes alight with fury.

He stopped five feet from their gathering.

'What is it?' the question was out before Ruvin could stall his curiosity, his eyes taking in the Ven guards who fanned out behind Kian.

'It is the Five Kings, my friend,' Kian shook his head. 'I know you are anxious to return to Bastion, all of you are. But I'm afraid you'll have to wait a little longer.'

'How long?'

Kian lifted a hand to scratch an ear. He took a moment to gather his thoughts, then opened his almond-shaped eyes. 'For the time being, indefinitely,' he put his hand palm out to stall their outcry. 'They have agreed to travel to the portal, though, to speak with Ahriman. I will travel with them, and they have consented to allow another.'

'Another?' Ruvin asked the question on all their tongues.

'Aye, one other can accompany me to the portal.'

'And who will that be?' Kayla's voice almost cracked.

'I'll take Jarred,' Kian said, looking to the boy who was becoming a man. 'He is young and agile enough to travel with us and not be a hindrance. He is strong and capable. And if he is willing, I'll see him through the portal and into Bastion.'

Ruvin expected shouts of defiance and disbelief, but instead only silence reigned.

Then Jarred spoke. 'When do we leave?'

'You have three days to prepare, Jarred. I'll see you then.'

*

Jarred watched with mouth agape as Kian left their quarters.

Like everyone else in the garden, he was stunned. The prospect of travel, the allure of returning to Bastion, there was a great deal to think about. But above it all hung the reality of leaving his friends behind. Friends who had become family. Friends he would die for if the need arose.

Neema patted his shoulder. 'Are you alright, Jarred?'

He nodded, although his thoughts were scattered. What would he take on such a journey? How much was he expected to carry? Who, besides the Five Kings and Kian, would accompany them? So many questions tumbled inside his head, and a single glance at Kayla saw his heart falter. More than anyone else, she wished to return to their city. Deep down, he knew she still believed Tarsin Va was alive. He was their king. And without him knowing, he now had an heir.

'It's alright . . . Jarred,' Kayla's words were said between sobs. 'With Rastan to care for, I could not make the journey at the pace I expect you to travel.'

Jarred took a step towards her and gave her a hug. Before he knew it, Donal and Neema were patting him on the back, then crowding in to share the embrace. Ruvin, who still held Rastan in his arms, caught his eye as he, too, sidled close. 'There will be certain items for you to take on your journey, Jarred,' Ruvin said. 'Neema and I have spoken with Kian on several occasions about what might occur if we returned to the portal. If you are step back into Bastion, you need to realise how dangerous it may be. Things will have greatly changed, and the men in charge may not be familiar to you at all. You will need documents penned by Neema and I to validate your claims.'

'Will there be anything else?'

'Aye, a great deal, lad. You'll need a weapon, so I guess you'll take my sword with you.'

'And I have maps,' piped Donal, 'that I took from the king's study beneath Highcastle. They show certain structures. I'm certain they are portals surrounding Aston's Tear. Such information will be greatly prized.'

'This is too much. You should all be coming with me.'

'Nonsense, Jarred,' Ruvin leant forward and passed Rastan to Kayla. With his hands free, Ruvin gripped his shoulders tight. 'This is what we have planned for, albeit the timing is sudden and the personnel a little different. Kian will instruct you as you journey, on a great many things. Listen to him, Jarred. He is wise, and he is caring. He will look out for you.'

'Thank you, Ruvin.'

'And be respectful,' mentioned Neema. 'The Five Kings are not all they appear to be. Like Kian, they are wise, but there is something deeper within their souls. Be careful around them, Jarred. I mean it.'

'Yes, Neema.'

'Do you remember their names?' she asked.

'I believe I do,' he returned, his eyes narrowed as he concentrated. 'Ik'omi is the first and eldest, followed by Shien, Vega, Ky'elk and Solaii.'

'Well done. You listened when Ruvin taught, it will hold you in good stead.'

He knew there would more instructions in the coming days. He could see the look in Neema's eyes, feel the importance in Ruvin's words. Three days of preparation. Three days to organise himself.

'Will we be riding?' he asked, sharing his thoughts with everyone present.

He watched Ruvin glance towards Neema. She shrugged her shoulders. 'I have seen no horses since our arrival,' she answered. 'If they ride something other than a horse, I have yet to see it.'

'It will be a long walk if we don't. It took an age to reach *Ayoshos*.'

Ruvin nodded his head. 'The return journey will take less time. You have my word. Kian led us through hostile terrain for a reason, often backtracking to keep pursuers off our trail. This time, you'll make for the portal by the fastest route possible. From what Kian has mentioned to me before, he believes he can travel there and back again within eight months on foot.'

'That is still a long time, Ruvin.'

'I know, lad, only you won't be returning with Kian. If all goes well, you will have been in Bastion for some time when he returns to us.'

Once again there was something extra to consider. Reaching the portal would be their goal, but there was still the fear of Ahriman and his witch. The Five Kings and Kian were prepared to confront them in some fashion, but there was no guarantee such a venture would turn out as expected. And the prospect of other survivors from Bastion being in the vicinity was also to be considered. What plans did they have for the thousands of people who remained behind on the day they fled?

So many questions with so few answers. And his head already hurt. But he had three days to spend with his friends who felt like family. Three days to cherish every moment and every conversation. He could do this. He would be brave.

'What's going on?' the question came from behind. Jarred opened tear-rimmed eyes to see Reefe O'Bannon walking in from the garden. 'What's happened?'

'Nothing, Reefe,' Jarred choked on his words, tried to compose himself. It was difficult, and he could see Kayla and Neema were struggling with the same emotions. Donal was already crying. Somehow, he found the strength to say the words he feared to say.

'I'm leaving.'

CHAPTER SIXTEEN

Isabelle knew the cupboards were bare, but she looked once more, just in case.

Nothing had changed. They remained empty. She sighed, deeply for a six-year-old, before moving back to the table. She'd placed everything she could scavenge from the chapel into a neat pile, hoping to have enough to feed herself and the demon named Ra'tor. Five jars of pickled carrots, three jars of salted cabbage and a wooden bucket of apples comprised her first few hauls from the cellar. Next came the dried herring, also in jars, placed in a crate so she could carry it easily up the stairs. Three jars at a time she carried, until she'd gathered eighteen in total. A substantial amount, so she thought.

Only that had been five days earlier. Now, her dried herring jars were down to six.

She moved away from the table and stepped into her room. Well, it had been her room, but Ra'tor now lay on her cot, cramped, for sure, but it was the only way he could rest his leg.

He was sleeping again. It seemed he slept often. She didn't mind, for it gave her time to tend the garden out back and take care of the chickens. Luckily, they produced a dozen eggs each day, which helped ease the burden of feeding her patient. He had such an appetite, could consume vast quantities of food in such a short amount of time. Yet she was always mindful of making certain Ra'tor was fed. For if he became hungry, she feared he might one day eat her instead.

She found herself once again in the kitchen, stepped onto a wooden step and moved the jars of herring onto a shelf in the cupboard. They could stay there for a day or two. When he woke from his slumber, she would feed him the eggs gathered this morning. There were ten today, large and speckled. Perhaps, if her luck was with her, she might even catch a mouse to add to his meal.

She reached for a small cloth parcel on the bench, opened it carefully. Inside was a handful of seeds gathered from the garden. This was the second parcel of seeds she had opened, but there was an entire crate brimming with seeds down in the cellar. The sisters and brothers kept a well organised garden at the rear of the chapel, and their harvest included keeping seed for the following season. Some of what she found was old - she could tell from the crumpled cloth - whilst some was neatly tied with colourful ribbon, and this she believed to be the most recent. The recent harvest of seeds she left, for it would be silly to waste them to catch a mouse, but the old seed, especially the larger pumpkin seeds, would work wonderfully.

She chose six seeds and placed them in her petite hand, then walked to what she called the garden door. A gentle push saw it open to the courtyard and the garden beds beyond. The sun was shining, which was pleasant, although she feared not for much longer. Thick clouds were billowing to the west, heading towards Bastion on a coastal breeze. She was protected here, within the chapel's high-walled yard, but not from the rain. She hoped her task would be over before the weather changed.

She made her way to where a wicker basket leant against some wooden stakes, a small seat, and a plank of timber. She sat, placed the seeds before a crack in the garden wall, then knelt with wicker basket in hand, a foot from the ground. Then she waited, patiently, for a mouse to come sniffing.

The first drops of rain were beginning to patter against the stone tiles when a pointy nose poked out from between the crack. About time, she thought. She knew there were many mice scampering about the chapel, of differing size and shape. This one sniffed constantly, whiskers twitching, until his tiny feet stretched into a run towards the scattered seeds. Isabelle let the wicker basket fall, trapping the mouse. She then reached for the thin piece of timber leaning beside her stool and began to slide it beneath the basket. This was the careful part of her operation. Too fast, and she would leave a gap for the mouse to scurry through. And if her hand shook — again - the mouse would find a way to leap from confinement. She took a breath, slid the timber panel slowly. It was the same width as the basket, but she needed to be precise. No gaps, she told herself. Keep a steady hand.

And then it was done.

She gave a small squeal of delight. This was mouse number three. She flipped the basket upside down, left the timber on top to keep it trapped. She had only thought of catching mice two days ago, to help feed Ra'tor. Not all her efforts had succeeded, but her skills were improving. And she was glad she remembered the mice were here, for Ra'tor looked very much like a lizard with all his scales, and she knew lizards could eat a mouse if they found one.

With steady hands and a smile on her pretty face, she carried her quarry back to the kitchen. The difficult part was over. Now came the sad part.

A wooden bucket sat a foot inside the door, full of water from the well. With a heavy heart she placed the basket atop the water and let it sink downwards. The piping squeals of the mouse began immediately as it fought to swim. It couldn't escape, for the timber sat above. It could only scream with its tiny lungs. Thankfully, it didn't scream for long.

She offered a silent prayer to the gods. She didn't know if the mouse believed, but it didn't matter. It was nice to know his sacrifice would help another in a time of need.

A moment of preparation saw her gather a wooden plate. On its surface she placed the chicken eggs and the damp mouse, which she shook once to be certain it was dead, and twice to dry it somewhat. She thought of cooking it, but she wasn't sure she could manage the smell. Also, once cooked, she feared there would be little left to eat.

With the sound of rain pattering against the tiled roof, she made her way into the sleeping quarters. It wasn't overly cold, but she decided once she fed Ra'tor she would add some wood to the glowing coals in the fireplace. She knew he liked the warmth. It would make him grin.

'Ra'tor,' she spoke with a soft voice, her hands holding the plate before her. "Ra'tor, I have food.'

He roused, nostrils flaring, eyes opening. The iris of his yellow eyes contracted; his focus narrowed. He saw the offered food. She watched his large, clawed hand reach for the tail of the mouse. Then it was gone, into his mouth whole. There was a single crunch, then he swallowed. The eggs followed seconds later, one after another. Like the mouse, they were devoured whole, including the shell.

'Good,' she said, offering a smile.

'Good,' he replied in return, his eyes on her own.

He remembered. Since his arrival, she'd made an effort to teach him how to speak the kingdom language. It hadn't been easy, for his teeth were large and so was his tongue. He kept hissing his words at first, but he was learning. If her counting was correct, he knew almost twenty words now.

'Show me your leg,' she said, placing the empty plate on the floor and pointing with her hand. He gave a nod in understanding, shifted his weight so she could peer at the bandages. They were bloodstained, again. She poked his flesh around the wound, heard his teeth clamp shut. It obviously hurt still. 'I think I need to change the dressing again,' she said. It was not her favourite task. Washing blood from his wound made her feel queasy, caused her stomach to churn. She knew if an adult were here, they would suggest a stitching of the wound, but she was too frightened to attempt such a procedure. If she kept it clean and changed the bandages, it should heal, especially if she applied a splash of vinegar. That was the trick, she knew, because she had grazed her elbow once when she was younger. Her father had brought her to the chapel, and the sister had tended to her. She remembered, because when the sister splashed the vinegar on her elbow, she screamed. But it was for the best, she heard her say, for it kept out the bad stuff.

Nimble fingers untied the bandage around Ra'tor's leg before checking for bad stuff. It was usually yellow and green in colour, seeping from the wound and smelling awful. If there was any, she would have to clean the wound with water and vinegar, and she knew Ra'tor would not like it.

She peered close, poked her finger against his flesh again, just beside the cut. It was tender still, slightly raised and a different colour to his scaled skin. But it was almost fully closed, and the blood that seeped from the wound when she pressed close was red, not yellow or green. She leant in and sniffed once. Thankfully, it didn't smell awful.

'It is clean, Ra'tor,' she said, looking into his large eyes. 'Good.'

'Good,' he replied, his voice deep like rumbling thunder. 'Hungry. Mouse.' He lifted his hand, mimicking a mouse dangling from above.

'Another,' she sighed, 'really?' She looked over her shoulder towards the garden door. It continued to rain outside. Still, if she fed him one more mouse, then sang him a song, he would most likely sleep. And sleep was good for him right now. It made his wound heal quickly. Hopefully, it would enable him to walk soon without any pain.

And if she were lucky, he might just walk out the door and be on his way.

*

'Anything?'

Cale Griffith looked over his shoulder. He was below ground, currently sitting inside a circular chamber with a familiar dais situated at its centre. Like the one he first saw on his way to Highcastle, this one also featured strange markings and drawings on the walls. With light from several lanterns highlighting the area, he could see the faded shapes of ancient Panthians painted on stone from thousands of years ago.

'Nothing,' Griffith responded, moving his large frame so his king could sit next to him. 'How goes above ground?'

Tarsin took the offered seat. 'It remains quiet,' he looked thoughtful, if a little tired. 'It's been twenty days since we returned, a dozen since we forced our way back into Bastion. I imagined we would be fighting on multiple fronts at this point in time. The inaction disturbs me.'

Griffith felt his concern. He, too, feared the worst. He remembered their first night in the city. A violent storm raged overhead; sheets of rain pounded rooftops. Amongst it all came the sounds of hunting beasts roaming deserted streets. Yet the buildings they had claimed during that first day were left alone, and the soldiers within saw the night through. Since then, little had been seen of the Deios. Some suggested they'd retreated to surround Aston's Tear. Others wondered if they had fled back to their own world. Either way, the following days were made easier as Tarsin led his men further into the city. Now they held the Queen's Way and everything either side for nearly a mile. And from what he heard this morning, Lord Beaumont and his Captains Devin Kayne and Randal Quinn were equally well placed in the Southern Docks. If it weren't for the other strange beasts roaming darkened streets each night, he might have thought they were close to taking back what was rightfully theirs.

The sound of shuffling feet caused Griffith to look beyond the painted walls. An arched doorway, the only one leading into the chamber, lay sixty feet away. Nearly thirty soldiers, hand-picked for their strength and loyalty, kept vigil without. Like himself, they'd been informed of the danger below the city. Barricades had been erected within the corridors to protect their position, but they knew otherworldly creatures could appear at any time, screeching in the black and thirsting for blood.

'Did you speak to Lord Beaumont's physician about his latest autopsy?'

'I did,' Tarsin eased his legs before him, stretching his hamstrings. 'Alwin, for all his quirks, knows how to dissect a beast when the mood is upon him. Six now lie open on his tables. I've not seen them myself, yet, but Alwin says they all share similar traits on the inside.'

'You mean they're like us?'

'Apparently. Structurally we share many similarities, although the length of certain bones varies, along with the surrounding muscles. Depending on the beast, both its weight, height and physical size will determine the strength it can wield. But within, once you cut through the tissue and reveal the internal organs, they are all familiar and placed accordingly. Take away the feathers and scales, forget about the horns and hoofed feet, and we are very much the same.'

'Is that what Alwin said?'

'In a roundabout fashion.'

Thick fingers twirled a strand of his red beard. 'I'm not sure such similarities sit well with me.'

'I know how you feel. It's why I haven't mentioned what Alwin discovered in front of Tahu and Zai. I'll leave such an episode for later. After much contemplation, I might add.'

'Where are your personal guards, by the way? It seems few are the times they aren't by your side.'

'Where else would you like me to send them?' Tarsin met his gaze, the lantern light casting shadows across his handsome face. 'With me they are safe.'

'Aye, you're right. I know.' Griffith twirled his beard even tighter. 'It would be nice for me to look out for you some time, though. I am still a member of the Unseen. It's my duty to protect you.'

A smile crept across his king's face. 'Are you jealous, big man?'

'Perhaps,' Griffith lowered his eyes, felt his cheeks begin to colour like his hair. 'Perhaps striding about the streets beside my king feels a damn sight better than sitting in a hole in the ground waiting for who-knows-what.'

'Well, that was a mouthful,' a short laugh accompanied Tarsin's observation.

'It's true. And you never answered my question. Where are they?'

His king looked towards the archway. 'They are socialising with the soldiers. Learning to speak the language. The more they interact, the less our men will be shocked when Inesco reaches us.'

Griffith gave a nod of approval, not that it mattered what he thought. Tarsin was always one step ahead, always had been.

Gods above, even when he was fifteen years old, he could outthink almost every other swordsman learning under Henrickson and Du Weng Sai. If ever there was a man more suited to the task at hand, he'd never heard of him.

'You think Inesco will arrive soon?' he asked, realising Tarsin probably wouldn't even be here if he didn't think it was possible.

'He should arrive sometime today. We spoke at length during our stay on Aeth. He promised to send aid. As you are aware, time runs differently between the two worlds. Twenty days here will have been almost three months for the Panthians.'

'Any time, then?' Griffith shifted his bulk, sat a little straighter.

'Any time, big man.'

He returned Tarsin's smile. It was good to see the king in better spirits. And if Inesco arrived today, as Tarsin believed he would, a slice of the burden would slide off his shoulders to ease his load. Gods alone knew how difficult times were right now. But the aid of the Panthians, however many walked through, would be a pleasant distraction.

A gentle vibration began to permeate the chamber, originating beneath the tiled floor and spreading to the outer wall. Griffith stood and offered his hand. Tarsin gripped it tight, stood beside him. It appeared Inesco's arrival would be sooner than he thought. Together they walked to stand before the dais. The vibration continued, joined now by a hum. Soldiers peered from the archway but declined to enter. A sliver of orange light snaked up from within the golden circle on the dais. It twirled, reached higher, sinuously climbing to greater height. Motes of vibrant colour popped into existence, droplets of ruby and splashes of sapphire. Emerald streaks joined the dance. A sense of calm pervaded their surroundings as the orange light bulged and formed into an oblong shape that pulsed with raw energy.

A moment passed.

Griffith held his breath, waited for the shadows to appear within. He could hear muttered voices in the background, could feel the tension of expectation emanating from his king. Where was the Nepharii named Inesco? Where was their aid?'

A glimmer of darkness manifested at the centre of the light. It grew, solidified. Griffith took a lungful of air, exhaled slowly as he saw the smiling face of Inesco appear before his eyes.

'Welcome,' Tarsin grabbed Inesco's hand and shook it, then pulled him forward and wrapped his arms about the ancient one. 'You made it.'

'I did, King Tarsin, as I promised,' he patted him on the shoulders as he spoke, gave a nod in recognition as their eyes met. 'And I have gathered allies for the battle to come, my friend. Let us step back a pace, so you can see them arrive.'

They did so, keeping their eyes on the portal of orange light. They waited, breathed deep, then relaxed as Panthians, one after another, began to file into the chamber.

They were attired for war, weapons slung over their shoulders, satchels hanging from their hips. Cloaked in grey, cat-like eyes observed as clawed hands twitched in anticipation. Tahu and Zai stepped into the chamber to greet those arriving. Words were spoken.

'This is all I can provide at present,' Inesco's voice cut through the chatter, 'but more will follow when the time is right. Twenty will remain here to help guard the path between our worlds. But for now, you are free to utilise sixty of the finest Panthian hunters I could find.'

A sense of deflation swept through Griffith's soul. Sixty? He'd hoped for considerably more. He knew Tarsin felt the same. Although he could see with his own eyes the Panthians were taller and stronger than most of the monks he'd previously been acquainted with. One look told him they could fight.

'Sixty will be fine, Inesco,' he heard Tarsin raise his voice. 'Come, we have work to do.'

*

'Have you seen what he's done?'

The voice was loud, disruptive. Of course he'd seen what the king had done. He expected nothing less.

'I have eyes, Bardell. I can see.'

'So you have, Will Tolsten, but what are you going to do about it? You said yourself the king was insane.'

Will frowned at Bardell's choice of words. He couldn't recall calling the king insane. He may have felt it, but he certainly didn't say it. At least not aloud. He looked at the swordsman from his perch, saw Bardell standing with his elbows resting on the battlements. They were above Farmer's Gate, looking inwards at the city. A dozen guards from his Knights of Salvation were on duty, keeping an eye out for any unusual activity. The real soldiers, under the king's command, were further in, sweeping the streets as they reclaimed the North-East of Bastion.

Bardell waved his arms above his head. 'You saw him, clear as day, walking with his cat-demons. What in Hell's name does he want with them?'

'Why don't you ask him?' Col Farren raised his own voice as he moved to stand alongside.

'I don't need to. I was there, you know, on the other world. Imprisoned by the cat-demons for months, we were. Never trusted them. But the king . . . well, didn't hear much from him whilst we sat and wondered. Methinks he may have been bewitched; his mind twisted so they could control his actions. Makes more sense if you ask me.'

'No one is asking you, Bardell,' Col couldn't refuse the barb. Will bit his lip to stop himself from smiling.

'Pah! You'll understand, Col, when they come for you in the night. You won't be laughing then.'

He noted Bardell's eyes were brimming with pent-up frustration. He was serious about his time spent on the other world, had spoken of it before. What he thought was nothing more than a rumour was fast becoming a reality. The king was not a loved man. He was an unknown. And with Bardell preaching his dislike for the king amongst the masses, more than a few were leaning towards the same path Bardell trod.

In times of disaster, the people needed someone to blame.

And that someone would be the Bastard King.

'You've a valid point, Bardell,' soft words sought to calm him down. Although the men on duty were hand-picked for having a like-minded belief, Will couldn't risk word of their dissent reaching unnecessary ears. 'But I'm not sure I understand what it is you expect me do. Our numbers are mostly conscripts, and they mostly city folk. The rest are all that remains of the Nocturnals. We are thieves and cut throats, Bardell, not an elite force of soldiers ready to usurp the kingdom of Dervae. At least . . . not yet.'

'Then do something to rid our city of the cat-demons. They make my skin crawl.'

'How, exactly?'

He watched Bardell screw his face into something even uglier. 'I don't know. Place a saucer of milk on the street, then stab them in the back when they stop for a drink.'

Will laughed, and so did half-a-dozen men standing within ear shot.

'Just do something, Will. You're our leader, you need to make a stand at some point.'

There it was. The big mouth talking nonsense. The one Col warned him about.

'He'll make a stand when he's good and ready,' Col was equally predictable. Like a guard dog protecting his master. He wondered if he walked away, right now, whether the two would come to blows.

'Just make sure you do something soon, Will. If you don't, someone else might.'

A veiled threat, perhaps? Doubtful. He might be a braggart and a swordsman of standing, but he wasn't a thinker. Will gave him a nod, more to acknowledge the exchange of words than anything else, then watched as he spun about and walked away from the battlements. A handful of seconds passed before Col voiced his displeasure.

'The nerve of the man!' he knew Col searched for an excuse to cut him down, he could see murder in his eyes. 'If I ever hear him talk to you again in such a manner, I'll slit his gods forsaken throat!'

'No, you won't, Col. We need him. As much as you don't like it, he has his uses.'

'So you keep saying. I don't see it.'

'No, not many do.' Will took a moment, thought about his dreams for the future. He would need luck if all his desires were to fall in place. A man like Bardell: rash, boisterous and unruly, could see it all unravel in the blink of an eye.

'A man like him is dangerous, I've said it before, Will. But with what you are trying to accomplish here, it makes him even more dangerous. He knows too much. And from what I've seen, he's gathering men of his own. Like you said earlier, there are men and women who are desperate, who have nothing to lose. A firebrand like Bardell can ignite into something sinister.'

He was right. Col had a way of seeing inside a man's head. Had a knack for understanding what made them tick. They'd spoken of Bardell several times, knew they'd need to keep him on a tight reign.

'He's no different to the Pillars of Bastion, you know. Cast from the same mould if you take my meaning.'

'I know, Col. He has a black heart, just like those men my father killed.'

'They were evil men,' Col continued, 'the sort of men you kill quickly before their darkness spreads. We shouldn't be in league with him. We should end this.'

And yet he had his uses. He could be used. And he'd been close to the king whilst imprisoned. For all his faults, he dreamed of using Bardell like a tool, the sort of tool one utilizes to eradicate a problem. Like an axe, he mused. An axe to the head.

'I'll keep my eyes on him,' Will replied, turning to look down Queen's Way. There was movement, but he could see it was merely soldiers returning from a patrol. As they came closer, he could see a group of six cat-demons walking in unison at the rear. They'd been integrated seamlessly into the king's ranks, appeared to be able bodied and slightly intimidating. He wasn't sure how many had crossed into Bastion, but it didn't appear to be many. At least not enough to offset the number of swords he'd been adding to his own ranks.

He looked back at his closest friend and aide. Col was still shaking his head in anger, no doubt his mind fuming whilst he continued to look for his own answer.

But he had his own answers. Had them all so long ago. He'd watched his father, the greatest general of the kingdom, work a lifetime battling others to keep them safe. Then he watched him die. Just like his older brother died, on the very streets his father saved. And now his sister was missing, perhaps never to return. All of them, gone. And for what?

Will had his answers. He'd lived it for the last five years with the thieves of Bastion. You took what you could and enjoyed the rest. For no-one lives forever.

And if the leaders were poor, or distrustful - or as Col said - evil, then you did what any sane man would do. You killed them. Just like Derrick Tolsten did when he killed the Pillars of Bastion.

There was no other way.

CHAPTER SEVENTEEN

It wasn't exactly the Eye of Bhral, but the small yellow sun did provide warmth during the middle of the day.

Ra'tor eased his body onto warm tiles, felt the heat tingle across his scales. He was sitting in the courtyard, surrounded by green plants and vines, a multitude of brightly coloured flowers and growths sprouting from the foliage. Isabelle had told him the names of certain oddities the day before, but all he could recall were the striped, ribbed gourds and the enormous sunflowers ranged along the back wall. The remainder, an assortment of red berries of differing shape and a selection of green tubers hanging from vines, he could not recall. But it would come to him, he knew, for the words Isabelle said never left his mind.

'Are you comfortable?' Isabelle asked, walking from the shelter to stand by his side. Ra'tor took a moment to think about the words and her tone. She was asking him a question, that much he knew.

'Com-ta-bil,' he repeated, knowing this was her word for relaxed, or at ease. And he was, he thought, for the first time since he staggered into the shelter. His wound was healed, although his range of movement was still limited, and if he stretched too far the pain returned. But he was making progress. Within days he would be walking without any discomfort.

'Good,' Isabelle smiled, showing perfectly white teeth. She passed a water vessel made of hard clay into his hands. 'Drink this as I gather some carrots and beans.'

He cocked his head to the side, watched her carry a small wicker basket into the garden. He took a sip of water as she began to pull slender tubers from beneath the soil. They were yellow and purple, some almost black. Carrots, he assumed, from the words she spoke. He took another sip, saw her move towards the vines that raced up slivers of wood with twine stretched taut between them. These, then, would be the beans. Green, like the plants themselves. For Isabelle, they were food. For himself, he preferred the meat of an animal. She tried to make him eat some of the plants once. He'd spat the food from his mouth, the taste and texture not to his liking.

He recalled the loose, red soil of his own world. Rarely did it hold any life, and the sad, twisted plants that did grow were quite often poisonous. Few dared try to consume them. Even the Patriarchs, in all their perceived wisdom, seldom took the time to gather the unusual growths. Some things were better left alone. He knew plants to be one of them.

He drank the last of the water and placed the vessel on the stone tile next to him. A few more days and he would be strong enough to return to his brood. The thought was comforting, but he also knew much would have transpired in his absence. The Deios would not mourn for long, it was their way. Within a day they would have been hunting again, looking to feed whilst they searched the dwelling place.

Isabelle began to sing whilst she continued to pluck food from the garden. The sound was like water trickling over smooth stones. Crystal clear and pure, just like the sacred places back home. It made him feel at peace. Settled his mind from the torture of leadership and the fear of reprisal. Nothing else mattered when Isabelle sang. Nothing at all.

It was why, when he left this shelter in the coming days, he would take Isabelle with him. She didn't know it yet, but he couldn't imagine a day where he didn't hear her voice. He needed her.

Such a treasure was not to be taken lightly. Nor, once found, was it to be left behind.

He wondered if she would be upset when he took her. He knew she was content here at the shelter, and it appeared she had everything she needed to survive. But he would not leave her behind. Alone, she had no defence against a hunter, at least no physical defence.

He would be her protector. He owed her that much. For without her, he wasn't sure his wound would have healed as fast or as well. There was a possibility it may not have healed at all.

Ra'tor closed his eyes for a moment, concentrated on the warmth washing over his face. He couldn't even recall the blade striking his flesh during the battle. The rage was upon him, the smell of blood thick, his veins bulging. It cost him. He'd lost his way. Not just the path he was following in the night, nor his Deios who he vowed to lead. He'd lost his vision of who he was to become. He became reckless, let the anger take hold.

To be brutally honest, he didn't even know if his Deios were victorious. They could even now be lying on stone paths, rotting in the midday sun.

And if they were, he could only assume the Aquilans were now crawling their way inside the temple of blue light.

A shudder of disappointment swept through his body. It brought his focus back to the Aquilans. They were obviously obsessed with the temple, much like he and his Deios. He wondered if there was something else they craved. Wondered if they knew something he did not. The temple held enormous power; that much was obvious. To travel between worlds, to link them together in a single chamber, was beyond his comprehension. But he had seen it with his own eyes, had been one of the first to step through and savour the scent of another time and place.

And yet the Aquilans appeared obsessed with reaching the temple. He heard them, listened as their leader shouted unfamiliar words in agitation, or possibly fear. And they'd been willing to fight for it, to sacrifice their lives. Commendable, he thought, if there was a purpose behind their actions. So, what did they know that he didn't?

Ra'tor searched for an answer, but it eluded him. The sun was beginning to wane, its heat dissipating, when he finally lifted his body off the tiles. Isabelle was no longer gathering in the garden, but he could hear her humming from within the shelter. He took a handful of long strides, stretched his leg before massaging it with a knuckle. The pain was bearable, nothing more than a sharp twinge. Perhaps he could leave in two days, not three. So long as he was strong. If he limped back to his Deios, they would not accept him. If he was to return, he needed to arrive with purpose. He would need to be the commanding leader he'd been before.

He gathered an armful of timber from the rear wall. It was cut into neat rounds of equal length, suitable for what Isabelle called the fireplace. She knew he liked the warmth of the flames when the sun set. He also liked to lose himself in their hypnotic dance. Fires were few and often brief on the world of Dei, and never required for heat. But here, he could admire the flickering orange light and wonder at the grand scheme of things.

He ducked his head as he walked into the preparation room. Isabelle was placing speckled eggs on a plate. She smiled as her eyes met his own. He tried to smile back, but even he knew it would be nothing more than a revealing of sharp teeth.

'We have food,' Isabelle said, her voice a delight. 'You can eat the eggs, Ra'tor, and I shall eat the carrots and beans. I also have one jar of salted herring in the cupboard. If you like, you can eat that, too.'

Her words were fast, as they often were, but he understood her tone quite well, and realised her talk was centred on the food she was preparing. He could see the eggs, which he enjoyed, and as he stepped closer to what Isabelle called the table, she reached for the jar of salted herring. He breathed deep. It was unlike anything he'd eaten before, the taste almost as hypnotic as the dancing flames. A vicious smile creased his mouth as he remembered how many he'd devoured the first time she brought them to him. A memory to treasure.

He could smell the herring as soon as she unstoppered the jar, but he held his nerve and walked to the fireplace instead, laying the timber to the side. Small flames already licked a collection of twigs and leaves, grey smoke floating towards the dark hole at the rear.

'Here,' she placed his plate of eggs and herring by his side, then sat with her own plate of food. He offered a nod of acceptance, something he rarely did for anyone, and placed the first of the eggs in his mouth.

Hours later he still sat there, watching the flames. Isabelle was asleep, curled beneath her blankets, golden hair splayed across a pillow. She'd sang for him after their meal, a song of beauty, her blue eyes alight with wonder. He could feel the energy of her voice still coursing through his veins. So like the blood-rage he felt when fighting, yet somehow so very different.

A spark jumped from the flames to land on the floorboards, accompanied by a crackle. It was sun-bright yet faded seconds later. He cocked his head to the side, gazed at her sleeping form. Was Isabelle the same? Would her voice shine bright and then fade in time? He hoped not. Then again, maybe her talent was fashioned by blood. He'd heard of Patriarchs performing certain rituals to empower individuals. Was Isabelle's voice granted during a pact with dark forces? Was she a sorceress, using her skills to entrap him?

He shook his head. He'd heard her mention a name several times since their first meeting. She used it often to describe her talent, her songs. The word was angel. Voice like an angel. That was it, he heard her say it. Like an angel. Was that what she was? An angel. When he presented her to the brood in the coming days, was that to be his introduction? This small creature is Isabelle: she is an angel.

He didn't know for certain, but it felt right when he said it. It also felt right in his chest, in his beating heart. Somehow, Isabelle was now a part of him, their paths entwined. She caused his heart to soar; he protected her. That would be the deal.

But he couldn't help thinking there was more at stake here. There was a purpose to their meeting, a greater role yet to play out. He never asked for direction in the past, but it didn't mean he didn't look for signs. His Blood-God was not where he thought he would be, nor did he appear to be anywhere else. Perhaps finding his Blood-God was not his path. Perhaps there was something else to be discovered.

For all his life, Bhral had been his purpose: his reason for existing. Eventually it led him here, to Isabelle. But what if his purpose were now to change? What if Isabelle were to become his purpose. What if she now led the way? Was it possible? Was it plausible?

He scratched his head, looked deeper into the flames. Despite his confusion and the countless unanswered questions, he felt at peace. And the fireplace was a marvel, kept him warm through the night without burning down the shelter. So clever to build a chute at the rear for the smoke to escape.

Later, when the fire in his blood subsided, he would think back to his time before the flames. He would question whether he subconsciously heard the footfalls on the roof; or thought of his smoke giving away their position first. How foolish, he now knew, to have lit a fire during the past four nights. It was folly to believe no-one would see his smoke winding sinuously into the night sky, or to accept its scent would go unnoticed. Unfortunately, his time to ponder such a mistake was now past.

He left Isabelle sleeping in her cot and walked into the preparation room, picking his cleaver off the table as he did so. The sound of many feet echoed from above. He offered a snarl, then ducked under the doorframe that led to the garden. He stood motionless for ten heartbeats, listening as he let his eyes adjust to the night.

The soft thud of feet landing on soil sounded to his left. He hefted his cleaver, saw starlight glint from the silvered blade. He squinted at the weapon, watched its mirrored surface as he turned it slowly about. A dark figure materialized along a brick wall, feathered like the Aquilans he'd already fought. Another leapt to the ground to land alongside a moment later.

Ra'tor crouched as he saw their gaze sweep the garden. His leg ached from the stretch, but he ignored the pain. Instead, he focused his mind to the task at hand. He was a hunter, one of the greatest living amongst the Deios. His brood now numbered over a thousand, a feat not heard of for generations, and his rule was unquestioned. Most importantly, though, he'd found himself an angel. He didn't exactly know what an angel was, but he knew the finding of one would prove to be significant. He was a hunter, a leader, and a protector.

And he vowed to never let an Aquilan cause his angel harm.

He held his breath, crouched lower, began to creep across stone tiles. Another Aquilan landed in the garden, close to the first two. He could hear soft clicks in the night air as they spoke to each other. Another thud.

He kept his body low, slowly let out his breath. He could smell them. A quick glance to the skyline revealed no others. Four of the creatures, then. He could do this, even without the blood-rage. He was strong.

And he was cunning. For that is the hunter's greatest strength.

A wooden bucket sat beneath a row of green vines. He lifted it by the rope handle, then flung it low towards the rear wall of the garden. As it sailed through the air, he sprang from his crouch and took long strides towards his foes. The crash of splintered wood saw Aquilans turn their heads, startled, before the crunch of bones sounded as his cleaver hammered into the torso of the one closest to him. A faint click sounded from its beaked mouth before he lifted his blade and brought it down again. He was taller than his foes by a foot, broader and gifted with rippling muscles beneath hardened scales. The Aquilans could not stand against him, not so tightly packed together. The garden was cramped, the raised beds of timber covering large sections of the yard. He needed only to swing his cleaver again, and again, and again.

He stopped his last swing an inch from the bloodied body. The chest was exposed, ribs already splayed and splintered. Blood black with the night covered his forearms. There was no movement from his enemy. They lay butchered on the ground, staining the garden with their malcontent.

'Ra'tor?'

He looked over his shoulder. Standing at the garden door was Isabelle with a candle in her hand. Her white dress draped her ankles, but her arms were bare. She was a pale creature, so slender, so innocent. He looked at his clawed hands, stained with death.

She couldn't stay here, not now. The Aquilans were aware of their shelter. They needed to flee this place. This very night.

'Come,' he motioned with his left hand whilst his right clipped his cleaver to his belt. He knew two score words, at the very least, of her difficult tongue. He would learn more in the days to follow.

'Come, Isabelle. We run!'

*

'Have you ever seen anything like it?'

Tarsin Va, King of Dervae, shook his head. He was below ground in a narrow disused cellar beneath the Southern Barracks. Lined along the far wall rested a dozen wooden benches, dissected corpses of varying degrees occupied six of them. Kelt Alwin, physician to Lord Beaumont, stood with arms spread wide, what was once a white jacket covering his torso and thighs. Tarsin noticed the darker stains about his cuffs and the numerous splashes of red about his midriff. There was also a belt holding numerous steel blades shining at his waist. Alwin had been busy.

Tarsin stepped closer to the benches, shared a look with his aides. Inesco and Cale Griffith both appeared as interested as he, although Lord Beaumont's face looked to have drained of colour.

'We have four species represented here,' Alwin pointed to the dead. They were split down the middle, their insides visible if one were to lean close. 'Three Deios, as you've described them, and three others yet to be named.'

'I know them,' Inesco took another step, lifted the wrist of a creature with black feathers about its face and a pointed nose that looked almost like a beak. The skin of the beast was pale, the arms thin. Black nails, long and sharp, extended from its fingers.

'Would you care to elaborate?' Tarsin asked, looking to the ancient Nepharii.

Inesco placed the hand of the corpse on the bench, stepped towards the next. 'You have seen the markings engraved on the *Nepharii Uranometria*,' Inesco began, looking him in the eye. 'They represent the constellations of the Nepharii, and yet they also represent the people who reside on the world associated with each constellation.'

Tarsin moved to his side. 'So, what are they called?'

'The Deios you already know,' Inesco shifted his eyes to the three heavy corpses at the far end, legs stiffly hanging over the wooden benches. 'This one here is called a Murdan. It hails from Ether, a world dominated by what you would call crow-men. The next is a Lupan, from a world called Mona. They are as they look; wolves who walk as men.'

'They are quite different in appearance,' Griffith let his eyes roam over their features. Tarsin agreed. The Lupan was tall and rangy, thick fur covering its head and shoulders, but only lightly covering the rest of its body. The Murdan, on the other hand, had feathers instead of fur, and only from the shoulders up. The rest of the body looked very much like that of a man.

'The Lupen are hunters still, much as the Deios,' Inesco continued. 'The Murden are not. You can see their physique is smaller, their muscles less developed. They are smaller in height and weight. Whatever they do to survive, it is not by hunting game alone. As men have learnt to harvest crops, the Murden have done the same.'

'He is right,' Alwin moved to a cupboard along the far wall. He opened a door, pulled some clothing from the top shelf. 'The Murdan was wearing this when killed,' he passed over the clothes. Amongst the bundle was a shirt and leggings. 'As you can see, they are of fine quality, using skills like our own weavers. This pouch was also in its possession.'

Tarsin took the offered pouch. It was made of leather, the skin incredibly soft. He untied the thong, looked inside, then upended its contents onto the table.

'Quite a collection,' Griffith peered at the oddities.

'What are they?' Lord Beaumont was equally curious.

Tarsin used a finger to search through the trinkets. He counted six metal pieces, all copper and circular, each with a hole in its centre. There were also five polished stones, dark blue in colour, with flashes of orange and red igniting just below the surface. 'I would suggest they represent their monetary system,' he said, admiring the coins and stones.

'And these?' Griffith used his thick finger to push three ivory bones, knuckle thick and blackened with runes, to the side.

'Fortune telling, perhaps,' mentioned Lord Beaumont. 'I've seen cunning folk implement such tokens before.'

'Witchcraft!' Griffith snarled, snatching his finger away.

'In any case, the items are the hallmark of civilization,' Tarsin offered, his fingers twirling the last piece to be found in the pouch. It was a steel cylinder, no bigger than his little finger, stoppered with red wax. 'Do you know what's inside this?' he asked Alwin, shaking the vial before the physician's eyes.

'No, I've not been game to open it. Besides,' he looked to the remaining corpses, 'I've been preoccupied with other interests.'

'Inesco?' he showed the Nepharii the steel vial.

'Alas, King Tarsin, I have no knowledge of its contents. If we break the seal, though, I may deduce its purpose and properties given some time.'

'Perhaps, when we are finished here, you can work with Alwin and do just that.' He placed the cylinder back on the table.

'This was also found in a pocket,' Alwin placed a parcel next to his hand.

Tarsin opened it by unfolding the wax-paper. Inside was a hard bread, nut-brown in colour. He pulled some apart, lifted his hand to sniff the morsel. He could see it was made of nuts and seeds, could smell something sweet, like honey, mixed within.

'Food made from a selection of gathered goods, some of those refined. It was also baked. Another reason to believe they no longer hunt for sustenance alone,' Tarsin was tempted to taste the bread, but he knew he couldn't afford such liberties. Dying of some unknown poison when his people needed him most was not an option.

'They are not savages, then,' Griffith was coming to the same conclusion as he.

'No, unlike the Deios, who seem to live for bloodshed, I doubt the Murden will be as volatile.' Tarsin looked to the third corpse in line, the one before the three huge Deios. 'And what is this last one?' he asked Inesco.

'This is an Aquilan,' Inesco replied, leading the men a further two steps towards the dead beast. It lay on the bench much like the Deios, almost as tall, but not as broad. Its head was covered in feathers like the Murdan, but its eyes were larger, its mouth beaked. Enormous feathers lined its long arms, all the way to its wrists, and likewise its legs. 'Aura, is its world, home to what you would call eagle-men.'

'It has a remarkably savage appearance,' Griffith leant close, opened its beak to look inside its mouth. The beak was serrated along the sides, flattened slightly at the rear.

'I dare say it would slice flesh with ease,' Lord Beaumont leant next to Griffith.

'Aye, I would hate to be bitten by one,' Tarsin heard the big man reply. 'Can it fly, do you think?'

'I do not believe so,' Inesco commented. 'They may be able to glide from high places, though, if their feathered arms were outstretched.'

'Interesting,' Tarsin put one of the Aquilan's exposed ribs between two fingers. 'The bone does not feel as dense as ours. Are they hollow, Alwin?'

'Very perceptive, my lord. You are quite correct. The bones share similarities with birds, incorporating a honeycomb cross section. It provides strength, but also lightness. I believe it's conceivable an Aquilan could glide from some height.'

'Something else to worry about, then,' Griffith didn't appear to be pleased.

'Perhaps,' Tarsin shared another look with Alwin. 'Do they have any weaknesses?'

'They are formidable, each in their own way. The Lupans and the Deios are fierce adversaries, for they are strong and agile. We can see it clearly. The Aquilans less so, although that doesn't mean they are less vicious or difficult to face in combat. As to the Murdan we have here, who can say? He was pierced by a crossbow bolt from twenty paces, straight through the throat. He died instantly. We have no others to gauge our curiosity. Until we can find them in number, and observe their behaviour, we have nothing. For all we know, they could be as resourceful as men, maybe even more so.'

'Why more so?' Tarsin asked.

'Because there have been so few sightings. It leads me to believe they are cautious, or possibly curious. They could also be strategizing, which lends favour to the Murden being civilized.'

'You're not serious, are you?' Griffith looked to Lord Beaumont, who appeared equally bemused.

'Absolutely,' Alwin moved towards the trinkets on the table. He picked up the steel cylinder. 'Care to explain to me what metal this is, my lord?'

'I have no idea,' Griffith shook his head.

'Exactly. Nor do I. The metal is lightweight, and yet it resists my every effort to squeeze or mark. For something so small and delicate, it is incredibly strong.'

'And that makes them more civilized, does it?'

'No, but it highlights skills we are unaware of,' Alwin placed the cylinder back on the table. 'But much could be said for every race in that regard. Like I said, the Murden *could* be civilized, and they could possibly utilize certain techniques we have yet to discover.'

Tarsin found himself placing a hand on Griffith's shoulder. 'It makes little difference to us, my friend. We need to be prepared, regardless of their skills. Nothing changes.'

'Like the Panthians,' began Inesco, 'some races will seek peace and the sharing of knowledge over bloodshed. The

Murden may be so inclined, although with one of their number dead, dialogue might now be difficult. Accident or not, this creature has been killed. It could complicate matters.'

'Matters are already complicated,' Tarsin muttered as he made for the stairs. He sensed his aides following on his heels. The visit to see Alwin had been a priority now the northern sector of Bastion had been stabilized. The physician had requested an audience five days earlier, but this was the first time he had felt it safe to journey to the southern sector. Apart from visiting Kelt Alwin, Devin Kayne and Randal Quinn had also asked for his presence. And from what he'd been told by Lord Beaumont, the news was bitter.

He climbed the stone stairs, reached the ground floor and moved out into a courtyard. Twenty men stood to attention as he swept past them, standing straight, looking alert. They were dressed for battle, swords at hip, armour polished. They knew death could visit at any moment.

Tarsin reached a wooden gate trimmed in steel, waited for his aides and men to fall in line. Beyond the gate wound a cobblestoned street, narrow, but remarkably intact despite the upheaval. Devin Kayne and Randal Quinn were only a short walk away, awaiting his arrival at the Southern Barracks.

The walk was brief.

Soldiers greeted him as he reached the Barracks. He smiled, shared a laugh with a handful, then made long strides towards the office. Devin Kayne met him at the door with a salute and ushered him inside.

Cale Griffith, Inesco and Lord Beaumont followed.

Inside, Tarsin found himself in a square room with a single desk and chair. On one wall rested mahogany shelves reaching from floor to ceiling, a central door marked the other. Behind the desk rested a cabinet, also fashioned from mahogany, whilst a thick-set man with a bald head and a stern look stood before it.

'Your majesty,' the bald man had a thick voice, which came as no surprise.

Tarsin watched as the man offered a bow. When he raised his eyes, Tarsin returned a nod. 'You must be Randal Quinn. I've heard a great deal about your exploits, captain. You appear to be a resourceful man.'

'Only doing my duty, my lord. You'd expect nothing less.'

Tarsin knew not all men shared such a sentiment. Still, Quinn sounded genuine, and looked the part. 'So, Captain Quinn, what do you have to tell me that reeks of urgency?'

The faintest sigh escaped Quinn's lips as he shuffled parchment on his desk. Then he grabbed a leather-bound journal, thicker than his forearm, which was considerable, before he opened it and spun it about in one motion. He peered at the script written within.

'What you see here, my lord, are entries. The written names are those of prisoners locked in cells beneath the city, primarily the cells known as The Cesspit. As you all know, the Cesspit lies beneath the Courthouse, which lies a stone's throw from the Barracks. But since the earthquake struck, the cells within the Cesspit have been empty.'

'Empty! How can they be empty?' Griffith was beginning to turn red in the face. Being Captain of the Citywatch, he'd been responsible for his fair share of prisoners being escorted to the Cesspit without any chance of return.

'What I'm saying, my lords, is that the building has been compromised. Walls have fallen, steel bars have warped, and entire sections have caved in. We have committed an extensive sweep of what is left, with this journal for a guide. From our reckoning, two hundred and seventy-three men and women should have been locked behind bars. Some were destined for the noose, others confined for life. We found seventeen dead: men crushed by falling debris. Another twenty-five were still chained in their cells, only they're now dead from starvation.'

'And the rest,' Tarsin's voice was calm, yet he felt anything but.

'The rest have escaped, my lord. All two hundred and thirty-one. We cannot tell you where they have gone.'

'They could be anywhere,' Griffith snarled, his hand tightening about the haft of his hammer.

'They would have escaped the day of the earthquake,' Quinn surmised. 'They may have fled the city with the populace, or they may have scampered to old dens to hide. Some may have even sought gain in such turbulent times.'

A sense of frustration was fuming behind Tarsin's stoic façade. With all that was occurring in his city, he now had thieves, cutthroats and murderers on the loose.

'There is something else you should see, my lord,' Devin Kayne moved to the desk. He flicked back several dozen pages in the journal, traced a finger down the entries. 'Here,' he said, moving the tome closer.

Curious eyes swept over the entries. The script was neat, easily read. On the left-hand side of the page were listed names, whilst beside the name read the prisoner's offence and recommended sentence. Tarsin read the name next to Kayne's finger. Clive Bardell.

He looked at his captains. 'Is this who I think it is?'

'It is,' Kayne stepped back a pace. 'The man named Bardell who fought beside you against the Deios, and who survived the imprisonment on the world of the Panthians, was once imprisoned in the Cesspit. He was in for kidnapping, attempted murder, thuggery, and extortion. He was serving a ten-year sentence, of which four years had passed.'

'He was a criminal, my lord, and still is,' said Quinn. 'It is also written in the journal that he was a known ringleader and organizer of crime. It is not known whether he was at the top of the food chain, but he had links with The Dockland Bruisers.'

'And now he is loose, wandering amongst the people of Bastion when they are at their most vulnerable.' Griffith said what they all thought.

'Aye, he is,' Tarsin clenched his teeth after his words. 'We need to find him, and quickly. 'I've a feeling Will Tolsten might be able to help on that score. I believe it's time we paid him a visit.

'Time to see if his Knights of Salvation are everything he hoped they would be, or whether he's recruited nothing more than the dregs of society, hungry for mischief.'

'What does your gut tell you, my king?' asked Griffith, moving to hold open the door.

'Trouble, my friend. My gut says trouble.

CHAPTER EIGHTEEN

Tired eyes surrounded by a scarred, wrinkled face, starred back at her. Coarse hair, at least the strands that remained, dangled white like the snow that fell overnight.

Avra Creswick was on her bony knees, her body bent as she peered into a puddle of water. Around her, the ground was frozen, but her voice had spoken words of power to melt the ice. Now the puddle was still and mirror-bright, allowing her to see events and people from afar. Provided she could keep her concentration from wandering.

It was becoming difficult, for her mind was scattered. Everything she had dreamed during her tortured years was still far from reality. The revenge she sought, the power she craved, neither had been fulfilled to their full extent. And now she was old and exhausted, floundering on an unknown world whilst her summoned god raged about a woman with many souls.

There was nothing she could do. She was as crippled as her Dark Lord, possibly more so. And she could feel her power ebbing, ever so slightly, draining from her ancient body. It would be only a matter of time before her contribution to their cause became negligible.

She pushed such morbid thoughts aside, focused on the puddle of water. She waved a shrivelled hand riddled with sunspots across its surface. The image blurred, replaced her disillusioned eyes with the strong physique of Jed Ironmonger. He was crouched beneath a tree, his eyes scanning the horizon. He was alone, his animalistic men had either fled or died. It didn't matter. Ironmonger was powerful and had proven tenacious. She shared a half-smile, then twirled a crooked finger, watched as the image shifted so she could see what Ironmonger saw. Vertigo caused her to place a hand next to the puddle for balance, but she steadied herself, blinked once to focus. He was partly shaded by the tree, his bald head visible beneath broad leaves. He was looking across a field of green towards a city shining golden in the morning light. He hadn't moved, then. It was the same as the time before, and the time before that. He was still waiting for the woman he was charged with delivering. He still waited for Kayla Tolsten.

Another failure. Even if Kayla Tolsten left the city and was captured by Ironmonger, it would be months before he could return with his prize. If Ahriman thought his journey here on the new world was going to be swift and rewarding, he was grossly mistaken.

Avra sat back, let her mind detach from the spell of seeing. There was nothing more for her to see here. Numerous times she'd attempted to focus on Kayla Tolsten to learn her whereabouts, but she was either protected via unknown trinkets, or Neema, canny as always, was countering her scrying. Quite possibly it was both.

Avra looked to the puddle of water at her feet. It had frozen within seconds.

What was her purpose now? She looked right and left, saw the abandoned huts and log houses to either side. The remnants of Sanctuary were silent. The survivors of Bastion, so desperate in the early days, had fled into the forest. It had taken time, but they eventually became aware of the Dark Lord's presence and his ominous designs. Countless had died during the first year, erupting in flame so Ahriman could consume their souls. It fed his undying hunger, provided strength to his diseased body. He became more God-like. But at some point, the people began to acknowledge those who were missing. They asked questions, some even looked for answers. First amongst them was Archbishop Treventos, a man Avra believed to be responsible for the people's sudden awakening.

The fear exuded by Ahriman was felt by those who dwelled in the make-shift town below. It became tangible, seeped like blackened treacle into every aspect of their survival. They sensed the change, felt the threat hovering over their souls. And then one day, as Avra hobbled down the rocky track to look for another victim, they were gone. Not a single individual remained. Everyone, from the young to the elderly, had vanished. And their tools and supplies went with them.

Avra had died a little herself when she saw they had fled. Once every ten days she had made the journey from Ahriman's camp to the survivor's town. There she would find a frightened soul, an outcast, or someone alone. She would entice them to follow, use words tinged with power. And then she would offer the individual to her lord once the journey back up the mountain was complete.

She took a deep breath, felt icy air sweep into her lungs. It settled there, felt like cold-dead fingers clawing from the inside. Perhaps she was dying. She had nothing to live for. All her dreams . . . gone, unfulfilled. This place, this world, was not what she envisaged when she summoned her Dark Lord. She already dreaded returning to the mountain; trembled at the prospect of providing him with empty hands.

Only he expected her. And she could not disobey.

It was midday when Avra finally completed the climb. She saw the firepit first, glowing orange still as tiny flames licked at dry timber. The pock-marked caves beyond were dark and sombre, many lined with the carcasses of wild animals. Skeletal trees, devoid of life, stood guard about the encampment, whilst the stench of death permeated her surrounds. It was pungent, cloying, ripe enough - she thought - to form a second skin to drape her body.

A shadow moved to her right. She twisted; knew her lord was waiting before she even saw his ember eyes blazing beneath his cowl.

'What have you found, Avra Creswick?'

She swallowed her fear, diverted her eyes away from his own. 'Nothing of interest, my lord,' she whispered the words, too afraid to say them out loud.

'Expected, at least,' he replied. He moved closer, almost engulfed her with his darkness as he towered over her bent form. 'I have made a decision, witch. I've decided there is little to entice me to stay on this world. I believe it's time to return to the city you call Bastion.'

The words startled her from apathy. Return to Bastion? Could his words be true? Did her lord have the power to reignite the portal connecting the two worlds?

'How will we accomplish such a task, my lord? The workings of the portal are beyond me. Do you have knowledge concerning its operation?'

He moved closer still, more a glide than a step. Silent as always.

'I do not, Avra,' he whispered, 'but there are others approaching who do.'

'Others . . . approaching?'

'Yes. Several men, powerful. One amongst them, Kian of the Nepharii, travels with them. He will open the portal for me when he arrives. He will not be able to refuse my request.'

Avra shook her head. Why would Kian the Nepharii be traveling towards this place? Did he not know of the danger lurking here? And who was travelling with him?

'Who are the others?' she asked, excitement in her voice for the first time in an age. The prospect of returning to Bastion was invigorating.

'They are also Nepharii. I can feel them. They come to ask questions as to why I am here.'

'And what shall you tell them, my lord?'

'Whatever it is they wish to hear. I care not. My strength is growing, but it will grow faster when I set foot back in Bastion. When the time is right, I shall come back for Kayla Tolsten. I am patient, but I will not forget. Her time will come.'

Avra could feel the vitality surging in her body. To walk the streets of Bastion again, to gaze upon stars she could name. To find her purpose, to rule with her lord over the weak and fearful. It was as it should be. It had been a journey of discovery, hardship and longing. But it was about to come to an end.

'How long until they arrive, my lord?'

Ahriman raised a twisted hand from within his black cloak. 'They will be here soon, within days. The talk will be brief. Once the portal is ignited, I'll leave.'

Avra tilted her head to the side. 'What will be our plans when we arrive back in Bastion?'

A dread pause hung in the air. She tried to swallow the lump in her throat, but it refused to budge, felt like some cancerous bulge that grew with each passing second.

'I travel alone, witch. You shall not accompany me any longer. My use for you has waned.'

The words ripped into her body like Hell's bladed chains.

'What am I to do? What can I do to please you?'

'Nothing. I am done with you. In fact, you may leave now . . . of your own accord. Linger longer than I care for, and you will find your body wreathed in flames. The sight of you turns my stomach. Begone!'

Her feet shifted atop the coarse ground, scraping as they turned her about. The spark of renewal had already fled, chased away at frightening pace by the sinister words of her lord. She was no longer required. Her services, her sweet revenge, little more than delusions of grandeur destroyed in a moment she'd never forget. As she walked from the mountain-top camp, silent laughter followed, prodding her forward, pushing her away. Even now, with thoughts of his betrayal simmering into hatred, she could not refuse his command.

Four times on her descent she paused at the edge of the cliff, eager to let it all go. Four times she summoned the strength to walk on. Despite everything she knew and felt, despite all the years she'd dedicated to her cause, it was all for nought. She had nothing. Had been nothing. Perhaps she would die as nothing.

The forest lay below, a blanket of white snow above a shadowed interior. The people of Bastion were somewhere within, surviving as best they could. She knew Archbishop Treventos would be amongst them, leading them. He would always be there to care for his people. Perhaps she could seek them out. Perhaps she could find solace amongst those she once dreamed of ruling.

Or she could find a gnarled tree, one as old as she, and lean against the trunk. She could lie there, alone, and sink into the forest floor, never to be seen again.

The choice was hers. Perhaps, for the first time, she would make the right one.

*

Jarred couldn't remember ever feeling so cold.

He was crouched near a snow-capped boulder, sheltering from the wind whilst the Ven worked with numb fingers to light a fire. Grey clouds drifted overhead, swept onwards by a gale that howled to the heavens. The day, like every other lately, looked to be overcast and grim, the prospect of snowfall high. He couldn't even recall the last time he'd seen the sun.

He clenched stiff fingers, then rubbed his gloved hands together to encourage circulation. The Endless Forest surrounded them, reminding him how small and insignificant he was. One step off the sodden path could see him lost in their twisted confines. Alone, he would not survive for long. Thankfully, he was not alone.

He stepped closer to those hard at work. The Ven were thorough, he noticed, quickly gathering their bundles of sticks and twigs so they could start a fire. Each carried a small collection, gathered during their walk each day. Strips of bark and dried lichen from ancient trees added to the kindling. Sparks formed within moments, protected by hunched bodies and large boulders hemming them in. Smoke and flame followed.

Jarred looked to his right, saw other Ven completing the same routine. A dozen fires sprang to life down the line, providing heat to the hundred Ven who accompanied the Five Kings on their quest.

He could see the Five Kings standing with backs straight as their entourage did their bidding. The cold did not seem to bother them, nor the howling wind. So strange, he thought. They were like nothing he'd ever known. Even Kian seemed a world apart from those he called his brothers. Ik'omi, Shien,

Vega, Ky'elk and Solaii. Immortals all, and arrogant to the core. He feared them, for their power was palpable, their presence nerve-racking, but he refused to worship them as the Ven were inclined to do.

He returned his eyes to the Ven, saw them step back as flames took hold. Jarred moved closer, watched as hands placed larger branches to build the fire. So much of what he experienced on his four-month journey was strange. Their first forty days were spent walking in pleasant sunshine, the days calm, the heat of the sun sublime. Then they reached the mountains to the north, where the trees disappeared, and the grass grew coarse. They spent the next ten days walking along mountain tracks formed by wild beasts, rocks and stones littered about their path. It was tedious, sometimes difficult, yet they strode onwards with a determination he couldn't place.

And then came the wind and the rain. Within days, the snow.

Kian had explained the seasons to him as they retreated from the mountain foothills and crept back into the sheltered forest. It had always been their plan to make haste in the early part of their travels when the weather was clement. But winter was coming, and the forested valley, although frightfully wild, would provide enough shelter. They would survive, for the Ven knew how.

He took it all in. The entire journey was one of learning for the young man. He spent his days walking beside Kian, listening to the intricacies of Ven life, studying their behaviour, savouring everything his Nepharii tutor explained. He learnt of the *ser-ti-ven*, the wild Ven, who first helped his party escape the forest after Kayla gave birth. They were different to the *vos-ti-ven*, those who dwelled in the golden city called Ayoshos. Much like the men and women who lived south of Dervae, he mused. Their skin, eyes and hair were mostly darker in colour. As the Rykedians east of Dervae, he heard, had skin of bronze, black hair and were considerably shorter in stature. The Herkosians to the north were giants in comparison, being six to seven feet tall. And so it was here on Vidae. Different Ven, with their own customs, mannerisms, and style. It was obvious when he thought about it. In fact, he noticed the lack of antlers on the male Ven the first day he set foot in the city. He spoke to Kian concerning their differences. He explained how the *ser-ti-ven* were stronger, more robust, because their lifestyle lacked the comfort of permanent shelter. They hunted and gathered every day, sometimes without reward, whilst the *vos-ti-ven* farmed and traded. The environment, he said, dictated a great deal about who they were and who they were to become. Jarred found the entire discussion enlightening and learnt more about his own world and their people in the process. And it continued every day as he watched the Ven hunt and dress their kill, watched them gather nuts and berries. He learnt how to make deadly weapons, discovered which wood to use for spears and arrows. He learnt to climb trees to look for feathers in abandoned nests. Then he learnt how to fletch.

As the days became shorter and the nights long, he would sit about the campfires and discover the names of beasts, both domesticated and wild. He knew the beasts of burden, called *aurri,* for twenty of them carried their supplies on their venture. Their appearance reminded him of wide-backed goats, for their footing was exceptional, only they were five times larger than any goat he'd ever seen, and their horns twisted down and then swept backwards. Likewise, their coats were different, shaggy all the way to the ground, and a peculiar blue-grey in colour. Many of the wild beasts were taught to him when found, ranging from the countless birds of differing hue and the smaller, scurrying animals that frolicked on grass plains. Of the forest predators, he saw little. The wildcats, known as *serrin,* were never seen, only heard. And the *vhaetin,* which he believed to be a cross between a deer and a giant lizard from what he was told, were thankfully avoided. It had been said a single *vhaetin* could kill a dozen Ven in the blink of an eye. Even if found, no one truly hunted the dangerous beast. It always hunted you.

It had all been so interesting, so informative and rewarding. And now they were at their destination, and winter was waning.

But it was cold, still. It settled in his bones and mingled with the fear already present.

Kian told him countless times about his role once they reached the portal. He was to return to Bastion, at any cost, with information for whoever was in charge. Failing such a venture, he was to find the *Nepharii Uranometria* inside the pyramid and set it free. Such an action would cease the portals operation. It would strand Kian and his friends here, on Vidae, but it would also prevent any more creatures from seeping into Bastion. And if what Kian said was true, it would keep Ahrmian here, where he could be dealt with. Such an outcome was likely, and it would provide Ahriman with no chance of escape. It was dangerous, for so much rested on his young shoulders, but he could do this. It was imperative he did so. And with the survivors of Bastion ahead, he found the difficulty of his task tempered due to having others by his side for the return journey.

He was nervous, though, as he checked the maps Donal had entrusted to him. They were still in the cylinders Kian provided; the parchment secure. He also carried what Kian called a glow-stone: a polished stone that looked like quartz and waxed golden when rubbed vigorously. He would need it once he stepped into the portal, for he would arrive beneath the city of Bastion in the dark confines of a temple not seen by man for thousands of years. It would provide a light, long enough for him to find a way clear. He also wore Ruvin's sword at hip in case he needed to defend himself.

A hand settled on his shoulder. 'Gather your pack, Jarred,' Kian's voice cut through the icy air, 'we go now to see the portal.'

'Already?' he looked into Kian's unusually shaped eyes. 'But we only just arrived. I thought we'd camp the night before walking up the hill.'

'No, Jarred, the Five Kings see no point in delaying their meeting. I will join them, and you will join me. We have spoken of this, Jarred. When I realign the portal, you are to step within as soon as it blooms. Today will be that day. If we delay, we'll need to wait another fifteen days before the portal reconnects with Bastion. If we are fortunate, the rest of the survivors will follow you through. Then the Five Kings and I will deal with the Dark Lord and his witch.'

'Are you sure it will be safe? You said yourself he has considerable power.'

'The Dark Lord does, I agree, but the six of us will be enough to persuade him to pursue another course. Failing that, even though it is against my nature, we will destroy him.

'That is why I wish you to be gone as soon as possible. The ramifications of a battle between us will be considerable. It is best you do not loiter.'

Jarred did as he was asked, picked up his pack with its parcels of food, tools and trinkets and, of course, his maps. If what Kian said was true, he was on his way back to Bastion. Possibly within hours.

He shouldered his pack, faced the hill he still had to climb. Then he cast a final look at the Ven as they went about their tasks. 'I'm ready,' he said, turning towards the hill. 'Let's do this.'

Kian patted him on the back, then motioned to his brothers. The Five Kings joined them as they began their walk. Ik'omi strode at the front of their procession, with his broad shoulders and golden hair, for he was the eldest. The rest followed. Shien with his long black braid, Vega with his twin swords, Ky'elk with his unruly swagger and Solaii with a look of disdain. Jarred walked by Kian's side, silent – he hoped - like the *vhaetin* when hunting prey. An hour later, they stood within a deserted village, vacant huts and log houses already succumbing to the encroaching forest.

'Where are the people?' Jarred couldn't stop himself from spinning around. Gaping doorways led into empty abodes, dank and silent and completely bare. The wood was rotting from excessive moisture, the unseasoned timber warped or split. There was nothing to see, little to discover. Not a sound could be heard other than the constant drip of water from hanging lichen.

Kian was equally perplexed, his brows knotted as he contemplated the worst.

'You don't think the Dark Lord has killed them all, do you?' Jarred whispered words laced with fear. His body began to tremble, visibly shaking. The prospect of returning through the portal, alone, was daunting.

'I do not know, Jarred,' Kian looked to the Five Kings. Ik'omi, with eyes suddenly alert and watchful, gave him a nod.

Kian raced towards the tiled dais that rested on a small rise, knelt onto the snow-covered ground. His gloved hand swept across a section of stone before he lifted a square piece and placed it to the side. For ten heartbeats he worked with nimble fingers, twisting and probing, before he returned the stone and stood to his feet. 'It is done,' his voice cut through the silence. 'Now we need only wait.' Kian looked to the sky to seek the sun. It was obscured by thick clouds, but he seemed content with his finding. 'We'll not need to wait for long.'

Jarred willed his legs to move, walked towards the Nepharii he called friend and mentor. 'I'm afraid, Kian, more than ever before.'

'I know, Jarred. Just remember what we planned.' Kian looked over his shoulder. 'Here, stand beneath this overhang, and keep to the shadow.' Kian walked towards an abandoned hut shrouded in gloom. It was sixty feet from the dais. Grey lichen hung from rotting timbers, thick strands glistening with frost. As Jarred stood beneath as told, Kian bent low to trace a circle about his position. 'Stand within this circle, Jarred,' he said, 'and do not leave it until the portal blooms. When it does, run into it as fast as able. When you arrive in Bastion, do the same. Run for the surface, hide, then find your way to those in command. If you cannot find them, seek the pyramid. You can do this. I have trained you well, and you have learnt accordingly.'

Jarred felt Kian push the cowl of his cloak back from his brow. He ruffled his long hair, then pulled him into an embrace. 'Stay safe, Jarred. Until we meet again.'

A tear slipped down his cheek as Kian walked to stand with his five brothers. They appeared to be impatient, almost agitated. As Kian reached their side, Ik'omi pointed a hand towards the mountain. 'He comes,' he said.

A tingle raced down Jarred's spine; his stomach sank low. The hairs on his arms and neck stood on end. He glanced towards a section of trees, old and knotted. There were no leaves, their branches blackened by fire. A shape moved within, almost unseen. A darkness detached itself and stepped onto level ground.

A scream caught in Jarred's throat. He found he couldn't breathe.

Ahriman, the Dark Lord, walked towards Kian and the Five Kings.

Silence walked with him.

The desire to look away was fierce. Yet Jarred felt compelled to watch his advance, to see the Dark Lord and know his power. A wave, endlessly crashing against his sanity, pounded into his thoughts and emotions. He could feel his own insignificance. Understood how inferior he was to the Dark Lord. He knew there was no escape. If the Dark Lord wished it to be so, he would die where he stood. Even though he was hiding in the shadow, he would find him and make him suffer.

Ahriman reached a spot ten feet from Kian and the Five Kings. Then he spoke with a voice loud as thunder and equally unnerving.

'Finally!' he cast his arms out wide and Jarred swore the overcast day turned to night. There was no sun, perhaps there never was one. There was only darkness surrounded by shadow. And in its midst was pain.

'You've come, as I knew you would,' Ahriman's voice cut like a blade. Jarred tried to cover his ears, but his arms failed to move.

'We have arrived,' Ik'omi took a single step forward. Even the eldest king looked pale as he stood opposite Ahriman, his golden hair lacking shine.

'You didn't believe I was here, did you?'

Ik'omi cocked his head to the side, looked at Kian. 'We did not,' he said, turning his attention back to Ahriman. 'Kian explained what occurred, we did not believe him. Now we do.'

The cold seeped into Jarred's motionless body. The words of Ahriman chilled him further. He didn't know if he could stand within his circle any longer. He needed to move his body, to stretch his arms and legs before they became numb. He focused on the dais. It rested between he and the Dark Lord, a fact he only now realised was deliberate. When the portal bloomed into life, Kian had known he would have a clear path to run. He hoped it would be soon. Prayed it would be so.

'Are you here to stop me?' Ahriman's voice boomed once more.

Silence followed. Ik'omi seemed to contemplate the question for considerable time. He shared a moment looking at his brother-kings. 'We are not here to stop you, Ahriman.'

A spark appeared at the centre of the dais, an emerald-green swirl of energy that twined like a flame, reaching higher with each second.

'So wise of you, Ik'omi,' Ahriman's voice stole his attention. 'You could not stop me if you tried, but you knew that already. Didn't you, brother?'

Jarred almost stopped breathing. Brother? What was he saying?

'It is true,' Ik'omi replied. 'We can sense your growth, but we do not understand it. We know your path is not ours, but it is also not here. You must return from where you came.'

The emerald flame swelled to encompass the dais, bulging outward as it continued to swirl higher. Shining motes of jade sparkled within, reflecting what little light remined. It was almost complete.

'It is where I wish to be,' Ahriman replied. 'I am done with your world for now, but I will return to claim the woman known as Kayla Tolsten.'

'You will not!' Kian growled, stepping closer. Jarred could hardly see him, for the portal was expanding rapidly, a spinning vortex of green light.

'Ah, Kian, so much younger than the rest of us. Is that the defiance of a child I see in your eyes?'

'I am no child, Ahriman, and you should be dead!'

'Yes, I should be. First to be born, first to die, is that not what they say?

A gasp forced Jarred's mouth open. It was true. Ahriman was their brother. He was Nepharii.

'I'll not let you return if destruction is your goal,' Kian bristled. 'You need to find another cause, seek a greater path.'

'If you stand against me, Kian, I will kill you.'

'This was never our way!'

'But it has become my way. I have grown, discovered pleasure and pain only dreamed about. If you step aside, Kian, I will teach you one day. I'll teach all of you.'

The portal reached its height of ten feet, then spun into itself to create an ellipsoid of pure green energy. Knowing Ahriman's intention was to also return to Bastion, Jarred dove deep to rouse his flagging courage and stepped out of his circle. His first step was difficult, for his legs felt encased in ice, but his next was more fluid. With a beating heart he began to run across sixty feet of frozen ground, fear driving him forward.

He leapt up the final steps, his eyes aware of the multicoloured tiles. He hoped Kian could stall Ahriman long enough for him to find an exit once he passed through. He would need time. He would need to flee as fast as able.

As he reached the portal, Jarred paused and sought out Kian, found him standing between he and the Dark Lord. The Nepharii sensed his look, turned to meet his eyes.

Tears streamed down Kian's face. 'Go, Jarred,' he yelled. 'Run!'

CHAPTER NINETEEN

Ahriman could see the fear in his brother's eyes.

He wondered if they had ever experienced such an emotion before. True fear: the sense of knowing your entire existence is at peril. He doubted it. They had never suffered as he had. They had never died and been reborn. What did they know of fear? What did they know of life? Only once it had been taken from you could you appreciate that which you had lost. He spat to the side, felt the anger brewing inside his body, churning with an intensity that sought to be released. He'd seen the young man plunge into the portal, saw him share a look with Kian. What game was the young Nepharii playing?

'You still seek to defy me!' he bellowed, eyes blazing with fury.

'Everything you represent is flawed!' Kian raged back. 'You died, thousands of years ago. You had your time. This is not our way!'

A smile creased the corner of his mouth. It mattered not if a child paved his way back into Bastion. He would be a herald of doom, nothing more. What harm could one so young be to a Lord of Darkness?

Ahriman felt his mouth twist into a smile. 'But I've returned, Kian, stronger than before. And I will continue to grow. You and your brothers cannot stop what I have become. You should not feel obliged to stand against me.'

'We will do everything we can to stop you, Ahriman. I'm not sure why you would believe otherwise.'

The smile Ahriman shared grew larger, stretching across his mouth until he bared his perfectly arranged teeth. He looked towards the Five Kings standing to his right, Kian unaware of their aloof manner.

'You will stand against me, Kian, but who will stand with you?'

The fear in Kian's eyes magnified as realization sank in. His five brothers had visibly separated themselves from his side, stepping back as the confronting words escalated. They appeared to have made a decision of their own, albeit one Kian was not privy to.

Kian, Guardian of Vidae, stood alone.

Ahriman flexed his hands. 'You are not strong enough to oppose me, brother, and I wish to return to Bastion. Step aside.'

Desperation flooded Kian's features. There was a look of longing as he spun towards his kin. 'Why?' he asked, his voice barely above a whisper.

'He does not belong here, Kian,' replied Ik'omi. 'We wish him gone. This world belongs to us.'

'But he seeks to destroy it. How can you let him walk such a path? We are not gods!'

'Are we not?' Ik'omi spread his hands wide. 'To the people of this world we are exactly that. We have power, greater than any other being on this world. We are immortal. Even you, the youngest of us here, have lived more than ten thousand years. Why should we not be considered as gods?'

'You are acting out a role, Ik'omi. Our purpose is to observe, nurture and guide. Nothing more. It has always been our way. If you pursue a path of power, how are you any different to Ahriman and his volatile nature?'

Ahriman continued to smile. The conflict swarming within his brothers was intoxicating.

Ik'omi took a step towards Kian, raised a fist. 'You need to step aside, Kian. Ahriman does not belong here. This world belongs to us!'

'You didn't answer my question,' Kian growled. 'How are you any different?'

'We are not! It is our right to rule, and Ahriman's right to conquer if he chooses. This is now our way. Everything we have learnt over the centuries has led to this.'

Ahriman locked eyes with Ik'omi, shared a nod of approval. Of course, he also knew the Five Kings feared his presence. The longer he remained on their world, the more dangerous he'd become. If he lingered, eventually, the world would become his. Ik'omi and his brothers knew this. It was the only reason they supported his desire to leave.

Kian spun away from the Five Kings. He knew he couldn't persuade them any further. Anger simmered in his eyes, filtered throughout his body as his fingers twitched near the blades sheathed at his hip. For a moment, Ahriman wondered if Kian had the nerve to draw his weapons and seek to strike him down.

'You must cease this madness,' Kian spat words in his direction. 'You have no right to kill innocent people for gain. It goes against the natural order.'

'But I am not the natural order,' Ahriman took a step closer. Green energy pulsed and swirled only ten feet away, directly behind the young immortal. 'I am the Lord of Chaos, brother. I choose my own path. Step aside.'

'I will not!'

'Then you will die!' Ahriman lifted his palms face up, drawing energy from the earth. Heat began to filter from the icy ground, causing meltwater to bubble and steam beneath Kian's feet.

'Step away, Kian,' Ik'omi beckoned. 'Let him pass, then you can close the portal. He will never return, and you can stand by our side. Become the sixth Nepharii king of Ayoshos. Rule with us, brother.'

The torment behind Kian's eyes was raw. Ahriman could see the conflict, could almost feel the angst coursing through his veins. The young Nepharii mumbled words, spat vehemently to the side. Incredible heat continued to build.

'Step aside, Kian!' all five brothers called to him at once. 'Let him pass.'

A yell of pain escaped Kian's lips as he stepped away from the scorched earth. Ik'omi reached out and pulled him close.

Ahriman allowed the heat to dissipate with a thought, leaving a dirty puddle of water still steaming into cold air.

'It is done,' Ahriman stepped towards the portal. He could feel the power. One step and he would return to Bastion.

As it should be, he thought. It had been a mistake to leave the warring city in the first place. His growth would have come faster if he'd remained, but the witch had muddled his motivation and desire. Now she was merely an irrelevant memory. One he could dispense with as he moved forward alone.

He cast his gaze over the swirling, emerald ellipsoid. A single step was all he needed. It had been a city of death when he left, confusion and anger riddled with desperation causing chaos. If the situation had calmed in his absence, he would reignite the flames of hatred in the days to come. Death and destruction would accelerate his rise to power. And this time, there would be no mistakes.

He shared a final look with his Nepharii brothers. Kian stood with head down, looking at the ground beneath his feet as if there was something of interest to be found. The kings said nothing.

'One day,' Ahriman said, a smile on his face, 'I will find a way to return. When I do, you will have a choice. You will bow before me . . . or you will die!'

He took his single step, felt the energy engulf his body.

Then he was gone.

*

Kian slumped to his knees as Ahriman stepped into the portal and disappeared.

With the Dark Lord's departure came a return of nature's sounds. The howl of winter winds, the sigh of snow slipping off laden branches. And a return of the light, he mused, looking to the distant sky. It was overcast and incredibly cold, snow clouds rolling over the mountains to the north. But the sun had not yet set to the west. They had less than an hour of light, but it would be enough to return to the Ven camp.

Ik'omi reached out a hand and pulled him back to his feet. 'How do you fare, Kian?'

Kian met the elder king's eyes. He looked deeply, searching for the spark of life he knew once existed in his brother. It was absent, lost, perhaps irretrievable. There was no compassion left in his soul. No laughter to be found. Just an empty void.

He shrugged the hand off his elbow. Ik'omi's concern was not relevant right now. His only concern was Jarred. The young man had fled as ordered, making his way to Bastion, but Ahriman followed. Now he thought back to their conversation, hoped he'd stalled the Dark Lord long enough for Jarred to make his escape. He had to believe the lad was resourceful enough. Prayed he'd taught him well.

'Come, Kian,' Ik'omi interrupted his thoughts. 'It is time to disengage the portal. Then you can join us back at camp.' He looked over his shoulder at the rocky path leading down the hill, spoke to the encroaching night. 'Tomorrow, we leave for Ayoshos. If you wish, you may stand with us as the sixth king. This I promise.'

Kian almost laughed at Ik'omi's absurdity. He had no desire to become the sixth king. Had never even contemplated such a role. He had always been a Guardian of Vidae; a protector. Not just a protector of the portal and its operation, but a protector of the world and the life it harboured. Sitting on a throne before a subjugated people was not how he envisaged spending his life.

He walked to the dais and the swirling portal. An emerald glow bathed multi-coloured tiles as he knelt and removed a square stone. Like he did previously, he tinkered with the mechanism that controlled the portal's operation, and within ten heartbeats the spinning ellipsoid winked out of existence. The portal was closed, the path to Bastion barred.

'It is done,' he said, standing to his full height. He looked at his brothers. They still appeared resplendent in their finery, as if they were going for an afternoon stroll through palace grounds.

'Then join us, Kian,' said Ik'omi, 'and let us forget this ever occurred.'

Kian shook his head. How could they forget? Why would they choose to forget? 'I'll return to Ayoshos with you,' he replied, 'to gather those I delivered from the other world. I'll lead them here, and we will step back into Bastion.'

He saw the Five Kings bristle at his words. They certainly didn't enjoy being told of plans they hadn't devised themselves.

'Those you delivered stay where they are, Kian,' Ik'omi glared, defiantly, so it seemed. 'I'll not risk having the portal reopened.'

'You do not own them, Ik'omi. They have a life of their own. They do not wish to stay at your palace.'

'We make the choices here; it is our right.'

'And how long do you propose to keep them locked away?'

'For as long as we desire, Kian. Have you not grasped the full extent of our power? Do you not realise the reality of this world is shaped by us?'

Five sets of eyes stared balefully at his own. He couldn't win here. They were united in their ignorance. He looked over their shoulders to the gloomy forest beyond. Winter was waning, but this far north, the cold winds would blow for some time to come. It would be a harsh environment to embrace, but he knew he'd survive. He'd been doing so for centuries.

'Then I shall not accompany you back to Ayoshos,' he said as calmly as he could. 'I will seek out the *ser-ti-ven*: those who dwell in the forest and find my own way. The portal I shall leave alone, until I decide otherwise. When the time is right, I will come for the people I delivered. You will not be able to stop me.'

Ik'omi's face became perplexed, twisted as he thought about the words he'd heard. There was a bewildered look about him so out of place on the king.

'You speak as one vested with power you choose not to share,' Ik'omi replied. Ky'elk and Solaii were already moving their hands to their weapons. They appeared equally unimpressed with what he had to say. Eyes narrowed as fingers curled about hilts.

'I speak the truth,' Kian responded. 'You are not aware of what is transpiring here. You have lost your way, and in doing so, have lost your ability to read what is before you.'

'Liar!' the fury in Ik'omi's voice would have levelled a lesser being, but Kian kept his feet and held his ground. But the outrage fuelled a need in the Five Kings. They drew their swords as one, let them breathe icy air.

It was as he feared and what he believed. From what he had witnessed, they were regressing into something inferior to their true state of being. Like Ahriman, they had fallen from lofty heights. What they had descended to, he was only now discovering.

'I am no liar, Ik'omi. I am Kian, Guardian of Vidae. I am Nepharii.' He raised his voice to the approaching night, felt the power surge within him. 'From the skies we came, long ago, to observe and nurture, to teach and be taught. We were Nepharii: those who came from the clouds.

'But you,' he pointed a hand at the Five Kings, 'have lost your way. You no longer have purpose. You have fallen. You are no longer Nepharii.'

'You do not know what it is you say!' Ik'omi yelled.

'I do know. You have changed, and not for the better. Now, you are Nephilim!'

The word hit the kings like a thunderbolt.

They stood there; their faces contorted to resemble masks of pain. Nephilim, he called them. Those who had fallen.

'You will die for your poor choice of words, Kian!'

'No, I will not. You have no power over me. I will walk from this place and seep into the forest. If you wish to be fortunate, you will release the men and women I delivered, and never see me again. If you choose to be obstinate, you will die.

'For an immortal, such a prospect is dire.'

He could see their hands tightly gripped about their weapons. The blades were expertly fashioned, and he knew from centuries past they knew how to employ them. If they attacked, he would not be able to stand against them for long. But his words carried the seeds of doubt for the Five Kings.

Never had they been spoken to in such a manner. They were on the edge of losing control, but they were also unaccustomed to having so many emotions sweep through their bodies.

In the end, it was confusion that kept their hands at bay.

'I will leave you here and be on my way,' Kian kept his eyes on Ik'omi as he walked to his right, the dark forest his destination. The silvered blades began to lose their shine as the sun slipped behind a mountain ridge. Shadows grew quickly.

He reached the closest tree, a gnarled specimen trailing lichen and icicles, blanketed in snow. He knew the Five Kings watched him, but they did not follow.

Kian looked over his shoulder. 'If we ever meet again, your lives will be forfeit,' the words eased out of his mouth with a life of their own. 'Now that you are Nephilim, you are no longer my brothers.'

Then, like Ahriman, he stepped away from the Five Kings and was gone.

*

Jarred paused to catch his breath.

He'd been running for some time, running ever since he stepped away from the swirling portal of green energy. How long he could not say. Possibly an hour. Maybe longer.

He let the dank air expand his chest, spared a look at the glow-stone held tight in his fist. He'd rubbed it with vigour the moment he arrived, watched the light intensify and bathe his surroundings. Kian described them well, a circular chamber marked with faded artwork, a dark hole in the wall his only egress. Knowing he couldn't linger, he'd leapt through the hole and began to run, his stone lighting the way.

Endless corridors and narrow, winding pathways lay in wait, most ankle-deep in fetid water and . . . other things. He'd felt the shift of slithering creatures against his boots on more than one occasion and spied countless rats scurrying before his golden sphere of light. They made his heart skip a beat each time he saw them, brown and black fur moving with frightening pace, sometimes a mere inch from his nose as they traversed ridges in the stonework. But the fear they evoked paled compared to the thought of Ahriman striding behind him. He didn't know if the Dark Lord was following him. Couldn't even know if he'd stepped into the circular chamber, just like he had. But he could feel the hairs on his neck standing on end. And he could feel the thud of his heart beating inside his chest, urging him to run faster, pleading with him to find a way out of the labyrinth that was Bastion's Undercity.

He took another deep breath, craned his neck to the side to ease a tightness. At some point he hoped to find a ladder - or a staircase - that would lead him to the surface. Even a door would raise his spirit, provided he could open it. He shook his head, remembered not to make any unnecessary noises. Sound travelled easily in the corridors. Those hunting in the dark would be alerted in quick fashion. He hoped there weren't any Deios nearby.

His legs began to shake. Uncontrollably. Why did he think of the Deios? A whimper eased past his lips as he placed a hand on the stone wall to brace himself. He shifted the pack on his back, slid a finger beneath the strap biting into his shoulder. His heart rate quickened, sweat beaded on his forehead. He inhaled several times, short and shallow, seeking to calm his nerves. He'd never felt so alone.

Never felt so afraid.

He looked to the stone in his hand, realised as he did so that he was on his knees. Water lapped almost to his waist. The stone in his hand was an inch from being submerged. Darkness crowded his senses, crept closer every second. The whimper became a sob, tears mingled with his sweat.

Something long and slimy slipped between his legs.

He scurried forward, crawling with one hand aloft to light the way. He couldn't tell how far he travelled before he found the ladder, but he was exhausted, spent, beyond tired when he did so. The cold winds of Vidae seemed so long ago.

The stone was pale in his hand, the smallest hint of a flicker all that remained. He could see five feet ahead of him at best. And five feet above. He lifted weeping eyes, saw the rust-stained ladder built into a wall. He couldn't see where it led, or how far he would have to climb, but he didn't hesitate. With one hand he began to ascend, his fading stone held tight in the other. His booted feet hit the rungs with a squelch, water dripped from his clothes. But he didn't mind, never gave it a thought. All he saw was a possible way out.

At least he hoped it was a way out.

The muscles in his shoulders burned and his neck continued to be a discomfit, but the ladder was sturdy, despite its appearance. So he climbed, and climbed further, until he moved past the curved ceiling and up into what he could only assume was a chimney. It was here the ladder ceased to be. Now he was surrounded by a circular wall, black as a raven sitting in the dark and slick with muck. Protruding stones provided a grip, and the stench, when he finally noticed, was ripe enough for him to hold his breath. But he climbed ever upward, even when his glow stone expired, feeling his way with grimy fingers and a grimace plastered across his face. Eventually, he felt a wooden board, also circular, lying directly above his head.

He paused for a moment and inhaled, hoping he could trick the stench from entering his lungs by doing it quickly. It didn't work, and he almost gagged and fell from his perch. But somehow his fingers, all slick with slime, managed to grip a stone and hold tight. Then he took a moment and tried to imagine how far he'd climbed, but without his vision, he couldn't tell for certain. It was a long way, though, further than he thought possible. Still, with his patience lost and his lungs burning, he heaved against the wooden board and was quite surprised when it lifted with ease.

If he'd been a heavy man, he swore he wouldn't have been able to squeeze past the opening he'd found. The rim was made of stone, like the wall, and the thought of his body all grimy from the chimney's soot was at the forefront of his mind. But it wasn't an afternoon breeze that touched his clammy skin when he crawled out into the open as expected. Nor was he sitting high above the city on a tiled roof, bathing in the sun. He was in a room, dark as the sewers, with flies buzzing within earshot. And the stench was horrendous. In fact, it was possibly worse.

And then he realised where he was.

Bile flew from his mouth to strike the cold stone floor. He retched and heaved and retched some more. The smell clung to him, smothered him, seeped down his throat every time he vomited. And then he'd vomit again, and again, until his insides were raw and his stomach was empty.

At some point he began to stir back into life. He lifted his aching body, one limb at a time, and found a wall with which to balance himself. Then he moved his hands across its surface, seeking a door so he could leave the privy chamber he'd unfortunately discovered. Because that was where he was, he was certain. He'd climbed out of the sewer and straight up the shitter inside some bastard's house.

Jarred moved forward, but he'd crawled no more than three feet when his knee bumped into something soft. He paused, held his breath and attempted to listen, only his heart continued to beat rapidly. He reached out with a hand, slowly, touched heavy cloth. His other hand followed. There was something here, yet it was heavy enough that he had trouble moving it. His hand followed the curve he felt, then touched something cold.

It was someone's face.

Jarred scampered back on all fours, thudded into the stone privy. Pain flared in his shoulder as his backpack struck a wall and his sword wedged into his ribs, but the thought of a dead body lying inches from his face was more startling. He now knew where the horrendous smell was emanating from, wished for a moment he'd never climbed the ladder in the first place.

He sat for only a few heartbeats before he set out in the opposite direction, following the wall until he could find a door. It didn't take long, and he was thankful the handle was just as easily found. It opened with a gentle push, but the light he hoped to find on the other side was absent.

His eyes adjusted to the gloom, and he saw he was at the far end of a small corridor. Before him sat half-a-dozen more wooden doors, all leading to what he knew were called long drops: or shitters, as those on the docks named them. He still couldn't believe he'd climbed out of one.

A deep breath eased his fears and he moved towards a steel embossed door at the end of the corridor. He opened it, found it led him into an open hall where large stained-glassed windows let starlight shine from above. Night had fallen outside, but as he moved to the window and gazed at the sky, he realized he was indeed back in Bastion, for he could make out the constellation of the Harper resting on the horizon, flanked by the Graceful Swan.

'I'm back,' he said to himself, for he knew he was alone, 'but where exactly am I?'

He looked about the hall, but in the dark, he could see little. There were no fires lit in the hearths at either end, although several large tables with bench seating did suggest he was in an eating hall, possibly an abandoned tavern. There were three closed doors across the room, but he couldn't hear any noise coming from behind them. Standing where he was, dripping in filth and smelling like the sewer, he decided he would need to search around, find a well outside so he could wash himself, and hopefully find a wardrobe inside where he could change into some clean clothes. It wasn't overly cold when he thought about it, nothing like the icy winds and snow back on Vidae. There was a gentle heat in the air, like a summer's night. Knowing he wasn't about to freeze to the core, he decided to find a well and wash himself first, for the thought of searching the establishment in his current state was not an option.

The first door he opened led to a kitchen, lined with stone benches and a hearth for cooking and another for baking. Another door at the rear led outside, a stone well positioned ten feet away. A bucket sat with rope attached, waiting for him, so it appeared. He dropped it down into darkened depths, heard the splash as it hit water. With tired arms he twirled the lever, lifting the full bucket so he could place it on the ground. Next, he unshouldered his pack then peeled off his grimy clothes and threw them to the side. He would burn them, or bury them, he wasn't quite sure which, yet. Then, standing naked under familiar stars, he upended the bucket of water over his head and braced for the cold.

It was invigorating, although he felt it was more cleansing, if the truth was told. The shivers racing through his body were welcomed, the grime washing from his hands, arms and face was delightful. And his hair, so long and blonde, was once again clean of sewer muck. He felt like a new man, newly birthed into the world, still naked and innocent.

He thought walking about the building to dry off would be a good idea before stepping back inside. There was a large stone wall wrapping itself around the establishment for as far as he could see, and as far as he could tell, no sounds were forthcoming from close by. He was still alone. A short walk to learn about his surroundings would be ideal.

Casual, quiet steps with bare feet took him to the edge of the rear kitchen. He peered about the corner, saw an overturned wagon with a broken wheel. A handful of hessian bags lay on the ground, their contents - an assortment of fruit - blackened with rot. They'd been sitting here for some time, untouched.

He glanced across the yard. Another building sat opposite, the large wall working its way behind it. It was an enclosed area, well protected. The walls were fifty feet high, if he were to guess. A portion of the wall had crumbled inwards, a wedge of stone lying at its base. Where was he?

He lifted his eyes and spun about in a circle. There she was. The tower he hoped to see. Tall and circular, once with an observatory nestled at its peak. Now it was broken, with some bricks missing and long, dangerous cracks visible even in the poor light. But it was still standing. It would provide a great vantage for his young eyes once daylight arrived. Like he did on the *Lioness* for Ruvin Ciricello, when he climbed the crow's nest and scouted for activity on the high seas, he would do the same here. He would climb the staircase inside the tower and search the city for signs of his people. Hopefully, he would learn something of importance when he did so. Perhaps he could be reunited with men he knew.

But for now, he was pleased, for he knew where he was. He was at Irongate, once a lookout tower for a fledgling city, now home to the Brotherhood of One.

And if Elder Cappitus wasn't dead, like Neema and Kian feared, then he might be here. He could be in his tower, looking out at the night, even now peering with interest down at the young man standing in the courtyard.

A naked man, Jarred realised.

Hasty steps returned him to the kitchen, an overwhelming urge to find some clothes his only thought.

CHAPTER TWENTY

They'd been hiding for four days.

Ra'tor looked over his shoulder, saw Isabelle curled up in the corner of a couch, asleep for the moment. A soft blanket covered her bare arms and feet, a cushion beneath her head. He sat beside a window, as Isabelle called it, that overlooked a square courtyard lined with cobblestones. The shelter they hid in was once a merchant's house, four levels of comfortable rooms above ground, with another, called a cellar, below ground. They were both currently on the third level, where they'd kept hidden since they fled the chapel. He was pleased the shelter provided protection from prying eyes and nocturnal hunters. He was even more excited to find the cellar provided food in the form of bottled goods and preserves.

And salted herring.

Ra'tor had swooned with anticipation when he cracked the first wax seal covering a bottle. The salty aroma, so unique to this world, caused his mouth to salivate and his nerves to fire. He devoured three bottles of the dried fish the moment they found them. Thankfully, and much to his delight, there were crates brimming with the delicacy. Enough, he mused, to satisfy his needs for many days to come.

And yet he couldn't know how many days they would remain in the merchant's house. The pyramid was visible in the distance, enticing him, so he believed, only the streets were crawling with hunters. If he could find a clear path to his brethren, he would leave in an instant. Yet he needed to feel confident he could protect Isabelle from the dangers outside if they left their shelter. And the paths in the city were many, twisting and turning, accompanied by flights of steps, bridges, and tunnels. Even if he left, he'd be lost within moments.

He shared a frown with the approaching night, pushed thoughts of winding paths aside. Below sat a patchwork of dusty stones, easily spied from his vantage. Isabelle had called it a cobblestoned square, a place she said was used for market stalls and festivals. He wasn't sure he understood her meaning, but it appeared to be a place for locals to gather. Four main pathways provided access to the area, whilst four smaller paths, or lanes, were positioned at each of the corners, also providing entry. With Isabelle asleep, he kept watch, for he knew they couldn't become complacent. Their flight from the chapel had seen him carry Isabelle on his back as he ran down darkened paths. He remained committed to protecting his angel from harm. The rear door to their current shelter had been barricaded with a heavy wooden table, and the main entrance was likewise barred with timber shelving. He vowed nothing would gain entry whilst he kept watch.

Only the sun setting beneath heavy clouds invited darkness to arrive quickly.

His furrowed brow deepened. Ever since they found the shelter in the dark and scampered within, he'd sat at this very window to watch shadowed creatures traversing the night. He hoped to see his own Deios hunting in the process, but so far, they remained absent.

Others filled the void, though, more than he cared for.

He saw Aquilans on numerous occasions. They would appear from the shadows, tall and feathered, moving with intent as they clicked words to each other. And he could see slivers of shiny steel gripped with delicate fingers, always ready for a confrontation. He didn't know who they hunted at first, but they appeared eager and willing, looked to have purpose. After an evening of observation and some silent contemplation, it didn't take him long to realise he and his angel were most likely their prey.

But it was not only Aquilans who stalked amongst the shelters. Rangy hunters covered in fur, like those he saw on the cold, white world, had arrived in number. They eased from the shadows in packs, sniffing the night air, issuing guttural sounds. Then they moved on, loping with easy strides, tall yet with a sense of primal strength evident in their gait. They were wolfen creatures, the same as the statue he thought he saw on the first day - after the battle before the pyramid. True hunters.

266

Responsible for the deaths of his own Deios on the world that took your breath away. Not to be feared, for he feared no one, but to be respected. When the time was right, he would deal with them in his own way. With his Deios beside him, perhaps, eager for a kill.

Such thoughts kept him sane. To be able to hunt, to provide and protect, to have purpose. Such things were important, especially to the Deios. Despite his current predicament, he would adhere to his craft and the teachings he'd been taught. At the forefront of a hunter's lesson was the ability to adapt to any situation. He would adapt, he always had. And those who adapted well lived to tell the tale.

He peered down at the vacant square made of stone. Lengthening shadows swept without hinderance as he flexed a clawed hand and cast a quick glance at Isabelle as she slept. Satisfied she was comfortable and content, he returned his gaze to the outside world. With eyes accustomed to peering in the dark, he narrowed his vision to the pathways entering the courtyard, searching for any sign of movement.

Then he waited, patiently, like the hunter he was.

The single moon, a crescent of silver, had crept more than a hand's width above the surrounding rooftops to pierce the clouded sky when the convergence began.

He blinked twice as he swivelled his head from side-to-side. A pack of wolfen creatures had crept from one pathway, silently - as usual - whilst a group of Aquilans, six in number, materialized from the opposite direction. It took a second for the hunters to acknowledge each other, before clicks and snarls broke the night's silence.

A surge of blood pumped through Ra'tor's veins as he moved closer to the window ledge, clawed hands pressing hard against the wooden panelling. He could hear the wolfen creatures sniffing the air as they walked further into the courtyard, branching out to give each other space. They wore an assortment of robes and kilts, similar to his own, with thick hide belts supporting sheathed blades. As the Aquilans shifted closer, clicking to each other whilst brandishing their silver weapons, the wolfen creatures drew their own steel: hunting knives a foot in length, curved like the crescent moon that shined above.

Bristling fur was matched by ruffled feathers as the two parties circled inwards. Ra'tor could smell the battle to come. Could almost feel their quickened heartbeats. One swift motion, one careless step, would be the only signal needed.

It came with a sound, a short howl to the night.

And blood began to flow.

The bite of blades into flesh and the ripping of claws against skin began with a flurry. Blood scattered like dew on a cold night, sprinkling across cobblestones in earnest as the fight was joined. The hunters swayed and side-stepped, plunged and danced amongst grunts of exertion and cries of pain. It was fierce and brutal, both sides striking with a force forged in hatred. There was no hesitation, only a lust to see the others vanquished. The two races had obviously met before, and the meeting had not been beneficial.

Within moments the fighting was reduced to five. Three wolfen creatures against two Aquilans, and one of them severely wounded. A momentary pause ensued as they measured each other. There would be only one victor, and everyone knew who it would be. A smile crept into the eyes of the largest wolfen, a black-haired specimen standing six-and-a-half feet tall. He pushed his huge shoulders back whilst gripping a hunting knife in each hand. It was almost over.

A flash of silver arced through the night, thudding into the chest of an Aquilan. Feathers flew before another flash, this one striking the lead wolfen in the neck. Confusion led the survivors to seek the attack, only for half-a-dozen shiny hatchets to strike from the darkness, felling those in the courtyard within a heartbeat. Aquilan and wolfen fell together, hitting the stones beneath their feet in an instant.

The howls of pain subsided as Deios entered the bloody arena to slit the throats of those not quite dead. Ra'tor was about to shout to his brood when he heard a noise from behind. He spun to see Isabelle sitting upright, her eyes wide with fear as she clutched a blanket to her chin. He motioned with a finger pressed against his lips, a signal to remain silent shared by both her kind and his. Satisfied she'd make no more sounds, he returned his vision to the carnage below, eager to acknowledge his brethren.

But they were already gone.

He spat a Deiosian curse, swept his gaze to each of the pathways, seeking a sign of their whereabouts. They had struck with skill from the cover of darkness and disappeared just as quickly. He couldn't see them, nor could he smell them over the stench of death.

'What is happening?' Isabelle whispered from the rear.

He waved her question away. She obviously understood the meaning of his gesture, for she remained silent.

Ra'tor calmed his breathing, sought out the corpses below. The hatchets were gone, he noticed, just like his Deios. They'd been retrieved from the fallen, their task complete. It had been a successful hunt. Only his brood had not taken time to drink the blood of their victims, a custom practiced since the *Beyond*.

He wondered why.

Perhaps the hunt had only just begun, he mused, and there were others in the vicinity. Perhaps the Aquilans and the wolfen were not the only hunters in the night.

He longed to leave his vantage inside the shelter, to feel the wind on his scales, to smell the blood spilt on stone. He felt an urge to grip his cleaver and swing it with vigour. Isabelle would be safe inside, wrapped in her blanket. He would be absent for a short time, long enough to search for tracks left by his Deios. She would be in no danger.

He gripped the window ledge so tight he heard it crack. It brought his attention back to the room, back to the small angel huddling in fear behind him. He looked over his shoulder to find his Isabelle.

Wide eyes, glistening with tears, stared back at him.

He would not leave her. Not ever.

He was about to rise from his position and stride to her side when he felt a chill in his bones. He paused, slid his tongue between sharp teeth to taste the air, sensed an unfamiliar scent. It was something other than blood and death, yet still smelt of corruption. Powerful enough to stall his thoughts.

Ra'tor felt his eyes drawn to the square made of stone. He couldn't see anything abnormal, but the sensation remained. There was something out there. He could feel it.

The crescent moon slipped behind a thick cloud; its light extinguished in an instant. He squinted down at the corpses. He could barely see them, a dozen mounds of dead flesh seeping blood. An urge to lift his eyes towards the far pathway prevailed upon him. There it was, hiding behind the splintered shelter. He couldn't tell how he knew, he just felt it deep in his soul.

A whimper sounded from Isabelle. He caught her eye, went to hold a finger to his lips, noticed it was trembling. A cold, numbing sensation swept through his body. He returned his eyes to the pathway.

The creature moved. In his mind's eye he saw a figure as black as a starless night, a shadow born from shadows, moving towards the dead. It seeped forward, dragging the darkness behind it like a protective garment. The reality was far worse. It was merely a single figure, heavily cloaked, moving fearlessly despite the slaughter.

And it moved alone.

He almost whistled at its audacity. Was it a hunter? Few would dare travel amongst the shelters without aid. Ra'tor narrowed his eyes, seeking features that might provide an answer. Yet as he focused on the individual, he felt a coldness settle in his soul. There was an abnormality to the creature, a tangible aura surrounding its form. It called to him, sang a song of despair. It was an opening maw, lined with dagger teeth, providing entry to a bottomless pit. There was no light. It was fashioned from anger and hate. There was only darkness and death.

It took his breath away.

A tremble sufficed his body. Ra'tor's heart was beating frantically, thumping hard against his ribcage, like it was about to burst from his chest. For one ridiculous moment he believed the blackened figure was pulling the life from his body.

'Ra'tor?' Isabelle whispered. He fought hard to pull his gaze from the darkness. He managed, although the muscles in his neck screamed their displeasure. 'I'm scared.'

He could barely see her, even though she was ten feet away.

He moved one hand across the floorboards, then the other. He was crawling on all fours when he reached her, straining to put distance between he and the creature outside. He placed quivering feet beneath him and picked Isabelle up at the same time, sat her on his hip as he held her tight. There was a doorway on the far wall, leading to the rear of the merchant's house. He knew he should run.

But the pull was strong, and he found himself turning to look out the window once more.

Only this time, when he peered down at the courtyard below, two ember eyes stared back from the darkness.

Ra'tor felt Isabelle shudder, heard her sob. It was enough for his protective instinct to take over, for his blood to burn with action. Without her, he may have succumbed.

He spun away from the horror, leapt towards the doorway. He kept a tight grip on his angel as he moved, took large strides down a hallway and two sets of stairs. His free hand smashed aside the table blocking the rear door before his foot pounded it open. A terrible boom sounded against the door leading into the merchant's house behind him.

The Darkness was coming.

He ran like he'd never ran before. The tight pull of his wound was forgotten, his fear of running into Aquilan's or wolfen irrelevant. His only course was to run, and then run some more.

He didn't know where he was going. He didn't care. He had his angel, and that was all that mattered.

And his life.

He ripped a wooden gate from its hinges, ran down a pathway hemmed in by tall shelters.

And ran some more.

*

Ahriman stood at the rear doorway of the merchant's house.

It was dark, the sliver of moonlight had yet to return, and only a handful of the brightest stars in the night sky could be seen between thick clouds. Yet his vision was keen enough to see the splintered door lying on slate tiles at his feet. And as his sight followed the tiles to an archway at the rear of the property, he could make out the broken gate ripped off its hinges.

His eyes squinted as he focused his breathing, inhaled deeply. He could smell his prey, smell the one who ran in fear.

A Deiosian, he concluded.

Ahriman placed a foot on the slate tiles, crouched down on one knee. Since his return to Bastion, he'd encountered all manner of beings. Some, who he found alone, he killed by hand. It was a simple matter of stepping in close, knowing the power he exuded would wash over his victims. They would tremble and quiver, some would fall to the ground and weep. Those with the most courage would stand immobile and wait for the inevitable.

Others, hunting in packs, he would follow through the city's labyrinth. He would watch their progress, study their ways. And being near, he would project his anger and fury, encourage the hatred he knew simmered beneath the surface of every mind he touched.

Eventually, the hunting party would encounter another, blood would flow. The victors would stand for a moment to witness their savagery, smelling the death orchestrated by their hands. Then a darkness would sweep in from the shadows.

Those who survived would burst into pillars of flame, consumed in hellish fire.

He would take his time as he drew in the souls of the dead. One-by-one, he would patiently absorb their life force and with it, all their memories. In this manner he could learn who they were and where they came from. He could begin to understand their culture and even speak their language. Mannerisms would follow, especially when he consumed more individuals, and every soul added to his own black maelstrom would enhance his power.

And yet none, so far, had the courage to run away once he was close.

But this one had.

He was sure it was a Deiosian. They were primal hunters, fierce and strong of limb. They exuded an energy of their own, as wild as the hot deserts they roamed on their own world. The Deios souls he'd already gathered were like molten balls of fiery energy, charged with a lust for life and the chance to prove oneself under the relentless hammer blows of a raging sun. Only this one differed. He could sense it, even now. Was it tainted? It was certainly unusual. He sensed an element of compassion, like a swirl of sky-blue energy mingling throughout the vibrant flames of desire. And something else. Almost, he thought, like the piercing white light of innocence.

Strange. Not what he expected. Perhaps this Deiosian was greater than those he'd devoured previously. Perhaps he was a leader, or a preacher. He knew about the Patriarchs, knew about their beliefs in following the lessons of Bhral: the Blood God. Was he one of them?

Searching eyes once again spied the broken gate ripped off its hinges at the end of the path. He was physically strong, that much was evident. Perhaps he was also mentally strong.

Ahriman breathed deep once more, caught the scent a final time, held on to it for a moment. He would remember its composition. When he caught up with him next time, he would know.

His pulse quickened with excitement at the prospect of finding his newly found prey. It would only be a matter of time before their paths crossed once more. It was inevitable.

Moving back into the merchant's house he took long strides to the main door. He hadn't forgotten the creatures lying dead on the cobblestones out front. More than a dozen, their souls even now beginning to vacate the flesh and swirl into a new existence.

He stepped into the cobblestoned square, his footfalls soft and soundless. He could see the souls as they emerged from the dead, saw them flicker as he approached. Without even studying the corpses he could tell who they were. Glowing, pale yellow balls of light belonged to the Lupen, a reflection of the moon goddess they worshipped. The magenta balls of light belonged to the Aquilan, those who were feathered like the eagles they resembled. He'd consumed both in the past few days. But he was always hungry for more. In fact, he was ravenous.

A dozen strides took him to the first. He bent a knee, waved a hand in the air. A magenta soul swept into his chest, disappearing in an instant. With eyes closed he felt the soul merge with his own. He concentrated, found the newcomer. Ath'ak, was his name. An Aquilan hunter, young. His life skills were few, his experiences limited. This venture to the new world was his peak.

He waved another magenta soul forward. It shivered as it approached, then sank quickly into his chest. Older, this one. Ath'cha, brother to the first. His life was more complex, his experiences greater, more defining. The sensation of the joining was pleasing.

Ahriman was growing stronger.

He could feel the power surging in his veins. Ever since his return, he'd fed frequently. Aquilan, Lupan, Deiosian, Murdan and Man. He knew others were out there, roaming the streets and filtering through the sewers. He would find them soon enough.

He waved the remaining magenta soul-spheres to join his own. After a deep breath, he moved a step closer to the fallen Lupen.

Even in death they were impressive specimens. Descendants from the wolf, they shared a wild, savage look so prominent amongst true hunters. Large teeth, clawed hands and strong limbs coupled with a body designed to run almost indefinitely. If the Lupen caught your scent, he imagined they would catch you soon after. And yet like the Deios, they crafted weapons and clothing, wore coloured beads and assorted trinkets fashioned from feathers. It showed a sophistication beyond merely hunting prey in the wild. From the Lupen souls he'd already devoured, he knew they shared social structures not unlike the Deios. So similar in disposition and manner, he thought, and yet the Deios lived beneath the heat of a smouldering sun baking desert sands, whilst the Lupen hunted within gloomy forests under snow-capped jagged mountains that sought to touch the sky.

He sent a mental command to the first pale yellow soul-sphere, a bauble of shining light only now seeping from the body of a large black-haired Lupan. It sank into his chest, merged with his thousands of souls already gathered. He discovered Ka-Voth, a leader amongst the Lupen, strong and agile, feared for his ferocity. A welcome was offered as Ahriman learnt from Ka-Voth's memories, then he consumed him.

Once again, Ahriman felt his power grow.

The remaining five Lupen followed their leader, their souls unable to resist his call.

The cobblestones were hard against his knees as the sliver of moonlight broke through the clouds. He placed a hand on the chest of Ka-Voth. With his power increasing so rapidly, Ahriman thought it time to test his capabilities. The streets were now quiet. He sensed there were no creatures lurking close by. Closing his eyes, he focused his thoughts on Ka-Voth and created the image of the Lupan in his mind.

He felt his skin crawl, felt it stretch and twist, felt long coarse hairs form and then burst from his shoulders and arms, then his torso. Ahriman lifted his head, opened bloodshot eyes to see the night sky above. Fingers cracked as his nails lengthened into claws. His legs lengthened, so too his nose and jaw. His mouth became a maw lined with teeth. Throughout the change he kept his focus, despite the sensation of whip-fire lashing his tendons and tearing his flesh. Somehow, he remained as silent as the empty streets.

He finally stood on trembling feet, swept his arms wide for balance. The cloak he wore still covered most of his frame, so too his trousers, only his legs were now visible from the calves down. He'd grown a few inches during the transformation.

He took a step, felt the muscles ripple as they adjusted to his new physique. He was lean, yet strong, felt fierce and capable.

A shudder rippled through his body, caused him to double over and heave bile onto the stones at his feet. Nausea swamped his senses; the bright stars above became streaks of light across a darkened sky. He heaved once more, spat wads of acidic phlegm from his mouth. Pain raced like wildfire through his veins, and the sensation of tingling skin morphed into a relentless barrage of hot needles stabbing into his flesh. He cursed with a swollen tongue, then pressed both clawed hands on the ground to stabilise his torso from the sudden convulsions wracking his body.

The assault lasted a handful of minutes. When it finally abated, he was once again himself, his bronzed flesh hairless. The transformation back to his human form had been horrendous, but it was over.

He wiped a hand across parched lips. His power was growing, but it was not enough to control his merge. But it would come. A smile crept into his eyes, bloodshot as they were. Within ten days, if he continued to consume at such a rapid rate, he'd be able to take the form of any creature he saw. Ten days later, he'd be able to hold the merge indefinitely.

Still crouched on the ground, he looked to the body of Ka-Voth, pulled him close with a clenched hand. The enormous Lupan slid across the stones as if it weighed no more than a child. Ahriman leant towards the neck, traced a fingernail across Ka-Voth's throat. Blood seeped from the wound, for the kill was still fresh.

Ahriman placed bone-dry lips against the throat and slurped with hunger.

It was sometime later when he finally sat back content. The corpse was almost drained of blood, and only a handful of ruby droplets had escaped to fall on cold stones. He sat back, licked his lips with a black-stained tongue. The feed had been necessary, for after his torturous ordeal with the merge he'd felt weak. Now satiated, he could continue his hunt. The night was still young.

He gathered his feet under him, looked to the shadowed pathways leading away from the courtyard. He had choices; knew whichever path he took he'd find a quarry. All living things were now his to hunt, for he was Ahriman, the first born Nepharii. He was the first thought of creation. The first to manifest.

But of all the Nepharii, he was also first to die.

So long ago, he thought, moving towards a crumpled building to his right. But somehow, when the choice to return to the light of the universe came, he refused. For thousands of years, possibly more, he endured as an insignificant spark of life. A spark that refused to acknowledge the finality of death. A spark that somehow learnt to feed in a shadowed world of his own creation.

In time, he grew. And as he grew, he visualised his return.

Now he was here, and the possibilities fuelled his desires. Now he could become the eternal god he felt was his right. Through his eyes the universe would see. Through his ears it would hear. Through his touch and smell, through the tastes on his tongue, the universe would learn.

And it would continue to learn until he was the only one.

CHAPTER TWENTY-ONE

A sigh eased past Tarsin's lips. It wasn't a deep sigh, yet it was laden with doubt, felt heavy as it passed into a sombre room.

The king blinked in an attempt to focus his vision, hoped sought after clarity might stimulate his wandering thoughts. Since dawn he'd sat in his makeshift war room with a dozen of his aides, reading through the population's grievances. The health of his people was a concern; the bickering, thieving and assaults more so. He was doing everything in his power to filter the citizens back into the city to reclaim a semblance of their lives, yet the situation was dire, the entire process balanced on a knives edge. One slip, one miscalculation, and whatever gains they'd fashioned would disappear in an instant.

A shaft of light slipped between boards covering a window to his right. Dust motes swirled before a glint of silver caught his eye. His chain mail shirt lay folded on a wooden chair, his jaguar embossed breast plate resting atop. He couldn't remember the last time he wore the armour.

'My king?' someone's voice cut through the murkiness.

Tarsin shook his head, looked across a table riddled with newly sketched maps. Lit candles danced from a candelabra, smoke from several pipes formed miniature clouds of grey. The smell of steel and leather mingled with sweat.

'My king, Captain Randal Quinn is here.' The voice belonged to Lady Jenna.

He gave a nod, allowed another sigh to ease past his lips. Cale Griffith shifted his huge frame to his left; Lord Beaumont placed his elbows on the table.

'Show him in, Jenna,' Tarsin could see the concern in her eyes. He quickly swept his gaze around the table. Setorious sat between Griffith and Lord Beaumont, Inesco sat to his right. Casian, still copying maps, sat beside him. The Map Makers dining room was currently their war room, crowded, as always, yet convenient. He noticed two younger ladies standing along the far wall, taking notes for Jenna, whilst the Panthian monks,

Tahu and Zai, with their cat-like features and inquisitive eyes, stood either side of the only door.

A slight smile edged the corner of Tarsin's mouth. The two monks followed him everywhere, insisting they were here to protect him from harm, adamant their duty to him was governed by a higher source. Inesco had mentioned their beliefs to him several times, suggested he accept their protection and loyalty as a gift. Despite their apparent differences, both physical and cultural, it was evident they would die for him if the situation arose.

Further musings on his behalf ceased once Randal Quinn entered the room.

Silence greeted him. Word had reached them at first light concerning an altercation at the Southern Docks and the loss of soldiers. Quinn was here to elaborate.

'What news do you bring?' Tarsin gestured to a chair next to Casian. Quinn sat with a clink of chain and a creak of leather.

'Nothing good, my lord,' he began. The man's hands clenched tight; his eyes were red rimmed from lack of sleep. 'There was an attack in the early hours of morning. We lost six men.'

'Attacked by who?' Griffith asked, his eyes already smouldering.

Quinn cleared his throat, then took a sip of water from a pewter goblet. 'Something new.'

'Something new?' Griffith sat back.

'Aye,' Quinn shook his head, wiped his brow with the back of his hand. 'A ten-man patrol was sweeping through the Southern Docks, heading towards the river Atvia. There's a smithy on the corner of Fenwick Lane and Coal Seam Road. As the patrol passed the forge, they heard movement and investigated. Inside they discovered a horned beast, broad as two men and heavy set. It towered above them, bellowed so loud they lost the ability to react. A second later it charged, hammering heavy fists into bodies. Six men died within the blink of an eye before the remaining four men found the courage to flee.'

'It doesn't take courage to flee,' Griffith rumbled.

'It does when the alternative is death,' Quinn defended. 'They could have stood their ground and died, and we'd be none the wiser.'

'How tall was the creature?' Inesco asked, his eyes curiously alight.

'The survivors said it was dark in the forge and difficult to tell exactly, but one of the men said he heard its horns scrape against the wooden ceiling. I returned with twenty men this morning to retrieve the dead. The ceiling is twelve feet high.'

'Gods above!' Jenna placed a hand over her mouth.

'My thoughts exactly, my lady,' Quinn rubbed his temple with a finger.

Tarsin looked to Inesco. 'What are your thoughts?'

Cat-like eyes stared back at him. 'The creature is a Tauran,' he replied, his words firm. 'Its size and the horns on its head make it so.'

'What in Hell's name is a Tauran?' Griffith yelled his words as his fists pounded the table. It was clear he was agitated.

'A species like any other,' Inesco placed his hands together. 'In your language, it represents a powerful beast of burden - what you would call an aurochs.'

'Are you saying the demon looks like a bull?'

'In a manner of speaking, yes.'

Silence gripped the table for several heartbeats, adding tension to an already tense room. Tarsin could feel it in his bones, see it in the eyes of his subjects. He knew what they were thinking. Another threat to add to the pile, a pile already reaching for the sky. When would it end? At what point could they reverse the trend?

'Continue your patrols, Quinn,' Tarsin broke the silence, 'only double their number and be wary of engaging.'

'Yes, my lord. Is there anything else?'

'Not for now. Keep hold of what you have and continue to clear the harbour. The *Leviathan* should be here within days.'

Quinn gave a nod as he stepped away from the table.

'Is that it?' Griffith asked once Quinn was out of earshot. 'He brings news of another demon, this one a killer like nothing we've heard of, and you just send him on his way.'

Tarsin felt the eyes of his aides searching for his own. What could he say to appease their angst? To be decisive he needed men, resources, and information. At present he lacked all three. He cleared his throat. 'He will be careful, which is all I can ask for, and he will stay alive. Randal Quinn is a resourceful man; his men praise his leadership. He knows what is required.'

'The king has the right of it,' Lord Beaumont puffed a cloud of blue smoke from his pipe. 'We are stretched thin, it's plain for all to see, but we have purpose. So long as we keep our minds focused and our swords sharp, we'll find a way.'

Tarsin offered the older man a nod. He was grateful for his calm nature and timely words, had been since he returned from the world called Aeth.

'Aye, I know it,' Griffith smacked the table with a fist once more. 'I meant no disrespect, my lord. I feel helpless, is all. I should be out there clearing the streets. Sitting around a table wears thin on this frame.'

'You'll have your time, Griffith,' Lord Beaumont shared a smile. 'We all will.'

Tarsin's own mouth mirrored Beaumont's smile before he caught the eye of Jenna as she marked notes on her supply list. 'Is Will Tolsten due to arrive?' he asked, aware midday was fast approaching.

'He is, my lord,' she replied, a frown creasing her forehead. 'I'll see if he is here.'

Jenna left the crowded table and exited the room, her footsteps carrying her past Tahu and Zai and down the hallway. Only a handful of minutes passed before she returned, Will Tolsten and his aides Col Farren and the man known as Patrick by his side.

Jenna showed Will Tolsten a seat at the far end of the table. His aides stood behind him.

Tarsin locked eyes with the man, saw confusion swirling within. And why wouldn't there be, he mused, after everything Will had endured this past ten days.

Tarsin recalled his return from the Southern Barracks, armed with the knowledge Clive Bardell was an escaped prisoner and a wanted man. It hadn't surprised him, but the fact he'd been by his side for an extended period on Aeth infuriated him. Several times Griffith had calmed his nerves and stayed his hand from striking out at the arrogant Bardell when they were imprisoned. He now wished he'd followed his instincts and carried through with his threats, doubly so when they discovered Bardell had left Will's mercenary company to form one of his own.

The news came as a shock, left a sour taste in his mouth. With Griffith and thirty hand-picked soldiers by his side they had converged on Will Tolsten's tent after their discovery, eager to find Bardell so they could clap him in chains. Instead, they found Will sitting at his table, head in his hands. Col Farren stood near the entrance, equally distraught, whilst Will's lady, Tessa, sat on the bed with tear-filled eyes.

Unbeknownst to them, Clive Bardell had undermined Will's authority and taken command of his Knights of Salvation. Several hundred mercenaries had quietly left the employ of Will Tolsten and shifted to the northern outskirts of Bastion, eager to follow the charismatic Bardell. From what they gleaned from the score of men who remained loyal to Will, the brigand promised untold riches from amongst the abandoned noble palaces and merchant houses lying empty within the Northern Quarter known as New City.

That was his aim, had been all along. Will had been nothing more than a tool, his own conflict of interests clouding his judgement concerning the man he thought to use. As expected, Col Farren was furious, and the look of disdain on his face spoke volumes. Now Will Tolsten and his dreams of recognition and power were merely whispers on a fast-fading wind. He had his *Shadow Brethren*: a dozen men, no more, but his band of misfits had fled.

Tarsin shared their anger. Bardell's betrayal was another thorn in his side. He would have loved nothing more than to seek him out and put an end to his ambitions, but the size of his mercenary band prevented any such action. Numbering close to a thousand, Tarsin couldn't pull enough men from within the city to deal with the threat. For now, the traitor would live, but when the dust settled, Clive Bardell would answer to the king.

His thoughts awhirl, Tarsin looked at a man he barely recognised. 'Will Tolsten,' he began, 'I've a proposition for you.'

The youngest son of Derrick Tolsten looked perplexed. He couldn't blame him. Three days earlier he'd mentioned he was returning to the family estate, only he'd been ordered to remain in Bastion, and not alone. Several guards were positioned close to the tent he shared with Tessa, their every move shadowed. Now he was here, unsure of his future and obviously sceptical of the newly crowned king before him.

'What do you require of me?' he asked.

There was a gasp from the ladies present, whilst Setorious and Griffith both pushed their chairs back, hands moving to daggers belted at their waist.

'What do you require of me, *my lord*, I believe you meant to say,' chimed Lord Beaumont with a frown. The old warrior sat without moving a muscle, but there was a focus in his eyes that suggested the man was poised to act. His presence was a boon, for he was wise enough to see through the shite so many people believed to be important.

'I apologize, *my lord*,' Will sneered. He was apparently not in the mood to be propositioned.

'Do you have a problem with the king?' rumbled Griffith.

Tarsin watched the man squirm in his seat. He might have his own beliefs concerning the crown, but here, in this environment, he was clearly all alone.

'No, I have no quarrel with the crown or the man who wears it,' Will shifted his eyes to meet all those at table. 'Far be it for one of my station to discuss such matters. If Tarsin proclaims to be the bastard son of the late Arkos Vantos, who am I to say otherwise.'

The words were barely out of his mouth before the dagger at Griffith's hip was brandished with a flurry.

'Are you threatening me, Cale Griffith?' Will spat the words as his eyes focused on the pointed blade of steel ten inches from his face. 'I'll speak the truth if I please. Have you not heard the people in the fields? If they don't call him the Bastard King of Dervae, they call him the Thieving King. Tell me it isn't true!'

'Enough!' Tarsin slammed his hands on the table as he stood, his own chair falling over to clatter on the floorboards. 'Is that your gripe, man? Does following a bastard upset you?'

Will sat back; his eyes clouded. Tarsin wondered if the man cared whether he followed a bastard or not. So long as the man in question provided sensible leadership and set achievable goals, it shouldn't matter in the slightest about his lineage. And yet such matters tended to rear their ugly heads at the most inconvenient times.

'I have no quarrel with your claim,' Will began, 'nor do I particularly care about your birth status.' The heat of his earlier words was forgotten as Griffith sat in his chair and sheathed his blade. 'My father fought his entire life for Dervae. He gave everything, including his marriage - or lack thereof - to the crown. He deserved more than to die beneath the city against a horde of demons. His name should be remembered and honoured. And I, being his son, should be held with greater esteem. I am not some farm boy swinging a sword for the first time. I am a proven tactician and leader of men.'

'You were a leader of men,' Griffith rumbled. 'Last I checked, your men abandoned you to be led by Clive Bardell.'

The words stung the younger man, a deliberate attempt by Griffith to test Will's resolve. But after a moment of silence and a deep breath, Will offered a single nod in recognition of the big man's barb.

'I lost them, it is true,' Will spoke hesitantly, 'but they were never truly mine to begin with. I used them to achieve my original goal: the rescue of my people from beneath the city.'

'Which you achieved admirably, it must be said,' added Lord Beaumont, 'and yet if Tarsin and his men had not intervened during your escape, it is quite possible you may not have made it back alive.'

Griffith slapped his huge hands on the table. 'Aye, you owe the king your life!'

'I'd have made it,' Will narrowed his eyes.

'But would your men have made it with you, Will? Or would you have left them behind because they'd served their purpose?' Griffith continued his tirade, seeking to offset Will's demeanour.

Nervous hands clenched tight about the table and eyes darted left and right. Both Col Farren and Patrick had stood silently behind their leader so far, but subtle movements suggested they'd had enough. It was all Tarsin needed to know. Would the men who knew Will best stand by his side when the heat was applied, or would they leave him to flounder all alone. Tarsin felt he knew the answer.

'You share your father's name,' Tarsin's voice carried easily across a now silent room, 'but what, Will Tolsten, have you ever done to suggest you are a man of valour? You were given everything as a child. You lived in comfort and safety, you ate with royalty, you were one of the privileged and educated.

'What, dare I ask, have you given back?'

'You dare sully the name of my father!'

'I've done no such thing,' Tarsin knew his eyes resembled those of an approaching storm cloud, rife with energy, crackling with intensity. 'Your father was a great man. An honourable man. I even asked to be by his side when he took his last stand. So, I'll ask one last time. What have you done for the kingdom of Dervae?'

Will brushed a hand through his hair. 'I was there, you know. I watched him die as the demons raced in. I couldn't save him. If I hadn't been concussed shortly after, I would have died on the floor with him. Sometimes, late at night, I wish I had.'

It appeared the fire in Will's eyes dimmed at the proclamation. His hands unclenched and rested calmly on the table. His shoulders slumped, as if a great weight had become unchained. Tarsin wondered if Will had grieved at all since his father's death.

Will met his stare from across the table. 'My father, Derrick Tolsten, lived for Dervae. And I lived for my father. I obeyed his orders without question. I trusted him. That is what I have done for the kingdom.'

Tarsin felt a half-smile crease his face. 'That is all I ask for, Will Tolsten. Trust me. We have all suffered loss, some of us more than others. But what makes a man or woman great is their willingness to step forward to create something new, especially after significant hardship.' He looked to the others in the room, seeking confirmation, perhaps, because his own doubts were greater than at any other time since the destruction of Bastion. 'If we cannot unite and share the same goal, then we are doomed to fail before we even begin.'

'And what goal do you have in mind?'

Tarsin shook his head, aware even he still harboured doubts concerning its validity. There were so many factors to consider, so many variables that could stifle his ambitious plan. What he needed most, what he craved more than anything else right now, was loyal men who would heed his call. Clive Bardell was a lost cause, and his men were of dubious nature in any case. They could possibly be a disturbance, but they weren't a serious threat. If push came to shove, he would deal with them with a hammer fist.

And yet those who patrolled the streets of Bastion, protecting homes and businesses, weren't increasing in number, nor were they enough to muster into a single armed force without jeopardising their hard-won gains. If he were to abandon their advancement now, it would prove difficult to reclaim lost ground later. What he needed was another force of men, a thousand and more in number, who could act separately to those patrolling the city.

And such a force was only five days away.

'I've received word from Admiral John Rhys and Lloyd Henrickson aboard the *Leviathan*,' Tarsin shared his knowledge. 'If all goes well, they shall be in our waters within five days.'

'I thought they were fighting a war against Prince Rahesh?' asked Will.

'It never eventuated. As soon as the *Leviathan* was spotted off the coast, the prince and his men retreated to the Southern States. It was as we feared. His foray into Dervae was reckless and ill timed, but a distraction, nonetheless. If he is privy to the disaster we have before us, then he'll return after the winter months have passed, rested, and quite possibly with a larger force.'

'So, what do you wish to achieve with Lloyd Henrickson's men?' asked Will. 'And where do I come into the equation?'

Sparkling eyes shared a look with Inesco who sat to his right. The Nepharii, with his vast knowledge and equally significant views, was proving to be a godsend he couldn't live without. And despite his otherworldly appearance, most of his aides were warming to his presence. For several nights the two of them had spoken about a great many things, almost to dawn on one occasion, as they plotted a way out of the quagmire that sought to consume them.

'There are multiple factors to consider,' Tarsin began, speaking not only to Will Tolsten, but to all who sat at table. 'Lloyd Henrickson will arrive with a thousand men eager for action. I'll seek to use them wisely. But as you may have noticed, those who we believe to be the enemy have been unusually quiet of late.'

'They are fighting amongst themselves,' offered Griffith.

'They are,' Tarsin gave a nod. 'Reports from our scouts suggest the otherworldly creatures are concerned with something other than us. They have moved inwards, away from our outer walls and the buildings we occupy, to swarm about Aston's Tear.'

'Why?' Will Tolsten asked, engaged with what his king had to say.

'We are uncertain at this point in time, although we sense it has something to do with the portal lying within the pyramid.'

Inesco moved his chair back, soundlessly, and stood tall. 'The king and I have spoken on this matter,' his words were clear and precise, although a faint accent could be detected. 'We believe the races stepping into Bastion are confused and excited, possibly inspired. Everything they thought they knew, all their beliefs and teachings, their promises, their dreams, have been shattered. In their place are multiple new worlds brimming with opportunity and danger. It is a feast for the hungry and a way forward for the resourceful. And amongst it all swirls the tendrils of chaos.'

Heads nodded in understanding.

'The excitement is childlike, and greed has become a motivating factor,' Inesco continued. 'I fear the races swarming throughout Bastion will descend further into violence and warfare in the months to come. If we wish to save the city, we cannot allow such madness to persist.'

'What Inesco says is true,' Tarsin wiped his brow. 'I am eternally grateful to have the wisdom of a Nepharii by my side in such turbulent times.' He motioned for Inesco to take his seat. 'We need to act, sooner rather than later. Every day we sit idle denies us the opportunity to realise our goal. And every day we spend inactive marks a day closer to dealing with Prince Rahesh and his southern horde. They have returned south for the winter, but my gut feeling suggests they will return in the spring. We need to be ready for such an eventuality. I wish with everything I have that Cappitus was here to share the burden. A part of me acknowledges he may be dead, for we found several corpses before the portal when we crossed over to Aeth. And yet another part of me suggests he is still here, hidden from sight, waiting for his moment to return.'

'He could also be protecting my sister,' Will voiced his opinion, 'on the other world, that is. You said yourself he could be with her.'

'I did, Will, and you are right. But until we reclaim Aston's Tear, we'll never know for certain.'

'So that's your plan,' the light in Will's eyes rekindled. 'You seek to reclaim the pyramid.'

Tarsin shared a look with the ceiling, wished he could see the heavens above. If he could see a sign splashed across a cloudless sky, he'd feel vindicated. But deep down he knew the sign he sought needed to come from within. It was what his heart felt. What his soul craved.

'It is,' he said, 'I believe it has always been our plan, we just didn't acknowledge it. The madness that grips our city began when the pyramid sprang into life. It cannot end until we return and take control. There is no other way.'

'You asked me to trust you, but what role am I to play?' Will spread his hands out wide.

Tarsin moistened dry lips with his tongue. He and Cale Griffith had spoken at length, and neither shared the same view. And yet he knew Will was a good man at heart. He needed direction and purpose to justify his existence, much like his father.

'The days ahead, Will, shall be dangerous. When Lloyd Henrickson arrives with his thousand men, I intend to make our presence felt. But I need eyes around me, eyes that will be alert to any danger that may manifest. When I was your age, I served the king as his eyes and ears. I was part of an organisation known as the Unseen. I need the Unseen once again, Will. Cale Griffith, John Rhys and Jeagar the Herkosian are all who remain. I would like you to join their ranks. And I would like those Shadow Brethren who serve you to also be by my side.'

'My Shadow Brethren are to become Unseen?'

'They are, Will. You have the evening to gather your men to explain the situation. If they are willing, you are to offer them what I have offered you. If they accept, you'll meet here at first light for your assignments and your Shadow Brethren will be no more.'

'We are to be your eyes and ears?'

'And his sword and shield,' Griffith slapped his hands together. 'This is the greatest honour you'll ever receive, lad, don't mess it up.'

All eyes swung to Will Tolsten. He sat in silence for a moment, beads of sweat blooming on his brow. Like he did earlier, he moistened suddenly dry lips with his tongue.

'I agree,' he finally found the courage to reply. 'I'll see you at first light . . . my lord?'

CHAPTER TWENTY-TWO

A storm was brewing on the horizon.

Tarsin could see angry clouds swirling to the west as he stepped onto the street. Dark curtains of rain trailed beneath, promising a final downpour, the last of the summer storms.

'We have an hour, my lord,' Lady Jenna said as she moved to his side. 'I suggest we make the most of our time before we seek shelter.'

Tarsin offered a solitary nod before peering towards the centre of the city. The silver-blue glow of the pyramid's peak was visible in the distance, ominously bright under a darkening sky. It was where he longed to be.

'My lord,' he looked behind to see Tahu and Zai step from beneath the porch of Casian the Map Maker's house. Like Will Tolsten, both Panthians had been appointed members of the Unseen. For the foreseeable future, they were to be his personal bodyguards. Zai, the taller of the two with his tiger-like features, spoke in the kingdom tongue. 'Where do we travel?'

Tarsin placed a hand to his brow, adjusted the golden crown resting there. Most days he forgot he even wore the symbol of office. On those days he did remember, he wished he could dispense with the authority it invoked. On occasion, he dreamt of throwing it away.

And yet he knew the people of Bastion needed a leader. They needed someone with power to make decisions, someone to stand for their rights, and someone to promise a better future. They also desired a figurehead to vent all their frustrations at.

He had become that figure, and the reality of being king sat heavy on his shoulders. He never asked for it, nor did he desire the position. He did believe he was the right man for the task, though. He knew all his teachings under Lloyd Henrickson and Du Weng Sai were directed towards such an outcome. Why else had he been instructed in the intricacies of warfare, the logistics involved with managing large numbers of men and the sheer number of personal required for operations? Everything he'd been taught was now coming to fruition. He was young and competent, he knew, and the desire was there. But he wondered if his decisions were the right ones. Like anyone, he could make mistakes. And in such an environment, any mistake he made could be catastrophic.

He shared sombre eyes with the two Panthians. He was about to lead them to the armoury for an inspection, located close to the Southern Gate, but the shrill cries of a young boy running in the street stopped his motion.

'Sire, sire!' the boy practically sang the words as he ran towards them. Behind him, labouring after the fleet-of-foot child, followed half-a-dozen soldiers.

Tahu and Zai stepped in front of him, hands drifting to their weapons, although they did not draw them forth. The child slid to a stop ten feet away, his mad dash complete.

The king looked at the scruffy blonde-haired child and shared a smile before casting eyes towards the soldiers who gave chase. 'What is it, child?' he asked, returning his eyes to the boy. 'Why do you run so fast through streets that are supposed to be sealed?'

The child took a deep breath, his small chest expanding, before he shrugged his shoulder to avoid a soldier's hand. 'I come on important business, my lord,' he spoke with an exuberance not commonly found in one so young. He couldn't have been more than eight years of age. 'My name is Cal, and I come on behalf of Sister Tahlia of the House of Isha.'

Tarsin nodded his head. He recalled the sister requesting a moment of his time only a day past. Like many of those invested in serving the gods of Dervae, taking care of those in need was now their priority. 'What do you require, young Cal?'

'We need more white sheets, my lord,' his eyes were fixed on the stones at his feet, but his words were spoken with intent.

'White sheets?' Tarsin creased his eyes. 'May I ask why you require white sheets, Cal?'

The boy nodded his head, then met his eyes. His cheeks were still ruddy from his run, and he darted his tongue across his lips in a nervous manner that brought a smile to the king. 'They are necessary for the dead, my lord. You promised every corpse pulled from the wreckage of Bastion would be cloaked in a blanket of white before burial. Sister Tahlia said we have exhausted our supply. We need more, and we were told you know where they are to be found.'

The smile on Tarsin's lips vanished in an instant. The reality of where he now stood and what was occurring reminded him how precarious their situation was. His soldiers had found useful items for clothing, discovered food supplies and equipment as they cleared the streets, but they'd also uncovered a growing number of dead amongst the ruins. Some died when the ground shook, and were decayed beyond recognition, whilst others had been killed by unknown hunters in the night; some partially eaten. A disaster such as the falling of Bastion was never going to be an easy fix. And stifling weather was only going to make matters worse. Griffith had mentioned earlier in the day that summer was officially over, yet there remained enough heat to cause one last storm; and enough heat to decompose the dead.

He stepped towards the boy, knelt so he could speak to him on his level. 'We will deliver the white sheets you need, Cal. We have a supply at the Southern Barracks. I'll send word to my men, but I need to know where to send them.' He gave the child a pat on his shoulder. 'Where is Sister Tahlia at this moment?'

Cal spoke with a rush of air. 'She is at the Orphanage of Saint Ryke, on Candle Street. The roof has collapsed, along with an outer wall. There are many bodies within.'

Tarsin felt the blood drain from his face. Tahu must have noticed, for he took a step closer. 'Are you well, my lord?' he asked with his thick accent.

Jenna also saw the change in his appearance. 'What is wrong?' she asked.

He swallowed his shock, closed his eyes for a moment. When he opened them, he saw all eyes fixed on his own. 'I spent my first years at the Orphanage of Saint Ryke,' he began. 'I have fond memories of the place, despite the hardships I endured. Come, Cal, I'll send word for the sheets, whilst my friends and I accompany you back to the orphanage. Maybe we can help the sisters in their task until the rains arrive.'

The young boy gave his nod of approval and fell in beside his king, a look of wonder in his eyes and a youthful smile stretching his lips. It remained plastered across his face for the entire journey back to the orphanage.

Yet as he and his followers arrived, they were greeted with a scene of horror.

More than thirty bodies had been pulled from the wreckage to lie on the street. The sound of flies buzzing in the air could be heard a hundred feet away, forming small black clouds of dread as they hovered above the corpses. Sisters dressed in the white cloth of Isha moved back and forth from what remained of the building, dragging the dead with minimal fuss, a look of determination crossed with sadness marring their features. Even from a distance, Tarsin could see their white clothing was stained with blood and ash, dirt and grime.

And a storm was coming.

A dozen carts were ranged across the street, currently sheltered beneath the overhang of what was once a merchant's shopfront. A wooden signboard swayed on rusty chains, the words, Nelson's Provider of Fine Goods, splashed in yellow. Tarsin remembered the store from his youth. Nelson had been a wily fellow, fast on his feet for one so old. He walked with a cane, but Tarsin knew it was to strike at the thieving hands of those bold enough to steal his produce.

He looked at his own hands. Only once had he been struck. A sharp whack across his knuckles that stung like Hell's own whip of fire. Back then, you learnt fast or suffered the consequences. He'd been a fast learner.

The king returned his vision to the orphanage, watched young Cal race to a sister's side and pull her dirty sleeve. He said a handful of words then pointed in his direction.

'Sister Tahlia,' Tarsin acknowledged the lady as he walked towards her. Jenna, Tahu and Zai ranged behind him; their eyes locked on the dead bodies littering the ground. The majority were small children, anywhere from four to twelve years in age. Tarsin swallowed his anger, met the sister's gaze. 'I've brought some help,' he waved towards the twenty soldiers who followed their footsteps, already lifting the dead onto the carts. 'I hope you don't mind.'

'Of course not, my lord,' she offered a bow, yet her eyes remained hard as slate, just like her face. Tarsin felt a lack of compassion on her behalf, noticed her lips were little more than a slash of contempt.

'Your sheets for the deceased will arrive shortly,' he said, 'hopefully before the storm arrives.' He looked towards the long three-story building, saw the broken wall and caved in roof. Red clay tiles lay scattered about the small yard, and bricks sat like a pile of scree, looking every bit the remains of a mountain avalanche in the corner. 'I spent more than ten years of my life housed in this building,' he continued, oblivious to who was listening. Tears formed in his eyes as he recalled the lessons in the hall with Old Smithy, his master of letters and numbers. For a moment he wondered if he could still be alive. Almost two decades had passed since he was pulled from the orphanage and ushered into Highcastle as a twelve-year-old. Smithy had been old back then.

'You lived here, my lord?' Sister Tahlia's voice cut through his musings.

'I did,' he replied, catching a glint of life in her eyes. 'I'm not sure how old I was when I arrived, but I was here until I was twelve,' he paused, shared a thoughtful look. 'At least I spent most of my time here. I had a habit of jumping out the rear window during Old Smithy's lectures, so I could roam the streets of Bastion with fellow footpads. We never hurt anyone, but we surely caused mischief.' A distant look swept across his face, almost a longing for simpler times. How easy life was as a youngster, running the streets, pinching apples from Nelson's barrels and loaves of hot bread from the windowsill of Aunt Carla's Bakery. He and a handful of other children would sit on the steps leading to the Handorff Canal, eating their fill whilst fishermen pulled in their netted hauls.

Life was simple back then. Full of golden sunshine, the occasional full belly and pleasant laughter amongst friends.

Now the children of Saint Ryke's orphanage were dead like so many others, yet barely a soul would remember who they were. The enormity of life's foibles was clearly apparent. Nothing lasted forever, no matter how hard you tried to cling on. Perhaps, he thought, the city of Bastion was lost. Perhaps she couldn't recover her dignity, no matter how hard he tried. Maybe their time had arrived; maybe their grip on life was now forfeit.

Was their destruction to be complete and irreversible?

'It must hurt you, then, to see your previous home destroyed?' Sister Tahlia placed a hand on his arm. It was a comforting gesture, came from the heart. Her face softened, the lines about her eyes appeared to melt away. He thought to guess her age, believed her to be mid-forties.

'It does,' the words fell out of his mouth, laden with grief. A tear slid down his cheek. He shivered, looked to the western sky, saw dark clouds circling. The rain would be here soon, a torrent to wash away his grief, or possibly to drown him in sorrow. 'I feel so cold, like I am far from where I need to be.'

'I believe you are exactly where you need to be, my lord.'

'Really?' Tarsin wiped the tear sliding down his cheek with the back of a finger. He sniffed the air, smelt dampness on the wind. The rain would fall in minutes. He cast his gaze towards the fallen building. 'I was born with nothing, now I have everything. And yet everything I have is broken.'

Silence reigned until the first drops began to fall, softly, like a child tiptoeing across polished floorboards. Sister Tahlia took a step closer, looked into his eyes. 'Your spirit is not broken, my lord. This I can tell.'

He smiled, sniffed the cold air once more. 'For now, perhaps, but I feel strained,' he shook his head, felt the crown atop his head. 'I have my doubts, sister. I doubt so many things.'

'Having doubts is healthy. It makes you question your decisions, hones your thinking. Every path we choose comes with its obstacles. Some are walls we need to climb over, others to walk around. Every now and again you'll find an obstacle that appears insurmountable. At this point in time, you may have to turn around and trace your path back, find another way.'

'What if there are no other ways?'

'Then you'll know you're on the right path; no matter how dark, how dangerous or how frightening it may be.'

Tarsin clenched his hands together, felt raindrops sneaking beneath his collar to slip down his back. The glow from Aston's Tear was to his right, reflecting from dark clouds hovering above the city. Daylight had been devoured.

'These two,' Tahlia swept her hand towards Tahu and Zai, 'are not from around here. They are different, like the demons killed by some of your soldiers. Yet they follow you, King Tarsin. Why is that?'

He was momentarily lost for words. Having the two Panthians by his side had become second nature, their presence never questioned. Still, he was caught off guard. Tahu and Zai were close, and their grasp of the Kingdom tongue was advanced enough for them to understand Tahlia's words. Besides, he could see the subtle twitch of Tahu's pointy ears, knew he'd have to choose his words carefully.

Sister Tahlia placed her grimy hand on young Cal's shoulder, patiently waiting for an answer.

'The Panthians believe I am a representation of a saviour,' he began, knowing the trust placed in him by the Panthians was a result of their faith. 'They refer to me as the Chosen One if you acknowledge their claim. The lore behind such a proclamation is unfamiliar to me, as are so many of their customs. Yet after considerable deliberation they requested to help, although such help was, at first, quite minor. From what Inesco, their spiritual leader, has explained, they believe the struggles we face here will be a precursor to troubles on their own world. Talk amongst the Panthian monks suggests a victory on this world will negate their predicted doom.'

'Yes,' Tahlia patted Cal's shoulder, sent him with a gentle push towards the overhang across the road. The rain continued. 'But what have you done, my lord, to evoke such trust from the Panthians?'

'I . . . I'm not sure. Perhaps I watched and listened. Perhaps I did not judge them harshly after our first encounter. I feel a kinship with the monks; I understand it was reciprocated.'

With Cal now absent, she stepped closer, once again placed a hand on his forearm. Tahu's ears twitched; his muscles tensed. Zai placed a clawed hand on the pommel of his sword. Yet her words were softly spoken. 'Coming here, to serve and protect you, requires unquestionable devotion. If you can garner such trust from a foreign species, you can evoke the same spirit in the people you swore to save. You are a young king, granted, but your words carry great weight. Cease being indecisive and no longer doubt your judgement. The people will listen, your words will unite them. If you can trust the Panthians who walk beside you, you can surely learn to have faith in yourself.'

He gave a solitary nod, aware the sister was wiser than he first believed, and possibly older. 'I hear the truth in your words, sister, and I thank you.'

'It is nothing. I have a gift for seeing what lies within. You have heart, King Tarsin. And a man with heart is an easy man to follow.'

Her words brought a faint smile to his face, briefly, before he ushered her towards the old store and its shoddy overhang. His soldiers stood in small groups, their task of lifting the dead onto laden carts complete. Small, dark puddles began to form along the road.

'I have need of your services, Sister Tahlia,' he said once he'd wiped his damp face.

'I have a duty to my goddess, Isha, as you may well be aware.'

'I am aware of your duty,' Tarsin replied with a grin, 'but as your king, I am being decisive. I need your counsel and your wisdom. I need to know I can call on you when I am most pressed. Unlike Tahu and Zai, you will not be required to follow my every step. But I would like to believe you will respond when I beckon.'

'Do you think I am worthy, my king?'

'You are, and you know it. I place my trust sparingly, but it is always well placed.'

'Then I accept your invitation, King Tarsin,' she replied.

They shared a smile whilst the rain continued to fall. For a moment, it appeared the worries swirling within his mind were no more dire than the last of the summer storms. Dark in patches, but certainly not permanent, although he was aware there was a price to be paid. The stiff bodies gathered from the orphanage were a stark reminder. He held a hand above his eyes, looked at the corpses piled high on the carts. He saw dead eyes staring at his own, asking questions he knew he couldn't answer. Children, mostly, and they paid the highest price of all.

He tore his gaze away from the deceased. 'The rain looks to have settled in, sister,' he said, waving a hand towards heavy clouds. 'I have taken more of your time than I intended, but I thank you, all the same.'

Sister Tahlia offered a slight bow. 'Thank you also, my lord. I'm sure we'll talk again soon, no doubt. I look forward to it.'

Tarsin watched her return to the orphanage across the street, her sisters and their helpers huddled beneath the roof of a stable, its walls precariously perched. Their task for the day appeared to be complete, the rain making certain of it. If the weather cleared tomorrow, they would commit to a final sweep of the ruins. Then they'd move on, seeking those lost amongst the carnage.

He did not envy them.

'We should move on, King Tarsin,' Lady Jenna stepped to his side, her face glistening with moisture. 'We were to arrive at the armoury by now.'

He shook his head. 'Send a soldier to the armoury in our stead. Apologize on my behalf, but I am needed elsewhere.'

'Elsewhere?' she asked.

'Aye, back at Casian's house. We need to plan our next sortie into the city.'

He could see the confusion cloud her eyes. She tilted her head, made a movement to retrieve her notes from a deep pocket, then thought better of it with so much rain about.

'It's alright, Jenna,' he tilted his own head, heard his neck crack, 'I've decided it's time to reclaim Irongate. With Henrickson due in days, it would be best - I believe - to be prepared to strike out as soon as possible.'

'Will you wait for Henrickson and his thousand men, my lord?'

He narrowed his eyes, a sure sign, so he'd been told by Griffith, that he was concentrating. 'Yes, we'll wait. It will allow us time to prepare the men, including Will Tolsten and those most loyal to him. Come tomorrow, we'll know where we stand concerning his Shadow Brethren. I hope they concur with their lord and accept my offer. The gods know we need every sword we can find.'

The rain intensified, hammering the surrounding buildings as the sky threatened to turn into night. The soldiers behind him jostled against each other as they sought to move further beneath the overhang. Puddles thickened as black rivulets swarmed across every surface.

'So, Irongate it is,' Jenna put her back to the wall, and yet fat drops of water still managed to find their way onto her skirt. 'You do realise Irongate is still behind enemy lines, my lord. Quite a distance behind, in fact.'

'I do,' he replied, 'but we need its strategic position, as well as the knowledge housed within. The elders kept all manner of maps and charts that could potentially help our cause, and besides, the tower also provides a clear view of the city. It's an advantage we could utilise once we decide to make for the pyramid.' He shifted his feet; aware his boots were becoming increasingly wet. 'In fact, it's an advantage we cannot live without.'

'A strategic position, then,' she said.

'Aye, and there is a possibility Cappitus may still be alive,' he continued. 'If he is, he will be at Irongate. It is a faint hope I have concerning his survival, but I'll never know until we reclaim the old watch tower.' He saw Jenna nod her head. Whether it was approval, or merely acknowledgement, he couldn't tell. 'Elder Cappitus is wise, his presence will be most welcome,' he suggested, not sure if he was trying to convince himself, or his aide. As soon as he said the words, he thought of Sister Tahlia; knew she would scold him for his lack of conviction.

'It remains a dangerous proposition, my lord,' Jenna reminded him. 'Clive Bardell is a thorn in your side, I agree, but we cannot disregard him altogether. And the men required to advance on Irongate will test your reserves. The creatures,' she cast a subtle glance towards Tahu and Zai, careful not to offend their sensibilities, 'are becoming more prolific every day. We are aware of their increasing number, and the number of species continues to grow. If you seek Irongate before you're prepared, you may very well never return.'

He shook his head once Jenna's assessment came to its conclusion. A wry smile creased his mouth. 'Well said,' he placed a hand on her shoulder. 'You've a sharp mind and a tongue to match, which I am grateful for. But it appears everywhere I look danger lurks. Irongate can solidify our position within Bastion. It offers hope. And there is no better stronghold to launch an attack towards Aston's Tear. If we are to reclaim the pyramid, Irongate is where we need to be.'

He waited for a rebuttal, but all he heard was the patter of raindrops. If Jenna disapproved, she would tell him. She had a way of letting him know what she thought, usually with a subtle suggestion contrary to his present thinking.

'I need to do this, Jenna,' he finally broke the silence. 'I know you believe it a foolish endeavour, but if we don't make ground soon, it may be too late.'

She was peering intently at the ground, watching the toe of her boot as it formed patterns in the mud. 'I know,' she raised her chin, met his eyes. There was fire amongst the green, blazing with furious energy. 'I know you need to be king. I know you need to be proactive. It doesn't mean I have to approve,' she flung a hand towards the sodden street. 'If you die out there . . .'

'I don't plan on dying, Jenna.'

'But if you did, do you know how angry I'd be?'

He watched the fire in her eyes simmer for a moment, then dissipate. It appeared her vigour for the argument waned accordingly. For a second, he believed he saw something else in her eyes, a glimpse behind her façade of steel.

'I'll not be the cause of your anger, Jenna,' he said his words with a smile, an attempt to keep her fire at bay. 'You have proven to be my most trusted advisor in a short time. I do listen, you know.'

'Then you are set on Irongate, my lord?'

'I am.'

'Then I suggest we return to Casian's, rain or no rain. If you seek Irongate in the days ahead, well, like you said earlier, we need to prepare.'

He looked towards his men, waved a hand at his soldiers to move out. Then he offered his elbow to Lady Jenna and led her onto the street. The rain continued to fall, yet its intensity eased as Tahu and Zai fell in behind, barely five feet away.

'Irongate it is, then,' he said, yet this time, he didn't smile.

Because he knew, as Jenna did, that danger lurked amongst every shadow.

CHAPTER TWENTY-THREE

'Is that it for the day, my lord?'

Cale Griffith gave a nod, took as single step to pat a hand on the soldier's shoulder. 'Aye, take your men to the hall for food and drink, let them rest until morning.' Griffith looked to the sky, saw the sun sinking to the west as it dropped behind broken towers. 'We'll have another long day ahead of us.'

The soldier returned the nod, then waved his men towards the hall further down the street. A sigh eased from his chest as Griffith let his warhammer slide through aching fingers to rest on the cobblestoned street.

He watched the soldiers disappear inside the hall, it's brickwork mostly intact, although several gaping holes in the roof and a rear wall with a slight lean were testament to the earthquake. But it was large enough to accommodate a hundred men and repairs were already being discussed. For now, it provided space and shelter.

A door opened to his left, allowing a young lady dressed in a plaid skirt access to the street. She met his eyes with her own, offered a smile. 'My lord,' she curtseyed, then fumbled the leather-bound books she held in her arms.

He thought to help her, only his legs were stiff and refused to move. As the door behind her closed, she steadied her books and sauntered away with a sway of her hips.

Another sigh, this one accompanied with a crack of his neck. He was feeling old; old and broken. And he hadn't even used his hammer in the past twenty days.

He shook his head, willed his legs to move. The building before him was timeworn, yet it remained structurally sound. Before the earthquake it supplied storage for incoming trade goods from the north, along with rooms to house a family and a handful of workers. Wooden sheds ranged from the rear of the establishment within an eight-foot-tall wall of stone, and a sizeable stable kept horse's and their wagons well maintained.

Whilst only a stone's throw from New City, she was south of the river Atvia and thus out of Clive Bardell's reach.

Men and women moved amongst idle chatter and the rustle of papers as he walked inside. Lanterns were already lit, heralding the night to come, and pipe-smoke drifted from one end of the long room, seeking to escape the building's confines through the open door behind him.

'Evening, Griffith,' the words came from Lord Beaumont, seated amongst the grey-blue haze. 'Anything?'

'Nothing of importance,' he rumbled. 'Where is he?'

A thumb jabbed upwards, directing him to the roof. Griffith moved to the staircase; a grand affair of polished oak shrouded by smoke and cluttered by those still dithering with reports.

He eased himself past and walked up three flights of stairs to the top of the building, sharing a view with the city skyline. It was darkening, yet golden highlights bathed the underside of soft clouds and tall towers. For some, the view would be a wonder.

'My king,' he announced himself, aware King Tarsin was standing at the rear of the building, a looking glass pointed towards the west. Will Tolsten and the Panthian, Zai, stood ten feet away, their eyes also on the horizon. He knew they weren't enjoying the view.

The looking glass was lowered.

Nothing was said. Then king merely stood there, his gaze still on the horizon.

'Keeping your gaze on Irongate will not bring it any closer,' Griffith broke the silence.

'I know,' Tarsin replied with a wave of his hand. He spun about, faced him. 'Anything to report?'

'No, nothing of value. Clive Bardell remains behind closed doors.'

A shrug from the king was his only response. Griffith couldn't blame him. A month had passed since he first suggested they seek out Irongate. Plans were formulated, men gathered and equipped. Once Admiral John Rhys and Lloyd

Henrickson arrived with a thousand men, they would march on the old watch tower and claim her as their own.

Then news arrived concerning Bardell. Lieutenant Setorious was the messenger, a man aware of the king's desire to delve further into the city. Yet he couldn't not tell him. So he did so, knowing what he said would change their focus and their plans. And Griffith was there, standing beside his king, when Setorious revealed his news.

Clive Bardell had purpose, that much was clear. Having undermined Will Tolsten by stealing his mercenaries, the traitor quickly sought refuge inside Bastion, claiming New City with its palaces and grand estates as his own. At such point in time, King Tarsin had acknowledged the betrayal, content to deal with the brigand in due course. And yet days later word arrived of Bardell's true intent.

The man had proclaimed himself the New King of Bastion. His number of men and women fighting for his cause had grown considerably, and he'd opened Northgate, along with Rivergate, to the public. Thousands of survivors were suddenly streaming into the city, eager to claim a residence of their own at the behest of their new lord.

It was madness, and a madness to be stopped. Tarsin was beyond furious. His plans for Irongate were forgotten, his fuming hatred for Bardell was magnified. By the time he'd alerted his men, changed tactics and awaited the arrival of John Rhys and Henrickson with his soldiers, he'd already moved to seal the northern gates and halt the influx of citizens into Bastion.

It had taken time, though, time the king was unwilling to spare.

Now there was a standoff between the two forces. The king was not prepared to wage war against his own people, and Clive Bardell was adamant he was going nowhere. For the last twenty days Griffith had been reduced to running patrols along the river Atvia, peering towards New City, looking for a sign that could potentially end Bardell's ridiculous reign.

'They must be nearing the limit of their supplies,' Tarsin took steps towards him, Will Tolsten and Zai followed.

'Aye, I agree. With the gates locked and manned by our forces, they've not received any food supplies from the north. Unless they have managed to infiltrate beneath the city, they should be close to starving.'

'Any deserters?'

'A handful yesterday. Possibly more today. Lloyd Henrickson should arrive any moment. He may have information regarding those seeking to flee.'

Tarsin shifted closer, kept his voice low. 'Those who arrived from the north, who were let into the city by Bardell,' his face was hard, unreadable in the dying light, 'any signs of the plague?'

It was the news his king feared the most. Talk of the plague striking Benwith was past, the small city having survived the worst, but three small villages between Benwith and Bastion had succumbed in the last month. Latest reports suggested there were few survivors. Fear of the plague spreading inside Bastion was eating at the souls of those who wished her healed.

'No, nothing, thank the gods,' Griffith replied, knowing full well he'd make certain he wouldn't be the one to tell him otherwise.

'I'd spare your thanks on that score, my friend,' Tarsin said, moving to the staircase. 'The gods do not appear to be interested in our plight, nor do they seem overly concerned about lending a hand.'

Griffith didn't reply. He agreed. Placing trust in the gods was a fool's game. Like most men raised with a weapon in their hand, his faith tended to be placed in those able to forge their own path. Sometimes, faith in his ability to make the right judgement was all that kept him alive.

He moved towards the staircase to stand close to his king. 'So, we'll starve them out?' he said, knowing such an action could take time.

Tarsin remained silent, passed the looking glass to Will as he and Zai joined them. The last of the evening light twinkled far behind them, the sun lost below the ruined cathedrals and those outer city walls that still stood. With clouds blanketing the sky, night would arrive quickly.

'Did you know, Griffith, that Will's looking glass once belonged to Captain Jarvis Vasco?'

'He was the man you sailed south with,' it wasn't a question. On those rare nights when the two men could sit together and speak of better days, Tarsin would often recall his time sailing aboard the *Lioness*.

'He was, and a damn fine captain,' Tarsin watched Will place the looking glass in a deep pocket within his jacket. 'Will and his men found him after the earthquake,' he continued. 'He survived for only a short time before his injuries took hold. It's a shame we don't have the wisdom of his words to guide us.'

'You have enough support, my friend, if you're seeking words of wisdom.'

'I believe you, Griffith. It just saddens me that he didn't survive.'

'You knew him well enough, though,' Griffith replied. 'What do you think he would say if he were here to guide you?'

Tarsin took a step, looked out across the city. Griffith knew it didn't matter what he or anyone else thought, for Tarsin had come to trust his own judgement. Yet he also knew prodding his king with ideas and asking him to think from another angle were more helpful than harmful. It never hurt to acquire another view, from the living or the dead.

'He would be decisive,' Tarsin said with finality. 'Captain Vasco was never one to mince his words, nor did he ever take a backward step. He knew where he wanted to be, knew who he wanted to be.'

'Does such knowledge help you? Can it help us in the coming days?'

'I believe so,' Tarsin motioned to Zai. 'Check the stairwell,' he said, 'and make certain we are alone.'

The Panthian disappeared down the staircase, silent like the dead of night. He returned a moment later, gave his king a nod.

'Listen,' King Tarsin moved a step closer, huddled the men together. 'At this point in time, I'd rather be at Aston's Tear, in control of the pyramid and its oddities. Failing that, Irongate is my next choice, for if we control the old watch tower, we are one step closer to taking the pyramid. We are currently at neither, as you're well aware, due to Clive Bardell and his ill-timed proclamation. And yet if we dally here, like we have for nearly a month, we'll continue to lose ground and ultimately, ownership of our city.'

'I hear you, my king,' Griffith could feel the blood in his veins surge, felt the aches in his legs and hands fade.

'So, I have a new plan,' Tarsin placed an arm over Will's shoulders. 'Will has been kind enough to detail a number of paths beneath the city, paths that should lead to New City and her grand estates.'

'Are we to finally engage the traitorous Bardell?' Griffith's voice was low, yet there was a sense of urgency in his gruff voice.

'In a manner of speaking,' Tarsin smiled, barely seen. 'I'm done with waiting. We need to be at Irongate, and shortly after, Aston's Tear. I'll entrust the gathering of a small warband to you, Cale Griffith. You have a day to assemble your hand-picked men. No more than thirty. Then you'll sneak into the sewers below Bastion and make your way to New City. I'll grant you five days to extract the thorn from my side.'

'Anything else?' Griffith showed his pearly-white teeth.

'No. I no longer have any desire to be tactful, nor do I have the patience. Just bring me the head of Clive Bardell. Preferably on a platter.

*

The platter slid across the wooden table with a screech.

Jarred cringed, realised he'd pushed a little too hard with his unfinished meal. He'd made a habit of not making too much noise since arriving at Irongate. It was a cautious approach to survival, a method to avoid detection. The thought of beasts hunting in the night, listening for their prey, sniffing for a scent, still sent shivers down his spine. And for nearly forty days and nights since arriving through the portal, he'd excelled at keeping himself hidden from prying eyes. He gathered food from the garden before the rising sun, kept indoors whilst the day was bright, and spent each night making minimal sounds as he crept about the tower and her various rooms.

It was a challenge at times, but one he couldn't afford to disregard. Until men of Bastion came to rescue him, he was on his own.

Several activities caught his attention in the early days of his arrival. Honing his sword skills was paramount. He could almost hear Ruvin's voice in his head after every sweep he made, prodding his movement, questioning his pace. Memories of laughter would follow, Donal with his high-pitched squeal, Ruvin his fatherly chuckle. Jarred understood his sword lessons were imperative, not only for his wellbeing, but also his sanity. It gave him purpose and focused his thoughts. The blood coursing through his veins made him feel worthy. And yet other pastimes were just as rewarding, and it was the Depository where he found himself spending most of his days. A place to rummage through numerous books and unfurl countless scrolls. He was amazed at the enormous space devoted to shelves, and the shelves devoted to books. Thousands of them, leather bound and dusty. From the floor to the ceiling in most cases. It took him an afternoon of observation to realize he knew so little about life. And about words. And numbers.

It hurt his mind just thinking about it. Celestial charts were found alongside poetry, wise words from elders were inscribed next to the mutterings of the damned. Books on herb lore, weaponry, husbandry, dancing, dining etiquette, socialising, womanising, forging, needlework and more. So many books, so many ideas. So much he didn't know.

He sighed, stuck his fingers in the congealing wax from his fluttering candle. From the height of his flaming stub he could tell night had fallen over an hour ago, yet the remains of his meal sat heavy on his wooden board. A thick piece of dried mutton, black as charcoal, and a half-eaten carrot he picked from the garden just before sunset. It didn't amount to much, but neither was he hungry. Besides, he'd eaten well first thing in the morning. Three raw eggs from the pen, followed by a bowl of oats mixed with water and sprinkled shavings of cinnamon bark. He couldn't believe his eyes when he found the cinnamon at the rear of the pantry, remembered Ruvin showing him the spice on their return from Al-Za'im. From what his old master had described, it was worth a fortune.

'I wish you were here, Ruvin,' he whispered to the night.

He shook his head, sought to shrug the melancholy he felt settling in. It was always the same, an hour after sunset, just as thoughts of retiring for the night surfaced. A deep breath calmed his nerves as his fingers sought out the candle wax. He rolled it between his finger and thumb, worked the wax into a ball. Then he carved two eyes and a mouth with his knife and sat it on the edge of his platter. It stared back at him, eyes wide, mouth open. He wondered if it was asking him a question.

Jarred blinked back tiredness; knew he should listen to his body. Yet the questions he asked himself during the day were now back to haunt him.

What were the men of Bastion doing to the north of the city? And why was he still here, hiding within Irongate, when he needed to be somewhere else?

He couldn't answer the first question. His looking glass allowed him to see quite a distance, but it couldn't pierce the hundreds of buildings sitting between Irongate and New City. Why the men had turned about so suddenly to head north, when he felt they were a day from marching on Irongate, he couldn't know. It still pained him. In fact, he clearly remembered the tears that flowed the following morning.

He knew their whereabouts initially, for he had climbed the watch tower the second day after his arrival. It was a precarious adventure, for the walls were unstable and the stairs had fallen between the third and fifth floor. But being a curious lad, and one used to climbing the rigging on a ship, he'd managed to hoist himself to the tower's upper level with deft hands and well placed feet. At its penultimate floor he found a room full of trinkets, much like any other within Irongate, for the brothers appeared to be as curious as he, amongst which he discovered a looking glass like Captain Vasco used on his ship, the *Lioness*.

Within an hour he could see soldiers on Bastion's outskirt, deployed in the field beyond her Southern Wall. His heart thumped with joy at his finding, only for it to slow to a depressed whimper once he realised how far away they actually were. The journey to reach the men would take him past dozens of streets and laneways and countless alleys crowded in shadow. And as he discovered later, as he thought to plot his course through the city, the streets of Bastion were no longer the domain of man.

He sat back from his table. He should retire for the night, only the thought of being in his cell, behind a locked door, gave him chills. It wasn't the first time, and he'd come to believe the voices inside his head, those same voices he heard when he first touched the pyramid, were somehow responsible for his feelings of dread.

Barely a week had passed before his visions returned. This time, though, he managed to keep his wits about him. The suggestions were minor, the sights he saw when he slept were knowledgeable. He learnt about the pyramid and its portals, discovered names for the beasts that suddenly roamed Bastion's streets.

And he saw patterns. Patterns in the design of the pyramid and the portals surrounding her. Patterns in the layout of an ancient city. Intwined within the patterns were methods of time, and intwined within the timing were patterns of space.

It was enough to send him over the edge, except the voices fed him slowly, one infinitesimal piece at a time, until he grasped the enormity of what they'd created.

A shake of the head. Jarred grabbed his candle and the sheathed sword that once belonged to Ruvin and stepped slowly towards the kitchen door. The hall beyond would lead him to his cell below ground, near the cellar, a haven for when he was fearful. But on occasion he'd climb the tower and sit high above the city as night fell, watching those who scampered in the shadows, hunting each other. Somehow, he felt safer knowing he could watch their movements from above. He felt safe knowing he could keep an eye on them.

The hall greeted him, dark and silent as usual. The candle in his hand flickered, cast its meagre light a mere ten feet. He had a choice to make. His cell was to his right, at the end of a corridor and down a handful of stone steps. He spun to his left and began his walk to the tower instead, hoping the exercise would clear his mind of its swirling questions.

He wasn't so lucky. The thoughts stayed with him, his doubts and fears gripped tight. Ever since he watched the men of Bastion move to the north, away from Irongate when they were so close to claiming it, he sensed it was time for him to leave. Three times he'd watched beasts climb the outer wall of Irongate and stalk her interior. Three times they found nothing of interest and moved on.

But one day, he feared they would find him. It was only a matter of time.

An iron door led him into the base of the tower, a circular space sixty feet in diameter. The staircase wound itself along the inside, twirling up towards the peak, one hundred feet above. He blew upon his candle flame, watched it wink out of existence with a puff of smoke. There were slits in the wall of the tower, vantage points to see the outside world. A candle flame, even one so small, would be easily seen by creatures nearby.

He began the climb, taking each step carefully, his left hand pressed against the stone wall for balance. For several minutes he wound upward, until he reached the third floor. Here he was forced to improvise, for the stairs had fallen when a large section of the wall had caved in. With deft hands he unclasped his sword belt and swung it over his shoulder. He found the blade was better placed across his back when he was climbing, away from his legs as they sought footholds on the broken wall.

Trembling hands reached for those bricks he knew remained firm. Having made the climb so many times in the last forty days, he was hoisting himself onto the fifth floor in moments.

A steadying breath allowed him to take an instant to look below, searching for any movement in the shadows. If a creature followed behind him and watched his ascent, he'd be in trouble. The type of trouble that would see him dead or trapped. And neither appealed to him. Thankfully, the stairwell was empty.

Three more twirls up the staircase saw him reach the penultimate floor, a room once below the enormous bronze telescope that allowed the brothers of Irongate to gaze upon the stars. It was still there, perched precariously above, but the floor had tilted and the wall had crumbled, denying him access. Any thoughts about reaching the top floor were quashed by its unstable nature. Instead, he made himself at home with what he had discovered. It was enough. On this floor rested a cabinet housing an assortment of bottled wine and spirits, whilst another series of shelves held a collection of tomes and journals, heavily bound in dark-stained leather.

He moved to his left, where a small window had fallen when the earthquake struck. He'd swept the broken glass into a corner on his first day in the tower, along with cleaning the fragments of brick and mortar blanketing the floor. He remembered the small writing table found on its side, a shattered ink bottle staining an area beneath it.

Everything was tidy now, in its place. He could close his eyes and still find what he needed, grab all his gear even when the sun went down. He needed to, because if the beasts came for him in the dead of night, a fast escape would be his only chance.

Starlight shone through the window, providing enough illumination for him to navigate his room tonight. With soft footfalls he moved to his left where he'd laid out his most prized possessions. After every ascent to the watchtower, he made a habit of studying the maps Donal had entrusted to him. They were of the inner city of Bastion, both above and below ground and detailed unlike anything he had seen before. What Donal found in King Arkos Vantos' chamber was something priceless. In the right hands, it could very well provide control of the city. In the wrong hands . . . well, he didn't like to think what would happen to Bastion should the maps fall into the wrong hands. The fact he was in possession of them now meant they were safe. If someone else came to possess them . . .

If he passed them to the leaders of Bastion, to someone like Tarsin Va - if he were alive - then he could sleep at night knowing his duty had been fulfilled. But he'd seen the soldiers move away from Irongate to pursue some other purpose to the north. And now the days were sweeping by, rushing towards the winter months as the heat dissipated and mornings became cool. When he agreed to return to Bastion, Kian and Neema had stressed to him the importance of his mission. Return and place the maps into the hands of a leader who could use them to advantage. Failing such an outcome, he was to use them himself and seek entry into Aston's Tear. There he was to disengage the portal by retrieving the *Nepharii Uranometria,* thus cancelling the influx of creatures into the city. Those in charge could then seek to reclaim Bastion and put measures in place to save her misplaced citizens.

He squinted at the maps, traced their lines from one portal to the next. Twelve balls of golden energy, surrounding the pyramid and her gigantic sphere of light. Then he moved to the lower map, looked at the markings, memorized the paths below ground that would lead him to the monstrosity. Forty days and nights he had paced the halls and corridors of Irongate. It was too many. He should have left by now. He should have found the courage to reach Aston's Tear.

A scream broke the silence, cut through his thoughts like the king's blade he once carried. He peered over the windowsill and down at murky streets below. Movement caught his eye, a flash of silver reflecting starlight. A roar followed. The thud of flesh being struck reached his ears, he saw bodies heave and sway and eventually fall. He heard the cries of death.

It made him feel ill. Even from where he sat, crouched behind a broken window within a broken tower, he swore he could smell the carnage. And come morning, he knew the crows would feast with the rising sun.

'I've been here too long,' he said to the night. 'I cannot wait any longer.'

Quick, sure steps took him across the room. A steel peg held a backpack, prepared days in advance, waiting for him to decide whether he should go or stay. Inside were strips of salted pork, dried beef and a pouch brimming with walnuts: food from the larder he found on his first day. In a pocket on the side rested his glow-stone. Kian had informed him a day in the sun would rekindle its power, and a simple rub of the stone when surrounded by darkness would emit a gentle glow. Jarred had sat it out in the sunshine as soon as possible, checked its power five times now, at night, when screams woke him from slumber.

He shouldered the pack over his sword, strapped it tight. The cold steel of the looking glass jabbed into his ribs. It sat in another pocket outside the pack, a silver buckle holding it in place. He had no wish to leave it behind.

Another three steps to his right. This time he reached for a waterskin with a long leather strap. He placed it around his neck, balanced the skin against his hip. Standing straight, he tested his ease of movement. His shoulders bore the most weight, yet he felt he could swing his arms admirably. Knowing his journey beneath Bastion could turn sour at any moment, the ability to run freely was paramount. It was another reason why he'd dispensed with the jacket. It wasn't cold enough yet to justify wearing it to begin with, and Aston's Tear was less than a day's travel from where he now stood. All things going well, he would be on the outskirts of the pyramid by tomorrow, and if

Frey: Goddess of Luck and the Four Winds looked favourably upon him, he'd be inside a short time later.

Tired eyes shifted to the staircase and the maps to the left. He took a pace, cast his gaze over the paths he was forced to memorize. 'Do I take you with me? Or do you burn?'

The thought of burning the maps broke his heart, but he knew he couldn't afford to leave them behind, nor could he take them on his journey. The risks were too high. Besides, the voices inside his head had been forcefully clear when suggesting he burn them. They knew the paths as well as any. If asked, they could show him the way.

He reached for them, rolled them tightly before placing them in a cylinder. He would take them below when he left and burn them inside the baker's oven at the rear of the kitchen. The light from the flame would be impossible to see from the outside, and the smoke would be invisible before the sun rose. Knowing he was now ready; he took one last look at the room he had come to call home.

Heavy eyes struggled to focus. He was tired and scared, wished Kian or Ruvin could stand beside him for encouragement. Even Neema, with her strange powers and crackling energy would be a delight. He would have such courage with a companion to share the burden.

But he was alone. Felt like he'd been alone his entire life.

He pushed his back against the wall, slid to a sitting position. 'I'll rest my eyes for a moment,' he whispered, 'then I'll make my way downstairs and into the cellars below.'

He closed his eyes, expecting to see Ruvin's wizened face smiling at him. Instead, he saw the beautiful green eyes of Kayla Tolsten, her babe, Rastan Va, sitting in the crook of her arm.

'I hope you are safe,' he mumbled, barely coherent. 'When I am ready, I will save you.'

Her image shifted, blurred, then merged into the face of Donal, followed by Ruvin, Kian and Reefe. It finally settled on Neema, the wisest lady he had ever known. She smiled; spoke words he couldn't hear. He tried to understand, asked her to repeat herself.

'Have faith,' he believed she said.

He shared a brief smile . . . then promptly fell asleep.

CHAPTER TWENTY-FOUR

Her fingers tightened about the shaft of wood.

Kayla took a breath, assessed her stance with a thought, slid her left foot back two inches across soft grass. She offered her right shoulder to Ruvin, her three-foot wooden sword held at eye level, unwavering.

'Good,' the old man smirked, although she could see he was pleased. 'Now, lunge!'

She did as bid, stepped forward with pace, her wooden sword lancing towards his grinning face. He slapped her practice sword to the side, took a wide step so he could bring his own sword in an arc towards her midriff. A twist of her wrist angled her sword down, slapping his thrust before it could strike. They circled.

'Your speed has increased, lass, along with your strength,' Ruvin kept smiling, which was his way when sparring.

'Are you surprised,' she replied. 'I've been training for more than a year. I've never felt so strong.'

He flicked his head to the side, more to rid himself of the sweat beading on his forehead, although she knew he always followed such an action with an overhead attack. He stepped forward, as she predicted, but instead of going high, as she planned for, he came in low with a sweep. The crack of wood hitting her thigh was drowned out by her curse.

'Hell's balls, Ruvin!' her face was flushed, more from embarrassment than any pain. 'I thought I had you.'

'Aye,' he continued to smile, 'I thought you'd guess my attack. I've only presented it five times already today. It is all well and good to observe patterns, my dear, but you must also be aware you aren't being set up for a trap. A canny swordsman is canny for a reason. Never underestimate your opponent.'

The wooden sword lowered until its tip hit the ground. A deep breath followed. Always with Ruvin there was a lesson to be learned. She wasn't certain if she'd learnt them all, but she was possibly close. The gods above knew she'd been hit enough times.

'Do we go again?' she asked, wiping her brow.

'No,' the smile faded, 'that's enough for today. Besides, you have company.' He tilted his head to the side, towards her rooms.

Kayla took another deep breath, wondered if she could merge into the trees in her garden and disappear. She spun about instead.

'Greetings, Kayla,' the voice belonged to Nae-oki, a female Ven with auburn hair to her waist, a slender willow-like body and beautiful eyes the colour of sapphires.

'Good morning, Nae-oki,' Kayla replied in the Ven tongue as Ruvin took his leave. 'How are you this fine day?'

A curtsey followed, for Nae-oki was always polite. 'I am well. You are sweating,' she observed, 'have you been running?'

Kayla placed the wooden sword behind her back, although she was certain Nae-oki knew what they had been doing. 'I have done some running,' it wasn't a lie.

'Well,' Nae-oki placed hands on hips, 'it is nearing noon and you have been summoned to the Sunshine Hall. Would you like help choosing your attire, or should we bathe you first?'

Kayla shook her head. Neither would be preferable. She knew today was an important occasion to the Ven, but she'd hoped not to be associated with their rituals. Neema hadn't shared the same views, though. The old matron had insisted on attending the festivities, for the occasions afforded the survivors of Bastion to be within earshot of the Five Kings were few. From what Neema mentioned earlier, it was a chance to observe and possibly learn more about the immortal lords who held them captive.

'I should bathe first,' she said, watching as Ruvin vacated her rooms to return to his own. He would be accompanied to the Sunshine Hall in the same way, with a young male Ven to lead and inform.

'I shall gather your new clothes and a towel, then,' Nae-oki was already retreating the way she had come. 'I'll meet you in the water.'

Another shake of her head, but she was aware of how sticky she felt since her sparring with Ruvin ceased. The thin hide shirt she wore for practice covered her torso only, and beneath the glistening sweat on her arms were a handful of bruises waiting to shine. She would have to cover her arms before reaching the Sunshine Hall. Questions would be asked otherwise.

She looked over her shoulder. Nae-oki was absent, probably searching for the garments she'd placed on her mattress earlier in the morning. Kayla had thrown them behind the wicker chair when she first saw them, vowing not to wear such an elaborate ensemble. The colours were garish and the style distinctly Ven. Neither was to her liking.

Still, she knew she had little choice in the end. Neema had said so, accompanied with the sternest look possible. Today was a chance not to be trifled with. If they were alert, something profound could occur.

With a raise of her eyebrows, Kayla walked the fifty feet to a pool of water nestled amongst the rocks. Tall, weeping trees swayed gently in the background, sturdy guardians to a small waterfall fed by a bubbling spring deeper in the garden. A ring of sky-blue flowers bordered the pool, interspersed with narrow sprigs of what she called red-velvet grass. It was picturesque, inviting, and she couldn't help but love the serenity each time she approached. There was a sense of calm in the air, noticeable with every step she took.

The wooden sword in her hand fell to the ground without a sound. Her tight-fitting hide shirt, once she untied the laces along her ribcage, was peeled off with a sigh a moment later. The air, even though it was warm, cooled her skin. The rock pool water, once she submerged, would soothe it.

Aching fingers unbuttoned her leather skirt. It fell upon the ground before she delicately placed a toe beneath the shimmering surface. A slight shiver raced down her spine, provoking a subtle twist of her shoulders as she took another step.

This was the one place where she could truly become lost. After everything she'd been forced to endure, this pool of water in a garden of exquisite workmanship could peel away the layers of hatred swirling just below the surface. Her cares would crumble as she waded naked into the middle of the pool. The worries she held onto, the concerns about her companions, the fears for her son. Everything she fought so hard to control would simply float away. Peace and quiet, a space to be mindful.

'I have your clothes,' the words intruded on her emptiness, forced her eyes open as she spun to watch Nae-oki, her own clothes lying pristine on the grass, wade into the water as naked as she. 'Shall I wash your hair, Kayla-mother? I have scented sand and petals.'

A smile formed beneath her baleful eyes, softening her visage. Nae-oki meant no disrespect, or harm. She was young and beautiful; a servant to the Five Kings. Possibly a plaything. Like every other servant within the palace, she adhered to her duty without fault. It was banishment from the palace if you were found to do otherwise.

'I believe it would be best, Nae-oki. If I am to present before the Five Kings this day, I should at least look the part.'

The smile on the young Ven widened. She moved closer, a gentle sway to her hips, her small breasts barely moving. Her lustrous hair looked aflame.

'I will make you even more beautiful than usual, Kayla-mother,' the glint in her eyes suggested specific plans had already been made for this day. 'We have time for a massage first, then I shall enlighten your hair. May I proceed?'

A nod of consent followed before Kayla took a step towards Nae-oki, then sank to her knees.

An hour later, with the sun now a murmur behind the tall, shading trees, she was ready.

'Thank you, Nae-oki, for all your work. I feel presentable, at least.'

'You look wonderful, Kayla-mother. You look like a queen.'

A bell sounded deep within the palace, reverberating for all to hear.

It was time.

*

A chime rang, clear and piercing.

Kayla Tolsten shook her head, her long raven tresses swaying halfway down her back. She was in the company of Neema and her son, Rastan Va, who held her left hand with his right as he walked beside her. She glanced at her little man and smiled, watched his balanced steps, then returned her eyes to the old matron. 'Do they have to be so loud?' she asked, sharing a look of disdain with her friend.

Neema snorted in reply, which eased Kayla's fears somewhat, then shook her head as they passed another assembly of garishly clothed Ven mingling in the hallway. She stifled a laugh, put one foot in front of the other. If her memory served her well, there was only one more staircase to traverse before they reached the Sunshine Hall.

Hopefully, the noise of chimes and pipes and cymbals struck with vigour would lessen. And if the gods smiled upon her, the riot of colour would fade with the volume.

Yet she knew her wishes wouldn't be answered. Colour bloomed from every avenue as they continued their walk. Ven in their outrageous outfits of mauve, teal and amber clashed with banners of cherry red and sunflower, whilst silk ribbons provided bursts of citrus and moody skies. Never had she seen the Ven celebrate an event like this. Not once since her arrival.

'I'm not sure I wish to do this,' her words were barely above a whisper, but they carried to Neema all the same.

'I'm not sure you have a choice, my dear. When the Five Kings ask for your attendance, you do not refuse. You know how demanding they are.'

'How controlling, you mean,' Kayla raised her eyes to the ceiling, noticed scarlet ribbons dangling in the shadows.

'Aye, they are that, my dear. Come,' Neema grabbed her hand and led her and Rastan to the final staircase.

Their steps quickened in rhythm with their heartbeats. Chimes and cymbals continued to sing in the hallway, and a new melody, composed of string instruments, drifted from behind the enormous entrance to the Sunshine Hall.

Kayla paused to admire the intricate woodwork winding sinuously about the rose quartz pillars flanking the doorway. Slender tendrils of blackwood mimicked creeping vines soaring to the ceiling, whilst elaborate carvings of the small dawn birds she'd come to love peeked from behind emerald leaves. Having only been admitted to the Sunshine Hall once since their arrival, the sight certainly hadn't waned in beauty.

A splash of forest moss and ocean blue caught her eye as Nae-oki danced towards them from within the hall. Her dress billowed as she approached, her vibrant auburn hair sparkled as if touched by the sun.

'You have arrived,' Nae-oki sang the words in her own tongue. 'This is truly a momentous event, Kayla-mother. Come, the festivities are about to begin.'

Nae-oki's enthusiasm was infectious, and her doe-like eyes practically swept the three of them across the threshold. Yet Kayla felt Rastan grip her hand tighter as they entered the sprawling space filled with lilting music. He was nervous, she could sense it clearly by the strength of his grip, although a sparkle in his eyes caught her own as she looked at her son. She smiled, then felt her attention being drawn back to the hall. It was everything she remembered it to be. Polished marble floors, flared windows, heaven-reaching pillars and a thousand brightly coloured ribbons hanging from a domed ceiling. Pale blue sky shone from the outside, offering a horizon unblemished by the surrounding city, for as Nae-oki explained, one had to traverse thirteen flights of stairs to reach the Sunshine Hall.

'There is so much to take in,' she explained, letting go of Neema's hand. She felt Rastan begin to pull away, his eyes already focused on the Ven playing their instruments. They sat on the far side of the entrance, both male and female, a dozen musicians working in harmony. Thirty feet to their left began a raised dais, a series of five steps to reach a platform for the Five Kings to sit and observe. To their right lay an open floor, a patchwork of coloured tiles bordered by gaping windows. There was room for three hundred Ven, she was certain, perhaps more if you included those wandering the hall with platters of expertly prepared delicacies for guests to satiate their appetite.

'This way, Kayla-mother,' Nae-oki gestured, leading them towards an area reserved for honoured dignitaries. 'There are cushions for you to sit upon, and refreshments if you are so inclined.'

Nervous eyes sought out Neema as they were led to their place in the hall. It was obvious Nae-oki was very pleased with herself, a direct result of her being a Ven of importance on this special day. From what Kayla heard and witnessed since their arrival, the majority of Ven rarely spoke with the Five Kings directly. Yet with such an occasion being orchestrated on their behalf, the possibility of Nae-oki exchanging words with a king was high. In fact, she was convinced she could see the answer in Nae-oki's cheerful eyes.

With Rastan still clinging to her hand, she took a seat upon a cushion, sitting her son in her lap as she made herself comfortable. Neema did likewise, and within moments a platter of delicate morsels was swept before their eyes, followed by crystal glasses offering flower-scented water and berry-stained juice.

Nae-oki stood before them as the platters disappeared, her affable nature not lost on Kayla. 'Those chosen to attend today's festivities have arrived,' she begun, her hand sweeping back the way they had come. 'The Five Kings will present soon and take their place above,' a finger pointed to the marble steps. 'A number of . . . favourites, may accompany them. Pay them no heed, for they are merely playthings for our immortal lords.'

Another shared glance with Neema as Nae-oki finished her words. Neither knew anything of importance concerning the kings, for contact had been minimal at best. Months had passed since the kings returned from their venture to the portal. Jarred, they knew, would have stepped back into Bastion. But there was no sign of Kian, nor any word from the kings to explain his absence. Entire scenarios had been played out and discussed by the survivors, yet any truth they sought to hold onto was mere speculation.

'Ruvin and Donal have arrived,' Neema said, lifting her mind from darkening thoughts.

Kayla sought them out, beckoned with a wave. Ruvin caught her movement and tapped young Donal on the shoulder. As they made for their position, she took a moment to observe her companions. Ruvin had aged, it was true, for the lines surrounding his eyes were long and varied, and the vigour in his step when she first met him in Bastion was completely absent. Although he continued to instruct her in swordplay, his involvement was sporadic, his lessons becoming shorter each day. Verbal instructions were becoming more frequent. It was obvious his health was failing, yet he never spoke of it. Neema knew he carried an ailment, but even she refused to comment.

And then there was Donal.

He still looked every bit the young boy. Whereas Jarred had grown tall and rangy as he transitioned from boy to man, Donal had barely added two inches to his height since arriving on the New World. Fear of his past flickered behind his shadowed eyes and talk of monsters in the dark troubled his sleep. Reefe spoke of it often, suggested this world and its people to be the cause. A return to their home would put Donal's demons to rest. She wasn't so sure, but like Reefe, returning to Bastion was her only desire.

'Welcome,' Kayla held out her hand, offering a place on the cushions ranged about them. 'Where is Reefe?' she asked, noting his absence.

'We have no idea,' Donal smiled as he sat next to her, his fingers wiggling before Rastan's eyes. 'He was in the garden this morning, like he always is, perched amongst the branches of the largest tree.'

'Aye,' Ruvin also sat, 'he still yearns for home. I think he looks beyond the city, imagining the road he'll one day take.'

She nodded, but in truth, she'd stopped listening. Any discussions concerning Reefe fell by the wayside from her perspective. The man thought it his right to hound her every step when they first entered the palace. Proclamations of protection and honour dribbled from his tongue, and his puffed-out chest and self-righteousness gave her sweaty palms and nausea. After a series of unsuccessful attempts to win her hand, he'd resorted to sending hand-written notes. Again, when words such as "desire" and "love" began to leap off the parchment, her stomach would turn sour in an instant. And when he wrote of being a father-figure to Rastan, it took all her will power not to vomit right there and then.

But she endured, and countless sessions with Neema calmed her anger at his insistent nature. Now, she barely saw him, and the past few months had been tolerable.

'How are you this day, Donal?' she asked, aware her mood was rapidly falling. Nae-oki had failed to inform them how long today's proceedings would likely take.

Donal lifted his eyes to meet her own. His blonde hair was long, tied at the nape with a dyed ribbon the colour of a deep forest. 'I feel well, Kayla.'

It was a lie. The lines around his weary eyes told her the truth. The lad couldn't sleep, not since they fled Bastion and arrived on the world Kian called Vidae. Neema and Ruvin had spoken several times concerning the boy and his health. Yet their thinking always returned to his uncanny ability to remember everything he saw. Everything in incredible detail, it was noted. How anyone could sleep when they closed their eyes - if the Deios were always there to devour you - was beyond her comprehension.

She offered half-a-smile in response. It was a strain on her behalf, but the look in his eyes softened. She was about to probe deeper, to ease his fears, if she could, when blaring trumpets and stained hide drums drowned all conversation. The group as one looked to the marble dais where elaborately carved wooden thrones ranged along its length. A moment later, with rhythmic sounds still pounding, Ik'omi: first born of the Five Kings, led his brothers to their seats.

She didn't know what to feel as they moved with sublime grace and confidence to their appointed place. Their attire was conservative, and yet at the same time practical. It was also incredibly evocative.

'They look the part,' Donal lent close and spoke into her ear.

She agreed with a nod, kept the kings in her sight. Beautifully fashioned leather vests: so old they were polished white, were part of an ensemble showcasing the kings lean, muscular bodies. Belts studded with fire-rubies added a glaring contrast, whilst Ven daggers sheathed in midnight blue sat comfortably at their hips. Each king wore a cape of gossamer silk, also dark as night, and yet their perfectly formed feet were bare.

'Can you see their pendants?' Neema's voice this time, from her right.

Kayla saw them, how could she not. Golden circles on golden chains hanging about their necks. Each was polished sun-bright and set with an azure gemstone the size of a plump cherry. 'They appear like angels,' her words voiced what they all thought.

'Perhaps they are,' Donal looked as transfixed as anyone.

A flicker of movement caught her attention. Behind the kings flowed a stream of Ven, the favourites Nae-oki spoke of, she assumed, blessed to partake in the ceremony within proximity of their lords. As Nae-oki claimed, they were pretty creatures, young and blemish free, a true example of youthful vigour and charm. And to her surprise, they were not all females. Half-a-dozen males with flaxen hair mingled amongst the group. Kayla watched as they settled in quick fashion, aware their lords could see every movement. But her attention wavered as she looked to the rear.

'What in Frey's name is Reefe O'Bannon doing with the chosen?' Kayla's words carried to her companions despite the echoing drums. She narrowed her gaze, saw the man she despised sitting on his knees, as the Ven so often did. His hair was tied into three braids, also like the Ven, and his shirt was loose and free, in line with his spirit. A ridiculous smile split his clean-shaven face, and his eyes, even from where she sat, suggested he'd taken a Ven narcotic before the event.

'He's sold his soul, I reckon,' said Donal, none too happy with his comrade.

Ruvin appeared equally displeased. 'I have seen the man sporadically the last few months,' he began, an aged finger stroking his chin. 'Perhaps Donal is right. Perhaps Reefe is tired of sitting in his room and the garden beyond. Perhaps this is his means of escape.'

'Or he has caved in,' suggested Neema. 'Betrayed us and our people.'

Speculation would be rife in the days to come. Kayla could picture the group sitting on manicured grass, tall branches swaying above, the sound of water tinkling into the rock pool. She could hear the anger in their words and see venom in their eyes.

'We don't know what he has said or done,' Neema explained, seeking to calm growing frustrations. 'But we'll certainly find out when he returns to us.'

'Aye,' Ruvin chimed in, still rubbing his chin, 'we'll ask him, alright.'

Further talk was stalled as another blast from bronze trumpets blared from the dais. Flags swept past the kings on silver poles and flower petals of differing hue were scattered over the marble floor. The sweet scent of honey and sunshine permeated the room.

A Ven herald took to the dais, his flowing emerald robe woven with golden flowers at the hems. Long white hair, braided twice, was twined with pale blue ribbon and his right hand held a wooden staff bristling with sparkling gems. He stood with authority before the Five Kings and their entourage, spoke with a clear voice in the language of the Ven. His words took on a life of their own, rolling together until they sounded like water sliding over moss-covered stones. Kayla could understand most of what he said, although his tone shifted on occasion, causing confusion at times. After a lengthy introduction to those gathered and an even lengthier proclamation of the Five King's immortality and divine presence, talk drifted to the cause of the gathering and why those from another world were invited to attend.

'It is our custom,' continued the herald, 'to announce the arrival of a newborn soul to the world on their third day. It is also custom amongst the Ven to celebrate the growing child who leaves infancy behind. At three years of age, it is to be so.' His eyes sought her out. 'Today we have the pleasure to announce Rastan Va, son of Kayla-mother, from a world other than our own. This has never occurred before. It is, and will be, a momentous occasion.'

All eyes fell on the survivors of Bastion.

She could feel the gaze of more than three hundred Ven seeking her and her son. Rastan squirmed in her lap, also conscious of the attention, his small hands squeezing her wrist as she kept a tight grip about his waist. Nae-oki had informed her of the importance of today numerous times during the last moon cycle. Still, the preparation involved was considerably more than she expected.

'Come, Kayla-mother,' the herald was talking in his sing-song voice once again, 'gather your child and present him before our immortal lords. Allow their benevolence to be shared with your son, so that he may grow tall, strong, bright and compassionate.' His arms spread wide, his emerald robes with golden embroidery shimmering in the light of day. 'Present Rastan Va so that our lords may catch a glimpse of his full potential.'

Shaking, she felt herself rise from her seat, Rastan in her arms. She took hesitant steps towards the dais, heard Neema offer words of encouragement from behind. The thought of offering her son to the kings was not her soul purpose as she crossed the marble floor. To simply be close, close enough to look deep into their immortal eyes, was her true purpose. She needed to see if the kings truly harboured souls within their immaculate bodies, or whether they were nothing more than power hungry individuals concerned only with their own self-importance.

Her steps ceased at the top of the marble stairs.

Five immortal kings locked eyes to her own.

She trembled. From her feet all the way to her hands, she trembled. It wasn't fear that evoked the tremors, though. It was awe. Awe at being in the presence of beings far older and wiser than herself. The realisation hit her like a thunderclap. This close, as she wished a moment earlier, was more than enough for her to feel the energy coursing through their veins. It was raw. It was tangible. It was, from her new perspective, terrible.

'Offer the child, Kayla-mother.'

The words jolted her into action. She held out her arms, offering Rastan to the Five Kings. Beginning with Ik'omi, they each took a step forward and looked into his storm-blue eyes. Nothing was spoken. No hands reached for the child. There was only silence.

Her arms began to shake. Holding a solid three-year-old in the air was taking its toll. As Solaii, the last and youngest of the Five Kings took steps away from Rastan, she bent forward and placed Rastan's bare feet on the marble. He stood there, straight-backed, his black hair plaited into a single tail. Bronzed skin from days frolicking in the sunshine was glimpsed beneath his white shirt. He looked up at the kings without flinching. Held their gaze with his own.

'The kings have looked into the eyes of the child,' the herald waved his staff in the air, its many faceted gemstones glinting with multi-coloured light, 'and the child has glimpsed immortality.' A cheer sounded from the gathered Ven. 'Rastan Va will grow tall, strong, bright and compassionate. It has been ordained.' The beating of drums began with earnest. Flower petals continued to be strewn about the hall. Kayla backed away, her body still tingling from the Five King's aura. She motioned towards Rastan, but he remained rooted to the floor, his tiny fists curled at his side. His eyes continued to blaze.

'Rastan,' her voice sounded weak. She looked at Ik'omi, but the king's focus was locked on her son. 'Rastan!' she shouted, seeking his attention.

Ik'omi heard her, for he tore his gaze away from her boy to seek her out. 'You!' the king's voice reverberated throughout the hall. She met his eyes, felt her legs shudder uncontrollably. 'Why does your son not speak?'

She felt her heart wither. Here she was, presenting her son to the Five Kings for acceptance, and somehow, unbeknownst to her, they'd discovered his inability to talk.

'Well, Kayla-mother,' Ik'omi smiled, making her feel incomplete and terrified. 'Why does your son refuse to converse like the rest of us?'

Silence. It bore into her soul, smothered her thoughts. What could she say? The boy was gifted, it was easy to see, but Ik'omi was right. Rastan did not talk. Never had. For three years she raised her son with Neema by her side and friends to help guide her. And for three years the only sounds Rastan made were gentle whimpers whilst he slept. He didn't cry, he didn't scream when hurt, he never demanded to be heard. He was silent. Always silent.

'I do not know the answer to your question, my lord,' tears welled, her voice choked. 'I have asked, but he does not reply.' A hand curled within her own. She looked down at her son, saw compassion and understanding, but also sorrow in his eyes. 'Perhaps he will talk when the time is right. Only he can know when that time shall be.'

Ik'omi nodded, although she sensed his disapproval. There was a notable shift in his demeanour, a glimpse of agitation in his gait as he walked back to his brothers. Something had passed between her son and the eldest king. For an instant, she wondered what it was.

Drums rolled to a crescendo, strings were plucked with light fingers. Music flowed. Within moments countless bodies began to sway as Ven, both young and old, chose to dance.

Neema, Donal and Ruvin reached her side. They placed comforting hands on her shoulders, squeezed her tight.

Rastan, three years old, stepped away. He walked to the centre of the hall where a dozen female Ven twirled and leaped with agility and confidence. Subtle movements accompanied bold fluctuations; lithe bodies became infused with raw energy.

A small bare foot began to tap. Hands clapped in rhythm. Those on the outskirts stood in silence.

The boy began to dance.

CHAPTER TWENTY-FIVE

The scent of spice and honey swamped him.

Reefe O'Bannon inhaled with a smile, aware his own senses were heightened due to a Ven powder called *spryx*. It was deep purple in colour, smelt like morning berries and mint and gave first-time recipients the sensation of bleeding eyes due to its sour taste. Of course, his eyes had never bled - so he'd been told – although tears had slipped across his cheeks unchecked. Now, he was used to the facial tightening one experienced after placing a thumbnail of *spryx* on the tongue. His eyes might not bleed, but he knew with certainty they'd be bloodshot.

It mattered little to the former thief. He no longer cared deeply about his wellbeing, and his past life was mostly forgotten, a distant memory of a time and place that offered much yet rarely delivered. Living in Bastion was hard, uncompromising, and quite often a struggle. He remembered having to fight every day just to be acknowledged, and knew he'd have to do it all over again lest he lose his privileges in the pecking order. That was his life: a constant battle pleasing others.

And yet he never caught the prize he'd always sought.

Kayla Tolsten.

His eyes found her to his left, seated amongst plush cushions, her companions surrounding her. She sat with a rigid back, eyes locked on her son, Rastan Va, the three old still dancing with Ven women in the centre of the hall. Those beside her thought her gaze was one of admiration for the youngster, but Reefe knew she carried a burden she was unwilling to share.

He didn't bother seeking out the boy. He could hear Ven laughter following him, practically see the wide smiles as they danced beside him. Yet it was all for naught. Rastan didn't talk, had never uttered a word. Whatever Neema and Kian thought they saw in the infant child had proven to be a fallacy. For Reefe, he was nothing more than a distraction.

He focused bloodshot eyes on Kayla, admired the gentle curve of her neck, her black tresses so elegantly twirled. If possible, she was more beautiful than the first day they met.

An image of dark corridors and dancing flames popped into his consciousness. A memory from Bastion, one he believed forgotten. A young Kayla, innocent, pretty, a country girl entering the city in search of her father. Word led her to Undercity and the headquarters of the Nocturnals. He led her to her father, the Underlord, Derrick Tolsten.

'I have done everything for you, Kayla Tolsten,' he whispered, 'yet it's never been enough.'

A hand offered a silver goblet. He raised his head, saw Ik'omi, firstborn of the Nepharii kings. The smell of sweet wine hit his senses.

'Drink, Reefe O'Bannon,' the words suggested he didn't have a choice, 'for it is unwise to be so melancholy on such a day.'

'You have guessed my mood, my lord,' he returned in the Ven tongue, his hand shaking as he reached for the goblet. He concentrated, took a deep breath, managed to sip the sweet liquid without spilling a drop. He raced a tongue over his bottom lip, satisfied the taste was to his liking.

'You have an obvious desire for Kayla-mother,' Ik'omi began, 'and I assume it has not been a fleeting one. Does she not return your interest?'

Reefe placed the goblet to his lips, took another sip. With the *spryx* coursing through his veins now accompanied by the wine, he was having a difficult time assembling his thoughts. How long had he lusted after Kayla? Since they first met, he was certain. Emerald eyes, luscious midnight hair and a body promising the vigour of youth. He clenched his left hand tight, raised his goblet for another swallow. 'It's complicated.'

'Truly,' Ik'omi smiled, and for a moment, Reefe swore his eyes sparkled with mirth. 'I have seen love aplenty and lovers scorned throughout my life, young man, but those who persist generally win the day.'

'I have persisted, believe me,' he finished his drink, sat the silver goblet on coloured tiles. 'I have watched her blossom from innocent youth to the beautiful mother she is today, yet her true desires are a mystery to me.'

'Do you watch her still?'

Reefe raised his eyes. The question was not as flippant as the king suggested. There was a curiosity beneath the surface. Did Ik'omi know he watched her every day?

'The spyglass you asked to be made for you,' Ik'omi twirled his own silver goblet under his nose, poorly masking his smile, 'do you use it to watch Kayla-mother from your perch amongst the trees?'

The blood drained from his face, his fingers became numb, and his heart thumped a rapid staccato within his chest. Did Ik'omi truly know of his infatuation, or was he probing for an unlikely answer? And did he know of his initial plans to escape the palace?

'I watch her when I can,' it was the truth, he felt it prudent not to lie to the immortal king. 'I desire her, always have. If I knew how to make her mine, I would do so.'

It felt good to open up, to say the words out loud. For longer than he cared to remember, he'd kept his feelings chained within. His companions listened in the early days of their confinement, but no-one supported him. Everything they did was based around keeping Kayla and her infant son happy. Reefe O'Bannon was an after-thought at best.

And so thoughts of escape consumed him shortly after their arrival. The palace and her kings overwhelmed him to the point of panic, yet having been born and bred in a city, the lure of green fields was not exactly his focus. He just needed to be free to roam where he pleased, preferably without answering to someone else for permission first. After seeing their quarters backed onto manicured gardens teeming with sky-reaching trees, ferns and lush grass bordering tinkling streams and gentle waterfalls, the prospect of clearing the fifteen-foot walls from amongst the tallest trees was a feasible idea.

His mind wandered back to his first attempt. Perched on a heavy branch amongst the tallest tree, he cast his gaze to the fields beyond the retaining wall. He was high, possibly twenty feet from the soft ground below. Yet his vantage didn't offer the means of escape he craved. The wall was too far away, his height a detriment to his endeavour. Furious, he sought another avenue, anything that might reveal a hint of freedom. To either side of his enclosure were others, similar in design, although the gardens appeared to have a theme, for the plants and trees were different in colour and shape. An impressive pond of water rested beneath pink foliage to his right, whilst a brook bubbled to his left, twining between two enormous redwoods and a collection of white boulders.

He sat and reflected on his predicament, seeking a solution, so he hoped, when movement caught his eye to the right.

And then he watched as Kayla Tolsten walked onto soft grass before dipping delicate toes into the pond, oblivious to his longing stare, unaware of his burning desire.

Months of confinement stretched into years, yet he never missed a day. He told old Ruvin and Donal it was his way of holding onto his past, a means to look beyond the wall in the hope of finding a path home. The reality was darker than his companions realised. He watched, and he schemed, and given the time he dedicated to his nefarious task, it was no surprise the tiny thread of goodness hidden deep inside snapped in two.

At some point his Ven guard, a young male with blonde hair braided halfway down his back, offered a pinch of *spryx* to alleviate his boredom. Within a short cycle he was hooked, and to his surprise, invited to several evening gatherings in the Sunshine Hall where the taking of *spryx* and other alleviates was encouraged. It was here he met Ik'omi in person for the first time, and with his use of the Ven language improving, dialogue between the two followed.

Gifts became prolific, resembling substance as well as outings to the city and beyond. Always accompanied by Ik'omi, they exchanged ideas about the world and its people, both the

Ven and those in Bastion. They learned much about each other, had continual discussions about Kian, the Nepharii guide who brought them here, and on occasion was prodded to speak about the powers he witnessed on the fields before Ayoshos, the City of Angels, when Neema defended Kayla with a sudden storm. And then there were questions concerning those who followed them to the city. Questions about the one called Jed Ironmonger who served under Ahriman. Yet he was reminded profusely to never tell his companions about the questions he'd been asked lest his privileges be taken away.

That part of his dealings was easy. He rarely spoke to his companions. They kept themselves occupied in their own way, whilst he kept to his own sordid routine.

A smile raised the corners of his mouth. At some point in his dealings with the king, he'd asked for a spyglass to be made for his own personal use. He advised Ik'omi on its design and function, was ecstatic to find it presented to him within days of his suggestion. A slender brass tube etched in gold and fitted with superbly crafted lenses was placed in his care.

He climbed the tallest tree early the next morning and waited for Kayla to emerge.

And like he did this morning, he watched her walk to the pond, strip her clothes, and step naked into the refreshing water.

The spyglass was effective, more so than he imagined. Pressed to his eye, the image of Kayla was close. He could see the beads of water glistening on her skin, the deep green of her moody eyes and the hint of a red rose in her full-bodied lips.

A small waterfall fell at the rear of the pond. It was here Reefe found his heart racing as Kayla lay back amongst the rocks to let smooth water slip over her toned body. She was exquisite, perfect. Full breasts, a narrow waist, athletic. She was like a she-cat, poised to pounce, a beauty beyond anything a thumbnail of *spryx* could conjure in the mind's eye.

Every day, without fail, he would watch.

'Here,' the voice startled him. He saw Ik'omi gather another goblet of wine from a servant. The pretty young Ven smiled at him, her face flawless, her almond-shaped eyes inviting. He'd pleased himself with many over the journey, he guessed she was one of them, only he couldn't recall her name. All he saw when he dallied with the young Ven women was Kayla. She was all he thought about.

'Thank you,' his reply was distant, aloof. He took a sip, felt a sharp bitterness that caused him to sit up.

'A fortified drink from the east,' Ik'omi patted his back. 'For the strong of heart, and for the lonely heart. Fitting, don't you think?'

Reefe winced, forced the bitter brew down his throat.

'You and I have a similar passion, Reefe O'Bannon,' Ik'omi waved a hand to encompass the hall. 'Like you, I watch those around me, always have. For a very long time, it was my duty. Watch and learn, discover new experiences. I wonder, Reefe, what it is you learn from watching Kayla-mother so often?'

The bitterness on his tongue almost manifested into a curt reply, but he stalled, aware such language could see his head separated from his shoulders. And then he realised the king might not be aware of his sordid secret after all. Perhaps Ik'omi merely thought he watched Kayla from afar on occasion, not at every opportunity as she bathed naked in the pond.

He met the king's inquisitive stare. 'She exercises frequently,' he replied, 'often with Ruvin Ciricello. He teaches her the art of swordplay when they believe no-one is watching.'

'Truly! Is she talented with a blade?'

'They use wooden poles, but her skills have improved. In all honesty, she is fast and agile, her strength an asset. If she were in Bastion, on our world, she would be greatly feared.'

'And what of her son? Do you watch him when you spy on Kayla-mother?'

'Rarely. He frolics in the garden most days, exploring his surrounds as any young boy would. He exudes the energy of a child, but as you are aware, he remains silent.'

Ik'omi tilted his head to the side, contemplating his words. 'Such silence from a young one is rare, I take it?'

'Aye, it is. I have never heard of such an ailment. On our world, babes usually cry when they are hungry and scream when lonely. Most are speaking words by the time they are weaned. At three years of age, as Rastan now is, children are well versed in their parent's language.'

'He is odd, that much I can tell,' the king looked to where Rastan continued to dance with the Ven women, 'although he has incredible energy.'

He noted a strange look come over Ik'omi's narrow face. Was he perplexed? Doubtful, for the Ven reminded him frequently that the kings were all-knowing. And yet there was something there - troubling him, perhaps - or offering intrigue.

A moment passed and the look disappeared. Replacing the unusual expression was the light of adventure. 'You said Kayla-mother was highly skilled in swordplay, did you not?'

'Yes, considering her relentless practice. I would not wish to fight her with a blade, and I have some skill. She has passed me in ferocity and technique, although I must admit I have not handled a sword since we arrived.'

'And why does she endeavour to learn such fierceness, do you think?'

Why did she, Reefe mused? Did she believe she could cut her way to freedom? 'I am not sure, my lord. Maybe she learns the blade to pass the time.'

Ik'omi gave a nod, but Reefe noticed a smile stretching wide on the king's face. Ik'omi passed his goblet to a Ven servant, then motioned towards one of his brothers, Shien. The immortal lord stepped lightly across the tiled floor.

'Are your blades sharp, brother?'

Shien looked to the silver-blue sheaths at his hips. 'Always, Ik'omi. What have you in mind?'

'A small demonstration of our expertise. It has been sometime since we employed the *Swift Steps to Eternal Night*.'

The two kings shared a grin. A moment passed before they moved gracefully to the centre of the hall. The dancing Ven backed away, creating a circle fifty feet in diameter. The stringed instruments ceased being plucked. The tanned-hide drums became silent. One last breath slipped through a flute.

It appeared everyone in the Sunshine Hall held their breath.

The remaining three immortal kings stood at the height of the five steps, their arms crossed as Ik'omi and Shien began to circle each other. Both kings had drawn their silver blades, one for each hand. They were slightly curved, two feet long and sparkled brightly as the afternoon sun shone through arched windows. For several moments, the silence continued as each king mimicked the other, hands lifting high as they stretched their shoulders, hips twisting as they placed feet in sequenced steps. It was beautiful to watch, mesmerizingly fluid. Twirls and leaps followed; blades sang as they sliced through air thick with expectation. Reefe couldn't believe how precise and daring some of their moves were, nor did he expect what was to come.

When the tempo lifted, the silence evaporated.

*

Kayla placed a hand on Ruvin's shoulder as the two kings stopped their circling and dived for each other, blades leading the way. There was a clash of steel, a grunt of exertion, shouts of fear from the crowd.

'Gods above, what are they doing?' the voice belonged to Donal, standing to her left.

She risked a brief look at the boy, saw him entranced with the spectacle like everyone else. Another strike whirled through the air to be met by a high-lifting blade. Kayla returned her gaze to hear a resounding ring as Ik'omi swivelled to block a blindingly fast thrust to the neck. He swayed next, slid his feet on the tiles, cut towards the midriff of Shien.

Gasps of delight, cries of disbelief and moans of despair mingled within the room. Ik'omi and Shien continued their dance, neither backing away, their movements entwined with the other, their steps coordinated with their strikes. For several minutes they spent turns attacking and defending, back and forth in harmony, both equally balanced. There was symmetry in every step, thrust and block.

340

And then the circling stopped. Both kings now stood side-by-side, their attacks combined against an imaginary foe. Light steps and twirls, feigned swipes and dashing cuts at incredible speed kept the audience breathless. When the kings finally ceased their demonstration of expertise, Kayla could feel her heart pounding in her chest to the point of bursting.

'What in the name of all the gods was that about?'

Ruvin and Neema both stepped close to her. She could see concern on their faces, saw alarm in their shadowed eyes. They exchanged a look that spoke volumes before Ruvin cleared his throat.

'A demonstration with layered meanings, my dear,' Ruvin's voice was flat. It appeared the spectacle had taken his breath away like so many others.

'Aye,' Neema grabbed a hand. 'Not only was the swordplay exquisite, but it was also designed to put fear into your soul.'

'How do you mean?' she was unsure of Neema's train of thought. The kings were talented beyond anything she had seen in her life, but she sensed no fear.

'Neema is right,' added Ruvin. 'There was a story to the dance we just witnessed.'

'Explain it to me.'

Ruvin gave a curt nod and lowered his voice as the kings moved away from the tiled floor. 'I have seen similar choreographed dances before, back home in the south, but never to such a standard. The story resembles the plight of one consumed with anger. They began as equals, circling each other, opposites balanced. And yet Ik'omi was a free spirit, his steps light, whilst Shien was moody and dark, his movements exaggerated and heavy. The light and the darkness. Good and evil.

'Eventually, Shien attacked, drawing Ik'omi in with his hatred. In the dances I saw in my travels, the light would hold its ground, then repel the darkness, often with a gesture of love or kindness. This was something different. It gave us an insight into their thoughts and beliefs. You could see Shien's face, snarling and cursing, his teeth bared like an animal. Instead of refusing the confrontation, Ik'omi complied and met him in a circle of fury. There they continued to fight with a rage born from survival. In the end, Ik'omi became one with Shien, consumed with anger and terribly frightening. He fell into darkness and became one with it.'

'A simple story, then,' Kayla thought she understood.

'Not so simple, my dear,' Neema squeezed her hand tight. 'It is also a message to those looking to betray or disobey the Five Kings. Step out of line and retribution will be swift and eternal. They have embraced the darkness, possibly because they believe they are beyond such emotions. And yet I believe any slight towards them will be met with terrible force. The demonstration suggests they do not fear anything, and for those who disobey, the promise of dire punishment awaits.'

Kayla felt her chest tighten. Was the message for her? Did they know she practiced swordplay in her garden?

She looked to where Rastan stood with a handful of Ven women. His eyes were wide, a smile on his face. Like those beside him, he clapped his little hands as the kings stepped towards the dais and their waiting brothers.

'The sword lessons must stop, Kayla,' whispered Ruvin in her ear. 'I swore to protect you when we crossed to this world, but I am no match against an immortal king, and neither are you.'

'You feel the demonstration was for us?'

'I do. Why else would they summon us to the Sunshine Hall if not to send a message. We are betrayed. Either Nae-oki or Reefe O'Bannon. You know it to be true.'

'So, my son being honoured is irrelevant, then?'

'It is not irrelevant, Kayla,' chimed Neema, 'it is merely an opportunity. Since Jarred and Kian left on their journey, we have been confined to our quarters. The Nepharii kings treat us like caged animals, a curiosity and nothing more. You have seen their pets in the garden beyond the palace. The only difference . . . our cage is within.'

'And I have taught you everything I know,' said Ruvin. 'If my life experiences were represented by a flawless diamond, then I fear the kings could fill this entire palace with diamonds from the years they have lived. Some may say my diamond is extraordinary when considered alone, but it is insignificant when compared to the whole. I can teach nothing more of value. Not physically, in any case.'

Kayla knew he spoke the truth. Whatever she thought to gain by practicing the sword, deep inside she knew it would never be enough. The kings were too powerful, too ancient.

'You are good, Kayla,' Ruvin squeezed her shoulder, 'but you'll never be good enough to defeat an immortal king. No-one is that skilled, nor as fast. And there are five of them. We could never dream of cutting our way clear of the palace and surviving.'

Her knees felt weak, her palms became sweaty. Kayla wasn't sure that was her plan – to cut her way free – but a part of her suspected it might be her only option.

'So, what do we do now?' she asked those she deemed more intelligent than herself. 'We have spent years here, and we've had no word from Kian, nor any sign of Jarred. How long are we to wait before we act? I'll not stay here for the rest of my days, nor will my son!'

Faces spun as she raised her voice, but she was past caring, nor did she choose to be diplomatic. Neema was right, they were nothing more than caged animals with minor privileges. She remembered Kian's words when they first arrived. He claimed they were to be fed and clothed, protected within the palace. But she also remembered him saying they were now prisoners of the Five Kings.

Nothing had changed.

Laughter caught her attention. She spun to see Ik'omi with Reefe O'Bannon by his side, standing atop the dais. Ven favourites swarmed about the king, sharing his laughter, mimicking some of his earlier actions. His eyes locked onto her own.

She swallowed back her fear. Ik'omi looked at her like a hungry dog, wicked, uncaring, ready to pounce no matter the consequences. Yet he stood with his straight back knowing the consequences would never scar him. He was king, he could devour whoever he chose. With her body trembling, Kayla wondered how she was going to resist.

'Come, Kayla-mother,' a hand fell on her forearm. It belonged to Nae-oki. Neema also placed a comforting arm about her shoulders. Would her friends fall for their comfort and support?

'I need someone to fetch Rastan,' she stammered, aware of the fear rising from the pit of her stomach. She looked beyond Nae-oki's worried expression, saw Rastan walking towards Ik'omi. The king beckoned him with a gentle wave, Reefe smiled like a puckered fish.

'No!' the sound didn't carry to her son, there was too much laughter and a dozen string instruments had begun to play once more. 'Somebody, grab him!'

Only they were too late. The boy danced towards the king, eyes alight with mischief and revelry.

Drums sounded from so far away.

Ik'omi narrowed his bright eyes towards the child as he approached. She watched Rastan hop up the steps. Kayla held her breath, not sure what to expect, but feared the worst. A sudden hum of energy manifested beside her, originating from Neema as words were quietly spoken.

Ik'omi glanced their way and smiled, then placed a hand beneath his vest and pulled forth a golden disc on a golden chain. He handed it to the boy, said several words and gave him a pat on the head to send him on his way.

Kayla exhaled, noticed Neema do the same. The energy she felt emanating from the mystic evaporated like dew drops on a summer morning.

'Nae-oki,' she found the Ven watching her closely, 'please, take me to my quarters.'

'Yes, Kayla-mother,' Nae-oki covered her pretty mouth with a raised hand. There was fear in her eyes, too. 'I will ask the kings permission first, lest we anger them further.'

Nae-oki slipped away on soft footfalls whilst Kayla stood and waited for Rastan to reach her side. The boy held his prize before him, all bright and shiny like a miniature sun. He was smiling.

'I feel faint, my friends,' Kayla's words were tinged with regret and sadness and the loss of hope. 'We are alone and forgotten. And when the kings decide it's time, we will cease to be.'

A tear slid down her cheek as Neema bent at the waist to pick Rastan off the floor. He continued to smile, reached out to stroke Neema's greying hair with the tenderness of youth.

'You are wrong, my dear,' Neema breathed deep, looked to the kings and their playthings with brimming goblets. 'Kian will come for us.'

'Will he? Tarsin said something similar before we stepped through the portal, then as you claim, he died defending us. Perhaps Kian has done the same.'

'No, Kian is still alive. The Five Kings are extravagant and unusual, but I do not believe they would kill their brother.'

Another shake of her head. 'Where is he, then? Why has he abandoned us? Nothing has changed since we arrived here, Neema. We have nothing. We are nothing!'

'My child,' she reached out to touch her cheek. 'We are so much more than you believe.'

Further talk was halted as Nae-oki returned. The Ven servant offered a short curtsey, her eyes downcast and lacking the light of merriment witnessed earlier.

'The kings have granted you and your companions leave, Kayla, so you may rest your son from an adventurous day of festivities. Come, I will lead you to your quarters.'

The group departed, slipping past the entrance liked whipped dogs barred from a feast. The joy of watching Rastan dance was forgotten, the tantalising morsels of food and sips of fruit wine lost amongst a fog of despair. But for Kayla, the memory of Tarsin Va standing his ground against a horde of demons so they could escape remained a dagger in her weeping heart.

Neema, still holding Rastan on her hip as they walked from the Sunshine Hall, stepped to her side and lent close. 'As dark as the world may appear right now, my dear, one thing remains true. There is always hope, no matter how dire life may seem. And sometimes, faith is all you need.'

CHAPTER TWENTY-SIX

The room was quiet.

It was early morning, cold, the sun yet to rise. Tarsin Va stood before his bed, looking down at his chain mail and the jaguar breast plate gifted to him from his father, whilst flames flickered from a small fireplace to his right. Lloyd Henrickson sat on a bench in the far corner rubbing his hands together, his eyes troubled. Will Tolsten stood looking out the only window.

Tarsin buttoned his thick shirt and slipped the chain mail over his head. It rested well on his shoulders, didn't pinch or scrape like most suits he'd worn in the past. The metal links were small and expertly fashioned, their strength and flexibility without equal. Coupled with the jaguar breastplate, he felt invincible.

He traced a finger over the embossed image of the snarling jungle cat. Even after his battles, the marks on his armour were few. He'd been struck often enough, especially during his stand before the pyramid, but whatever techniques were used to shape the metal had infused the plate with rare qualities sufficient to save his life. Without it, he wasn't sure he would still be here. It was certainly a kingly gift.

Like his chain mail, he lifted his breastplate over his head and began to tighten the buckles at either side.

'Do you need any help?' Henrickson was watching him, his white moustache twitching at the corner.

'No, I'm fine,' Tarsin tightened the last leather strap, raised his arms to stretch. The plate settled as he twisted and rolled his shoulders. Like his chain mail, it felt comfortable to wear.

'This is madness, you know,' Henrickson again, the old man still rubbing his hands together.

'I know what it is, my friend,' Tarsin moved to the mantle above the fireplace, reached for his sheathed sword. With a fluid motion he belted it to his waist, then rested his hand on the pommel. 'I gave Griffith five days to bring me

Bardell's head. Five days are up. Now the Unseen and I will go see what we can find.'

'If he and his thirty men are dead, what hope do you and your twenty have?'

The two warriors locked eyes. Tarsin didn't have an answer, at least not one that would suffice. It was why he prepared in the early hours of morning, away from the prying eyes of his aides. If Lady Jenna or Sister Tahlia knew of his plans, no amount of talk would placate their concerns. Besides, he didn't have a choice. If Griffith were trapped or captured, he would be there to rescue him. If he was dead, then he would avenge him instead.

He prayed he wasn't dead.

'I need to find him, Henrickson, you know that.'

'Aye, I know it,' Henrickson ran a hand through his hair. 'It doesn't make it right.'

'I don't have another option,' he placed his black gloves on. 'Whatever stalled the big man, we need to know. Bardell is a nuisance soon to be dead, you have my word, but I need to find Griffith first.'

Henrickson shook his head as he stepped away from the bench. There was concern etched on his face, and not just for his welfare. He was also worried about Cale Griffith. For five days they'd been waiting for word from their companion, dreaming he'd walk back with a smile plastered across his grizzly visage after accomplishing his mission. The secret pathways beneath Bastion provided by Will were a means to infiltrate Bardell's foothold to the north. If they could find a way into his court without being seen, the confrontation with his people could end. One death would be all it would take.

Five days passed and not a word had been sent. Everyone shared a concern, and thoughts swirled regarding Bardell's retaliation if Griffith and his men had been caught. And yet the patrols along the river Atvia claimed the upstart king and his men were equally quiet. If they had caught Griffith, most of his aides agreed regarding Bardell's actions thereafter. He would make it known, use the infiltrators to his advantage.

Will moved away from the window. He was attired for battle, leather amour and sword, a heavy brown cloak over his shoulders. 'There is danger behind every corner in Bastion right now,' his voice was sombre. 'Griffith and his men may have never reached New City for all we know.'

'That is why we leave this morning, before day breaks,' Tarsin added, crossing to stand before Will. 'Are the Unseen ready?' he asked.

'They are ready, my lord. Including myself and your two Panthians, we number twenty.'

The king tilted his head to the side, aware Tahu and Zai were still guarding the door outside his room. He spun back to Henrickson. 'Inform Inesco of our whereabouts come daybreak. Tell him he is to aide you in the coming days if we do not return. Stick to the plan. Lady Jenna and Sister Tahlia will also offer sound advice. Listen to them.'

'As you should, my king,' a brief smile stretched Henrickson's face.

'Aye, I should, but I cannot,' he clapped the Swordmaster on the shoulder. 'Trust me, old friend. The Unseen and I will survive. We'll be back before you know it.'

'You hope,' the hint of a smile faded.

Silence settled as the three men sought solace in their own thoughts, a moment to reflect on what was to come. As Will said, there was danger everywhere they looked, everywhere they travelled. No matter how prepared they were, there was no escaping the reality of what Bastion had become.

'It's time we left, my lord,' Will was the first to break the silence.

'You're right,' Tarsin replied, sharing a final look with Henrickson. 'We've stalled long enough. Let's move.'

*

The enveloping darkness consumed them to the point of panic.

Will Tolsten held out a hand, hoping he'd find a wall to lean against as he paused to take a breath. He knew his men were ranged behind him, for he could hear their movement, the sound of shallow footfalls the only constant to walk hand-in-hand with the darkness.

'Hold your ground,' Will whispered behind him, knowing Col Farren to be next in line. The words were repeated, each man whispering to the one behind him. He waited, praying everyone was accounted for.

He heard the reply from Col a moment later. 'We're all here.'

A sigh of relief eased from aching lungs. For more than half-a-morning they'd travelled beneath the city, cutting through sewers and traversing underground canals. They passed the river Atvia prior to the rising sun, then slunk below ground, easing into a cellar with access to the Undercity shortly thereafter. For a time, Tarsin allowed the use of flaming brands and two lanterns to light their way. But an hour into their journey, as they traversed a series of sodden, moss-covered steps, the first of several screeches rent the ripe air.

Flaming brands were doused and lanterns shuttered as secrecy became paramount. The line ceased moving forward as Will called for calm, although he could hear the men's heavy breathing as fear began to take hold. He knew they were deep beneath the city; he sensed the men felt it just as keenly. So much stone and timber lying above. Such a small, tight corridor they now found themselves in.

He slid a hand into a pocket and pulled forth his map. Col heard the scrape of paper, took a step closer and unshuttered the lantern he held. Pale light bathed his face.

Will took his time, checked the narrow lines he'd drawn, counting to himself the number of paces he believed they'd taken. By his estimation, they were approximately halfway to their destination.

Soft steps and the ruffle of clothing approached. 'How far?' his king asked, speaking as quietly as his steps.

'Halfway,' Will folded his map, gave a nod to confirm they were headed in the right direction.

'Good,' his king lent closer. 'Leave the shutter exposed for the time being. The men are barely holding it together. I'll send Tahu to walk with you. He can see well in the near darkness, almost as well as you or I in the daylight.'

'As you wish,' the relief in Will's voice was evident, but he didn't care. Leading the procession was nerve-racking, especially with his king amongst their number. He'd never felt more responsible, nor afraid.

Tahu's company was welcome as the procession continued. The Panthian was lithe of limb, his movements graceful. And for the time being he walked several steps ahead of the line, easing the fear that sought to tear his sanity down. For almost an hour they kept a respectable pace, until Tahu paused after a long stride, one hand pressed against the wall, the other curling into a high-held fist.

'What do you see,' Will asked, aware of his men crowding behind him.

Yellow eyes reflected light from the lantern as he swung his head about. 'Broken wall,' he replied, his accent thick. 'A silver door.'

'A silver door,' Will muttered, heard the words repeated down the line. King Tarsin made his way to his side a moment later.

'Open your lantern, Col,' the king gestured with a hand. 'Let us see where the door leads,' he shifted his focus, took tentative steps ahead. 'Are there any silver doors on your map, Will, or is this something new?'

'Something new, I believe.'

'Then let us be cautious. It could lead anywhere, and there is no telling what lies behind it.'

Will didn't need to be reminded. He knew all about the dangers now residing in Bastion. With Col crouched to his left and Tahu on his right, he approached with soft footfalls and several prayers to the gods.

'See here,' Tahu placed an arm out wide, preventing him from walking further. 'Many feet. Recent.'

Will peered at the dirt floor. Tahu was right, there were boot prints layered atop boot prints. Dozens of them, maybe more, their outline clearly seen. A large group of men had converged on the door, and if the prints were true, stepped over the threshold to whatever lay beyond.

'Could the prints belong to Griffith and his men, do you think?' asked Col, looking over his shoulder towards the king.

Tarsin reached their position, observed the door and the prints up close.

'It is possible. They followed an identical map to the one Will has. Unless they became lost, they surely would have arrived at the silver door.'

Will moved a step closer, placed a hand on its cold surface. 'Shall I see if it opens?' he asked.

'Aye,' the king spoke first, 'open it up. The rest of you, be ready.'

Will briefly wondered what they might need to be ready for when he twisted the handle. Could a hidden danger be lurking behind the door? He finished twisting, heard a mechanism issue a muffled click, then with a gentle push, the door swung inward. 'I'll need a light,' he said over his shoulder. 'It's pitch black in here.'

Col lifted his lantern, opened shutters wide in the process, then joined him. Together they peered through the doorway, sought clarification of what lay beyond.

'It's another corridor,' Will announced to those crowding behind. He stepped through, Col by his side. 'The floor is dirt, like outside, and the footprints are many. If you were to ask me, my king, the prints belong to Griffith and his crew.'

King Tarsin and Tahu stepped into the corridor as he and Col moved forward, their heads nodding in what he believed was confirmation. If Griffith did indeed lead his men this way, then he most certainly would have veered off course. The map he provided to the veteran showed no silver door or pathway beyond. In truth, they could be anywhere right now.

'We have no other avenue to pursue, Will,' King Tarsin stated the obvious. 'Like Griffith, we need to head this way.'

'You're right, although we'll keep our wits about us, look for another corridor branching from this one. If we find one, it may lead us back to our original route.'

'Or take us further away,' Col muttered under his breath.

'There is that,' King Tarsin slapped the old fighter on the back. 'So long as we find Griffith and his men, I don't care how far we travel.'

A sudden itch at the nape of his neck had Will wondering if there was more to the words of his king. Yet his contemplation was interrupted as Tahu moved ahead, a signal for the men to move on.

They walked a hundred feet, no more, and entered a circular room with a dome ceiling. At its centre was a circular dais, slender pillars ranged at its perimeter, reaching twenty feet high. A swirling, elongated sphere of sapphire light twirled within.

But it was the tall figure of an elegant lady, hooded in robes of pale blue, that took his breath away.

Will blinked; aware her robes were fashioned so fine they were almost see-through. Broad shoulders, a narrow waist, a face so fine it was practically flawless. As the men stood with mouths agape, she took an effortless step forward.

'I have been waiting for you,' her words were light, carried easily in the chamber.

'And you are?' King Tarsin made his way to Tahu's side.

'I am called Nen.'

'Are you Nepharii?' Tarsin asked.

A pause followed. The lady, Nen, lifted her hands to push her hood away from her face. She was bald, not a single hair could be seen on her pate. For a moment, Will thought it made her more beautiful.

'Long ago, perhaps,' Nen replied. 'Now, I am Elusian: a Walker of Paths. Come, I shall lead you to your men.'

'My men are with you. You have Cale Griffith?'

'I do not *have* him, King Tarsin. He and his companions are with us. They are safe and well, as you will be.'

'Why would we trust you?' There was an urgency in the king's voice.

'You will die if you do not. It has been written,' her eyes shone like the swirling light behind her, sapphire blue, piercing. 'Trust me. I have spoken at length with Cale Griffith. We touched minds, so I may know your language. You are King Tarsin, the men surrounding you are the Unseen.'

'Where would you lead us, then?'

'To a haven, a place not of this world.'

Will saw his king clench his fist. 'I'm not sure I can trust you, Nen. We have a mission to see through, an enemy to confront. If Griffith and his men are safe, send them to us so we can be on our way.'

Nen tilted her head to the side. 'I don't believe you understood my earlier words, King Tarsin. You will die if you do not follow. The danger here is very real, and not what you imagine. If you wish to find Kayla Tolsten in the future, your path lies with me.'

'You have my sister?' Will exclaimed, unable to control the passion in his voice.

'I do not,' Nen spun her gaze to settle on his own. 'What I have is a safe place and answers. But I cannot share them here. We are running out of time.'

The king took another step forward, peered with intent into her sapphire eyes. She was at least three inches taller, yet delicate and alluring. 'The portal behind you leads to your safe place?'

'It does.'

'And Cale Griffith is on the other side, alive and well?'

'He is.'

'Does he have a weapon by his side?'

'You refer to his warhammer, the one he calls *Bloodstain*?'

'I do,' Tarsin smiled, and it appeared a weight lifted from his shoulders. 'We accept your offer,' the king unclenched his fist, looked to his men. There was steel in his eyes as they swept over the Unseen.

'You have made the right decision,' Nen offered. 'Now follow, and do not look down.'

Will heard her words, felt another itch crawl up his spine towards his neck. Don't look down. But as he stepped beside his king and followed Nen into the crystal-blue light, he did exactly that.

And a bottomless pit of swirling light engulfed him.

*

It was terribly cold.

At least, Ra'tor thought it so. Not quite as cold as the white world where the wolfen creatures roamed, but it was certainly close.

He looked from behind iron bars to the pale light of dawn, the first hint of colour seeping across the city he now knew as Bastion. It wasn't pleasant, evoked no stirring hunger in his soul. It did remind him of the fear that still gripped his heart, though. Reminded him danger was ever-present. He knew if he stepped outside it would show itself. A cloaked figure with fire in his eyes, hunting through the streets, feeding at will. It chased him, chased him through the house and down a lane, chased him still when he closed his eyes.

For more days than he could remember he cowered here, beneath the city, in a tunnel of stone Isabelle called a sewer. It was circular in shape and ten foot in diameter. Above their position reached the clawed remains of a stone bridge, the remainder somewhere below the surface of a river. Water ran down a channel in the floor, the iron bars he stood before kept him caged from the outside world. Behind him, in the dark, were countless more tunnels dripping water and filth.

He knew when he arrived, he would need protection from hunters. As the water trickled into the wide river outside, it passed beneath iron bars wedged into stone. They kept him safe, but behind him, there was no protection at all. It took time, but with Isabelle's guidance, he moved countless heavy stones from deep in the tunnels and built a wall to shield them. Water still trickled past the barrier, but if a hunter came calling, they would have time to flee.

He looked to his right. A single ladder led to a recess on the far wall. It climbed to a wooden door; two bolts of iron kept it locked. The only other option was to pass the iron bars at the end of the tunnel. Isabelle could slip past easily enough, for she was small of stature and thin as a wisp. Squeezing his own body through was another matter. He could bend the bars with his hands, for he tried the first time they stumbled across the den, but he wasn't sure if he could bend them far enough.

So long as Isabelle could escape.

And yet the thought of her traversing the city on her own pained him. He would find a way to be by her side. He would never leave her.

'Are you alright, Ra'tor?'

That voice of hers; so soothing it calmed his soul. Where would he be if he hadn't found her? He shrugged his huge shoulders, felt her small hand curl about his fingers. So soft, so gentle.

'I look to the sky, little one, to see what I can see.'

'And what do you see?'

Did he dare tell her all he saw was death? The city was enormous, grander than anything he had ever seen before. From what Isabelle told him of her home, it was a place teeming with thousands upon thousands of men, women and children. Festivals and markets were commonplace, tasks were completed by those most apt. Vibrant colour, the smell of the sea and the noise of a city bursting with life.

Now it was vacant. The only noise they heard was the screams of the soon-to-be dead. Dust clouds billowed upon open thoroughfares; water dripped loudly from overhangs onto pavestones sprouting grass. The new inhabitants, including his own brood of Deios, kept out of sight during the day and were rarely heard during the night. Hunters everywhere, wary of each other, so often silent.

And they all craved the same prize.

Isabelle called the pyramid Aston's Tear.

He looked down at his angel. 'Tell me the story of your pyramid again.'

She tilted her head, beckoned to be lifted. He reached for her, placed his clawed hand about her waist, then sat her in the crook of his arm.

'I can remember only parts,' she began, 'but from what my father said, Aston was the First God, and he created Everything. Other Gods arrived and some chose to help with his creation. They agreed it was beautiful, and they were happy. But being Gods, they could not walk upon the world for their own beauty was too great. So, Aston created a mother to nurture all living things, for a mother knows best when it comes to caring. To support her, Aston then created a father, so together they could populate the world with offspring of their own. The offspring would help their mother and father in their duties, and for thousands of years it was so.

'As time passed, Aston saw the reality of what he created change. A Darkness crept into their souls, and people became divided. To remind them of their true purpose and instil a sense of hope, he asked his people to build a temple in his honour. They did so, and when completed, he was so overcome with gratitude he shed a single tear to fall upon its peak.'

Ra'tor nodded his head. Isabelle had related the story to him several times, and it was mostly the same, although she spoke too quickly on occasion. He knew most of the words, for Isabelle continued to teach him what she knew, but some words flew past like the tiny winged *darniks* back home. Fast, they were, and nearly impossible to catch.

'Your people built the temple?' he asked, knowing the pyramid she spoke of was the silver-blue pyramid sitting in the middle of Bastion.

'That is what the priests and their acolytes at the temples say,' she sighed deeply, scrunched up her nose. 'My father says differently. He says there are those in Highcastle who believe the pyramid was here before we even arrived. He says the first clans to settle here fought for the temple.'

Ra'tor blinked at the revelation. It was already here. It would explain Isabelle's earlier explanation of the pyramid's appearance. She said it was encased in granite, all the way to the top except for a small, silver-blue capstone. When the ground shook, the stone was splintered and discarded like a broken garment.

'It is prettier to look at, now,' Isabelle pinched his arm for attention. 'It shines all day and sparkles like the stars at night. What do you think lies inside?'

He knew what lay within, had walked many steps back and forth, scheming, cursing, and raging at his discovery. His initial prospect of finding Bhral, his Blood-God, had proven false. And the reality of losing his prey was equally galling. But the sphere of light spinning in its depths was mesmerising and beyond extraordinary. To be able cross to other worlds at will, with a single step, sent shivers down his spine.

Yet it was more than an adventure to another world. The power to control such travel, to have countless resources at your disposal, to be able to hunt indefinitely was unfathomable. Knowing his brood would never know the pains of hunger during a dry season was comforting. Knowing water could be found with ease was a blessing. There was so much to consider, so much to learn. A new age of discovery was upon them.

And his brood had control of the temple when he last saw them.

'When we find my Deios, I will show you,' he kept his voice low, aware they were in hiding. 'It is a wonder beyond imagining, Isabelle. I believe it's a godly gift.'

He moved forward, towards the iron bars at the end of the sewer tunnel. The sky remained grey; the sun hidden behind low-lying clouds. Other than a pack of feral dogs barking during the night, he'd heard nothing to suggest any hunters were nearby.

He bent at the knee and let Isabelle leap to the brick floor. She immediately reached for the net piled against the iron bars, dragged it clear. It had been here when they arrived, along with wooden buckets, a handful of knives and hooks. She slipped past the iron bars and stepped onto the ledge, cast the net into the water with a fluid motion. He wondered how many times she had done so since they arrived.

Still holding a section of rope, she stepped back behind the bars and offered it to him. She could cast easily, young Isabelle, but she wasn't strong enough to haul the net from the water.

'Thank you,' she said, as she walked past and sat on the upside-down bucket.

He offered a smile, which he knew was a mouthful of sharp teeth. His little angel laughed.

He felt the rope in his hand pull with the tide. It had been their only source of finding food. The fish were plentiful, a result of an empty city. With its people scattered, nature was reclaiming what was once hers. It was happening quicker than he thought possible. Birds flocked in greater numbers, squirrels scampered boldly, and rats darted everywhere.

And here he sat, in a sewer, too afraid to leave for fear of the Darkness.

How long was he going to sit and wonder? How long could he keep Isabelle safe? She couldn't live here indefinitely. At some point she would need to feel the sun on her face and the wind in her hair. And he needed the heat of the sun more than she. He was always cold. It slowed his thoughts and movements, made him feel sluggish. It wasn't something a hunter wished for.

The tug on the rope intensified. He gave it a pull, began to haul the net in through the bars. It was heavy. His muscles bulged and strained; his heart began to race. 'By the blood of Bhral,' he cursed under his breath, 'what have we caught?'

A grunt of exertion escaped his lips. His feet slipped on the damp surface. And then his heart sank as the reality of what he caught became apparent. A winged creature, as tall as he, sat with clawed talons on his net. It was lithe and scaled, snapped its heavy beak to create the sound of two daggers clashing together. Then it spread its wings wide.

A fifteen-foot wingspan was the result. It blocked out the grey sky behind it, a leathery flap sent in a rush of air.

A screech sounded behind him. It belonged to Isabelle. 'What is it?' she yelled.

Again, he knew what it was. A *terrovyn*. A creature from his own world. Rare and highly sought after. If it was here, it could only be for one reason.

He dropped the net and turned his back on the *terrovyn*, looked down the tunnel. The sound of splintered wood came seconds later.

A dark shape kicked what remained of the iron-bolted door to the floor. From the shadows moved a heavy body, clawed hands clutching steel. This was it, then. His time had come. Ra'tor, once a hunter of renown, was now the hunted.

He reached for his own blade, offered a snarl to fire his blood.

The creature took a step forward, entered an area of light that had slipped past the winged horror. His head and shoulders were covered in red scales.

'Ra'tor,' a deep voice beckoned.

'I am he,' he returned in his own tongue.

'I have come for you. The hunt has not been easy.'

Ra'tor chanced a look over his shoulder. The *terrovyn* couldn't reach him through the iron bars. He was to face the hunter alone. He spun back. 'You're a Hex?' he asked.

'I am. I am known as Kors.'

'Who sent you?' his words dripped venom, although he knew the answer before he asked the question.

'The Patriarchs, and those charged with leading the brood since your absence.'

It was as he thought. The lure of power had become too great. Always seeking to rise higher, were the Deios. Never content. And they sent for a Hex to track him down. That was an accomplishment. The Hex were difficult to find, especially if they didn't wish to be found. They didn't belong to any brood.

They hunted away from the Deios, their only companion a *terrovyn*. To capture one was close to impossible. To train one even harder. They were so rarely seen that most broods thought them mythical.

He locked eyes with Kors. The Hex were spoken of with awe. Supreme hunters, able to seek out the rarest and largest of prey on their home world. What twenty Deios hunted together, a single Hex could bring down alone.

'You can put your blade down, Ra'tor. It's over.'

'I'll not give in, Kors. I'm a fighter. I'll die a fighter.'

The Hex narrowed his eyes, shifted his focus to Isabelle, noticed her for the first time. 'What have you found?'

'Leave her!' Ra'tor growled. He knew the tales. He knew the Hex liked to hunt rare creatures.

'Does she live here? What is she called?'

'She is an angel. And she is mine!' He almost leapt at Kors such was the fury in his voice. But he was wary. The Hex were known to play tricks.

'Then bring her with you,' Kors replied, 'if you wish to keep her. I'll leave the decision with you.'

'Bring her? Keep her? What are you talking about?'

'I came to find you, Ra'tor, not kill you. The brood asked me to search for you and bring you back. Much has changed since you were lost in the streets, and your brood no longer holds the glowing temple.'

'You're not here to kill me,' Ra'tor said the words to himself, then looked to Isabelle.

'We need to leave, Ra'tor. There is a great danger lurking outside, I have sensed it. Something I've not crossed paths with before. We need to move now, before it finds us.'

The Darkness with fire in its eyes. He knew what Kors spoke of. If he only knew the fear it carried.

Ra'tor held out his hand. 'Come, my little angel,' he felt soft fingers curl about his own. He was about to be reunited with his brood. After so many days and nights hiding within the city, he was about to become the leader his Deios once yearned for.

He picked Isabelle up, sat her in the crook of his arm.

'Lead on, Kors,' Ra'tor snarled, 'and let's see what we can see.'

CHAPTER TWENTY-SEVEN

The sky was still grey as Ra'tor and Isabelle followed Kors out of the building.

He took a quick glance at their surroundings. They were standing in a buckled street, some of its stone pavers splintered. To his right an assortment of tumbled bricks lay in a small mound against a shattered wall, the river swept beyond. Ahead lay a twisted path, the subtle movement of rustling leaves their only company.

'You follow my lead,' Kors spoke low, but his deep voice carried easily.

'Lead on,' Ra'tor tightened his grip about the hilt of his heavy blade. For longer than he cared to recall, he'd kept hidden from Bastion's streets for fear of being found. Not only was his life at risk if they were caught, it was also the life of Isabelle he feared to lose. Innocent, defenceless, physically insufficient to survive against any hunter who chanced upon her. The thought of his angel with her stained white dress and dusty golden hair being ripped apart was too much. He needed her as she needed him. Walking the open streets wasn't part of his plan to keep her alive.

'Do you know how to reach our Deios?' he caught Kors' eye.

'It will take time,' Kors lifted a sharp looking slender blade from his belt. Like Ra'tor, he wore a kilt of leather embossed with steel rivets. He also wore a leather strap wrapped over one shoulder, small pouches dangling along its length, whilst cured hide bracers covered his forearms and lower legs. From his first initial glance, he was certain the Hex carried no less than a dozen assorted blades upon his body.

Kors lifted his chin to the sky, gave a soft call using the back of his throat. Then he waited.

The sound of flapping wings broke the silence a moment later.

Isabelle gave another small scream of fright as the *terrovyn* flew from the river's edge and placed its talons on the stone ground before them. Its scales reflected the grey morning, a hint of deep blue lurking beneath the surface. Enormous wings beat at the air.

'Settle, Sin-cha,' Kors continued to keep his voice low. The *terrovyn's* savage-looking beak, shining like polished ebony, snapped shut before the Hex stepped forward to stroke the beast above its eyes.

'He listens to you?' Ra'tor was impressed not only with the size of the beast, but also the potential ferocity it exuded.

'Sin-cha is female,' Kors didn't take his gaze from his companion. 'She listens when I speak, she understands much of what I say. And yet we have a connection beyond words.'

'She can read your mind, then?'

'No, it is more a feeling. A sense, perhaps, of what is to come and what is expected.'

Ra'tor gave a nod, but he wasn't sure if it was because he understood. At least Isabelle had calmed in his arms. She kept her eyes fixed on Sin-cha, although they were wide like startled prey being stalked. She'd obviously never seen anything like the *terrovyn* in her short life.

'Do you have creatures . . . like this?' he asked his question in Isabelle's kingdom tongue.

'No,' she squawked, 'we do not. Is it a dragon?'

He didn't know what a dragon was, hadn't heard the word before. He shook his head. It was to be expected. No matter how long he had spent learning the language of man, he still had some way to go. 'We do not call it a dragon,' he said, 'we call it a *terrovyn*. This one, I believe, is about as big as she will grow.'

'I think your *terrovyn* is the same as our dragon,' Isabelle said, keeping a wary eye on the creature. 'I have never seen one, though, except in a book. Do you have books on your world?'

He didn't know what a book was. As far as he knew, he'd never seen one.

'Come,' Kors interrupted their conversation, one hand still stroking Sin-cha's scaled head. 'We need to move quickly. It is not safe to stay in one position for too long. There are eyes everywhere.'

'Where are our Deios?' Ra'tor cast his gaze beyond the street they were standing in. There was little to see, and no obvious direction called them forward.

'Far from here,' Kors lifted Sin-cha's jaw, placed his nose against hers and breathed deep. 'Fly, and be alert,' he whispered.

Sin-cha gave a soft chortle, then flapped her wings once and leapt high. Another flap saw her twenty feet above, her wings tilting to catch the wind. Seconds later she was lost behind sandstone buildings.

'Will she come back?' Isabelle squinted at the vacant skyline.

Ra'tor offered a shrug, looked to Kors and repeated the question in his own tongue. 'Will she come back?'

'When I call her,' Kors beckoned them to follow as he began to walk in the same direction Sin-cha flew. 'Until then, she looks for any movement ahead of us. This way, we are rarely surprised.'

'What about behind us?'

'We are hunters, Ra'tor. We do not need to look behind. Now follow.'

There was truth in his words, but Ra'tor was experienced enough to know not all truths were infallible. To understand who you are and what you are capable of requires lessons. Some lessons can be taught by elders, most are learnt through life's journey. Ra'tor looked at Kors red scales. They were beginning to turn, shifting to become almost copper in the light. It meant he was younger, possibly ten cycles younger. Enough for Ra'tor to realise not all his words were full of wisdom. He might be an accomplished hunter, but it didn't mean he was the perfect survivor. There would be lessons to come on the streets of Bastion to sway Kors' thoughts concerning what lies ahead . . . and behind.

Knowing such truths, he followed the Hex anyway. For some time, they walked, the sun breaking through slate-grey clouds to herald midday when they stopped beside a high wall. Far to their left sat the pyramid, glowing brightly as she always did. To reach her they would need to traverse a conglomeration of collapsed temples and abbeys, an assortment of holy places destined to never reach the heights of Aston's Tear. They were elaborate in their design, though, all fluted columns and high arches. He knew without doubt there would be something of interest amongst their broken pillars.

'I can hear the sound of sliding feet,' he moved a step closer to Kors. 'We are being followed.'

'I know,' Kors looked to the sky. 'They seek to herd us along another path.'

'How do we escape?'

Kors declined to answer. Instead, he moved along the wall until he could peer around its corner.

Ra'tor caught him as he was about to cross another stone path. 'I asked you a question.'

Kors looked over his shoulder. 'There is a stone path-over-water not far from here. It will lead us to your Deios.'

'It is called a bridge,' he gave a nod after meeting Isabelle's eyes. He remembered a word, at least. 'What are they doing so far away? Our camp was close to the temple, amongst the ruins to our left.'

'They lost the fight the night you disappeared. To save numbers, they retreated to a shelter across the river.'

They lost? Without him to lead, they were unable to hold their ground. The Aquilans were canny, he knew firsthand, but he never believed they'd be strong enough to best his brood.

A red mist began to cloud his vision. Fiery anger pumped hot blood through his veins. 'So, who holds the temple?'

'The bird creatures, and some others. I do not know their kind.'

The Aquilans were not alone, then. It didn't matter. When he returned, he would seek them out and take back what

366

was rightfully his. All the answers were to be found inside the temple. He knew it, just as he knew his little angel had a bigger role to play in the fight to come.

'Follow quickly, Ra'tor,' Kors took a long stride, eased into a gentle run. 'The bridge is not far.'

He was right. They ran past a dozen stone buildings to either side and two small paths intersecting their own. Subtle sounds kept pace with their flight, suggesting there were several hunters tracking their movement, but the stone bridge appeared before them as they veered to their right. Large strides allowed them to leap the fallen debris barring their way, dust swirled in their wake.

'We cross here,' Kors was breathing evenly. He pointed a finger. 'Your brood lies beyond, where the red shelter lies.'

Ra'tor looked ahead. A rectangular sandstone building sat on a small rise, red tiles providing cover from the sun. He shifted Isabelle higher on his hip, then cursed as four figures materialised from behind marble columns halfway across the bridge.

They were wolfen, the same breed of hunter to kill his Deios when they crossed to the cold world. Tall, rangy, patches of fur covering their torso. He owed them.

He chanced a quick look behind, saw an empty street. It was what he hoped for. Whoever traced their steps still hid in the shadows. He placed Isabelle gently at his feet.

'I need to fight, little one,' he leant close, spoke for her ears only. 'The creatures on the bridge seek to kill us. I will not let that happen. But you should close your eyes.'

'I'm afraid, Ra'tor,' there was a quiver in her voice.

'Perhaps you can sing for us,' he suggested. 'Use your voice to lift our souls.'

She gave a solitary whimper. Tears already rimmed her eyes. She wiped her hand across her nose.

'Stay strong, Isabelle,' he turned to see the wolfen approaching at speed. He gripped his cleaver, tightened his fist. Then he stood tall and pushed back his shoulders.

They were swift and agile, the wolfen, but he was strong and precise. They sought to overpower him with a brutal charge, but he stayed light on his feet, ducked and spun to keep them guessing. Then he stepped in, cut with his blade, never overextending his reach as he used his height and size to advantage. The sound of heavy grunts and the ring of steel consumed the combatants.

The first to fall was a wolfen, split across the skull from his heavy chop. Another fell when Kors plunged his steel five inches between its ribs. A brief pause followed as the remaining two hunters assessed their foes, uncertainty in their eyes, nervous. But the sound of bounding feet slapping stone gave them cause to snarl with renewed vigour. Five new wolfen arrived to support the two, eager to avenge their fallen brethren.

A curse rolled off Ra'tor's tongue, then he gave a silent prayer to his Blood-God. The odds were not in their favour. He bent on one knee, picked up a wolfen blade for his other hand. He'd need two weapons if he was to survive against so many. He saw Kors follow his lead, drawing another of his many hunting knives.

'This will not be easy, Hex,' he snarled. Two against seven, and they were angry.

'I don't think running is an option,' Kors replied, looking over his shoulder. Ra'tor did the same, saw a dozen dark cloaked figures standing at the beginning of the bridge. They were silent, carried no weapons that he could see, but their posture was rigid. There was no chance they could retreat that way without provoking another conflict.

'We stand our ground, then,' he offered, flexing his arms wide. The blades felt light in his hands. Strength flowed through his veins.

The wolfen crept forward, cautiously, steel held at arm's length.

Isabelle began to sing.

Her voice carried to him as a wave of pure joy. He could sense his blood pumping, experienced thousands of lightning pulses racing up his spine. He felt taller, stronger, and faster. He thought himself invincible.

He charged into the mass of wolfen, spun in short arcs, blades leading, slashing and cutting. Growls of pain morphed into screams of agony. Kors settled beside him, his weapons a blur, defending his back against those slipping in behind. And then the sky went black.

He couldn't see the *terrovyn* when it attacked, but he heard the screech of a wolfen as an ebony beak plunged into its neck. The head listed to the side, almost severed, before the body slumped to the ground. Enormous wings beat at the air, the beast enraged, hungry for more.

Ra'tor chopped his cleaver into a shoulder. It struck true, wedged in the bone. He pulled the wolfen towards him, kicked it in the chest. The body crashed into another, sent arms and legs sprawling. The smell of blood was everywhere, and his angel continued to sing.

Then it was over.

Ra'tor wiped blood from his mouth, flicked gore from his blades. The wolfen were all accounted for, their bodies butchered and bleeding. Sin-cha still beat her wings, excited, he assumed. He spun to see where his angel was.

She stood behind him, small and innocent looking. Her white dress splattered with glistening droplets of blood, her face as pale as a full moon. Yet the fear in her eyes was absent. Perhaps she was no longer the innocent child he first found.

'Are you injured?' he asked in the kingdom tongue, looking over her shoulder at the dozen black cloaks still standing on the far side of the bridge. They hadn't moved during the fight, still held their ground. He had no idea who they were.

'I am fine, Ra'tor. And so are you,' she placed her small hand against a cut on his knee.

He put his blades away, lifted her to his hip. 'I think we should leave,' he said to Kors, who was picking through the corpses.

'I agree,' he sliced a strip of flesh from a wolfen thigh, tossed it to Sin-cha who swallowed it whole. 'The way is clear. Let us reunite you with your Deios.'

Ra'tor could see the red tiled roof from where he stood. He would be there soon, amongst his brood after being absent for so long.

He smiled at his little angel.

She smiled back.

*

A persistent hum permeated their every thought, kept them calm.

Tarsin blinked stars from his eyes, looked about a circular chamber identical to the one they just vacated. Like his previous venture through a portal, he'd stepped from one world to another in the briefest of moments.

'Where are we?' he asked, seeing the tall shape of Nen standing five feet away.

'You have arrived at a place called the Weeping Tower,' she replied, offering a hand to steady his vertigo. 'We stand at its lowest level, where its heart resides,' Nen glanced at the beating sphere of light they stepped from, its glare casting irregular shadows about the room. Within seconds the remainder of Tarsin's Unseen were present, hands raised to shield their eyes.

'And where is the Weeping Tower located?' Tarsin asked. 'Which world do we now stand upon?'

Nen declined to answer immediately. Instead, she walked gracefully towards an archway, beckoned with a raise of her eyebrows, then passed through. Tarsin gestured to his men, followed Nen's footsteps, his hand resting on the pommel of his broadsword. The hum he heard, the vibration he felt through his entire body, was soothing, yet his mind suggested caution.

Beyond the archway lay a hallway, curved as it circled the inner chamber. Walls of alabaster somehow offered a soft green glow for them to see by and the floor was polished marble. Above, highlighted by the glowing walls, rested an arched ceiling intricately painted with numerous figures. Some wore assorted garments of vibrant colour, others frolicked under the watchful gaze of elders, as naked as the azure sky. From where he stood, it appeared the fresco wrapped about the entire circular hallway.

Nen's sapphire eyes caught his own as they continued to walk. 'This place is called Omphalos,' she began, 'it is a world of our own creation.'

'You created an entire world?'

'In a manner of speaking, yes,' her eyes sparkled, as if they were alive. He wondered what sights they had witnessed and what truths they could unravel.

As he thought of her answer the reality of her power registered. Whether she acted alone or not was irrelevant. Nen was once Nepharii, and he knew from experience the Nepharii were extremely capable, especially if they were united in a common cause.

As questions fought for ascendency inside his mind, another archway appeared, leading further from the centre of the tower. It was a narrow room with a single staircase leading up, which eventually led to a long room reminiscent of a sprawling tavern. As enjoyable as it was to see such a familiar sight, it was Cale Griffith and his thirty men that brought a tear to his eye. Thoughts had plagued him ever since he left. Dire thoughts of torture and death.

Within seconds the red-bearded giant threw back his chair and enveloped him in a bone-crunching hug.

'Easy, Griffith,' Tarsin's words sounded faint, 'you had me worried.'

'My king, I apologise,' Griffith shared a nervous glance with Nen before she wandered to the rear of the room. 'We had nowhere else to go,' he elaborated. 'The tunnels were caved in, then the Lady arrived, said she was a Walker of Paths, suggested we follow her. I . . . said yes, but I'm not sure why.'

He understood, felt the same now that he was here with his men. She was pretty and persuasive, it was true, but such attributes would take you only so far. There was another quality about Nen providing uncanny influence.

'Be on your guard,' Tarsin said the words softly, yet they carried weight.

'Always,' Griffith's grin split his red beard. 'I'm surprised you arrived so quickly. Nen said you followed, but I didn't realise you were this close.'

'We gave you five days to find and kill Bardell. I wasn't waiting any longer.'

Griffith's grin faded as quickly as it appeared. 'Five days? We left this morning, several hours ago.'

'No,' he shared his perplexed look, 'you've been absent for five days. The Unseen and I left this morning to trace your footsteps. We were worried you had fallen foul in Undercity, or Bardell had captured you.'

'Trust me, my lord, we have been in this room no longer than an hour. I spoke briefly with Nen when she led us here. Then she left, mentioned she was going to find you.'

Griffith's confusion mirrored his own. Once again, there was more at play here than he realised. Possibly more than he could comprehend. He swung his gaze about the room. His men were relaxed, sharing in conversation with Griffith's hand-picked crew. Yet the reality of this morning's events was becoming apparent.

Nen caught his eye as she stood beneath an archway. He walked with Griffith to stand in front of her, hands on hips. 'You have much to explain.'

'I am aware. But I think some time to eat and recuperate would be to your advantage. Food has been scarce in Bastion, the quality poor. Please,' she waved towards the laden table, 'accept my offer.'

Tarsin could see the men already consuming roasted meats and bowls of stew. 'I'll have the men drink water only,' he said, aware of a barrel sitting at the end of the long table.

'The purest water is all we have,' she purred.

'And the questions I have? When shall they be answered?'

Her storm-blue eyes locked onto his. 'We will talk, you and I, and you will learn a great many truths, Tarsin Va. But I urge you to be patient. Eat, gather your strength, and prepare yourself. Time is going nowhere.'

He watched her walk away, swiftly and without sound. He had no words to chase her, no questions to tease his lips.

'Are we going to eat?' Griffith nudged him in the back. The big man's eyes were wide in anticipation. He was hungry, they all were.

'I guess so,' he replied, his own stomach growling. Nen disappeared as the wall curved away.

'Good,' Griffith flashed his pearly white teeth, 'I'll meet you in the middle.'

*

He couldn't recall how many days had passed since they arrived.

Tarsin Va, king of Dervae, shook his head. It did nothing to clear the fog he felt swirling within. He looked about the long room, saw his men, fifty in number since he found Griffith, content and at rest. Green-glowing walls provided subtle shifts in hue, what he first believed to be a difference between night and day. But he'd lost count how many times they had changed. Ten times, twenty? Did he really care? Apart from the hazy mind he felt strong. At some point, having eaten and rested, he'd gathered his men and pushed them through a series of stretches to ease any tensions. As one, they all agreed they had never felt better.

But did they exercise this morning, or was it yesterday?

Or was it an idea he dreamed of, something he could do with the men tomorrow?

He was having trouble latching onto his own thoughts. The aroma of sizzling meat distracted him. The casual conversations bubbling around him were enticing. It was an effort to focus, to even breathe.

He assumed he was drowning.

'King Tarsin Va,' the words cut through his stupor like a thunderbolt.

He lifted his head, saw Nen standing over him, tall, powerful, gossamer threads of pale-blue silk draping her perfect form. Her sapphire eyes blazed with intensity.

'It is time, King Tarsin. You have rested long enough. You have regained your strength. Now for your answers.'

He pushed his hands beneath him, stood on shaking legs a moment later.

'Follow me,' she swung away without a second glance.

Somehow, he found the will to move. One step, another, until he found himself in a curved hallway. The headiness of simmering food faded, the call of companionship and the lure of restful sleep subsided. His mind cleared, as if his quickening steps upon the marble floor were responsible, sweeping away the last vestiges of lethargy.

He caught Nen as she passed beneath a broad arch. The room beyond was spacious, its walls lined with wooden shelves nursing countless tomes. Thousands of them, possibly more, reaching for a ceiling lost in shadow far above.

'What is this place?' he asked, aware they were alone. In fact, now that his faculties had returned, he couldn't recall having seen anyone else like Nen since he arrived at the Weeping Tower.

'A place where memories and ideas are not forgotten,' she walked to the other side of the room, where another broad arch led into darkness. 'Come, Tarsin Va, there is something I must show you.'

He traced her steps, something he was becoming quite adept at, until they both entered the outer room of the Weeping Tower. It was slightly curved, for the tower was circular, yet this outer room was open to the elements. Arches swept from his sight in either direction, a sheet of water falling on the outside. It provided a curtain between the room he stood in and the world beyond. It was also the source of the hum he first heard when he stepped through the portal. It was persistent, provided a steady flow evoking a sense of peace.

Before each arch sat an Elusian. Everybody he saw sat with legs crossed, hands resting on knees. They appeared to be like Nen, bald heads, pale-blue silk shifts that did little to reveal the contours of their womanly bodies. Their eyes were closed.

'What are they doing?' Tarsin whispered, too afraid to speak above the sound of falling water.

'They watch, as we have always done,' Nen smiled. 'This is where we keep an eye on our subjects.'

'Your subjects?'

'The people of the worlds, Tarsin Va. And since your temple is now operational, your world, along with those connected to her, are available to us once again.'

Her words confused him. How could the Elusian's before him watch anyone if their eyes were closed? And how could anyone watch someone from another world?

'I know what you are thinking, Tarsin,' Nen moved to stand before a sitting Elusian. 'All those who sit here in the Weeping Tower are my sisters. We number over a thousand, watching others as they live their lives, walking paths already set before them. We can see their journey, and sometimes, we can see a portion of their future.

'When we deem it necessary, on occasion, we will seek out an individual and offer guidance.'

His eyes narrowed. 'That is why I am here. You seek to offer advice.'

'We seek to offer you knowledge, Tarsin, so you can make your own judgements in the days to come.'

'Why not offer aid? If there are a thousand and more Elusian's sitting here in this tower, why not join us in our fight to save Bastion?'

She smiled at his words. 'This is but one of many towers, Tarsin. And yet we cannot join you. Our path has always been one of observation. Since the dawn of our arrival we have watched, recorded, and when necessary, we have offered guidance. It is not our place to steer someone from their chosen path.'

'But you have done exactly that,' he interjected.

'No, we have plucked you from your path for the time being, but you will return and continue as before when we believe you are ready.'

He clenched his hands. 'I don't understand the difference. Offering help and guidance will surely alter my path in the future.'

'It is possible, but Fate has a way of righting herself. Perhaps we were always destined to guide you, our paths guaranteed to merge. We may have taken you from a certain time and place, but we will return you to that place so you can continue on.'

Their talk stalled as an Elusian moaned to their right. Both he and Nen searched out the noise, saw a series of shudders ripple through a sitting body.

'What is happening to her?'

'She dreams,' Nen seem nonplussed. 'We Elusian's have been gifted with the *Sight*. It enables us to see strands of light streaming through the cosmos when we close our eyes. The strands represent the path each soul is currently on. Some deviate over time, some are intersected or fragment. Some souls step off completely and are lost. Those which pulse with intent belong to people of power. They draw others towards them, some entwine, some shape into something of importance. Your thread, King Tarsin Va, is bright and vibrant. In a single year thousands of individuals will cross paths with you. You can influence them, enlighten them - if necessary, you can destroy them.'

'And you can see all this when you close your eyes?'

'There is a process,' Nen held a hand towards the curtain of water falling outside. 'Immersion in the pure water of Omphalos is just the beginning. But when protocols are followed, yes, we can see a great deal.'

'So why me?' he asked the obvious question. 'Of all the worlds you can scry, why choose me to offer guidance?'

'Because there is a darkness surrounding you, Tarsin. It seeks you with an intent to consume you. It was written long ago. And yet we need your path to remain strong and true,' Nen took a deep breath, lowered her pretty face. 'We can observe elements of the future when using our *Sight*, especially when our observation is shared. A possible future has been glimpsed where you no longer exist. That future is dark, and the prospect of our own survival is severely compromised.'

'You'll be in danger?'

'More than danger, Tarsin. We may cease to be.'

'But you are powerful, capable of feats I can only dream about. If you will not stand against what is to come, how can I?'

'You will have allies, Tarsin, as many as you can find. Because when the time comes, you will not be able to stand against a god alone.'

'Ahriman is the Darkness you speak of,' he offered, knowing it to be true.

'He is,' Nen sighed, then met his eyes with her sapphire stare. 'If you do not defeat him, there is a possibility he may destroy all of existence.'

'Is he currently in Bastion?'

'He is.'

'So, I'll need to find men and women to defeat a god?'

'You have already started such a process. You have already reformed the Unseen, you have Panthian allies. Others will join you in the days and weeks ahead.'

'What of Kayla Tolsten? You said our paths will cross in the future. I vowed to protect her, promised I would come for her and keep her safe.'

The sparkle in Nen's eyes intensified, which settled his nerves somewhat as she smiled. 'Kayla Tolsten is well, that is all I can say. I believe you will see her soon.'

A yearning deep in his chest almost floored him. To be able to place his arms around her, hold her tight, to stroke her midnight hair. He needed Kayla more than he realised. A companion. A confidante. Someone he could trust. She'd been absent from his side for too long. More than anything, he needed to take back Aston's Tear so he could seek her out.

'She is important to you, isn't she?'

He wiped a finger under his eye, tried to focus. 'She is,' he whispered, aware he was all choked up. He'd bottled his anger and frustrations for so long they'd masked his true feelings for her. But here, in the Weeping Tower, all the walls he'd built to keep out the pain were beginning to crumble.

'To acknowledge one's feelings is the first step to enlightenment,' Nen moved closer, placed a soft hand on his arm. 'Tell me about her, Tarsin Va.

'Tell me about the woman you love.'

CHAPTER TWENTY-EIGHT

Birdsong, so bright and cheerful, aroused him from slumber.

Rastan pushed his elbow beneath him, half sat up. He looked at the low branch above, saw a *wing-tail* sitting pretty, all scarlet feathers except for a yellow crest. He thought to leap up to catch the bird, because the mind of six-year-old boy thought it would be entertaining. He wouldn't hold onto it for long. He merely wished to stroke its feathers and hold it close. If he was lucky, he might even hear its thoughts.

Intrigued, he pushed himself fully upright and stretched his arms, realised the *wing-tail* was out of reach, despite the low branch. He shared a smile with the bird anyway, then peered about the garden. He'd spent the morning rummaging through tall fronds and emerald-leafed water plants, seeking insects to study and draw. His parchment, ink and quill remained on his small wooden table under the *roaring-tree*, hidden beneath the shade of broad branches and heavy green foliage. He managed to complete three drawings in the early hours, well before anyone else had broken their fast. Ruvin would be proud of his details, Neema impressed with his letters. He'd taken extra care this morning as he patiently waited for his ink to dry. No smudges, dirt smears or grass stains marred his sheet. He even drew the outline of a sun peeking from behind a cloud in the top right-hand corner.

Mother would smile when she saw his elaboration. She would smile and then ruffle his long black hair. It was a shame her smile wouldn't see out the day.

'*She still loves you; you know.*'

'*I know she loves me, but I can see the pain on her face growing as each day passes.*'

Silence, for a moment. The voices in his head knew how he felt about his mother. Kayla had given him everything he could have asked for in his formative years. Love, support, friendship, and laughter. She taught him everything she knew, allowed Ruvin and Neema to teach him ideas and truths of a different kind. He ran and climbed, as any young boy should, learnt his numbers and letters, as only the privileged could. Dancing forms were taught by the Ven women, at which he excelled, and the playing of instruments: percussion, string, and wind, came just as naturally. Donal, a dozen years older and now a man, was his best friend, though. He liked to share his afternoons by his side, thankful for the peace and quiet, content to sit and listen to the sounds of the garden. Together, they had written eight journals discussing the anatomy of creatures found in their garden. If they conversed at all whilst they worked, it was by writing letters to each other, something they were both fond of.

'We know you feel her pain as keenly as she does, Rastan. You hide it well, but you cannot hide it from us.'

'I have no wish to hide my pain,' his inner voice replied, a touch of anger at its source, *'at least not from the Core.'*

That was what he called them, the thousands of voices swirling inside his head each day. The Core. A collection of souls, too many to accurately count - and he'd tried on multiple occasions – that swarmed beneath the surface of his skin, twirling inside his mind and body. They were present when he first woke each morning, calling, asking questions, shouting to be heard. It was only when he fell asleep that he managed to escape their chatter. But even then, he rarely slept for long.

'My mother worries,' he ventured, knowing the Core were always listening. He'd learnt a great deal about their flight from Bastion when Ruvin taught him their history. It had been a stressful period in their lives, one which eventually consumed his mother. Ruvin and Neema, elders and wise, sought to keep the survivor's content and motivated during their imprisonment. Donal appeared to be happy with their predicament, and rarely spoke of Bastion and his life before. Reefe O'Bannon was another matter entirely. Somehow, he'd found comfort with the Ven, and whatever desire he had for home was lost within the haze he now lived. Ruvin said he yearned only for his narcotics, and then only when he was coherent. He was certain no-one had seen him for six months, possibly longer.

'Your mother has always worried,' the voice belonged to his favourite, an old man he called the Wise One.

'It still saddens me. Her smiles shrink each day, and the laughter I once heard is now absent.'

'Six years confined to a garden and an assortment of rooms will send even the sanest person over the edge. It is a wonder any of your companions share your optimism.'

'He doesn't know anything different,' chimed the Dancer. She was his instructor when he took to the floor with the Ven women. A hard taskmaster, but her expertise was appreciated, along with her enthusiasm.

And she was right. He didn't know any different. All his life had been spent here, in the Palace of the Five Kings, a watchful eye always focused on his wellbeing. This was his world. It was small compared to what his family once lived and knew, but it was his.

'If you let me speak to her, I could change her mood,' Rastan offered. *'She worries because she believes I am flawed. If I could speak and sing and laugh, she would be happier.'*

'Such notions are out of the question,' responded the Wise One. *'I have previously explained to you the danger of letting others hear you speak. You are young, but your voice has power, and so will your words. There are some who would use such knowledge against you.'*

It was the same old argument. The Wise One had never told him who might stand against him. Or why anyone would choose to. He was a young boy with an adventurous heart, skilled beyond his age thanks to the voices in his head. More so than Ruvin, Neema and his mother, they were his teachers. And yet there were some things left unsaid by the Core, secret things he truly wished to know.

'When you are older,' the words of the Wise One cut through his melancholy. Funny how he couldn't keep a secret from his Core, but they could keep one from him.

A clear note flew from the scarlet *wing-tail* above, piercing, concise, a call to a mate. He felt his own heart beat twice before he heard the return chirp, faint, for the female was perched higher, yet full of love. It had been a satisfying discovery between he and Donal when they realised the *wing-tails* mated for life.

'*You have stalled long enough,*' intruded the Wise One, the hint of a smile in his tone, '*the Instructor is here, ready to observe your exercise.*'

'*I exercised this morning,*' he replied, '*and you were with me when I climbed the* sallow *tree.*'

'*You climbed the tree to look over the wall, not for exercise.*'

'*It was still physical. I lifted myself higher than I'd ever been before. My arms still burn thinking about it.*'

He shared a smile with the *wing-tail* above as it launched into the air with a sudden flap. He couldn't win any argument with the Wise One, but he enjoyed the verbal jousting, nonetheless. It encouraged him to be creative, to think spontaneously and develop his vernacular in a manner conducive to leadership. Because that's what his mother - and unbeknownst to her, his Core - were grooming him for. The prospect of his little family of survivors returning to Bastion was remote, but if it could be orchestrated, he would arrive at the Holy City as heir to the throne of Dervae.

'*Start stretching, child,*' the Instructor had arrived. Not the most pleasant voice to converse with. He was harsh at the best of times. Spoke with a voice like a whip crack, snarled like a feral dog.

'*I'm stretching,*' he eased his arms out wide, twisted his torso. '*Where's the Swordsman? I'd rather swing my wooden blade than run and jump.*'

'*Later,*' cracked the Instructor's voice. '*Exercise comes first. Loosen your muscles, then you can swing about with your wooden stick.*'

He was sure he heard laughter in the background, faint, but it was there. It alerted him to a handful of others watching from within. Some he could sense, like the Carpenter and the Blacksmith. They were jovial most of the time yet cared about his development. And yet there were some who hid in the shadows of his mind and watched, never offering advice, nor speaking to him directly. If he could describe them with a single word, it would be Sinister.

It was another reason to be thankful for the Wise One. It was he who kept them in line, silenced them, even, so as not to disturb his learning. He recalled a voice from his past, a male voice he knew as Bruiser. Rastan had been four years old at the time, learning to write his words with a steady hand when Bruiser began to curse him for being a puppet. There was a rage in his verbal assault, a memory of a leather belt and lashings. There was so much anger.

The Wise One asked Bruiser once to cease his tirade. Bruiser refused, spat foul language in retaliation. A chorus of voices sang out for him to stop.

A moment later all was quiet.

'Where did he go?' Rastan had asked, as curious as any small boy.

'The Bruiser is no more,' the Wise One returned. *'He has left. He will no longer disrupt your learning.'*

Those were the only words he heard regarding the matter. There were others who voiced their displeasure at times, but they were quickly reminded of Bruiser's fate. The Wise One was always nearby, waiting, ready to pounce to protect the boy.

Ready to protect the future king.

'I'm waiting!' the Instructor barked. *'Finish your stretches and run, child. I don't have all day!'*

'I think you do,' chimed a voice he knew as the Jester. *'If I'm not mistaken, you have an eternity.'*

Rastan swung his arms and began to run as more laughter sang from within. He moved with casual grace towards the east wall, his feet stepping lightly over soft grass. The circuit he ran kept the fifteen-foot wall on his right shoulder, before he reached the end and spun about, retracing his footsteps with the wall now beside his left shoulder. Back and forth, from one end to the next. A weathered trail marked his route, worn from daily runs now years in the making. It was the only scar to blemish the beautiful garden, a reminder to the survivors of Bastion that they were imprisoned. A reminder that the Five Kings thought of them as a curiosity.

Caged animals, perhaps. Kept in a pen, fed and groomed. The prospect of freedom a dim reality.

Rastan took his eyes from the scarred ground to look at the sky, hoping to see the *wing-tail* soaring above, free to fly where it pleased.

'I'll fly free of this cage one day,' he breathed evenly, concentrated on his rhythm as he quickened his pace. *'One day, I'll find a way to take my mother home.'*

He didn't know how to begin such a journey, though. The Five Kings were powerful beings, their every wish seen to, all their desires manifested. They were highly skilled, incredibly intelligent and cunning beyond belief. He'd overheard many a Ven servant speaking out of turn, claiming the kings could read the minds of their subjects. He didn't know if it was true, but he was conscious of his thoughts when in their presence. Besides, he was a young boy who couldn't speak, with no experience of the outside world. From what Ruvin described, it was dangerous beyond the garden wall. Dangerous and impossibly vast.

So how was he, a young child, going to see his mother home?

He would think of something. Since the day his mother told him she wished to be in Bastion, he'd spent hours scheming of a way to escape the Palace of the Five Kings. If he could break down the doors and fly past the guards, he would do so. If he could commune with the wild beasts and ask for aid, it would be done.

But he still didn't know how to deal with the Five Kings. If they came for him, how would he escape them? And if they chose to destroy his family, how could he stop them?

'Patience, my boy,' the Wise One settled his nervous energy.

'Yes,' snapped the Instructor, *'listen to the old man. And concentrate on the task at hand. You should be running, and your breathing should be measured. Concentrate!'*

Rastan focused, brought his technique back in line with the Instructor's wish. Everything they taught him was important, so he'd been told. Everything had its place, and everything had purpose. It might not be relevant here and now, but one day, he would understand. So he'd been told.

He reached the end of the wall where it joined the palace rooms, twisted his body about and began to retrace his steps. He breathed clean air, noted his heart beating at a steady pace. He felt relaxed, felt his rhythm.

'Do you truly believe you'll free your mother one day, Rastan?' asked the Wise One. *'Can you really take her home?'*

'Obviously not yet, but one day I will,' he replied as his bare feet slapped the ground. *'If I can return her home, then maybe she will smile for me. Maybe she will smile all day long.'*

'That is good,' the deep voice of the Wise One echoed from the background. *'Because I'm counting on it.'*

*

The heat was stifling.

Neema eased her old frame next to Donal, who sat on a ledge beside the rockpool in her garden. His feet dangled in the water; his trousers rolled to his knees. His thin shirt was open at the neck. Long, broad branches of the *sallow* tree provided speckled shade, enough to keep the sun from burning their skin.

'Are you melting, yet?' Neema asked, a wry grin stretching the wrinkles of her face.

'Almost,' Donal responded, also smiling.

'Where is Rastan? I thought he was with you.'

'He is,' she followed Donal's finger as he pointed to a swirl in the water. 'He swims beneath the surface, searching for treasures, so his letter informed me.'

She nodded in understanding, pleased the young boy was behaving exactly like a young boy. Although she wasn't sure she wished to know what his collection of treasures was going to look like. 'How long has he been under?' her eyes narrowed in concern, aware she hadn't seen him as she walked towards the pool of water and sat down.

'Long enough, would be my guess, but he swims like a fish,' Donal didn't seem bothered by Rastan's absence. 'He can hold his breath for a long time. Longer than I, in any case.'

Neema searched for movement under the reflecting water. It was difficult, for the shade and sun flickered back and forth, causing her eyes to squint in some places, then adjust to the shadow in others. 'I cannot see him,' she finally said, a hint of panic in her voice.

A splash answered her worries as Rastan burst from below the surface. His long black hair shimmered; his sun-kissed skin glistened. There was the largest smile she'd ever seen shinning within his jade-green eyes.

'I was about to jump in to search for you, my mischievous boy.'

Rastan's mouth lifted to match the smile in his eyes. As did his hands. Neema could see they were full of silt and waterweed, dark rivulets running down his arms.

Donal shifted next to her. 'What have you found, Rastan?'

The young boy held his hands before him, stepped through the waist-high water so they could clearly see the treasures he'd discovered. It was difficult to discern what he cradled in his hands, except for the shell of a *sink-snail*. It's copper hue sparkled in the sunlight, looked every bit a piece of treasure raised from the depths.

'Oh,' Donal stepped into the water to share a closer look. 'You found a *sink-snail* and a patch of *hairy-rock-moss*.

She could see the excitement in Rastan as he nodded his head. It was a wonderful find. The *sink-snail* was a delicate morsel craved by the locals; its flesh pried from its shell with an equally delicate bone utensil. The Ven often ate it raw, allowing the slippery flesh to slide down their throat with a single swallow. Neema preferred it simmered in a pan with a hint of spice.

But it was the yellow *hairy-rock-moss* that caught her eye. Rastan still held the rock in his hand, but it was the hairy moss growing upright that was the true treasure. Plastered over open wounds, the rock moss would take a single hour to mould itself across the skin, protecting and then repairing the damage below. She had seen the miraculous remedy only once during her time on Vidae, after a male Ven servant was split across the forehead by Ik'omi, first born of the Nepharii Kings. It was his price to pay, suffering a retaliatory strike for a lack of enthusiasm at the king's humour.

The wound, though severe at first glance, was healed within a day.

She pushed sour thoughts of the kings from her mind. 'Such a marvellous find, young Rastan,' she squinted, looked to see if he held any other treasures in his small hands. 'Did you find anything else of importance?'

Sparkling droplets showered the pool as Rastan shook his head.

'Will you search for more?' she asked.

He smiled, then returned his gaze to his treasures, his little fingers cleaning the dirt and weeds away.

She placed a comforting hand on Donal's shoulder. 'Have you ever seen such life in a child's eyes?'

'No, they are full of wonder.'

'It is no surprise. Like you, he remembers everything he sees.'

'It is more than that,' Donal shifted his hips closer as he returned to his rock seat, spoke quietly, as if what he was about to say was for her ears only. 'He knows things he shouldn't possibly be aware of. Words, phrases, mannerisms. You saw him dance for the first time, as a three-year-old before the kings. How could he know the steps to a dance he only just witnessed? How could he move and twist with such precision? Even his letters and drawings are of exquisite detail. I was gifted as a child, Neema, but Rastan has talents far beyond anything I could manage.'

'I know, Donal, he is a very special boy. And I'm glad you are friends. It's important Rastan knows he is loved.'

There was a pause as Rastan looked up and searched their eyes, looking for something, perhaps, or merely curious.

He flicked his long hair over his shoulder a moment later, then dived back into the pool.

'I agree,' Donal continued to speak quietly. 'But every now and then he writes things he shouldn't know.'

'Such as?'

Donal took a deep breath, but his eyes seemed far away, as if he was recalling an event from long ago. 'I was an orphan,' he began, 'raised beneath the streets of Bastion by a collection of uncles and aunts. I shared blood with no-one, was taught life's lessons from anyone who had time or could be bothered. As I grew older my memory skills became a boon for certain individuals, and thus I was taught further skills relevant to a thief. But I discovered the greatest difference between those who scrounged below, as opposed to those who lived above, was the manner in which we conversed. Speech amongst thieves was a conglomeration of languages, signals and what we called gutter-talk. If a message needed to be sent secretly, we could do so without anyone above being the wiser. If someone didn't understand the message, then it was obviously not for them. It meant imposters were caught out with relative ease.'

'How is your past relevant to Rastan?'

'About a year before Kayla arrived to be with her father, Derrick Tolsten, a family of Rykedians from the east joined the ranks of the Nocturnals. They spoke the kingdom tongue poorly, had trouble enunciating a handful of letters,' Donal wiped a hand across his forehead, swept away his beads of sweat. 'A number of sailors helped our guild gather information regarding cargo from the docks. They cursed often and colourfully, garnered laughs as they did so. One of their favourite phrases was "Frey's Luck", except our Rykedian friends couldn't wrap their tongues around all the letters. Whenever they tried to repeat the phrase, it became muddled, much to our amusement. In the end, the sailors converted the phrase to "Fr'uck", to accommodate our new companions.

'Other than our guild, very few people were aware of our new phrase. Those who heard it would have no idea concerning its origin. And yet last week Rastan jumped from a branch and landed on a sharp stick that pricked his foot. I could see he was in pain, and when I asked how he felt, he grabbed the offending stick and wrote the word Fr'uck in the soil at his feet.

'How could he know the word? I have never said it in front of him, nor have I heard Reefe say it either.'

'Reefe may have said it once, in the early days of our arrival,' she replied.

'It's possible, but I doubt it. Reefe rarely had time with Rastan alone, if at all. And I feel I've spent more time with him than any other in the past two years, including Kayla.'

'Maybe Kayla said it in front of him?'

'Again, it's possible, but I've never heard her say it. When she arrived in Undercity, she spent most of her time with her father and his select group of advisors. He refused to let her associate with any undesirables. You know, the cutthroats and beggars, the whores and the bruisers. The words she heard were from the educated, not those from the street. After a year with her father, she was given leave to roam, but only with an escort. If I didn't accompany her, it was Reefe O'Bannon by her side.'

'There is truth in your words,' Neema sighed, knowing there were many mysteries surrounding the boy. She remembered when he was born. A Star-Born child: a child born with many souls. Could it be? Could he share memories with those who had already lived?

Another splash saw Rastan surface below her dangling feet. Once again, his green eyes sparkled with mirth. He flashed perfectly white teeth at Donal, then disappeared back under the water.

'I think he is part fish,' Neema laughed at the boy's antics.

'I'm glad he's happy,' Donal responded, but the tone of his voice suggested he wasn't so sure.

'Is there something wrong?'

He kept his eyes on the swirling water. 'Not with Rastan. It's Kayla I worry about.'

She should have guessed Donal would be concerned. Little escaped the bright young man.

'I'm certain it is just a phase,' Neema sought to comfort him with kind words. 'Kayla feels lost right now, but she'll recover.'

'I hope so. I said I had no blood family amongst the Nocturnals, but as a boy, I saw Kayla as my older sister. She was the first to truly show compassion to a scruffy blonde-haired street urchin.'

'Then hold on to the memory, Donal, and do everything you can to remind her of the connection you both shared,' she paused, lifted a hand to shade her eyes from the sun. 'Perhaps you can do something for me.'

'What would you like me to do?'

So many things, she thought, although she knew Donal, as clever as he was, lacked the courage for what was to come. 'You said Kayla acted as your older sister when she arrived in Bastion. Perhaps you could be an older brother for Rastan. I know you are both close, the bond of friendship is clear to see. You may not have the same blood, but that doesn't mean you cannot be brothers.'

'I would like that,' Donal forced a smile, but she could see the light in his eyes return.

'Kayla would appreciate it. Her concerns are many, and mostly deal with issues far from here. If you can be here for Rastan, it may just ease the pressure she feels gnawing inside.'

'Being here for Rastan is no pressure on my behalf. In fact, being here is the best thing that has ever happened to me. Here I am safe, Neema. There are no demons searching for me down broken streets, no sleepless nights or a belly rumbling from lack of food. Here, I have everything I need.'

'But it isn't home, Donal, it never will be. Here, we are no more than a curiosity. One day, we may no longer be even that. What do you think will happen when the Five Kings decide our lives are no longer important? Where will we go if they cast us out, or worse, decree we are merely playthings and separate our little family? Can you survive all alone? I fear it has already begun. I haven't seen Reefe for half-a-year.'

'No, I have not seen him either. Nor has Ruvin,' a rogue cloud drifted before the sun, blocking the heat for a moment. Rastan popped his head above the water, swam towards a collection of water ferns on the far edge. In his hands shone three *sink-snails*, shining despite the lack of sunlight. He spun about and sat down, gathered a small twig, and began to pry the flesh from his gathered treasures.

'One day, Donal, we may have to act and act quickly. You know this. We cannot pretend this is where we shall be for the rest of our lives.'

'Is that why Kayla still practices the sword in secret, despite Ruvin being unable to teach her anything new?'

'It is. Unlike you, she yearns for it. She wants nothing more than to return to Bastion. If she could escape the palace, she would flee today.'

'So, you're saying I need to be a brother to Rastan, but I should also be ready to support him should we need to flee?'

'I'm saying exactly that,' she replied, knowing there was so much more she wished to tell. But Donal was too clever for her to divulge all she knew. Too clever, but also too innocent. She couldn't afford him saying something out of turn; she also feared he may be overheard if he talked. Better to keep her secrets within, to reveal when the time was right.

'How long, do you think, before we need to be ready?'

Was there a quiver in his voice? Did he still fear the dangers back home more than being imprisoned by the Five Kings? Her heart wished to tell him of the note Kian entrusted to her before he left with Jarred. It revealed many truths, some deeply concerning. Ruvin was the only other to have read Kian's words.

But she couldn't. The truths were too frightening for the young man. His reality was already compromised, his fears never to be forgotten. His only hope was to embrace the concept of family, to revel in the nurturing instinct of an older brother.

'I have no idea when we'll need to be ready, Donal. Kian once said there will be a sign. It could be tomorrow; it could be years away.'

'I hope it is years away,' there was a sadness in his voice. 'I like it here.'

She knew he did.

For Donal, it was what she feared the most.

CHAPTER TWENTY-NINE

The sun was low on the horizon, sinking fast.

Jarred shed a tear, knew the night was only moments away. He felt like he was losing a long-lost friend, a friend only found earlier this day.

He shook his head, closed his eyes in preparation for the darkness to come. Like every other evening, it was a prelude to sudden fear and loathing. A reminder of his failed mission to reach Aston's Tear. A reminder of his lack of courage.

He had tried so many times to be brave. For countless nights he'd sat with his backpack around his shoulders, sword buckled at his hip. Strips of dried food and a pocket full of walnuts accompanied his waterskin. Maps and scrolls and his polished spyglass were placed within easy reach. He was prepared. He was always prepared.

Yet he never found the nerve to walk away from the safety of Irongate.

He told himself he was waiting for men of Bastion to arrive. He could see them patrolling the city, only a handful of streets away at times. From his vantage in the tower, peering through his spyglass, he thought to will them closer. The prospect of waving a flag or lighting a flame enticed him, yet he succumbed to doing neither, fearful his actions would be seen by Others roaming nearby.

So many Others, he mused. He knew them all, for the voices in his head reminded him each day of who they were and where they came from. Aquilans from a world called Aura, the Lupans from Mona, the crow-like Murdans from Ether and the Deios from Dei.

There were others amongst the hordes now crowding Bastion's streets, though. Some he saw on rare occasions, like the Venatian hound-men from Anubi and the Vulpan fox-men from Tricae. He saw a Tauran once, a huge beast twelve feet tall and broader than any doorway, twin horns twirling from its bull-like head. The voices told him it came from a world known as Labyrin, a strange world where cities were built underground to escape the harsh light of a dying star.

He was yet to lay eyes on a Verman from Trich or a Panthian from Aeth, and he thought he may have glimpsed both an Ursan from Sopor and an Ophidian from Ouro during an altercation ten days earlier, but he couldn't be absolutely sure. The only other to remain absent was the Ven from the world called Vidae.

They would not be seen any time soon, for he knew their portal to Bastion was closed. Kian promised it would remain so for some time, until he was ready to return and help cleanse the city of the Dark Lord they feared.

The one who frightened him greater than all the beasts in Bastion combined.

Twisted thoughts of Ahriman kept his feet firmly planted in the tower. The prospect of crossing paths with the ancient one on his way to the pyramid sent his heart beating in strange, irregular patterns. His hands would become clammy, his breathing ragged. The urge to vomit what little food he had sitting in his stomach was extraordinary. If he saw the Dark Man, as he thought of him, a single look would surely see him perish. Possibly in a burst of flame, maybe with his heart exploding from within his chest. Whichever way he looked at it, their crossing of paths always ended poorly.

At least for him it did.

Jarred rubbed his hands together, vigorously, hoping to instil some heat before the true cold of night arrived. Today's sunshine had been a welcome sight, a chance to feel alive in a winter of uncertainty. But he also knew the cloudless sky above to be a herald of frigid weather. Once again, he would need to burrow beneath the dozen blankets and fur-lined cloaks he'd salvaged from the cupboards of the Brotherhood, hiding, perhaps, from the reality of winter's savage bite. Up here, in the small room at the top of the tower, it was difficult to remain warm.

But he rarely ventured below anymore. Down there, amongst the corridors of Irongate, were too many nooks for a demon to hide.

The last flash of brilliant orange light flared to the west, sinking beneath blackened waves too far away for his eyes to see. He quickly moved to his collection of candles, snatched one the length of his finger from a wooden box now half empty. It was his only solace, a lit candle to help keep the darkness at bay.

A single candle would see through half the night. Then he would light another, always flickering, day and night, but out of sight of any window or slit in the wall.

He took a couple of steps, placed the wick of his new candle into the flame of the stuttering stub slouched on its copper dish. The flame flared for an instant, then settled. He offered a prayer and a smile, then placed it upright on a second copper dish before carrying it carefully to the far wall where his blankets lay.

The cold was already beginning to seep into his bones.

He placed his candle on a shelf, rubbed his hands together once more. It was too early for him to curl into his makeshift bed, although the appeal was strong. Maybe he could read his maps by the candlelight, the ones he promised to hand over to the lords of Bastion. He was certain he'd memorised the intricate location of all twelve portals lying beneath the city, but it wouldn't hurt to have another look.

Or he could check his path to the pyramid one more time, make certain he knew where he was going once he left Irongate. If he couldn't find a lord or a general to hand his maps too, then the pyramid would be his next option. Kian had asked him to retrieve the *Nepharii Uranometria* from within, ceasing the pyramid's function. A task he willingly agreed to accomplish should the need arise.

But it was too cold to leave now. The backpack hanging from a peg near the only door hadn't been touched in weeks. Any thoughts of attempting either of his goals was quashed by his lack of courage to step outside. Winter was his excuse, the early snow blanketing rooftops and icy paths a reason to avoid the journey he knew he should be attempting. An excuse that even his reflection thought was weak.

He found the rectangular mirror one day, hidden behind the bookshelf. He'd been looking for drafts in the wall, hoping to seal them before the winter winds arrived from the north. Instead, he found a gilded frame obscured with dust. He slid it towards him, carefully, saw it was taller than he and three foot wide.

Jarred blew across the surface, saw his reflection starring back at him.

It judged him. Judged him for being the coward he was. Judged him for being afraid.

He remembered. How could he not. His mirror image still scorned him every time he looked.

Maybe it will be different now that winter is truly here? He couldn't possibly head out in this weather. He would die so very quickly once the icy tendrils of night caught hold of him. Surely it was wiser to wait for a more clement season, possibly even summer.

He'd placed a grey sheet over its silvered surface, draping the gilded frame and the burning eyes that always sought his own. What if he looked now? It had been a month, at least, since he locked eyes with himself.

A trembling hand reached for the dusty cloth. Jarred pulled at the fabric, watched as it fell away to reveal a full-length image of a boy who should be turning into a man. Instead, he saw an emaciated individual, malnourished, frightened, alone.

'Hello,' he spoke softly, with a voice trembling in fear.

There was no answer, but his eyes revealed his inner thoughts. They still judged him, despite his gaunt appearance and dishevelled hair. Even without his lips moving, he could hear scathing words ripping into his soul.

'You are a coward, Jarred. You are nothing! So many people trusted you. So many people believed in you. And what

have you done with their trust and goodwill? What have you achieved since you arrived back in Bastion?'

A tear slid across a pale cheek. His hands shook, not with cold, but with disappointment.

'Are you crying, Jarred? Are you still afraid? If the city is to be saved, you need to complete your mission. Either find the men of Bastion, or head towards the pyramid. Make your choice.'

'I hate you,' he whispered, but it hurt him, all the same. Because it was true. He did hate himself. He hated everything he had become.

Trembling fingers found the sheet curled on the floor. He clenched them tight, covered the mirror with a sweep. There was nothing new to be found from his reflection. He remained the same. Bitter and brutally honest. A revelation he wasn't prepared to accept.

He wiped the single tear from his cheek, sighed deeply within the silent room. Alone and afraid, he didn't know how much longer he could remain hidden in his tower. The threads of sanity were already parting, in some places, they were being pulled with obvious disdain for his wellbeing.

He wasn't sure he could halt the untangling.

Shouts, barks and blood-curdling screams sounded from below, interrupting his darkening thoughts.

It took a moment for him to realise what was occurring. Three long strides took him to the broken window, where he carefully pulled aside the heavy blanket masking the outside world. He peered down at the darkened street, saw a flash of starlight on raised blades as heaving bodies battled against each other. Black cloaks and dark fur, silvered talons and claws. It was a frenzied assault between adversaries, no quarter given, no backward steps. Primal and terrifying. Brutal.

It was over in what felt like a heartbeat.

Two survivors, Lupan, from what he could tell, loped away to the west, slinking into shadows. They left nothing but silence and the dead behind.

Fear gripped Jarred's heart, squeezed tight. The dead lay ten feet from Irongate's entrance. If he left them there to rot, others would come sniffing. He'd rather not have hunters creeping so close to his hideaway. What if they sensed him, cowering in the tower?

Maybe it was the thought of being found that stirred him into action, maybe it was the voice in his head telling him how disappointing he'd been. Whatever it was, he felt an urge to recover the dead from outside Irongate. He would drag them inside, take them below to where the Brotherhood kept their embalming tools and flasks of fluid, neatly laid upon heavy wooden tables. There he would examine the beasts, learn what he could, discover information he could then relay to those of importance. And with the blades and scissors and scraping implements at his disposal, he'd fashion a disguise from whatever beast he claimed. Fashion a disguise that might see him slink back into Bastion's streets with a semblance of hope.

Perhaps a clever disguise that would see him reach the pyramid, Aston's Tear.

Adrenaline flowed in his veins, the first time in months. Excitement with a dash of purpose. Weak as he was, alone and distressed, he found the energy to climb down his broken staircase and from there, make his way into the main hall of Irongate. He kept his eyes focused on the large wooden doors across the expanse, was too afraid to search the shadows he passed with hurried footsteps. As he reached the exit, he fumbled the lock, then pushed with everything he had to open solid doors to the night.

Cold air slapped his face hard. He took a reassuring breath, plunged into the courtyard with wanning courage. The iron gates were sixty feet away, stone pavement already slick with ice before him. Lose his footing and he could crack his head like a melon hit with a hatchet. So he shuffled, slowly, taking his time, listening as the sounds of a winter night swept over him.

He reached the gate, fumbled with numb hands for the key, then twisted, listened as the mechanism released a locking pin with a click. A frightful gasp leapt from his mouth, fully aware Others may have heard, alerting them to the unusual noise.

Nothing stirred but the wind, a low, mournful sigh that did little to ease his fears.

He peered from behind the iron gate, his hands shaking, eyes wide as they sought the corpses he knew to be there. There were four creatures lying prone, blood blackening in shallow pools. Three were unmistakably Ophidian, serpent men with scaled hides, slitted eyes and a plethora of silver trinkets piercing their exposed bodies. The other was smaller in stature but covered in bloody fur.

A Vulpan, he noticed, after stepping with care to examine the body up close. A man with a head like a fox.

He must have been hunting with the Lupans, he guessed, for he certainly wasn't a friend of the Ophidians. Two wickedly curved blades belonging to the serpent men protruded from his body. One in his chest, the other skewering an eye. He would have died before he hit the ground.

He would do, though, Jarred mused. If he could skin the beast and cure the hide, he might be able to assemble a disguise convenient enough to see him pass close inspection.

With nervous energy Jarred bent to grab the collar of the Vulpan's leather shirt, then with both hands, began to pull. He was heavy, despite being a foot smaller than the Ophidians. But with gritted teeth Jarred strained until the corpse slid upon the icy ground. By the time he reached the embalming room beneath the dormitory with the last of the four beasts, Jarred was exhausted to the point of collapsing. He left the pile of flesh on the tiled floor, locked the door with a rusty key. Then he slunk with his back to the wall, his hands raw and bleeding, his breathing heavy. As his eyes closed, he imagined what he might find if he dissected the beasts. Then he thought of cutting the Vulpan, skinning it, so he could wear its hide. If he made the correct cuts, pulled back the skin with care, he could fashion it into something he could wear. And the face of the Vulpan? He would need to be precise, perhaps even cast a mould to keep its shape. Or he could cut away the lower jaw and hollow out the skull. It would take time, and there were half-a-dozen books on a shelf he could read detailing the process. Scraping, curing and stitching, all difficult tasks during a cold winter. Yet despite being a gruesome thought, the prospect of having something important to manufacture warmed his heart.

And the final result would see him become someone other than the malnourished young man living in fear. Someone who would not be judged when he looked in the mirror.

'I'll wear a demon-skin,' he spoke quietly, a smile creasing his face, 'and become something I'm not.'

*

He was deep below Bastion.

Ahriman's bald head breached the surface of the black water he bathed in. He was in a Nepharii bathhouse, an ancient, tiled room with a dozen pools, all empty except for the one he sat in. Above sat a domed ceiling, cracked in places, dust and grime marring its once beautiful fresco. He could barely see the painted figures, for the only light came from warlock's fungi, glowing green and clumped together in the dank corners of the room. It was enough, though, enough for him to notice the flesh piled next to his pool.

A nefarious smile crept unbidden as he remembered the souls he'd enticed to his new domain. So many had already heard his call. So many were still to come.

The Dark Lord shifted his heavy body, watched as black rivulets slid across his muscled arms. His skin was almost copper in hue, finally free of the welts and stretch marks, his bone structure and tendons once again in their rightful configuration. It had taken a great deal of time and countless souls to rectify Avra's mistake. When she presented Lucius Vupello as king, his heart had raced with excitement. Pain and suffering had been the result. Her error was now past, and she was most likely dead. Greater prospects were within his grasp.

He clenched a mighty fist, felt his strength build. He had never experienced such power before. It was intoxicating, cathartic. And it would continue to grow, to evolve and manifest in a manner of his choosing.

When the cold winter arrived with mind numbing ferocity, he feared his hunting of Bastion's streets was finished. The races scampering about the pyramid, battling each other for control, hunting in packs and scavenging amongst the ruins, suddenly ceased. As one they fled the bitting winds of sleet and the slick ice-covered lanes, burrowing deep into whatever shelters they had managed to erect or salvage. He sensed many had returned to their home worlds, stepping through their below-ground portals, vacating the broken, frozen city.

But enough remained, waiting, patiently seeing out the winter months until the thaw arrived and birds began to sing. A new offensive would be waged once the weather turned. He could feel it. In fact, he would make certain of it.

With a smile Ahriman sent a thought-pulse to the streets above, concentrated, probed the well-trod paths for signs of activity. The daylight hours were increasing, the desperate survivors were becoming bold once again.

And like those above, he was hungry.

He released a sphere of energy to bubble towards the surface, passing through rock and timber, seeking the living. Little sparks of light in his mind would alert him to an individual soul, a flare would signal a hunting party on the move. It was how he kept his hunger satisfied during the winter months. Here, beneath the city where he could keep his chamber warm with a thought, he would sit, sending a call to ensnare the weak willed. There were many, especially when the hardship of cold and hunger magnified. It wasn't difficult to entice them with images of food and warmth. Failing that, the prospect of discovering their most sought-after dream was just as alluring.

A handful of sparks caught his attention. He focused, found the mind of a female scavenger searching at the rear of a collapsed building. She was desperate, had survived the winter in a cellar, but her food supply was now exhausted.

Ahriman sent a pulse of warmth and satisfaction in her direction, flashed an image of a staircase hidden behind a crumbled wall. Protection, food and water, a safe place to reside. He kept sending subtle suggestions, delicately implanting ideas into her own consciousness, providing direction. Once the snare was cast, it took only minutes before she changed her course.

His mind took complete control long before she stepped into the bathhouse.

Soft green light bathed her body as she took gentle steps towards the pool. Her eyes were wide, unfocused, devoid of reasoning. He knew she was terrified on the inside, but her muscles wouldn't obey her commands, just as her will was crumbling to his relentless onslaught. She was his, now, a vessel brimming with sustenance. And her soul belonged to him.

The woollen jacket covering her body slipped to the ground. The grey linen shirt and leggings followed. She would have been pretty, once, a lithe figure, curved, strength in her thighs, broad across the shoulders. Now, her naked body was thin, her collar bone protruding, straw-coloured hair mattered and grimy. There was little flesh covering her frame.

He forced her to step into the black pool, slowly, her toes dipping beneath the surface with only the slightest ripple. Three steps forward saw the water lapping at her waist.

'Come, child,' his deep, heavy words sounded from every direction, reverberated about the room. 'Sit beside me, where you will be safe from the broken reality that lies above.'

She sank next to his toned body, placed slippery hands atop his muscular chest. His arm draped over her shoulders, puller her close.

'You and I are now one, child,' he began, 'as it was always destined to be.' He lowered his face towards her own, looked into her blue eyes. He could feel her hands as they played across his skin, plunging beneath the water. He brushed his own fingers down her arm, cupped her breast. His lips found her mouth, then her tongue.

He was patient, as always, for he was immortal and not constrained by time. And considering it was to be her final moment in this terrible life, it was only fitting he provide an exquisite moment of satisfaction.

His gentle caressing eventually saw her shift a leg across his hips. She sank with a soft moan, her hands digging into his chest. Ahriman shared a smile, watched her rock slowly forward and back, his strong fingers racing across her heightened skin. Blackened water splashed over her torso, slithered like oily snakes between her breasts. Her breathing quickened, her back arched, she moaned once more, this time for what seemed an eternity. A quiver shook her entire body.

His mouth found her neck, just below the ear. Spent as she was, there was hardly a reaction as he sank his teeth into her flesh and began to feed.

Ahriman swallowed the last drop of blood, curled his huge hand about her throat and casually lifted her from the pool. Her soul was now his, her bauble of light consumed minutes earlier. Satisfied, he walked three steps to the tiled rim, then tossed the empty corpse atop the mound of dead that continued to grow. Then he sank back into the pool, waited for the ripples to ease. His wet tongue raced across his lips.

Another figure took a step towards the pool. He lifted his head, saw an Ophidian, wounded, barely alive due to a viscous cut across its brow. He knew of the snake-men but had yet to consume one. Compared to some of the races now crowding Bastion, they had only recently become involved.

He enticed it forward with a mental command, watched it discard its attire. Then it stepped into the pool.

Sometime later he tossed the Ophidian corpse onto the rising pile.

Ahriman sat back down, concentrated on the new memories, emotions, images and reflections he'd just devoured. Streams of dialogue swam for ascendency, names and terms of reference shouted at him. But he sat without moving, consumed the knowledge, and within moments he knew he could speak the Ophidian tongue.

Black water slipped from his huge arms as he lifted them high. He concentrated, felt power surge from a bottomless well. A tingling sensation raced across his skin, scales began to appear, glittering as they crept along his arms and towards his neck and torso. His body shuddered, changed shape, became thinner. The merge into an Ophidian came easily.

There was no pain, nor any nauseous swirling in his stomach. A winter of feeding had seen his power grow considerably. He could perform the merge – shapeshifting into any species – with a single thought. And he could hold the form longer each day.

It would make hunting so much easier once the thaw arrived, for he could now become whoever he chose, could seamlessly shift between each race. His ravenous hunger would no longer be stymied by such trivial matters as the weather. And no one would be able to stop him. He would feed until he was the only one to remain on this sad, crumbling world.

Then he would step through the portal and continue his quest for supreme control, claiming every soul he could find until they ceased to be. And with every soul he caught, his power would continue to expand.

Forever.

*

Dawn broke over the city of Bastion, a pale light to herald another frosty morning.

Isabelle noticed the waning predawn darkness, took a moment to look to the east. 'We need to hurry,' she said to her companions, three burly Deios hunters, hastily hauling in a large net from the canal they stood alongside.

A grunt was the only reply. All three stood with feet firmly planted on the deck, straining as their clawed hands grasped their catch. It was considerable, she could tell, for her Deios hunters were short of breath.

A final heave was accompanied by a tremendous wet slap as the haul fell atop timber planks. The sound of flapping fish followed.

She smiled. 'Ra'tor will be happy,' she said in the Deios tongue. And he would be. There was enough fish crammed into their net to feed his brood for several days. Dozens of silvery scaled fish, long and thick, the result of a river having not been overfished during the winter months.

Her companions didn't reply. Instead, they set to work, separating the fish into wooden crates so they could eventually disperse them amongst Ra'tor's brood. By the time they finished, the sun had almost crested the townhouses near Rivergate. They would have to move quickly.

The Deios moved at their own pace, but it was fast enough for her to not question their efforts. She was thankful. Even though Ra'tor had explained to his brood the importance of having an angel amongst them, many were dubious about her usefulness. She exuded no raw power or cunning concerning the hunt, was small and weak - in their eyes - and did not wield a weapon of significance. And her input into daily matters was trivial. Apart from Ra'tor and a handful of his Patriarchs, few deemed her worthy of sitting at the side of their Bhra-vek.

That was Ra'tor's new title. They called him Bhra-vek, now. Similar, she assumed, to a king in her own language. She was there, by his side, when they stepped beneath the arched entrance and into the shelter covered with the red-tiled roof. She was there when they welcomed him back with open arms and the deepest sigh of relief she had ever heard.

The shelter was a warehouse. At least it had been. It was situated along the bank of the river Atvia with access to four jetties, a small trading house and a fenced in yard for stabling livestock. Access to another canal lay at the rear, where another wharf could see traders and haulers move about the city in their narrow rafts without the need for horse and cart. It was here she now stood, supervising the fishing. An area well secured and out of sight from those who might prowl in the night.

Isabelle thought of their past few months, as grim as any she'd known in her short lifetime. Her father always said a long hot summer was to be followed by an equally cold winter. He was right this time. The first frost came early, and once settled;

the snow was not far behind. Mount Ossa, overlooking the city to the north, was once again blanketed in a heavy cloak of white. And ice daggers hung from every overhang along every street, sparkling during the day whilst stretching longer each night.

The Deios fared poorly at first, for the cold was not to their liking. They had no reference to combat the extreme weather. If it were not for her small voice suggesting they gather blankets for cover and timber for burning, she feared many may have stepped into their portal to return home.

It was not an outcome favoured by Ra'tor. He had spent too much time in the broken city seeking his god to retreat now. The Patriarchs agreed, which was a first for Ra'tor. Animosity had been rife between the two parties initially. But once Ra'tor accepted the crown of blood to become the first Bhra-vek in centuries, the Patriarchs had found solace in their newly crowned king's words and proclamations. For he now spoke with the voice of Bhral. His words were now the words of their god.

The clack of crates being handled brought her attention back to her hunters. They were ready to move, their arms full, their biceps bulging. Isabelle smiled and waved a hand, watched them fall into line as she walked towards the steps leading to the rear yard. It was only a short walk, yet Ra'tor had stressed they complete their task before any unnecessary eyes spied their activity. If others saw how adept they were at finding food in the broken city, there was sure to be a confrontation. Hunting the traditional ways had been fraught with peril. Even the Hex known as Kors, with his *terrovyn*, Sin-cha, had experienced problems within the city. So many hunters prowled the streets. And each presented a danger to those who encountered them.

Heavy steps followed her light ones. As she reached the top of the stairs, she offered a gentle knock on a reinforced gate. It was answered with a grunt, and before the sun had risen another inch on the horizon, she and her hunters were moving through the rear yard and towards the warehouse. She could sense warmth from the sun as it caressed her back. The chance of the day being a fine one was high.

The hunters moved to her left, placed their catch before a wizened Patriarch for inspection, whilst she stepped into the warehouse. It had changed greatly over the winter months, become a place of rest for Ra'tor and those closest to him, but also a place for the Deios to strategize.

The hiss and snarls of the Deios tongue were already reverberating throughout the long chamber. Ra'tor sat atop a raised platform, his back against a salvaged wedge of marble from a nearby temple. Ranged about him were the Patriarchs and a selection of his favoured hunters, Kors included. The talk amongst the brood was animated, especially considering the time of day, and a sense of heightened activity swept over her as a result. It was no mistake that winter was coming to an end. The days were longer, the sun felt warmer. The morning frosts had been absent the last ten days.

A small ladder led to some shelving not far from where she stood. She reached for it, climbed so she could sit on a wooden shelf above the noise and watch the exchange.

Ra'tor was at the centre, as always, his voice booming to be heard by all. The Deios clutched to his every word, mesmerized, as her father would say. Since his return he had grown stronger, more commanding, a leader for a race in desperate need. His health had improved, she noted. When they first met, he was a demon of the night with long teeth covered in blood. But he was wounded, quite severely, and his days after were spent recovering. Her time by his side consisted of running and scavenging, always hungry, forever in fear. It showed in his eyes, it was evident in the way he moved. But a winter with his Deios had changed him.

He appeared larger, now, taller, more frightening. There was an aura of ferocity about his frame. His words were spoken with authority. He told her he had never felt so strong in his life.

She could understand the transition. Whilst so many of his brood cowered once winter arrived, Ra'tor had taken to moving his body, afraid his blood would freeze if he sat still. So he pushed his Deios outside, hunted with them for food, clothing and timber. Then he forced them into neighbouring streets and the buildings they harboured. They searched for treasures hitherto unheard of, blankets to keep them warm at night, flint and steel to light their fires. Bottles of spirit that kept the heat alive on the inside were highly sought after, whilst jars of preserved fish and vegetables from abandoned cellars were consumed with whatever else they could scavenge.

Busy as they were, the change in Ra'tor was noticeable. A part of her was glad, for he was with his own kind and they respected him. But a voice in her mind suggested he was no longer just her protector. He was responsible for so much more. Especially now, for the city was dangerous. She also sensed his priorities had shifted.

The room fell quiet. She looked up; aware she had become lost in her own thoughts. Ra'tor was still at the centre of his Deios, but the Patriarchs had formed a semi-circle about his position. It was that time of morning, a time for tradition to be invoked.

A large copper bowl was placed before Ra'tor. Silence remained, even when a large Deiosian stepped into the half circle with his fist curled about the neck of another creature. It was cloaked in black, hooded, yet she could see its eyes bulging from their sockets. Feathers lined its arms, visible as they slipped past their sleeves. Legs thrashed.

The large Deiosian stopped, held the offering high with an outstretched arm. Even from her position at the rear of the room, she could see his straining muscles.

Then he placed a silver blade against the creature's throat, slit it with a single, casual motion.

Blood began to pool in the copper bowl. The Deiosian held the creature closer, careful not to spill his offering. A low sounding hum began to emanate amongst those in attendance.

A Patriarch was the next to move into the half circle. He held out a clawed hand, waited for Ra'tor to pass his crown. It

408

was a circlet of steel, sharp edges protruding thorn-like from the rim. It was offered to Ra'tor the day he returned.

Ra'tor handed it over and sat back, his broad shoulders slapping against the marble. A wicked smile stretched his mouth.

The Patriarch waved the large Deiosian with his offering away, moved a step forward. Silence remained as he lowered the crown into the hot blood. He held it there, with his clawed hand, speaking unknown words. Eventually he rose from his crouch, his hands drenched in gore, and stepped forward to place the crown of blood atop Ra'tor's scaled head.

'Ra'tor Bhra-vek!' they shouted to complete the ritual. Isabelle wanted to smile, she really did, but she was tiring of the daily routine. Tiring of the blood and the sight of her protector wearing a crown that appeared to weep. Every day, as the sun cleared the buildings to the east.

She locked her eyes onto the Deios king. He was changing, that much was certain. With every ritual he appeared to hold greater sway over his subjects. They worshipped him.

Winter was finished. Any day now, she mused, and the Deios would set out to hunt once again. But it wouldn't be a hunt for survival. It would be something completely different. They were hungry. Hungry for battle; hungry for revenge.

And once the carnage began, she would be expected to be by his side, singing her hymns to raise his spirits and those of his hunting brood.

Singing songs so they could kill.

Isabelle wondered, and not for the first time, if an angel would perform such a task. Surely an angel focused on protecting and nurturing. Ra'tor was always nearby, protective as always, but if he expected her to roam the broken streets in the days to come and watch as his brood hunted and killed, well, her heart suggested otherwise.

He said countless times he would never leave her.

But what if she left him?

CHAPTER THIRTY

It was the sound of a door being locked that jolted Nae-oki out of her stupor.

She lifted her head, slowly, brushed a tear from her cheek. She knelt on cold tiles inside the entrance to Neema and Kayla-mother's rooms. Neither were to be seen. Neema, as far as she knew, was visiting Ruvin and Donal. Kayla-mother, at this time of morning, would be in the garden, most likely exercising or bathing in the rockpool. Either way, they weren't close at hand, nor witness to what just transpired.

And yet both women needed to know. Urgently.

She placed shaking hands on the tiles, next to her knees, rocked forward so she could push herself upright. It was an effort. Her strength almost failed her. Even her legs trembled, made walking the short distance to the wooden screen door problematic. But the garden beyond called her, suggested she find Kayla-mother as quickly as able. And yet, when she found her, what should she say?

The wooden door slid with ease, allowed her to step softly onto the grass. Nae-oki couldn't see Kayla-mother yet, but she wouldn't be far away. Perhaps she was running, following the same beaten track Rastan used when he ran alongside the wall that kept them confined. If so, she would be visible any moment, likely to emerge from behind thick ferns to her right.

She took a deep breath, settled her nerves, fixed her eyes on her hands and willed them to stop shaking. A cool breeze enticed the fine golden hairs on her arms to stand tall, sent a shiver down her spine. Was it an omen?

She took another step, found courage as her toes sunk into the earth. There was power there, in the ground, subtle. Was that why the Five Kings paved the streets with stone? Did they know about the power of the earth, and thus deny it to the Ven?

One more step. Nae-oki's strength was returning, her legs and hands at ease. A puff of wind caught her fiery hair, swept it out wide. So many questions leapt unbidden into her mind. Ever since she visited the market at daybreak, when she overheard the *ser-ti-ven* asking about the otherworldly child kept imprisoned in the palace.

The queries caught her by surprise, especially coming from those called the Wild Ones. It was rare to even see them visit Ayoshos, for they despised everything the City of Gold stood for. But they were known, once every few years, to wander into the city to trade their cured hides and abundance of herbs. On occasion, they even brought wild animals gutted and skinned, strung between wooden poles and dressed for the flame.

The exchange of words between the *ser-ti-ven* and the merchant were at first irrelevant. It was their appearance that caught her eye, for they were indeed wild. Half-a-dozen arrived for trade, animal skins barely covering their torsos. Their hair was matted or twined, yet either way, leaves and twigs jutted from random locations, speckled red, green and yellow to herald the fall. Sheathed hunting knives rested at their hip; recurved bows were slung over their shoulders. And they were muscular. Two women led the group, and their bronzed arms were as toned as those of the males.

Yet the male Ven were tall and strong, ferocious looking, especially with their many-pronged antlers reaching for the sky.

She felt her heart skip a beat. The Ven of Ayoshos were slight in comparison, and soft as well-worn leather, one might say. The temptation to reach out and touch a muscled arm was extreme.

Quick words were spoken with the merchant, and a word in particular, *Star-Born,* caught her attention. The haze of wonder from seeing wild Ven in Ayoshos cleared. Talk continued, eyes were locked, as the *ser-ti-ven* probed for answers to questions she had never heard mentioned before. Like all the Ven - civilized and wild – their past was remembered through stories of heroism and ingenuity, cunning and compassion. Most were fables, told to their children as they huddled about the flames each night, a means to teach them lessons concerning the foibles of life and its unpredictability's. Those who listened well would understand the cycles everyone would endure. Some would be seen as heroes, some merely respected for their honesty and ethics. But every Ven experienced the stories as children. Civilized and wild alike.

And every Ven, especially those deemed trapped in Ayoshos, knew of a prophecy concerning a Star-Born Child.

For he was to be the light the Ven would follow, their saviour during a time of oppression and doubt. When the world was deemed to suffer, and the Ven became lost, the Star-Born would arrive to set matters right. An otherworldly child. A hero.

So why were the *ser-ti-ven* in Ayoshos, asking questions about a child from another world?

'He is young still,' said a woman, her hair a riot of autumn colour, 'he will have seen no more than ten summers.'

'I'm sorry, Wild One,' replied the merchant, 'but if you seek to know what transpires inside the palace, you'd best speak to someone from within.'

Nae-oki heard the words, saw the look of defeat drift over the woman's weathered face.

The merchant wandered away, leaving the six Wild Ones standing in a circle. Nae-oki could see a skittish look manifest in their bright eyes, as if they feared the high walls and paved stones beneath their feet. They appeared like caged animals, she thought. Alone and afraid.

'I live inside the palace,' the words tumbled before she knew what she was saying. The skittish eyes narrowed, became focused. A sense of being hunted swept over her.

The woman with autumn hair stepped close, held out her hands. 'I am Thia,' she said with a smile. 'We seek word of the Star-Born. Do you know him?'

Nae-oki placed her delicate hands in Thia's. They were softer than she expected, smelt of honeysuckle. 'I am Nae-oki,' she replied, 'but I have not heard anyone called Star-Born,' she said with a shake of her head. 'But there is a child in the palace from another world, ten years of age, who is known as Rastan.'

Thia's shoulders slumped, but Nae-oki could see it was due to a weight being lifted. A smile followed; soft hands gripped hers tight. 'He is known to us as Rastan Va,' her words whispered back. 'I was there, you know, when he was named on his third day. I was there when he was born.'

'You said he was Star-Born,' Nae-oki whispered back. 'Is it true?'

'It is. The Guardian Kian confirmed it. It was he who sent us. We are here to discover word of his wellbeing, no more. And if we can, we are to send a message to his people. Can we trust you, Nae-oki? Can you deliver a message to his kind, a private message, one that must not reach the ears of the Five Kings?'

'I can do as you ask,' Nae-oki offered. And why wouldn't she. Almost everyone lived in fear of the Five Kings and their laws. They preached a life of comfort and satisfaction in a city of splendour and charm, but the reality was something entirely different. The facade was opulent, true, but two days travel into the hills and one would see the gaping holes in the ground where stone was quarried. It was here that Ven slaved cutting and hauling rock. And the holes being dug were like open wounds in the earth, growing each day, festering in the heat of the sun. Dust choked the pathways leading in, and stagnant, dirty water lay in numerous pools to blemish once green fields. For those who asked questions about freedom and prosperity, or for those who voiced their concerns regarding the Five King's decisions, it was here they were sent. A labour force of male and female Ven, comprising of those who apparently encouraged dissent.

Nae-oki's brother was there, digging and hauling, aged beyond his years. All because he cried his frustration at the kings when they increased their share of his seasonal yield.

'What would you have me say?' Nae-oki asked, casting a quick look behind her. The street was quiet, and in any case, few wished to walk too close to the wild looking Ven.

'Let his people know that Kian is preparing the way,' began Thia. 'He is well, and so are those who survived the fall of their city. They reside in the Great Forest with the *ser-ti-ven*, and those known as the Celestial Sisters are now strong in number. The one known as Neema will be glad of such information.'

There was a pause as Thia took a deep breath. She obviously had more to tell.

'Listen well, Nae-oki,' her wild Ven crowded close, to keep unwanted eyes from reading lips, perhaps. 'Kian is aware of the difficulties being experienced by those from another world, but he pleads patience. Please, let them know they are not alone. Everything Kian does, he does to see them free.'

Another nod of her head. There was a great deal to remember. She wondered if she would be able to retell everything she heard.

'Let them know the young man, Jarred, completed his passage to Bastion. Let them know the Dark Lord followed later and no longer resides on Vidae. Kian also mentioned when the time is right, he will seek them out to lead them home. They will know when it is time. Rastan, the one who is Star-Born, will light the way.'

Thia finished by planting a kiss on her forehead. It was an unexpected gesture, but the importance of Thia's words was not lost on Nae-oki. Rumours of unrest were common amongst the *vos-ti-ven*. But to know the *ser-ti-ven* were sharing the same doubts concerning the Five Kings was welcome. Perhaps they were not so different after all. Perhaps the only difference was the expectations imposed on them by their rulers. In their hearts, they were still one people.

'I will see your message delivered, Thia. You have my word.'

Remembering the smile in Thia's bright eyes gave her strength as she walked across the manicured grass to speak to Kayla-mother. She had been running, was lathered in sweat, and breathing heavily.

'Good morning, Nae-oki,' Kayla-mother waved a hand, forced a brief smile. It was more than anyone else received. 'Is everything alright? You look a little pale.'

What could she say? Thia's words were still fresh in her mind from their talk this morning. There was a great deal to tell. Yet discovering Kayla-mother's son was the one prophesised in legend took time to digest. So much was occurring, so many thoughts were swirling inside her mind. She lowered her eyes, saw her hands begin to tremble once again.

'What is it, Nae-oki? This is very unlike you.'

Nae-oki opened her mouth; found she couldn't speak. A tear slid across her cheek. How many had she shed since she arrived at Kayla-mother's rooms.

Kayla-mother reached for her, pulled her close.

'I'm sorry,' Nae-oki finally found her voice. A finger lifted to wipe a tear from under her eye. 'I arrived not so long ago, whilst you were running,' her bottom lip quivered. She wished she were somewhere else. Anywhere but here.

'And . . . what is wrong?'

'The Five Kings arrived behind me, entered your rooms,' there, she said it, although the burden on her soul didn't lesson as she hoped. 'They took him, Kayla-mother.

'They took your son.'

*

'Where do you think they are taking me?'

'Your guess, child, is as good as mine,' responded the Wise One. *'You have left the confines of your rooms on thirteen separate occasions since your third birthday. Every occasion saw you make your way to the Sunshine Hall for a celebration of some description. And yet the Palace of the Five Kings is vast, the corridors many. We have not travelled this direction before. I cannot answer your question with confidence.'*

Rastan scrunched his nose, lifted his face so he could see Ik'omi, first born of the Five Kings. His back was straight, his eyes focused. He sensed there was a purpose to his long strides down the hallway, although his bare feet were silent as he stepped upon the marble tiles.

Rastan looked over his shoulder, saw the remainder of the Five Kings a few steps behind. Like Ik'omi, their eyes were fixed on something far away. In their wake, visible only as a conglomeration of riotous colour, scampered a score of Ven aides and a collection of guards wearing their ridiculously elongated helmets. Comical at the best of times, more so when they were forced to march with intent.

'I've been in the presence of the Five Kings sparsely, I must admit, but there is a seriousness to their visage I cannot place.'

'Be wary of your actions today, Rastan,' the Wise One was equally perplexed, his words cautiously spoken. *'And remain mindful of your expressions. Something is different about the kings. They know something.'*

'Well, whatever it is, I am curious,' Rastan was about to smile, thought better of it. Perhaps he should keep his eyes on the tiled floor. *'I wonder why mother was not invited to come along. Or Nae-oki.'*

'Nae-oki appeared frightened if I'm not mistaken. Her hands were trembling.'

'Yes,' Rastan agreed, *'I did see her shiver as the door was slammed shut. The Five Kings paid her no heed, but she was clearly shaken by their brazen entrance and equally audacious exit.'*

A set of bronze doors appeared before the Five Kings and their entourage. Two Ven females, dressed in sky-blue robes, raced past to open them. Their copper hair was plaited into long tails, their ankles surrounded by tinkling bells. The sound of lilting music followed their every step.

An urge to dance forward and help with the large bronze doors was quickly quashed. They opened easily, despite their size, revealed an enormous square room of quartz tiles and twinning pillars. Arched windows provided an avenue for streaming sunlight, whilst magenta banners draped twenty-foot walls.

Ik'omi gestured to his entourage and stepped forward, making his way down a dozen steps to the elaborate floor.

Sunlight caught his face, glistened as it struck the gold trimmings of his white jacket. To the casual observer, he appeared to be glowing.

'Come, child,' Ik'omi's voice carried easily as he swept a hand towards another set of bronze doors. They were similar in design to the ones they just stepped through, yet half-as-large again. As before, the two Ven females opened them, only this time, it was the outside world that greeted him.

'Oh my, this is new,' Rastan couldn't hide the smile on his face this time. Beyond doors he could see a sea of green, a mantle of grass peppered with slender trees and delicate shrubs. Pools of water sparkled; the sound of buzzing insects was intense. But as he crossed the threshold and stepped outside for the first time since his arrival ten years earlier, it was the enormity of two red wood trees to either side that truly caused his mouth to open in wonder. They soared high, higher than he thought was possible. Two hundred feet, he guessed. Maybe taller. And their girth was impressive, their thick roots snaking into the earth like the tendrils of a serpent god. Everything about the sentinel trees screamed power and longevity. They were ancient and all-knowing, impressive beyond words. He could almost sense the thrumming energy within.

'The Twin Sentinels,' Ik'omi skipped towards the right red wood to place his hand against the coarse bark. 'They were planted by my brothers and I, over a thousand years ago,' he shared a knowing smile with his brother-kings. 'The red woods are evergreen and have stood watch since before the palace was built,' Rastan almost flinched as Ik'omi's eyes sought his own. There was a fierceness about his gaze, a feral glean, even. 'We share a bond,' he continued, 'some would say we can communicate with each other.'

Ik'omi stepped away from the sentinel tree, offered Rastan an opportunity to approach, if he so chose. *'Do you think he wants me to talk to the tree?'* he asked the Wise One.

'I would refrain if I were you,' the Wise One was quick to respond.

'I agree,' it was the voice of the Mystic, this time. As far as he could tell, the Mystic was once an elder of the Brotherhood of One. He had a broad grasp of life and its mysteries, knew many things of interest. *'Do not lay a hand on the tree, Rastan. They are testing you.'*

'Testing me for what, exactly?'

'Anything and everything,' both the Wise One and the Mystic replied.

He took their advice, stepped away from the sentinel tree and onto the manicured grounds. Like the kings, his feet were bare, and the cool sensation of autumn grass below his feet was most invigorating. As it was in his rooms, he chose to frolic outside whenever possible. Being here, outside the palace for the first time, was truly incredible.

Ik'omi reached his side, followed closely by Shien and Ky'elk. Vega and Solaii remained beside the left sentinel tree, their palms pressed gently against the red bark. Their eyes were closed.

'Would you like to walk the palace grounds, Rastan?' It was Shien who asked the question. It was the first time Rastan had ever heard him say a word.

He gave a nod, looked with eager eyes towards a protrusion of moss-covered granite and shrubbery beneath an enormous *roaring tree*. Its broad leaves provided adequate shade, allowed a plethora of ferns and thick-stemmed grasses to flourish. Rivulets of spring water trickled from amongst the highest boulders, falling into small pools that merged into lily covered ponds.

'Come then,' Shien waved him forward, took steps beside him. 'The grounds are vast. Two thousand feet lie between the palace doors and the entrance gate. Likewise, it is two thousand feet in either direction to your left and right. It you were to turn about and walk behind the palace, your steps would be considerably more.'

'The palace grounds cover a substantial area, is what he is trying to tell you.' It was the Mystic who interjected.

'Listen carefully to everything the Five Kings say, my boy. We may learn something of our own if we're observant.'

Rastan heard the Mystic's words, but he was already walking towards the *roaring tree* and the pond beneath it. There was so much life out here, so many creatures fluttering and flying, so many unusual sounds.

A roar sounded from within a collection of swaying willow to his right. He halted his stride, bent at the knee to dig his hands in the turf. He could feel the vibration long after the roar passed. Felt the beast creeping towards him before it parted the swaying willows.

'Calm yourself, boy,' Shien spoke with a smile, cast an eye over him, seeking fear, perhaps, as the *serrin* began a rhythmic lope in their direction. Nae-oki had explained many of the creatures of Vidae to him during their time together. It wasn't difficult to realise it was a wild cat approaching. Its size alarmed him, though. Nae-oki had said they were large, and Ruvin suggested they were comparable to a horse in Bastion, apparently. Only he'd never seen a horse.

He stood from his crouch, watched as the *serrin* made its way effortlessly towards their position. Its skin was an odd shade of ochre with a metallic tinge, causing flashes of sunlight to twinkle from its hide as it walked. A powerful neck with thick, corded muscles supported an equally powerful head. Large jaws designed to deliver a single death blow were lined with savage teeth four inches long, whilst flowing behind its ears and down its neck and shoulders was a mane of thickly mattered blue-green hair.

It crept to within sixty feet, paused to assess who stood before it. Rastan could see its eyes clearly, now. They were large, bright orbs of sunshine. A single glance told him the *serrin* would look right through him if he felt brave enough to stare.

'Careful, Rastan,' the Wise One could sense his blood rising to the challenge. *'It would be best not to startle the beast.'*

'I can feel it, even from here,' his reply was already on his tongue. He knew the Core were aware of his feelings. For as long as he could remember - be it small, scampering lizards or flighty birds darting between swaying branches – a connection between the animal and himself was easily developed. He need only pause and clear his mind, imagine the world through their eyes.

'The wild cat is not small and soft, Rastan, it is powerful beyond anything we have seen on this world,' he could hear the concern in the Wise One's voice. *'A false move on your behalf – an intrusion, perhaps – may trigger a response you're not equipped to handle. Surely you have noticed the dagger-like teeth and the silver claws. A single swipe would be enough to tear a man - or a Ven - in half.'*

'I see the weapons of the beast,' a smile touched his cheeks. *'Do not fear for me, I will cause it no angst. Besides, there is a Ven carer standing thirty feet away, under a willow. This powerful specimen has been trained to obey commands. It will not lunge for me unless ordered.'*

A soft hand clenched his right shoulder. For a blessed moment, he'd forgotten about the Five Kings.

'He will not harm you, Rastan,' began Shien, an equally broad smile manifesting on his flawless face. 'Not unless we ask him.'

'Was that a veiled threat, do you think?' he asked his Core whilst keeping his visage devoid of emotion.

'Poorly veiled if you ask me,' replied the Mystic.

'Aye,' the Wise One's voice was concerned. *'I said they were testing you. Give them nothing, my boy. Do not play this game. They are suddenly curious, searching for answers to questions we do not know. I sense a great deal of danger.'*

'Would you like to step closer, Rastan? Would you like to run your hands across its hide?' Shien was still smiling. To his right stepped Vega and Solaii. They, too, were smiling. He spun about, looked towards the wild cat. It sat on its haunches, rolled its head from side-to-side. Its mouth opened wide, revealed glistening teeth. Ik'omi and Ky'elk walked the sixty feet to stand at either flank, placed gentle hands on the *serrin's* shoulders. A subtle vibration sounded from its chest. They beckoned with a look, curled their elegant fingers deep into blue-green mattered hair.

'*I believe they wish for you to join them,*' suggested the Wise One.

'*And you think I should refrain?*'

'*Absolutely. There is nothing you can gain from being here. I don't know what has occurred for the kings to take an interest in you. Either they know something about who you are, or they seek to know more about who you are. I fear it matters little. They are dangerous, fickle creatures. Like I said earlier, give them nothing.*'

'*You are right, Wise One,*' Rastan's smile faded. The kings were indeed searching for something. He could see it in their piercing eyes, feel his skin crawl every time they looked at him. It was obvious, now. They wanted to see his abilities. Wished to see his interactions. For beings as old as those standing about him, a morning frolicking in the sunshine amongst flora and fauna could reveal a great deal.

'*I am done being a curio,*' his voice might have been silent, but his intent was clear as he placed hands on hips.

'*What are you doing?*' asked the Wise One.

'*I'm returning to my room. I wish to see my mother. If the kings wish to watch me, they can follow.*'

He turned his back on the *serrin* and the Five Kings, took long strides towards the double bronze doors. He was twenty feet from stepping into the palace when a rush of air swept past his shoulder. A blur of shimmering diamonds amongst heaving red flesh settled before him, barring the way. A shake of the *serrin's* enormous head with its blue-green hair stalled him. The wild cats pink tongue snaked over sharp teeth. Rippling muscles bulged in its forelegs.

Golden eyes glared, daring him to move. Rastan took a breath, heard the rumblings of a growl begin from deep within the *serrin's* chest. One paw flexed, tore grass from the earth with a scrape.

'Do not move,' it was the Mystic speaking. *'They continue to test you. You need to appear frightened.'*

'But I'm not afraid.'

'We know, Rastan, but we cannot allow the Five Kings to learn of your abilities. Tremble a little, as Nae-oki did before we left. Look at the ground, not directly at the eyes of the serrin.'

'Will the Five Kings believe I fear the creature if I do as you ask?'

'They will.'

Ik'omi walked to stand before him, a sparkle in his eyes. 'Where are you going, Rastan?'

Rastan shrugged his shoulders, looked at the ground as the Mystic suggested.

'As my brother Shien explained, the *serrin* will not attack you unless ordered. You have nothing to fear from the beast. It is under our control. Be at ease, child.'

He kept his eyes downcast, focused on his hands, made them tremble.

'You appear disturbed, child. Is the *serrin's* proximity causing you stress?'

Rastan lifted his head, gave a solitary nod.

'It is not unusual. Very few souls can stand before such a magnificent beast and not feel inadequate. Other than the *vhaetin*, the *serrin* are the most powerful of creatures.' Ik'omi paused, looked to his left towards a collection of trees and flowering shrubs. 'We have six *serrin* roaming our gardens here in the palace grounds.'

'A warning if I've ever heard one,' said the Wise One.

Ik'omi rested a hand on his shoulder. 'We were told you enjoyed the company of birds and lizards in your garden. We thought a *serrin* might be of interest to you. Maybe when you are older and less fearful, perhaps.' He lifted his hand, took a step towards the bronze doors. 'Come, we will return you to your room.'

'He ridicules me.'

'*He is still searching,*' the Wise One spoke gently, sought to calm the nervous energy coursing through Rastan's body. '*Keep your head down until you reach your room.*'

'*I don't want to be here any longer. I wish to take my mother home.*'

'*You are not yet ready. You need to be stronger, Rastan. You are not fully grown. Be patient.*'

'*How many years must I remain here, still? How long until I can flee to Bastion?*'

Silence greeted him. He had asked the question before, but his Core were uncertain of their answer. Maybe they didn't know. Maybe the decision was his alone. Was he ready? Would he ever be ready? Did he have the courage to flee the Five Kings? So many questions, yet the answers remained elusive. But he knew the time for action was approaching.

He could sense it, feel the murmur of thousands of voices bubbling in his veins. Building ever so slowly but building all the same.

One day, when he was strong enough.

One day soon.

*

Birds chirped in the branches above.

Kayla took a moment to seek out the *wing-tails*, hoping they wouldn't wake Rastan from his slumber. He was curled beside her, his unruly black hair draped over one shoulder, his small hands clutching her skirt. She traced a finger against his cheek, pushed a strand of hair that had fallen over his eyes. So peaceful, so innocent. A child, still. Her child.

She let out a sigh. Neema, Ruvin, Donal and Nae-oki sat in a circle with her, under the largest of the *roaring trees* in the garden. It was past midday, yet a bank of sombre clouds had drifted across the sky an hour earlier, darkening what had already felt like a terrible day.

It took only a moment to recall the fear, to recall the words Nae-oki stammered whilst shedding her own tears. '*They took your son.*'

A rage surfaced upon hearing the words. A rage that had been brewing for a decade, simmering beneath the surface, biding its time. Fear drove it up, forced it to explode outwards in a burst of anger and frustration. Through a red mist she saw the door to their room, remembered smashing her clenched hands against its surface, thundering kicks into the timber. Screams of pure hatred screeched from her lungs, flecked with spittle and the curses of one distraught.

At some point she sat on the tiles, a bundle of flesh beyond exhaustion. Tears streaked her face; her midnight hair looked a wild thing of its own. Swollen hands sat bruised in her lap. Nae-oki sat behind her, hugged her tight. She could feel her wet tears falling on her shoulder.

They cried together, uncertain of what was to come, afraid Rastan had been taken from them.

'He is sleeping well,' Neema spoke quietly, gave Kayla's knee a pat.

And he was. Kayla looked at his innocent face, unblemished, sharing features with his father. It was moments like this when she could picture Tarsin. But Rastan was only ten years of age, a boy in every sense of the word. He was alert, inquisitive, knew so much about so many things. Yet he rarely slept, seemed to always be searching for something to learn.

Nae-oki shared a smile, the first since Rastan returned. 'He exudes a great deal of love, Kayla,' she said. 'I could see it in his eyes when the door opened and he leapt into your arms.'

Kayla closed her eyes, remembered the sight of her boy racing into their room. His arms were reaching for her before the door slammed behind him, his eyes wide with what she believed was fear. She was as speechless as her son, held him so tight he could do nothing but squeeze her back.

'Aye, you have the right of it, Nae-oki,' Ruvin nodded his approval. 'He is special in every facet. Both an enigma and a prodigy.'

'But he is Star-Born, isn't he?' asked Nae-oki, her eyes sparkling with interest.

'He is, lass,' Ruvin nodded his head again, to reinforce his statement. 'Neema heard the words.'

She did. But I heard them also, thought Kayla. A time of pain and anger, followed by a blessing. A miracle. A child conceived on one world, then born on another. Star-Born, so they said. A child of light, a child of wonder. A bastard child.

Pain flared in her mind. How she wished to see Tarsin one more time. To touch his cheek, to have him hold her in his strong arms. If only he were alive to see his son, to see the wonderful child he helped create.

She looked at her circle of friends. Tired eyes stared back. Since Nae-oki revealed all she heard from the *ser-ti-ven*, a number of discussions had ensued. Yet the realisation Rastan was to be a saviour for her people was not what she expected. A future king of Dervae she had planned for, provided they did return to Bastion. But to be caught up in some Ven prophecy was beyond Kayla's comprehension.

'Our hopes of returning to Bastion appear to be entwined with the hopes of the Ven,' Kayla's voice was barely above a whisper. 'I'm not sure I understand how Rastan is involved in your prophecy, Nae-oki, or whether he actually is the child of light your people have dreamed about. Yet I sense a connection between your cause and ours. Until today, we had no idea the Ven felt oppressed by their immortal lords.'

'We dare not speak against them, Kayla-mother,' Nae-oki also kept her voice low, 'for fear of being sent to what we call the Scars. My brother is there, toiling beneath the earth. Few live longer than five years in such conditions.'

'Aye, and no one has the courage to stand against them,' Ruvin shook his head. 'I've seen it before, it will happen again. Eventually, someone will unite the people to hold their ground. Then they'll fight back.'

'And that someone appears to be my son, apparently,' Kayla shook her head. 'He is a ten-year-old boy, not a saviour.'

Nae-oki held out her hand. 'He is everything we have been told, Kayla-mother. Otherworldly, Star-Born, a silent child. He is the one. He will lead the way.'

'When will this occur?' she asked, anger threatening to surge once more. 'I've waited ten years hoping Rastan's father was still alive, hoping he would come and rescue us from this golden prison. Now you're telling me my son will be the one to free us all. How long are we to wait, Nae-oki? When am I to be free? I'll say it again, he is only a boy.'

The circle of friends remained silent. Donal appeared as distressed as anyone, his eyes clouded, concern etched on his youthful face. Neema and Ruvin both appeared older than she had ever seen them before, both refused to comment. If she wasn't mistaken, she felt they knew something profound about the situation, but at present, refused to elaborate. Nae-oki simply wished to believe.

Neema cleared her throat. 'We need to assume the Five Kings know who Rastan will one day become.'

'Assumptions are generally fraught with danger,' Kayla replied.

'Fine, then prepare for the worst. The kings will know. One day, they may come for him.'

'To kill him?'

'Perhaps. It depends on whether they fear him or not. If they do, I'm not sure we can stop them. If Kian was here, we may have a chance. But it would be a small one at best.'

'So, what do we do in the meantime? Are we to wait for the Five Kings to decide if they're interested, or do we look for a way out of here on our own?'

'The Star-Born will lead,' Nae-oki offered, 'when the time is right. It has been said.'

'She is right,' Neema appeared adamant. 'We protect the child, nurture him, love him. We offer every insight we have, teach him all that we know.

'And when the time is right, we will act.'

Kayla peered deep into Neema's eyes, searched for the faith she so desperately needed. Tarsin was gone, she knew, but her son was in her care. She wasn't about to lose him. Not ever.

For ten years she had placed her trust in Neema. If she believed they were on the right path, then she also believed.

'We will do this together, then,' Kayla said, one last tear sliding down her cheek. 'We'll protect the child, my son, until the time is right.'

'Aye,' Ruvin agreed, leaning his old frame close to pat her on the leg. 'Let it be so.'

CHAPTER THIRTY-ONE

Glowing green walls and the gentle hum of falling water calmed his soul.

Tarsin stood next to Nen in the outer corridor of the Weeping Tower, seated Elusians ranged before them - silent as always - hands resting on their knees, legs crossed beneath. He had asked to come and see those who sat and observed one last time, in the hope of understanding their significance in his plight. There was purpose in their involvement, yet at the same time they offered little to appease his soul. Other than having his men rested and fed, there was no discernible advantage to being here.

'You said you brought us here to save us,' Tarsin met Nen's sapphire eyes. 'You mentioned death was waiting for us if you did not intervene. Would you care to elaborate?'

The hint of a smile touched her lips. 'It is true,' she began. 'A darkness surrounds you, Tarsin. It seeks to find you, to consume you. If you continued your path to New City, to engage with Clive Bardell and his summoned men, Ahriman would have found you. He has been on the move throughout Bastion. He has grown strong, can now shapeshift and converse freely with any species he finds. Fate saw him arrive at the court of the newly proclaimed King Bardell. They have spoken, shared knowledge. Ahriman waited, for he believed you were heading his way. He has eyes everywhere, as does the False King. They knew you were coming.'

'And you thought we would have succumbed.'

'We knew you would. You are not yet strong enough to confront Ahriman. Not alone.'

'I have my men with me. We number fifty.'

'They are insignificant in comparison,' Nen placed a hand on his arm. 'They would have died with you, and all would be lost. It wasn't the appointed time, Tarsin. There are allies still to arrive, to join you in the fight to come. It is best to be patient. To be prepared.'

'So, when are we to return?'

Nen lifted her hand from his arm. 'Today,' she said, her eyes bright. 'Your men have regained their strength and resilience. Soon, we will walk you back to your halls under the city so you may seek your objective.'

'We will seek out the False King, still,' he replied. 'I take it Ahriman is no longer in attendance?'

'He is not. Hunger calls him. But you must be wary. Ahriman will not have left without bestowing certain gifts to those he deems worthy. You must know you are walking into danger.'

Tarsin knew it. Was prepared for it. Like his adversaries, he had eyes watching those of interest. Clive Bardell had set his throne in the Grand Hall of Benjin Auldstone's manor. The man, Benjin Auldstone, was speaker for the Guild of Merchants and self-proclaimed Lord of Antiquities. Wealthy beyond most men's dreams, his manor was the size of a palace, with paved grounds bordered by a twelve-foot wall and a tower gate. A trader in fine goods and a seller of exotic items, the man was on Ruvin Ciricello's list of contacts after their voyage to the south. Whether he was still alive was yet to be determined. Like most of Bastion's residents, Auldstone may have fled when the earthquake struck. As wealthy as he claimed to be, he would likely have a residence in the countryside or possibly south in the city of Octavio. Maybe both.

'We'll be careful, you have my word,' Tarsin gave Nen a nod of assurance, took a last look at the Elusians with their eyes closed. Waterfalls fell beyond the arches.

'I am sorry I cannot help you further, Tarsin Va.'

'Tell me,' he swung his gaze back to Nen, 'you said I may see Kayla Tolsten soon. How long will I have to wait?'

'For you, it will feel like an eternity. For Kayla, even longer.'

'No riddles, Nen. Can you give me a number of days, or months, perhaps?'

'It will be soon, that is all I can say. It is also dependant on certain outcomes. Nothing we see is etched in stone. Paths can be altered. We have given what we hope you perceive as wisdom, yet there are others who may feel obliged to do the same. You are a small spark in a universe teeming with life. Other sparks are also offered advice. Things can change.'

'And the Dark One? I have asked before how best to deal with him, yet the answers I received were vague. So, I ask you, Nen of the Weeping Tower, why is he so fixed on our destruction? What have we done for him to despise us so very much?'

He watched the life in her beautiful eyes fade. They became clouded, darkened under heavy memories, perhaps. He wasn't sure, but he sensed a chill permeate the corridor they stood in.

'You are aware the Dark One is known as Ahriman, first born of the Nepharii,' her words were softly spoken, a tenderness evident in her tone. 'He was the best of us, the most enthusiastic, a vibrant beacon for a race newly formed. He spoke words of wonder, miracles danced off his tongue, and the light in his eyes would instil a sense of belief and hope in all who gazed upon him.

'Thousands of years passed, Tarsin, and we marvelled every day at the beauty of the universe and the world we lived on. We . . . discovered the early tribes of man, watched them grow and learn. At certain times we walked secretly amongst them, taught them knowledge, a fragment, piece-by-piece.

'And they grew. At some point in history, they became aware we were different, sought us out in our city called Aos, long before we built the pyramid you call Aston's Tear. They asked for more knowledge, begged for aid when their hunting was scarce. We obliged because we felt compassion. We offered solutions because we saw no reason to abstain.

'I look back now, Tarsin, and I see the seeds of our demise. We were arrogant without knowing, a trait common to those who live for ever. Ahriman was the first to fall. He would not be alone.'

'How did he fall?'

Nen closed her eyes, contemplated his question. Tarsin wondered if she would divulge all she knew, or feed him information piece-by-piece, as she did with the early tribes of man.

'There was a king of Man, long ago, who sought trade with the Nepharii. He arrived with a retinue of warriors and aides, spoke of his will to see the tribes of Man united. He would lead, for he believed it was his destiny. This much he knew, so we were told.

'Yet he came for power, in any form, something we had not considered before.'

Nen grabbed his hand, beckoned he follow as she spun about to walk the corridor. She took several steps, continued her story.

'We took our time debating the idea of trading with the king. Our initial purpose was to observe and nurture the world and everything it encompassed. Aiding man with weapons to subjugate others went against our creed. Yet some Nepharii saw a united Man as a boon, suggested there was merit to the king's line of thinking. I believe the prospect of people dying unnecessarily swayed our judgement in the end. Common sense prevailed; our decision was final. The power he sought would not come from the Nepharii.

'At least that was out belief.'

'What happened?' Tarsin asked, sensing something afoot.

'The king's daughter arrived within our halls.'

Nen came to a halt, turned to look him in the eye.

'She was beautiful beyond words, Tarsin. So beautiful, in fact, that many Nepharii became enamoured by her appearance. We had watched the tribes grow over time, but her beauty took us by surprise. It was said by many, Ahriman included, that if the king wished to trade for power, it would cost him his daughter.'

'Did the king accept?'

'Initially, no. He returned to his tent in the fields with his retinue, sought council with his aides. Whilst he deliberated, the Nepharii schemed against each other, vying amongst themselves for the right to own the princess. It was a dark time in our history, Tarsin,' Nen's words ran thick with emotion. 'It was the first time we ever felt divided. It was the first time we had ever felt lust, anger, frustration.

'Few truly know what occurred in the following days. Voices were raised, unkind words were spoken. Ahriman, being first born, refused to acknowledge any claim other than his own. He stood defiant, challenged anyone to deny him his right. Yet there were other Nepharii, equally as powerful, who saw a way to exploit Ahriman's desire. It is said they had grown tired of listening to the first born dictate their existence. Now, an opportunity had arrived that could see him undone.

'It is here that many theories are speculated upon. The most revealing, and in my mind, the most plausible, revolves around the king being swayed by several Nepharii to accept Ahriman's offer. It is said the king was convinced to invite the first born into his tent, to offer his daughter, and then strike the eldest Nepharii with weapons of iron until he was dead. If power was what the king craved, a sip of Ahriman's blood would provide him with everything he desired.'

'And he believed them?'

'Why would he not?' Nen held out her hands. 'The Nepharii had never lied before, and even if they did, their words can be quite hypnotic, especially when seeking gain. The king fell for their subtle suggestions, carried out their wish. Ahrmian arrived later that night, alone, with a burning desire in his heart for a beautiful daughter of Man. He didn't notice the guards stationed within the tent, never saw the first blade strike him from behind. Or the second. Or the third. When the men had finished, Ahriman was a shredded mess of flesh and blood.'

'And the king? Did he drink his blood?'

'It is said he stepped close, looked down at Ahriman. He expected to gaze upon the corpse of a Nepharii immortal. Instead, he looked into the eyes of the first born, saw life still flickering within. Speechless, the king listened as Ahriman cursed him with his last breath.'

Tarsin was afraid to ask what the curse entailed, but felt he knew it anyway. 'What did he say?'

'Ahriman said he would come for him. He said, "One day, when I am whole again, I will come for you and all your people. I will not stop. I will destroy you all!".'

'And now he is here,' Tarsin replied, 'doing exactly as he foretold.'

'Now he is here,' Nen repeated. 'He is fuelled by anger and distrust, betrayal and vengeance. I cannot claim to know how or why he is still alive, other than his soul was once part of the divine. Somehow, he has been reborn after the seeds of Chaos played a part in his demise. Call it a whim of the Universe, call it chance, perhaps. Now Ahriman seeks to eradicate such folly. He is a creature of Chaos striving for his own sense of Order. So consumed by hatred, is he, that he has become blind to the notion of balance.'

'A terrible tale.'

'With lessons for us all.'

'Tell me, Nen, if I meet a Nepharii, will I be able to trust him?'

'If you refer to Kian and Inesco, yes, you may trust them. They do not seek power to rule or sway. They are guardians and teachers, seek only to nurture. But there are others, like Ahriman, who have fallen to become consumed by their base desires. They are known as Nephilim. You will know them by their actions and beliefs. Do not trust them.' She ceased her walk as she arrived at an archway on her left. 'It is time, Tarsin, for you and your men to return.'

He nodded his head, followed Nen as she stepped under the arch and down a set of stairs. After several minutes they arrived at the central chamber where Griffith and Will Tolsten mingled with their men. The spiralling vortex of energy pulsed behind them, bathing everyone with subtle shades of gold.

Tarsin turned to Nen once more. 'Thank you,' he said, as he watched her eyes turn from brilliant sapphire to molten gold. 'Thank you for your wisdom and this short reprieve from fighting and war.'

'It is our pleasure, Tarsin Va. We are here to guide and inform, nothing more, but we appreciate your kind words.'

'And Ahriman?' he asked. 'He is no longer on our path?'

'No, he has veered away from New City and the one you call the False King. But his path, at some point, will cross yours again in the future. You need to be prepared. Seek out your allies, Tarsin. That is all I can offer.'

Thoughts swirled as he took steps towards his men and gathered them close. They were excited, longed to return to the tunnels beneath Bastion. There was a mission to complete, a chance to infiltrate New City and the manor of Benjin Auldstone. A chance to take down the False King, Clive Bardell.

The first of his men, led by Will Tolsten, disappeared as they stepped into the golden light.

Tarsin paused, turned to see Nen watching from the rear. 'One last question,' he raised his voice above the murmur of his crew. 'Did the king drink the blood of the fallen?'

She dropped her chin to her chest, took a deep breath then raised her eyes. 'He did,' she replied, 'and it gave him power, just as the Nepahrii said. I told you, we have no cause to lie. The first king of Man had the blood of the immortals in his veins. It gave him power. It has been so ever since.'

An understanding passed between them. A collection of thoughts unheard by his men. It was as he believed. She fed him truths, piece-by-piece.

Sometime, in the future, she would feed him more.

*

Tarsin Va slipped past his men, smelt pungent sweat and oiled steel.

'We're almost there, my king,' Will Tolsten greeted him at the head of the line. Flickering torchlight revealed blonde hair plastered to his skull, nervous eyes darting from shadow to shadow. For hours they had been navigating the underground lanes beneath Bastion, following a path only Will and Griffith knew.

'Are you sure this tunnel will see us to Benjin Auldstone's manor?'

'Aye, this is the way,' Will replied. 'The Lord of Antiquities was a trader in fine goods, it is known, but he was also a smuggler of weapons. The Nocturnals aided his movements below the city for a fee, for the paths were ours. I know where I am.'

Tarsin was glad someone knew, for in all honesty, he felt as though they had been walking in circles since they passed from Omphalos back into Undercity. Yet he saw Will take charge with ease as he led them onwards, kept his focus as they traversed the plethora of hidden laneways and canals lying below the city proper.

Will took a deep breath, wiped sweat from his forehead. 'A short walk ahead lies an avenue that leads to what we call Smuggler's Way. Lord Auldstone has access to the avenue via a secret storeroom beneath his stables. Once we climb our way out, it's a short walk to the rear of the manor.'

Tarsin nodded confirmation, looked behind to see if Griffith was nearby. The big man was twenty feet away, his wild red hair reflecting torchlight. 'Have the men draw blades and prepare crossbows,' he kept his voice calm, although he could feel the tension emanating from those pressed close to him. From all reports, Clive Bardell had gathered a considerable number of men to his cause. Bandits and thugs, mostly, yet there were desperate families seeking shelter amongst them. The plan was to find the False King as quickly as possible and eradicate him. Anyone caught in the way was to be taken down. Negotiations at this point were futile. Dervae needed only one king to reclaim the city for Man.

'Should I lead us forward?' asked Will.

'In a moment,' Tarsin took a swallow of water from a skin handed to him. It was hot down here, stifling, even. He offered the water to Tahu, the Panthian standing to his right.

He'd kept quiet the last hour, yet his steps were never far from his own.

Tahu finished his mouthful, wiped a hand across his chin. 'Tell me, Tarsin King,' he spoke softly, a look of curiosity in his cat-like eyes. 'Why do men kill men?'

It took a moment for Tarsin to comprehend the question. 'I . . . it's complicated,' he stumbled, unsure if he even knew the answer to such a query. Man had always fought against each other. 'Actually,' he added, aware his answer was unworthy of the Panthian, '*we* are complicated. Man, that is.'

It was a terrible explanation. He knew, because he could see Tahu's eyes narrow, silently judging him, perhaps.

'Panthians do not kill each other on our world,' he replied. 'We fight, on occasion, but deaths are extremely rare and always accidental.'

Tarsin didn't know what to say. Their culture was obviously different to his own. He had seen firsthand how strange it was, but he'd only seen a small sample of Tahu and Zai's people at the temple. Inesco explained their customs and rituals in some detail, including their nomadic, wandering existence, but talk of disputes and war were never mentioned.

'Listen,' Tarsin stepped closer, 'the man who claims he is now king of Dervae lies ahead. He is a liar and a thief, a callous man with delusions of grandeur. He seeks to take what is rightfully mine. If I believed he could rule the kingdom better than I, then I would leave him be. But he will not. I know this because the man is consumed by greed and anger. If a man like Bardell seeks to unsettle proceedings during such a dire conflict, then he is a fool.

'I do not suffer fools, Tahu. If they cross me, they die.'

He couldn't tell if what he said made any sense, but Tahu's eyes closed in contemplation for a moment, followed by a subtle nod of his head.

'I will not ask you to kill for me, Tahu. Protect my back in the fighting to come, if you can, but the killing you can leave to me.'

'I can fight, Tarsin King,' Tahu drew the blade at his hip. Although the Panthians typically wielded wooden staves, they had quickly found a liking to the steel provided by the Dervani soldiers. 'As you have said on occasion, evil needs to be dealt with when it is discovered. Left to fester, it soon becomes a blemish on the world we live in. On our world, we care for our surroundings with a nurturing hand. This world is different, therefore our techniques for caring also differ. I will fight by your side, Tarsin King. I will kill for you, whether they be man or not.'

It was enough. He shared a smile, saw many of those standing close by nod their heads in approval.

'I guess we're ready, then,' Will drew his own blade as he took one last look at the map he held in his left hand.

The scrape of steel being drawn was his only answer. Fifty men, holding sword or crossbow, began to follow Will's steps.

'Keep your focus, lads,' Tarsin's voice was firm, carried easily to every man in the corridor. 'Very soon we shall find the False King and his court. When we do, we shall end his short reign.'

There was a moment of quiet before Griffith's burly voice echoed from behind. 'Good,' he rumbled. 'It's about bloody time.

*

It was eerily quiet as Tarsin and his men crept across paved stones between the stables and the rear entrance to the manor. A handful of men with crossbows had placed themselves beside an overturned cart, whilst three members of Will's Unseen had moved silently to the only door, one with his ear pressed to the oak, listening for any movement.

'There is something amiss here,' Griffith did his best to keep his voice low.

The big man was right. There were no sounds coming from Auldstone's manor, nor did they see anything resembling a residence in use. A discarded bucket lay next to the well along the west wall, a rake and a hoe rested against a wooden shed.

There was nothing of interest here, except for a layer of grey ash atop the marble steps leading into the establishment.

'Keep your wits about you,' Tarsin addressed the soldiers crowding near the stables. Like his men, he gripped his sword in a sweaty hand, his nerves tight. The sense of conflict was high, breathing was rapid. His heart kept pace.

'Let's do this,' Griffith again, his warhammer, *Bloodstain*, resting comfortably over his shoulder.

Tarsin took a lingering look at the clouded sky, guessed it was midday. If Frey smiled upon them, it could all be over by this afternoon. 'Aye,' he moved with the sound of his own voice, stepped with light feet towards his Unseen. His men followed without a word.

Tarsin offered a nod, saw Zai open the door as he approached. A hallway beckoned, silent, still. They stepped inside, crept forward, passed a kitchen and a sitting room to either side.

'Are you sure this is Auldstone's manor?' he turned to Will as they paused before another set of oak doors.

'Certain of it,' Will replied, sweat glistening on his brow. 'I have been here before, on business, I might add. I wouldn't forget this place. If you doubt me, check the kitchen we just passed. Three stone ovens bake bread each morning for the lord and his retinue. A larder lies to the side, meat hanging from iron pegs. There is also an enormous green slab of granite used for rolling dough. It is one of a kind, made purposefully for his lord by request and shipped from the Corphym Isles. I've seen it. He tells everyone how wonderful it is.'

'I believe you, Will,' Tarsin shook his head. It didn't make sense. The ovens weren't in use, the fires unlit. His reports suggested hundreds of people had flocked to Bardell's side when he opened the gates. If they were here, there should at least be some activity within the manor. Surely there would be people bustling about the kitchen and yards, people looking to help feeds the masses. Instead, there was nothing to see or smell, nothing to hear.

'Keep moving,' he motioned towards the doors with his sword.

Zai once again pushed on the door before him. It opened without a sound, allowed the Panthian to step into the Grand Hall.

'This is something,' Griffith craned his neck to follow the twining staircase to his left. Another was replicated to the right, both leading to a balcony that surrounded the Grand Hall. Rooms and corridors could be seen in the background.

'There are more than forty rooms in the manor,' Will took a step into the hall. 'And yet I would have expected this to be Bardell's throne room, for it is the largest and most accessible.'

'Perhaps it was,' Tarsin cast his eyes back to the hall, saw patterns in the marble tiles. To his left, at what would be the rear of the room, sat an enormous high-backed wooden chair. 'This looks to be his seat of office. I wonder where he and his people are?'

He took another step closer to the chair, saw blue-painted swirls arranged in a pattern on the floor. He caught a scent of decay as he took another step, sensed something was surely amiss.

'This place is not right,' Griffith lifted his hammer from his shoulder and slapped it into his palm. 'My bloody red hairs are standing on end,' he showed his hairy forearm to Tahu. 'Something's wrong.'

Tarsin was about to agree when a blinding sheet of light flared from the tile he stepped upon. He closed his eyes to reduce the glare, saw a thousand tiny stars blur his vision. Then the darkness between the stars began to grow. He opened his eyes, yet the darkness remained. He couldn't see his men, couldn't hear them. Silence engulfed him.

He calmed his breathing, cast his mind over his body. He could feel his feet on the marble floor, feel the sword in his right hand. He touched his armour, felt the cold steel protecting him.

'Welcome!' a voice boomed from nowhere and everywhere at once.

'Where am I?' his own voice sounded distant.

'You are in the Grand Hall, Tarsin Va. You have finally arrived. You are the king who should have been sacrificed.'

Tarsin tightened his grip about the hilt of his sword. 'Show yourself!' he snarled.

'As you wish.'

Darkness shifted to grey, merged to light. The voice was right. He remained in the hall, yet his men were nowhere to be seen.

'This is not the hall I walked in,' Tarsin shouted. The light from outside was dim when he entered, the day overcast. And there were markings about the throne, painted blue. All were now absent.

'So you say,' a shadow detached from the rear wall, floated towards the centre of the room.

'You are Ahriman,' Tarsin replied, 'once a dead man, soon to be dead again!'

Laughter. The shadow became a black cloaked figure, tall and commanding, its darkness absorbing the light. 'I was never such a simple creature, child. But you are right. I am Ahriman, the first born Nepharii. When I am done with you and your world, I will be the last.'

'My blade here might say otherwise!'

'You cannot strike me, child of Man, for 'tis but a dream you find yourself in.'

A dream? So . . . was this real? Could he even touch the black cloak swirling before him? A pain in his head began to manifest. His eyes began to sting.

'Difficult, isn't it,' Ahriman's voice mocked him from the shadows, 'to accept your dream as reality. This room you stand in, my image, all are constructs of your mind, not mine. And yet I am here, Tarsin Va. That much is real.'

'What is your purpose?' he asked, fighting the lancing pain behind his eyes.

'To assess your worth, to see what I must confront when the time is right. Clive Bardell and I have spoken at length. You interest me, Tarsin Va. When it is time for you and I to lock horns, as they say, I would like to believe I know who you are.'

'Well, I'm standing here and haven't fallen. Unlike you, I might add.'

'Pretty words . . .'

'That ring of truth, Nephilim! Are we done here? I've a fallen god to kill and a city to reclaim!'

Silence. Shadows swirled, bulged in agitation. The dark mass representing Ahriman grew, drowning what little light remained. The large room he stood in became smaller, darkness closed in.

'Few it is who know the true meaning of the word Nephilim.'

'I have friends, Ahriman, powerful friends who have explained more than you realise. You died once. You will do so again.'

'I decide when my time is up, child,' Ahriman's voice sounded in his head. 'No-one else has that right. The Universe tried to end me once, but here I am. If you come for me, you will die.'

He was so certain. And as Nen suggested, they did not lie. If Ahriman could bring the city to its knees, how was he going to stand before him with the belief he could cut him down?

'The seeds of doubt grow in the weak, Tarsin Va. Are you weak, child? Do your legs tremble? Will you fight me when you find me, or will you stand before me, like Clive Bardell, and die without a semblance of dignity whatsoever?'

Ahriman's words ran thick with sarcasm yet mentioning Bardell's death brought Tarsin's attention back to the conversation.

'You killed him?' Tarsin found his voice. 'You killed the False King?'

'Can you imagine the sight of a crowded Grand Hall in the dead of night, suddenly brightened by a hundred pillars of flame and the screams of the unworthy.'

'You killed them all?'

'I did. Why would I not? I was the first, I shall soon be the last. No matter what you think you know, Tarsin Va, I know more.'

Tarsin closed his eyes, remembered seeing grey ash piled high in the corners of the Grand Hall. In fact, it was everywhere. On the steps leading to the kitchen, a small pile beside the well, a smear covering planks of timber in the stables. Piles of ash, all that remained of those who chose to follow Clive Bardell, the False King.

How would he and his men fare differently if they sought out Ahriman?

He forced his eyes open, saw the makeshift throne to his left, noticed ash on the seat. He blinked, knew Clive Bardell was nothing more than dust, along with his followers. So many people of Bastion gone. If Ahriman wasn't stopped soon, so many more would follow. He sought the Dark One, saw black tendrils snake from the bulging cloud of darkness. Whatever light remained in the room was dissipating fast, along with air to breathe. It was stiflingly hot all of a sudden. He tried to swallow, found his mouth parched.

'Humbling, is it not,' Ahriman asked, 'to find yourself incapable of retaliating against that which drives you mad?'

Tarsin tried to speak but couldn't form the words. An oily tentacle stretched towards his mouth, brushed against his lips. His entire body became rigid, as if cast from stone. The tentacle stretched further, slid past his teeth and down his throat. He gagged.

'Perhaps I should kill you now, Tarsin Va. Perhaps I shouldn't waste any more time.'

Fear gripped his soul. Could he wield such power? Could he kill him through a dream? What was it he said when they first met? Everything was a construct of *his* mind.

Tarsin flashed his blade upwards, severing the tentacle. Hot, bubbling ichor oozed from the tendril to drip slowly upon the tiles. He spat the remainder from his mouth, sucked in a lungful of precious air. As his chest expanded, he raised his head to peer at the dark cloud of hatred. 'Damn you, Nephilim!' he snarled, brandishing his sword with a clenched fist. 'I will find you, then I will kill you!'

'Brave words, child.'

The cloud of boiling darkness flared from within. Tarsin blinked back hot tears, saw an image take shape. Black tendrils melted to the floor leaving a powerfully built figure, as if cast from bronze, standing poised with rippling muscles and chiselled features. He was tall and broad, hairless, completely naked. Black eyes glared.

Ahriman took a single step towards him. It sounded like a clap of thunder to herald a storm.

'Leave here, child, and seek me out when you believe you are ready,' his voice pounded into his skull. 'I'll be waiting.'

Ahriman began to fade as quickly as he arrived. His metallic skin shifted to grey, separated into thin, cloud-like wisps to float into the surrounding darkness. But his eyes remained, fixed onto his own. Two black orbs promising eternal pain.

Tarsin closed his eyes, but the soulless orbs remained, unwavering with deadly intent as they questioned his sanity. And the voice of Ahriman chased him into darkness.

'I'll be waiting.'

CHAPTER THIRTY-TWO

'Anok and Eli,' the words were gruffly spoken, 'you're alive!'

King Tarsin Va opened tired eyes to see Cale Griffith's face before him, a nervous smile splitting his red beard, concern in his eyes. 'What happened?' Tarsin ventured, his mouth dry, his tongue swollen. 'Where am I?'

'Outside Benjin Auldstone's Grand Hall,' the big man said. 'On the steps out front. I carried you here. We thought you were dead.'

That would explain the look of concern, he thought. Was that blue sky behind Griffith's shoulder? He sat up, felt more than one set of hands behind him, helping to prop him upright. Tahu and Zai were beside him, Will Tolsten as well.

'You stopped breathing,' Griffith explained. 'For longer than we cared for. There was a flash of light when you entered the hall, then you collapsed.'

Tarsin lifted a hand to rub above his temple. Dark images crept from the shadow of his mind, accompanied with fear laden words and the obliteration of hope.

'I spoke with the Dark One,' he offered, wondering whether he actually did, or if it was just a terrifying dream. His instinct told him to believe his vision. 'If what I saw was real, he has grown powerful.'

'Another concern, then,' Griffith snarled. 'Add it to the list.'

He heard bitterness in Griffith's words, an overbearing sense of anger. Something must have occurred whilst he was unconscious. 'How long was I out for?'

'Not too long, my lord,' Will Tolsten offered.

'Long enough for us to realise something is afoot, though,' Griffith suggested, evidently still unhappy with their situation.

'He is right, my king,' Will nodded his head.

'Aye,' Griffith scratched his beard, 'there is something you should see if you can manage.'

There was the concern again, deeply etched in the big man's weathered face, evident in the tone of his voice. Tarsin took another deep breath, held out a hand. Tahu gripped it tight, helped him stand.

'What would you show me?'

'Over here,' Will began to walk towards a stone wall. It was six feet high, punctuated with arched doorways leading into a manicured garden. Will headed for a doorway to his right, walked beneath the arch.

Tarsin followed, his first footsteps tentative, but as he reached the archway, he felt himself again. The fear gripping his soul lingered, though, along with his doubts. Whatever Ahriman was, or had become, his death was not likely to come easily.

He breathed deeply, felt warmth in the air. 'What is it you are showing me?' he asked Will, tapping him on the shoulder as he moved to his side.

Will pointed a finger towards the grounds. His eyes followed, spied an enormous mound of overturned earth where a patterned grass-bed should have been.

It took a moment of contemplation before he realised what he was looking at.

'Pray tell me that's not a mass grave I see before me?'

'It is exactly that, my king,' Will shook his head, held out a hand to stall his steps towards the makeshift gravesite. 'I wouldn't step any closer. We have inspected a handful of the dead from a distance. From our observation, we believe they died of the plague.'

'How many do you estimate?'

'Hundreds, my lord.'

A look of pain must have strained his face, for Will quickly added words to ease his conscience. 'They died some time ago. The handful of corpses not buried have decomposed, but we noticed the remnants of black boils under their armpits. We estimate the majority have been buried for months, but we'll not take a closer look for fear of infection.'

Tarsin gave a solitary nod, let the words sink in. He looked to the blue sky, saw shifting clouds on the horizon. Once again, he noticed how warm it was out here under the sun. Warmer than it should have been.

'Winter has passed,' he said under his breath. 'When we left to find Griffith and his men, a blanket of snow lay thick over Bastion.'

'Aye, you see it,' Griffith patted *Bloodstain*. 'A few of my men, farmers in a former life, suggest we have passed Midsummer's Eve. They know their seasons. I trust them.'

'Midsummer's Eve,' Tarsin repeated. 'That's half a year and then some.'

His words confirmed their fears. Blank stares resembled his own. The words of Nen suddenly meant so much more to him then. Wherever Omphalos and the Weeping Tower was, like the world of Aeth, time travelled differently. What seemed like a handful of days of recuperation with his men, now appeared to be vastly different to the passage of time in Bastion.

He backed away from the mass grave, aware of how many could be buried beneath the soil. His men fell in behind as he walked to the stone steps leading to the Grand Hall. He took a moment to examine its façade, noticed a line of cracks splintering the plaster. Damaged, like every other building. And then he saw grey ash piled in a corner, alongside a marble pillar. No matter where he looked, death greeted him. Plague and fire. Painful.

The clink of sword and chain alerted him to his surrounding men. They were waiting for word from their king. Waiting for direction and purpose. What could he say to them, here on the steps surrounded by death?

And then the real shock of Bastion's demise hit him.

Once the noise of his men shifting into position subsided, it became apparent. Alarmingly so. He was surprised he hadn't noticed it earlier.

The sounds of the city were absent.

Nothing stirred. Nothing at all.

He looked beyond his fifty men. There was no wind blowing through dusty streets, no sigh from heavily foliaged trees. He tilted his head to the side, sought the incessant twitter of birds on the wing. Again, nothing. Not a chirp, nor a song. Not a soul.

Silence.

'There is nothing here,' he said to himself, although he was aware those men directly before him would have heard his words. 'I cannot hear the birds, nor the buzz of insects on a summer's day. The city is silent, holding its breath.'

Tahu took steps to stand by his side. Tarsin peered into his tawny eyes, saw a depth of understanding in the Panthian. What would he make of the silent city?

'We are here, my lord,' Tahu said with his heavy accent. 'We will bring life back to this fallen city.'

Could they? His mind was racing. Councillor Tahlia would have heard word of the plague in New City across the river Atvia. Together with Lloyd Henrickson they would have seen the dead being buried in the hastily dug grave. Thoughts of engaging with Clive Bardell would have stalled, then become irrelevant. Within a day they would have retreated as far away from New City as possible. Most likely from the city altogether. There was a chance his people, especially those closest to him in his fight to reclaim Bastion, were safe in the Southern Fields beyond the cities broken walls.

And what of the Deios? And the Eagle-men? And those who looked like crows? What of the giant Taurans? Were they still roaming the streets, fighting for supremacy? Or had a single race taken hold of the pyramid and claimed the wonders within?

Was there anything remaining to fight for?

So many questions with unknown answers. And amongst it all, he sensed the most important question was whether it was worth it. Was the city of Bastion worth fighting for?

He looked further afield, sought those towers still standing after the earthquake, looked for the belfries and their bronze cast bells. Red-tiled peaked roofs jutted from behind walls of sandstone, pathways lined with cobblestones led confidently into the labyrinth of a city built a thousand years ago. And beneath her rested an older city, an ancient city fashioned by Nepharii hands.

She was still there, as the city of Bastion would remain whether he saved her or not.

A flash of sunlight reflected by a bronze bell caught his eye. He squeezed his eyes closed, momentarily blinded. An image of the Dark One manifested in his mind, lurking in shadow, laughing at his confusion.

And Tarsin Va, King of Dervae, realised an important truth.

It wasn't the city he needed to save. It was his people, first and foremost. Yet to save his people he would need to defeat Ahriman. He couldn't avoid the revelation, nor dismiss it. It was his only purpose. If the Dark Lord lived, they were doomed. Everything else hinged on this one fact.

He placed a hand on Tahu's shoulder, met his cat-like eyes. 'To bring life back to the city, my friend, we must take a life. The Dark One is here, most likely close to the pyramid where true power resides. We must defeat him,' his words carried to his fifty men, 'to save our people *and* your people.'

'I feel it also,' Tahu replied, flexing a clawed hand. 'You will lead us, Tarsin King, for you are our Chosen One.'

'It is written,' Zai confirmed as he walked towards them. 'It has always been written.'

Tarsin shared a smile. 'Nen said I would need allies in the battle to come, for I cannot defeat the Darkness alone. You are the first, methinks.'

'Hopefully,' bellowed Griffith, 'they'll not be the last.'

'They won't be,' Will Tolsten joined the gathering. 'The Darkness festers, grows, and our city decays. You can see it; you can sense it. The city is dying. But like the plague-riddled bodies lying in an unmarked grave, if we have the courage to lance the blackened boil that lies beneath our city now, we may avoid the disease and terrible death that follows. The other races crawling throughout our city will sense it also. Survival is an instinct. When death creeps close, you feel it in your soul. The Dark One will not hold sway over everyone.'

'I hope you're right, lad,' Griffith lifted his hammer and placed it on his shoulder. 'Gods above know we can't fight them all. What do you think, my king?'

'We'll fight them all if we have to,' Tarsin felt the anger in his words, 'but Will may be right. There are others, like us,' he pointed a finger to encompass Tahu and Zai, 'who will fight against Ahriman and his whispered half-truths. He cannot hide forever.'

Brave words. He hoped they were true. Still, if Ahriman did crawl out from whatever hole he now called home, Tarsin vowed to be prepared for the worst. And yet whichever way he looked at the coming confrontation, casualties were going to be high.

'So,' it was Griffith, looking over his shoulder towards the path leading away from Benjin Auldstone's manor, 'what is our next move?'

The sun was dipping to the west, yet the heat of the day remained. So unusual, so unexpected, to feel warmth when the mind assumes cold. He cast his eyes over the southern section of Bastion. New City was elevated enough for him to see a goodly portion, despite the mass of Aston's Tear blocking everything towards the harbour. They would make for the closest bridge, cross the river Atvia with all haste.

'Irongate,' he finally said, spying the old watch tower in the distance. It would take them almost to nightfall before they reached its position, but he longed to be inside its protective walls. Besides, the old tower, although damaged, was still standing relatively straight. She would provide the view they needed in the coming days. A view of a city falling to pieces, perhaps, but a view they could use to strategize.

And she was close to the pyramid and the centre of all their woes.

Close to the Dark One, he surmised.

'We'll head to Irongate, see what we can find,' his men listened attentively. 'She's placed well for any sortie we choose to make in the days ahead, both deep into the city, or possibly to the outside, where we'll seek aid from our councillors and soldiers. There is much to learn, I'll not deny it, but Irongate will provide for us. It's where I wish to be.'

'Irongate it is, then,' Griffith slapped *Bloodstain*. 'If you've no objection, my king, I suggest we move out.'

Tarsin gave a solitary nod to confirm Griffith's suggestion, placed a hand on the hilt of his Rykedian broadsword. The touch eased his worries, settled his nerves. With a blade in his hand, he always felt in control. There was a synergy between he and the weapon. It calmed him.

He wondered if he would draw his sword in the coming days.

Wondered if he'd remain calm when he did so.

'Lead the way, Cale Griffith,' he raised his voice, spoke with kingly authority. 'Lead the way to Irongate.'

There was a murmur of approval from his men. They could defend Irongate if they had to. It was pleasing to know they'd have someplace safe inside the broken city.

At least he prayed they'd be safe.

At least for one night.

*

He rolled the sleeves of his linen shirt to his elbow, aware of the stains and terrible stench of his garment as he did so.

'I must smell like a corpse,' Jarred said to himself, sniffing the ripe air.

If the fact disturbed him, he hid his disgust behind a stony facade as he walked towards a wooden bench pressed against the far stone wall. A conglomeration of implements used for curing hides arranged along its length, seen by the light of a dozen flickering candles congealing atop a silver candelabra. Three leather-bound tomes lay open for reading at the centre of the bench, a wooden high-backed chair sat in front. For months he'd been following detailed steps concerning the production of leather from hide and the curing process

450

involved. Having all the tools of the trade at his disposal was a boon he couldn't deny, and yet more importantly, the learning process had provided a distraction for the young man. A distraction that quite possibly kept him sane in a world of pain and suffering.

He lifted a grimy arm to wipe sweat from his brow. The winter months had tested his nerves, blanketed him in fear and the loss of hope. After dragging the four corpses from the street one winter's night and into the tanning rooms beneath Irongate, he'd spent the next three days roaming the cold chambers, trembling as he did so. He'd been too frightened to return above, too frightened to chance his luck returning to the pantry where his meagre food was stored.

And yet his roaming proved the Goddess of Luck still smiled upon him.

The chambers below Irongate were linked by tunnels, some with channels of water sweeping towards neighbouring canals, some paved with stone tiles that led to storerooms hitherto unknown. It was here, after finding a large brass ring with a dozen brass keys, that Jarred unlocked a room to find crates of bottled preserves and barrels of cider.

There was enough food for the young man to survive the winter and spring. Enough to see him grow strong once again, to regain some of the weight he'd lost whilst hiding in the tower.

Pickled cucumbers and salted herring became his staple, along with wedges of cheese after he discovered another storeroom with shelves piled high with waxed rounds of Irongate's specialty. And each room he unlocked provided something new. Salted pork in sealed barrels, pumpkins cradled in crates of straw, potatoes hidden beneath coarse sand in wooden boxes.

With sustenance came a renewed vigour to achieve his goal of reaching Aston's Tear. Whether his full belly provided the necessary motivation, he couldn't be sure, but there was a spring in his step as he set about learning how to skin the creatures he'd dragged below.

It was a gruesome task, more so considering he'd left the corpses for three days before attending to them. Thankfully the chambers below Irongate remained cold, especially during winter. After stripping them of their garments, he set about opening the beasts to see what lay inside, curious to see if their insides resembled the careful drawings he'd found in a book written by Gerald Riddicio, an elder of the Brotherhood of One. From the detailed text he read at the beginning, Gerald Riddicio was an adept when considering the anatomy of man. Diagrams of the body, both inside and out, were expertly detailed throughout the manual, penned with an immaculate hand.

It was here Jarred learnt how to perform the correct incisions with the proper blades. It took time, but his hunger for knowledge took hold, and once again he became the Information Gatherer he'd always been.

He began with the three Ophidians, for he knew any mistakes he made in the early stages could be rectified on the next corpse. It was bloody business, his arms covered in gore as he opened the chest to reveal the cavity below the ribcage. And it wasn't easy work. The cutters he used required strength of arm, something he was currently lacking. But he managed to hack through his first set of bones, albeit poorly, before revealing the inner organs.

Curious to see if the Ophidians contained workings like man, he began to extract the decomposing slabs of organ meat and arrange them on the bench.

Heart, liver, kidneys, lungs, spleen, and stomach. All were present, all present in a manner that mimicked the diagrams penned by Gerald Riddicio. Take away the Ophidian's facial features and its scaled hide, and the slight differences in hands and feet, and the creature was in every aspect identical to a man when looking beneath the skin.

Days swept by as he continued to cut and saw, to peel back skin and extract organs. The process was gruelling, the stench incredible, but the tanning rooms had drop holes for disposing any unwanted flesh and bone into the waterways below. With his mind afire with the prospect of knowledge, he began to draw his own diagrams, fuelled by a desire to record his observations. If he managed to find his people at some point, what he learnt now could possibly be of value to those in power. Perhaps his fascination was a means of finally making use of his time, perhaps it was his method of distancing himself from his original task. Whatever the cause, he devoured the works of the Brotherhood over the winter and strove towards creating a leather mask from the Vulpan to hide his identity. Because he knew with spring approaching, he would need to revisit his original plan. He couldn't hide below Irongate forever. At some point, he would need to recover his backpack from the tower, and his sword, and set out for the pyramid.

With his initial observations behind him he began work on the Vulpan, his first step to peel the face away from the skull. It took longer than he expected, but he was patient, for he had no other should he prove to be hasty. Once the skin was free of the skull, he delicately flipped the skin over and switched his scalpel to a scraper so he could dispense with the excess flesh, muscle, and fat. A handful of salt came next, a liberal amount to absorb the moisture whilst he kept the skin in a dry place. The process was relatively straightforward except for the curing time. From the notes written by Gerald Riddicio, twenty days, perhaps more, was necessary for the salt to do its curing work.

He checked his Vulpan mask every day, finally drained it of liquid and began the first of several washes. A handful of stone vats were ranged in one of the chambers, ideal for soaking hides in water gathered from the tunnels. After scraping one final time, he then moved to soaking the skin in a solution of his own urine. Another wash followed. Spring had arrived.

A week later he began working beeswax into the skin to make it supple, a final procedure before he gathered needle and thread to create a mask that would cover his face.

A desperate attempt, perhaps, to see him step into Bastion.

A leather satchel sat on the chair. He reached for it, knew his facemask lay within. It was time. Spring had passed swiftly as he dawdled beneath Irongate. His desire to reach Aston's Tear waned every day to be almost non-existent. He'd survived the winter without being found by the Others, he survived spring even though they were becoming more brazen with their roaming. Yet he couldn't stay hidden indefinitely. One day, they would find him. But more importantly, Kian was relying on him. He couldn't forget his mission, nor his obligation to the Nepharii. So much hinged on his ability to see the task through.

Midsummer's Eve had passed yet still he remained. It was galling. The time was now. He needed to forget about his days as a coward. He needed to put them behind him and focus on his next step.

He climbed the tower two days earlier to fetch his sword and backpack. The experience unnerved him, if anything, yet he used his time to scan the surrounds for any activity. There was no sign of Bastion's soldiers. That fact alone sent shivers racing down his spine, despite the heat of the day. Once again, fear began to take hold. With trembling hands, he reached for the mirror behind the bookshelf, seeking – he assumed - confirmation of his cowardice.

Shadowed eyes peered back at him. His mouth began to move.

'I have a mask to hide my face, a mask to hide my pain. Do I leave for Aston's Tear, or shall I go insane?'

Did he recite the words aloud, or was it all in his head? He couldn't tell. His hands still trembled. But he knew if delayed any longer, his nerve to act would disappear.

It rained that night, a gentle shower, nothing more, but it was enough for him to hesitate.

He opened the satchel and pulled out the mask.

'You will help me,' his words were softly spoken, but he sensed the desperation in his voice. It was taking everything he had and more to commit to the plan. Thoughts of setting out into the streets and crossing paths with Others was tearing his mind apart. Even with his sword by his side, he doubted he'd be able to fight to protect himself.

He shared a smile with his creation. It didn't smile back. Just as well, he thought, for I am about to leave the safe confines of Irongate. I doubt I'll ever return.

The mask felt soft in his hands as he placed it on the bench. He tended to it constantly over the past months, more than was required, he knew. And yet his devotion to the mask eventually led to a disguise of incredible workmanship. The fox-man, or Vulpan, as he was once told by the now vacant voices in his head, stood a similar height to his own. Its body was likewise similar in appearance, broad across the shoulders, lean arms and legs. Having taken care to extricate the Vulpan from his attire when he first began the autopsy, adding the garments to his costume provided a level of authenticity even looking in the mirror was difficult to fault. But travel during daylight hours would see him undone upon close inspection, and if his hood was swept behind him, his stitching would be visible. Two scenarios he was aware of, both creating problems. In the end, after countless deliberations, the two issues decided his path away from Irongate.

To stay hidden for as long as possible, he would need to leave via the tunnels beneath the old keep. A rusty iron gate barred one of the tunnels below, but having found the brass ring of keys, he discovered he could open it. Charts in the Depository clearly marked the passages snaking away from cellars and storerooms. Like the portals surrounding Aston's Tear, he memorized their position, their turns and their length. When he left, he would know exactly where he was going. With or without his fear.

His journey to Aston's Tear would take no more than a day for he knew the distance, even below the city's streets. Less than a day, even with a cautious pace.

It was time for him to leave.

A pile of clothes lay folded beneath the bench. He reached for them, unfolded the garments that once belonged to the Vulpan. A black leather jacket, hardened by some means and studded with metal rings, would serve as his protection. It smelt awful, despite cleaning it several times, but thankfully the hole he stitched remained tightly sewn. The trousers were also darkly stained and cut differently to his own. He pulled them on, tightened his belt, then stepped into his boots. These he would keep, for the leather was supple and the sizing was right. The prospect of fleeing Others with ill-fitting boots caused his heart to flutter.

He shouldered his backpack next, strapped his sword to his belt and covered all with a heavy cloak. It would be stifling wearing such gear, but his plan was to skulk into Aston's Tear unseen, not to race through the streets like the wind. Slow and easy, methodical, not rash.

He checked his pockets. His pouch of walnuts still sat in one, his other held his glow-stone gifted to him by Kian. As the Nepharii explained to him when offering the item, a day lying in the sun would see its power restored. Jarred did as bid when the summer days arrived, knew it had value if he ever found the courage to continue. It was a pretty piece, and the urge to rub the stone was overwhelming. But he stayed his hand and placed it back in his pocket, aware he would need it later as he traversed the tunnels. If he was fortunate, its light would see him to the pyramid.

He thought of the mirror leaning at the top of the tower, wished he'd moved it down here to the tanning chambers so he could see what he truly looked like. 'Perhaps I should,' he said to himself. 'Perhaps I should retrieve the mirror, just to make certain I look the part.'

He shook his head; aware he was stalling. Instead, he placed the fox mask over his own face, adjusted the fit so his frightened eyes could see through the slits.

A deep breath followed. It smelt fresh. The skin on his skin was soft, almost tender. He raised a hand, ran his fingers against his now red-haired cheek. He could feel the coarse hairs, both along his jawline and across his fingertips.

His hand reached higher, felt the pelt above his brow, the pointy ears. It sat well, didn't shift as he moved his head from side-to-side.

'This is it,' he said to an empty room. He lifted the hood of his cloak, draped it carefully over his newfound features. He was no longer Jarred the Information Gatherer. Now he was something wholly different. A fox-man. A Vulpan. He shifted his shoulders, let his cloak settle. The candles flickered with his movement, cast shadows on the stone wall.

He walked towards the tunnels, his right hand grasping the brass keys as he passed the vats, his other hand tightening about the hilt of his sword.

Within minutes the iron gate was behind him, the subtle glow of his magic stone shining on damp walls.

And Aston's Tear was ahead of him.

Somewhere.

CHAPTER THIRTY-THREE

Iron gates opened with a whine.

The noise was piercing, carried easily to the forty men waiting in the street. Tarsin Va felt his muscles tighten as he shared a glance, knew he and his men were poised for combat, anxious.

Will Tolsten stepped before him, a steel key gripped tight in his hand.

'You found a way inside, obviously,' Tarsin ushered his men into the courtyard of Irongate.

'Aye, my lord,' Will held a steel key before him. Tasked to find a way to enter the old keep, Will and nine of his men offered to scout beneath the city via the sewers. With Col Farren and the red-haired Patrick, they had set out an hour earlier. 'I had faith we would find a way in. Despite the Nocturnals giving the Brotherhood a wide berth when traversing Undercity, we are taught there is always a way inside if you know where to look.'

'Any trouble?'

'No, quite the opposite, actually,' Will offered a smile as Col Farren stepped to his left. 'We found an old rusty gate in one of the tunnels, happened to be unlocked and inviting. We moved in, found a handful of storerooms and a tannery within minutes. There is food aplenty for the men, I might add.'

'That is welcome news. I was wondering where our next meal was going to come from. Anything else?'

Will waved his key in the air. 'Found this in the kitchen, lying on a bench. Like it was waiting for us,' he said, his smile fading.

The last of his men passed beneath the guardhouse. Col Farren and Cale Griffith pushed their shoulders back and heaved the iron gate, slammed it closed as Will twisted his key to lock it once again.

Will waited for the men to pass. 'There is something else, my lord,' his kept his voice low. 'As we made our way into the tannery beneath the keep, we came across a table with a six-pronged candelabra. The candles were aflame.'

'Aflame?' Tarsin queried. 'That would suggest someone is here, in Irongate.'

'My thoughts also,' Will shifted his eyes to the tower.

'Gather the men,' Tarsin ordered Griffith, eyes suddenly narrowed. 'I want groups of five searching every room in Irongate. If someone - or something - is here, I'd like to know.'

'As you wish,' Griffith hefted his hammer, whistled once to the men. Within a minute he'd organised their numbers, then sent them searching the grounds outside the keep. 'They'll search the yards and stables,' he offered, 'then we'll move inside.'

'Aye,' Tarsin replied. 'Keep an eye on them.' He signalled to Tahu and Zai, placed a hand on Will's shoulder. 'You and I will venture to the tower. Farren comes with us.'

'Yes, my lord.'

A quick glance to the sky suggested dusk was approaching. 'Keep your eyes peeled,' Tarsin shifted his eyes to look at Griffith, 'and we'll meet you back here before the sun sets.'

'Aye, my king,' his voice was gruff. 'Stay out of trouble.'

The corners of his lips twitched, hinting at a smile, but the severity of his situation ceased further movement. Something was happening here at Irongate. He could feel it. Whether it was something to learn or discover, or a warning, perhaps, he wasn't sure. But he sensed being at Irongate was important.

Like Will, he looked to the damaged tower. If he was to learn anything about the city and how she fared, he felt it was within those stone walls where his answers might lie.

It was a feeling, nothing more.

A feeling he was desperate to latch onto.

He took a deep breath, knew he had to focus on the task at hand. Climb the tower and he could contemplate all he liked.

'Let's move,' he finally spoke to Will, Farren, Tahu and Zai. They gave a nod in response, and as one, followed his lead.

Within half-an-hour they were standing in a circular room, a single level below the observatory, although it was obvious significant damage suggested she was no longer operational. It was here elders of the Brotherhood would come to gaze at the stars each night. Something he doubted would ever occur again.

He looked at Tahu, the Panthian quietly easing his breathing. The ascent had been difficult, for a section of the staircase had fallen during the earthquake, but Tahu, having climbed the inside wall, found a coiled rope on the level above, making the risk of injury negligible for those still to follow. As Col Farren finished his climb, they stepped inside the circular room as one to find it empty.

Empty of life, perhaps, but there was a story to be discovered here.

'This place looks like a nest,' Will stepped towards the pile of blankets resting against the far wall. He reached out to touch the blanket hanging over the window to his right, saw another masking the one to his left.

Tarsin narrowed his eyes, watched Zai walk further into the room, sniffing as he went. 'What do you smell?'

'Man,' he replied. 'A man lived here for some time, but not recently.' He walked towards a bookshelf, reached out his clawed hand. 'There is much dust.'

'Aye, I see it,' Col Farren walked towards a cabinet, traced a finger across the glass. Goblets and bottles of wine greeted him on the other side. 'There has been little movement in here of late.' He looked to the floor. 'Except for these footsteps.'

Everyone looked down at their feet. Farren was right, someone in the last day or two had walked into the room and towards the bookshelf. There they paused, before returning to the only door. A section on the wall next to the doorway, where three wooden pegs sat at head height, was bare of any dust.

'Something was hanging from these pegs, Tarsin King,' spoke Tahu, leaning close to examine the empty space.

'Any idea what it might have been?'

'A cloak, perhaps,' Tahu sniffed again. 'Perhaps a belt or a pack.'

The king raced his tongue over his teeth, scanned the room once again. 'Search the place,' he motioned towards the bookshelf and the cabinet, pointed towards the pile of blankets. 'There must be something here to offer clues as to who roams Irongate. Find them.'

A flurry of activity ensued as the men and two Panthians searched the room. Seeing the men occupied, Tarsin moved towards the window and tore the blanket from its pegs, allowing the late afternoon sun to light their surroundings. It highlighted a thousand dust motes swirling behind their every movement, chased away the last of the shadows lurking beside the cabinet. He heard a heavy sneeze behind him, spun about. It was Col Farren, lifting a handful of leather-bound books from a shelf. 'Anything?' he asked.

Tahu stood to his feet. He'd been crouched over the pile of blankets. 'I have something,' he offered, his clawed hand holding something resembling a journal.

After three long strides Tarsin held out his hand. It was as he hoped, a bound journal, slightly larger than his palm. There was no writing on the blue-stained leather, but as he flicked it open, he could see the cream-coloured parchment to be enthusiastically written upon. Page after page, from the first to the last.

'Can you read it?' asked Will, looking over his shoulder.

'Aye,' he smiled as his eyes swept over the opening line. 'It's legible, although rudimentary at the same time.' He paused to continue reading the passage. Flipped a page, read some more.

'Is it of interest?' Col Farren moved away from the bookshelf.

Tarsin stroked his chin with his left hand, narrowed his eyes. 'Gods above!' he whispered to the room. 'Jarred was here. In this very room.'

'Who is Jarred?' Will met his gaze.

'A young lad who worked for Ruvin Ciricello. I taught him swordplay. I was there when he purchased his first blade. He was with your sister, Will, when they crossed through the portal. But from what I am reading here, he's been at Irongate for months.'

'And my sister? Has Kayla returned?'

Tarsin flipped through the journal with trembling fingers, searched for any mention of Kayla Tolsten. His heart raced; he even held his breath. Halfway through the journal a passage caught his eye.

He gathered himself, cleared his throat so he could read aloud.

'I am afraid,' he began. 'There, I said it. For more nights than I can remember I have convinced myself that timing is everything. Kian said I would need to be strong, regardless of which task I chose to perform. Yet I cannot see any men patrolling the streets during the winter months, nor, do I fear, will they return. The Others are all that remain.

'So, I am now tasked with stealing the *Uranometria* from within the pyramid. It is the only way to stop beings from other worlds entering Bastion. With the closing of the portal the Dark Man can be hunted down and the city reclaimed. Then, with peace restored, I can reopen the portal to allow the survivors to return from the world of the Ven.

'Yet I am afraid. I fear the dark. I fear the Others. I fear Ahriman. When I saw him last, I could feel the ice in my veins. I fear to see him again. If I do, I will not survive the encounter. And yet if I wish to see my friends again, I must at least try. I must try to enter Aston's Tear and steal the Nepharii disc.

'I must try, yet I lack the courage to take the first step. But timing is everything. And now is the time.'

Tarsin paused his narration, took a deep breath.

'How long ago was this written?' Will shook his head.

'During the winter months, would be my guess,' he replied, flipping to the last entry. 'Here,' he looked at the last page, began to read once again. 'Midsummer's Eve has passed. I have my disguise. I am no longer Jarred the Information Gatherer. I am now a Vulpan – part man, part fox. Tomorrow, I head for the pyramid. I have stalled for long enough. I no longer have any excuses. If the gods smile upon me, I may end this conflict. If they do smile, I may see my friends return.

'I am scared. But I have no other choice.'

The silence in the room suggested heavy thoughts and contemplation. It remained for several minutes as they stared at the floor before Will raised his chin.

'How old is Jarred? Is my sister here?'

'He is but a boy. Fifteen years, perhaps. Maybe sixteen. I don't think Kayla is here. There is no mention of her other than Jarred hoping to see his friends return.'

'And this entry, it could have been written recently. As little as a day ago.'

Tarsin breathed deep. 'It could have. Griffith said Midsummer's Eve has passed.'

'The candles in the tannery were lit when my men and I entered Irongate,' said Will, sharing a look with Farren. 'And the gate beneath the keep was unlocked.'

Eyes met as they stood in a circle. Realisation came swiftly.

'He left today,' the words sent a tingle down Tarsin's spine. 'Come, Will, lead me to the tannery. We must see if we can find a clue to his whereabouts.

'If we can, we will save him.'

A horn blast echoed from afar.

'What was that?' Will and Col Farren spoke together.

For a moment Tarsin was too afraid to answer. Instead, he took hurried steps to the window and peered outside. The streets remained eerily quiet as the sun began its descent towards the Bay of Pennants. There was no movement, no other sounds. He flicked a latch and opened the lead-framed window, craned his neck to peer towards the south.

Nothing, although he could make out the far Southern Wall.

Another blast of a horn, longer this time.

Tahu pulled the blanket from the remaining window, opened it. In the distance sat Aston's Tear, shining bright in the fading light.

'Here,' Will offered his looking glass.

Tarsin grabbed the brass tube as he moved to Tahu's side, placed the small end to his eye. He scanned the city, focused on the pyramid. There was movement in the streets below, barely visible between the monasteries and fallen temples.

'There is a gathering,' the king mentioned, explaining his vision. Another sound, a piercing call from an instrument he was unfamiliar with. Almost a high-pitched screech. 'I believe a battle is about to ensue. It is difficult to see from here, but there is more than one force approaching through the streets.'

'And young Jarred is headed straight for the conflict,' Col reminded him.

It was true. Somewhere out there, amongst the broken city, walked a young man consumed by fear. He was alone and desperate. Afraid.

'Do we search for him?' asked Will.

Tarsin thought about it. Almost agreed to the notion. Yet they had no idea where he might be, or how far he may have travelled. And they were too few to march brazenly down twisted streets. Like Jarred, they would need to keep out of sight, remain unseen. And somewhere out there roamed the Dark One. Nen said their paths would cross. It was foretold. It was his destiny. But before making any sortie towards the pyramid, Tarsin would need to seek out allies.

He lowered the eye glass, stepped away from the window.

'Searching for Jarred would be folly,' he shook his head. 'The lad is alone, I know, but we may best serve him by providing a diversion.'

'What do you have in mind, my lord?' Col bit one of his fingernails as he met his eyes.

He placed a hand on the older man's shoulder, locked eyes with Will who stood by his side. 'We need reinforcements. Fifty is not enough to engage with those merging about the pyramid.'

'You wish for me to gather aid from the Southern Fields?' asked Will.

'Aye, I do. I'll have you take me to the tannery first, but from there you'll lead twenty men to the Southern Gate. Find Lloyd Henrickson and the Lady Jenna. Search out John Rhys and Inesco with his Panthians. Rouse them, do whatever it takes to encourage a call to arms. Tell them their king requires aid. I want as many men as can be mustered, thousands of them. Come dawn, we march.'

'On Aston's Tear?'

'Aye, Will,' Tarsin flexed his hand, grasped the pommel of his Rykedian broadsword. 'When morning breaks, we march on Aston's Tear.

'For Bastion is our city. It's time we took her back!'

*

A roar sounded from the Deios as they marched towards the temple of light.

Ra'tor's mouth stretched into a wicked grin. The guttural expulsion of air and noise from his brood was welcome. Intoxicating, even.

And all because his angel, Isabelle, had shown him the way.

He tilted his head to the left, caught her eye as she sat on his shoulder. His little angel with her innocent face and golden hair. Priceless. With Isabelle amongst their number, they were certain to triumph in the battle to come. No one else claimed such a trophy. No one else could be whipped into frenzied action like his Deios. With Isabelle singing her battle hymns and stirring their blood, they were unstoppable.

He flexed his left shoulder, watched his angel swivel her gaze down to his own. He felt his smile return.

'You are happy, Ra'tor Bhra-vek,' she said. He knew it wasn't a question.

'I am, little one,' he replied. How could he not be? He was leading the largest brood in their history, seeking to claim a prize previously undreamt of. And in such a short amount of time he'd discovered so many new experiences, learnt so many lessons.

'I am happy for you,' she brushed her delicate fingers across his brow; a brow no longer burdened with his crown of blood.

Dark thoughts swirled, hinting at a time of confusion. When he returned to his Deios he was sufficed with power, called the Blood King and expected to lead in a manner befitting such a title. For days on end, he became the centre of a ritual harking back to days of lore. Doused in the blood of his enemies, he began to believe he was invincible, began to believe he was chosen to be the Hand of Bhral. With the Crown of Blood symbolising his worth, he would command his brood in battle and become the embodiment of his bloodthirsty god.

And yet Isabelle did not see his transition in a favourable light. She questioned his purpose, refused to watch his rituals. The blood and death she saw was frightening.

Fear began to manifest in her beautiful eyes, but he saw it not. He was blinded by his lust, consumed with a purpose dictated to him by his Patriarchs.

Until one day, as he walked with his most trusted Deios, he caught Isabelle standing at a gate leading away from their shelter. She stood alone, her clothing stained, her feet bare. Wild hair streaked with grime clumped half-way down her back.

'Isabelle,' he said, moving away from his Deios to step towards her.

She heard him approach, turned her head slightly, although she did not meet his eyes with her own.

'Why are you here?' he asked, his clawed hand resting on her shoulder.

She didn't respond at first. Instead, she stared back at the gate, her eyes looking through the wooden panels and beyond. When she finally spoke, her voice was so faint he found himself leaning close to hear her words.

'I miss my parents, Ra'tor,' tears rimmed her eyes. 'I miss my mother's arms about me, I miss my father's kisses on my cheek.' She raised her chin, stared at the crown sitting on his head. 'I have never felt so alone as I do right now. And I'm afraid, Ra'tor. Afraid you no longer care; afraid you no longer need me. I'm afraid I have no one to protect me.'

He listened to her words, wondered why she would be so distraught. She was surrounded by Deios. Few would dare seek her out to cause harm. An image of his morning ritual flared in his head. The smell of blood, the chants, the knife slicing flesh. A custom from a different time. Would Isabelle understand its worth? Could she see the ritual from their perspective? He hadn't given it any thought. Hadn't even contemplated the emotional impact on his little angel. So different, she was, so rare.

He remembered kneeling on one knee before her, placing both his hands on her shoulders. Tears began to steadily fall, her chest heaved as she sobbed.

Young, she was. Ra'tor had forgotten how innocent she was when he found her in the chapel. Even amongst the Deios, she would be considered a *bloodling*. To think of all she had endured in the time since. Hiding and running, constantly on the move. Surviving on instinct. And when she finally settled, finally found a semblance of safety, she was surrounded by Deios.

And for more days than he could remember, he'd been encouraging his brood to embrace the bloodlust.

Not once did he consider her feelings. Nor did he seek to placate her concerns.

He offered her nothing.

Now she threatened to leave.

'I am sorry, Isabelle,' he bowed his head, too afraid to seek out her eyes. 'I have failed you, my little angel. I have forgotten how important you are to me. I have been selfish.'

She lifted a hand, placed it over his. 'I know my family are most likely dead, Ra'tor, and you are all I have. Yet I feel alone. I have never felt so alone or afraid.'

He shook his head, snorted once for being both disrespectful and uncaring. He knew Isabelle was different. Knew she was special. Caught up in his own importance, he'd lost sight of who he truly was and how he came to be here. If it wasn't for Isabelle, he would have never returned to his Deios. He owed her his life. He owed her everything.

He let go of her hand, placed his own to either side of his head. Then with a swift gesture he lifted his bloody crown and threw it into the dirt.

'I am Ra'tor,' he said. 'I do not need a crown to define me, nor a daily ritual to remind me who I am. I beg your forgiveness, little one. I may have failed you, but now I am whole.

'I would die for you, Isabelle. I will always protect you.'

He watched her tears continue to fall, but the hint of a smile crept onto her face. A moment passed before she reached for him. Tiny arms wrapped about his neck. She clung to him with everything she had.

'I've missed you, Ra'tor,' she whispered into his ear.

'I've missed you, too, little one,' he replied.

That moment changed him.

For the better.

In the time since, he learnt everything he could from his little angel. She described the seasons to him, explained the difference between the cold, wet winter, and the welcome spring with its promise of life. Summer followed, the days long and the heat reminiscent of the weather on Dei, his home world. His brood grew with the daylight, wandering Deios summoned through the portal by his scouts, the promise of hunting for the Hand of Bhral inspiration enough. Skirmishes with Aquilans were commonplace. The occasional battle with wolfen a reminder of the dangers present. A handful of other beings were spied upon, lessons were learned concerning their prowess.

Everything he discovered, everything he'd been told, led to now.

He shaded his eyes from the setting sun, looked towards the pyramid as it glowed silver beneath a blue sky. It was to be his final prize. If he could regain control of the temple of light, his Deios would flourish. There was a chance, if he searched with intent, of discovering answers to the whereabouts of his Blood God.

If he could find Bhral, there was a possibility he could share the eternal hunt with him.

The heavy flap of leather wings sounded behind him. He looked over his right shoulder, saw Kors walking to his side, his *terrovyn*, Sin-cha, easing her taloned feet onto the tiled ground.

'Greetings, Hex,' he snarled at the lone hunter, thankful he and his pet were still amongst them. Ever since he found them, the hunter had threatened to return to Dei. But every day Ra'tor woke to find the Hex and Sin-cha peering with interest into the ruined city. The chance to hunt creatures never-before-seen kept Kors thoughtful. The prospect of gathering trophies equally so.

'The time has come,' Kors placed a hand on the pommel of his chopping blade, shared a glance towards the pyramid.

'Today we fight to reclaim the temple,' Ra'tor offered back, loud enough for those Deios lurking within earshot to hear. More than two thousand of his hunters ranged throughout the streets to either side, blades held in tightened grips. Five hundred more filtered through what Isabelle called the sewers, searching for neighbouring gates-between-worlds beneath the city. With their own protected, a chance to destroy or contain an enemy's gate was paramount. It could well dictate the outcome of the confrontation to come.

'The hunt will be most memorable, Ra'tor Bhra-vek,' Kors returned with a slight nod of his head.

He snorted his thanks. Even without his Crown of Blood, his Deios continued to call him Ra'tor the Blood King.

'The Aquilans will taste fear for the first time, Kors. Our blades will strike them hard; our feet will grind their flesh. And we will sing our battle hymns as one, a chorus of voices to drown out their screams.' He lifted his eyes towards Isabelle. 'Isn't that right, little angel?'

'It is, Ra'tor,' she smiled, her voice carrying on a gentle breeze.

A dozen of his strongest flexed their shoulders at his words. As he fell for the angelic sounds of Isabelle's voice, so too did his Deios when introduced to her hymns. As one they adored her, saw her as a gift from Bhral.

A horn blared from his right, signalling they were ready. Another followed to his left.

The sound of grinding chains echoed on the street ahead, a reminder of the Aquilan corpses they'd already caught and hung from wooden beams. Death lay before them, a path they willingly chose.

Pebbles scraped across paved stones as clawed feet became restless. The Aquilans, no more than dark shadows flitting before the pyramid, could be seen mobilizing, their ranks swelling. Another horn, shrill in the afternoon air, sounded from beyond their force.

'Was that an Aquilan call?' Kors asked, shading his eyes with a raised fist.

Ra'tor tilted his head, thought to recall the sound. He couldn't remember having heard it before. 'It might be theirs,' he answered, 'although it could be we are not the only force striking at the pyramid this day.'

Isabelle squirmed on his shoulder, a nervous twitch, perhaps, as the reality of battle became apparent. He knew she could feel the tension growing, just as he did. He could almost taste it.

He snarled, then raced his tongue over sharp teeth. With his two flanks ready, he could lead the charge. A signal was all they waited for.

Sin-cha flapped her leathery wings in agitation, restless to engage.

'Who is that?' Kors pointed a clawed finger towards a broken shelter ahead and to the right. A shadow detached from a stone wall, hooded in black, tall and broad. It moved to the centre of the cobbled path, then took long strides towards their position.

Its movement was confident. There was no hesitation.

Six of Ra'tor's Deios stepped before him, blades held before heaving chests. The creature came to a stop, a hundred feet separated them.

The breeze from the west ceased blowing. A heavy cloud drifted beneath the setting sun.

The creature was huge, stood at least eight feet tall with a straight back. Lost for words, Ra'tor watched scaled hands reach for its cowl.

The savage appearance of a Deios stared back at them.

A gasp sounded from his hunters. Eight ivory horns protruded from its head to form a circlet. Blood seeped from each, temporarily glistening as the fading sun shone one last beam of light before being swallowed by the clouds.

A Deios to his right fell to his knees. More followed, in quick succession, until every hunter who could see was now kneeling with head bowed.

'What is happening, Ra'tor?' Isabelle's voice quivered as her eyes swept to either side.

He didn't quite know how to answer. His tongue felt numb and heavy, he'd lost feeling in his hands they were clenched so tight. Kors and a dozen of his closest hunters still stood with him, but he could sense they were nervous.

'It appears our Blood-God, Bhral, stands before us little one,' he explained. And yet as he said the words, he felt a familiar sensation rip through his body. The one standing before them he had met before. He was certain it was he. The one who fed on the dying and the dead in a courtyard of blood. The one who chased them out of their shelter.

He was certain. He could feel the same numbing cold seep into his bones. The dread and the unknown. The power of one with incredible strength.

The one who carried fear as a cloak, ready to engulf you into the all-consuming black.

'Our Blood-God has arrived in our time of need,' he heard a Patriarch shout from his right flank. Ra'tor looked to the source, saw an emaciated Deios wearing a red cloth, scrawny arms held high in subjugation. 'We see you, my lord. We are here for you!'

'What is your bidding?' another Deios shouted as the one who was Bhral stepped closer. No other sound surfaced as he walked towards them. Only the heavy steps of their god crushing stones beneath his feet could be heard.

'We need to leave, Ra'tor,' Isabelle warned. 'I'm afraid.'

He felt her fear. Could feel her tiny hands digging into his shoulder. But as before, his body failed to respond. His mind screamed for him to turn about and run, but he couldn't move a muscle.

Bhral continued to close the distance. He was fifty feet away. The fear grew, morphed into an enormous wall of darkness that fell in behind the Blood-God, blanketing the city in the blink of an eye.

'Kill for me, my brood!' Bhral bellowed. His voice shook the ground. 'Kill everything you find. Embrace the red rage. Let the blood flow!'

Knees began to tremble. Ra'tor could feel his legs buckle. Bhral's glowing eyes locked onto his own. Hunters to his left and right suddenly ran into the darkened city, roaring their battle cries with brandished weapons. The will of Bhral was forcing him to the paved stones. Forcing him to lie down and surrender. Forcing him to die.

Isabelle's voice cut through the air like a silver blade. High pitched, pure, a sound to summon sunrays to pierce the darkness. Ra'tor felt his blood rush through his limbs, became aware he was holding his own blade with a clenched fist. He saw Kors standing with him, noticed a dozen of his strongest still on their feet.

'Come!' Ra'tor shouted, before stepping back a few paces. 'That creature is not our god. We must flee.'

'Are you sure?' asked Kors, doing his best to keep his hands from shaking.

'I am,' he replied. 'He is a shifter and an eater of the dead. We have seen him before. As your Blood King, I ask you to trust me. Come now, my brood. Follow me.'

Isabelle continued to sing with enough vigour to rouse those closest into action. As one they began to step away from the street. Startled eyes followed those Deios to either side as they swept with passion towards the pyramid and the guarding Aquilans. Blood would be spilt in a matter of moments.

Ra'tor took another step, then another. His pace quickened; his heart thumped in unison. Seconds later he was running away from the battle and heading towards their red-tiled shelter. Two score of his Deios ran with him.

But he knew he couldn't hide from Bhral inside the shelter. He would have to run further. He would need to flee into regions his Deios had yet to explore. Flee far from here in the hope the imposter would not find their gate-between-worlds.

He wasn't sure of his options once he stopped, though. He couldn't run for ever. At some point, he would need to turn about and face the one who called himself Bhral.

The Dark One.

The Imposter.

The Drinker of Blood.

CHAPTER THIRTY-FOUR

Laughter broke an awkward silence.

Ruvin lifted his tired eyes, saw Nae-oki and Rastan dancing together in the garden, golden sunshine bathing their twirling forms. The sight forced a smile to crease his weathered face, yet dark thoughts pulled it back seconds later.

He returned his attention to those seated about him. Kayla and Donal sat on the vibrant grass before him, their legs crossed, whilst Neema, looking every bit as old as he, sat next to him on a golden bench. The expansive garden spread beyond; the fifteen-foot walls hidden in the background.

It was the same view he shared every day for the last fifteen years.

'They have grown close over the years,' he commented, diverting their thoughts towards Nae-oki's laughter. Kayla peered over her shoulder, watched her son twine his body about Nae-oki's, his hands sweeping across her body. 'Do you think he's bedded her yet?'

'He's fifteen years old,' Kayla answered, although her words lacked conviction.

'Which means he is old enough,' Ruvin chuckled, despite the sombre mood. 'Besides, he is a man in every sense of the word. Look at him now, all fully grown. In all my years I have never seen such strength in an individual. Nor one with such poise. He has speed, endurance, flexibility. He has skills that defy belief.'

'We have taught him well,' Neema patted his bony knee.

'Will it be enough, do you think?' Kayla kept her eyes on her son.

Ruvin hoped so. For five years they'd prepared Rastan to be everything he could be. He was a Star-Born child connected in some fashion to the Ven. A herald of light in their most desperate time of need. At least so it had been written.

In some manner, Rastan was to free them of their imprisonment. He was to free them from the Palace of the Five Kings. He was to free the Ven from the Five Kings rule.

Until today, such notions of freedom were tied with the future.

Ruvin looked at the piece of parchment folded in his hands. It was a message handed to Nae-oki this morning as she wandered through the markets before daylight. Thia, the *ser-ti-ven* who helped Kayla deliver Rastan, passed it to her along with words from Kian. He was close, Thia mentioned, hiding on the outskirts of Ayoshos, the Golden City. It was said he planned to infiltrate the palace in the coming days.

He unfolded the parchment once again, narrowed his eyes to read the flowing script. It was written in the language of the Ven, yet he could read it as easily as any kingdom words. Like everyone else kept in captivity, the language of the Ven was now spoken with regularity and utmost proficiency.

'I'm still uncertain,' Donal queried once again, 'as to what we're supposed to be doing.'

Ruvin held the note close, read the words a final time. 'The Star-Born is ready. It is time.'

'Yes,' Donal held his hands up, 'but time for what? Is there something I should be preparing for? Or do we sit and wait for Kian to burst through the doors to rescue us?'

A hush sounded from Neema, followed by a stern look from the old matron. 'Keep your voice down, Donal,' she whispered back. 'We are as confused as you and share your fears, but the last thing you should do is panic. Act your age, Donal, you're not a young boy anymore.'

Neema was right. Donal was close to thirty years in age, a slight, slender man, one who seemingly refused to reach his full height. In fact, Ruvin mused, even at his age, with a crooked back and aching joints, Donal still only managed to reach his shoulder in height.

'I'm still unsure,' Donal returned. 'Are we certain leaving is our only option?'

'Aye, Donal,' Ruvin locked eyes with the young man. 'We can hide here until we take our last breath, but I wouldn't call it living. Here we are no more than pets in a cage. There is more for you to experience, especially at your age, for at its core life is about being challenged. There comes a time when you need to stand up and fight to survive. Now is the time.'

'And we're as uncertain as you,' Neema added. 'That's why we are sitting here contemplating Kian's words. Something is about to happen in the days to come. When it does, we need to be ready.'

'How are five of us supposed to escape the Palace of the Five Kings?' Donal wasn't convinced.

'There are six of us, including Reefe,' Neema reminded them.

'We've not seen him for years, Neema,' Donal shook his head. 'If we leave, he'll not be returning with us.'

Another burst of laughter from Nae-oki sounded from the garden. Ruvin tore his gaze from the parchment, saw Rastan holding the beautiful Ven woman above his head with his bronzed, muscular arms. One hand was on her waist, the other just between her shoulder blades. She squirmed, then rolled out of his grasp to land cat-like on the grass.

Rastan flicked his wild black hair over his shoulder and smiled, then held out his hand. No words passed between them, for he'd never spoken, but the look suggested they knew exactly what the other was thinking.

'The power of youth is a wonderful thing to behold,' Ruvin's voice remained low, yet everyone heard his words. How could they not? There was a stillness to the air, a calmness rarely perceived. It felt as though nature herself was holding her breath for what was to come.

'My boy is powerful, as you say,' Kayla also spoke quietly, 'yet I am more afraid today than at any other time in my life. I can't lose him, Ruvin. I'll die if I do.'

Ruvin stood to his feet, along with Neema, and stepped towards Kayla and Donal. Together they held out their arms, enticed Kayla and Donal to stand and share an embrace. For so long, all they had was each other.

Their arms entwined, tightly, as though no-one wished to let go. Tears slipped across weathered cheeks.

Ruvin was content to remain huddled with his family, but knew his words needed to be spoken. 'If it is time,' he wiped the end of his nose with the back of his hand, 'then I suppose I should take the boy into the garden.'

Neema stepped back, clutched her hands together before her chest. 'You speak the truth, Ruvin,' she offered a nod in confirmation. 'As Kian wrote, he is ready.'

The old man took a step, then another, convinced himself to walk towards the boy he'd taught for fifteen years. Everything he knew, every skill, every ounce of knowledge he could regale him with, had been given freely. Just as any father would teach his own son.

Rastan and Nae-oki smiled as he approached. He took his time, his aging body no longer conditioned to smooth movements with casual thought. Every step he took was one of concentration. A momentous effort to simply function without the consequence of pain. A product of an adventurous life. A life well lived.

'Thank you for your messages this morning, Nae-oki,' Ruvin offered her a smile. Her eyes changed from sparkling curiosities to moody storm clouds in an instant. Like everyone else, she knew their time here in the palace was about to enter uncharted grounds. As an oppressed *vos-ti-ven*, she was aware of the coming conflict. A morning frolicking with Rastan, a chance to dance with the boy she helped nurture into a man, was quite possibly her last.

Rastan's eyes locked onto Ruvin's. The boy was intelligent, incredibly so. It wouldn't take him long to decipher something was amiss.

'If you don't mind, Nae-oki, I need some time alone with Rastan if I may.'

Her eyes dimmed, simmered until they were a soft green, calming. Delicate fingers brushed across his frail hand as she passed. Rastan lent to one side, caught his eyes with an inquisitive look.

'Let's take a walk, my boy,' Ruvin pointed a finger towards a thick stand of trees in the middle of the garden. A *roaring tree* stood head-and-shoulders above the rest. He took tired steps in its direction. Rastan kept pace, the young man's hand reaching out to hold his elbow, helping him traverse the uneven ground.

The journey was short, yet he was out of breath.

A moment passed. He inhaled deeply to gather his courage. 'Dig here for me,' he nudged a tuft of grass between thick roots at the base of the tree.

Rastan obliged, knelt quickly, squeezed his fingers into the dirt. He worked tirelessly, his hands smothered with soft loam, copper-coloured worms wiggling between his fingers.

A pile of dirt formed to the side, rising, the smell of earth and life was strong.

A bundle of leather appeared beneath Rastan's probing hands.

'Pull it out, my lad,' Ruvin encouraged. 'Place it here,' he motioned towards a verdant patch of grass.

The bundle was teased from the earth and placed with care. Hiding his pain, Ruvin knelt beside Rastan and offered a smile.

'I hid this bundle when we first arrived,' he began, knowing Rastan was as curious as he'd ever been. 'It was entrusted to me by your father, before we crossed from our world to this. I was to keep it safe until he found us.' A tear slid down his cheek. The memory of Tarsin standing in a broken street, strong, defiant, a leader of men, sent a dagger into his heart. 'He was an incredible man, your father. A fighter like no other. Skilled beyond belief.' He placed a hand on Rastan's shoulder. 'I have never seen a swordsman to equal him.'

Ruvin leant forward, brushed a clump of dirt from the stained leather. It took a moment, and he was careful, but eventually the prize within was teased into the light.

'The twin swords you see here, Rastan, are called the Jaguar Blades. Although by right they belonged to your father, he never wore them. He had another blade, a Rykedian broadsword that he favoured. These beauties belonged to your grandfather, Arkos Vantos. They are also Rykedian.'

The sheaths were well protected beneath the soil, the blades within equally so. Ruvin lifted one before him, held it reverently for some time. Then he slid the blade from its sheath, marvelled at the balance, the beauty, the incredible shine of unblemished steel. Perfectly cut emeralds offered a glint of perfection, the jaguar's eyes resting in the pommel still lifelike after so many years beneath the ground.

A gentle nod suggested Rastan should take up the other blade. The young man reached for it, held it lovingly for ten heartbeats. Then he unsheathed the blade with a swift motion, allowed it to sing.

'The blades are yours, Rastan,' he offered his hilt first, wiped another tear bubbling along the lip of his eyelid. 'Your father, if he were here, would want you to have them.'

Rastan curled his fingers about the hilt and took the blade. Then he stood to his feet, a sword in each hand. Twin blades with a single edge, slightly curved. The Jaguar Blades. A kingly gift.

They sang for the first time in years as Rastan twirled them by his side. Effortless, cutting through the air without any resistance, sublime in both movement and balance.

Weapons of precision. Weapons of death.

'Look after them, my boy. I don't know what else to say, but you may have to use them in the days to come. Things are afoot. Our lives are about to become complicated. Be true to yourself, Rastan. We have taught you everything we know.'

The young man offered a nod, yet Ruivn could see the lad's eyes fixed on the twin blades, glassy as they contemplated his words. Along with everything else he taught him; the history of his father remained paramount.

'Your father sacrificed his life so we could escape,' he knew Rastan was aware of the details, but he said it again anyway. 'He fought for us to be free, to survive so we may return. Now it is our turn to save our stranded people. And you, my boy, will play an important role. You are the Dervani King. You will lead us back to the city of Bastion.'

Another nod of the head. It was enough. He was a boy no longer. Now, he would become the man they prayed for.

'Come, Rastan, it is time we returned.'

Ruvin watched him sheath the swords and roll them in leather before they made their way from under the *roaring tree* back to the gathering. Kayla watched their every step, Neema beside her with half a smile on her lips.

'It truly is time, isn't it?' Kayla took a step to embrace her son.

He was about to reply when the doors to their room opened to the sound of steel embossed staves cracking upon the tiled floor. Armoured Ven guards, a score in number, stepped into their abode with their conical helmets and vibrant plumes.

'By order of the Five Kings,' shouted the first guard to enter, a bright blue feather on his helmet denoting him as captain, 'those present are hereby summoned to the Sunshine Hall with all due haste. You have a moment to prepare. We will wait for you.'

*

He could see the panic in the eyes of his loved ones.

Rastan kept his own gaze low, swept the bundle of leather behind his back as he moved towards his mother. Together they stepped into their chamber, dressed quickly in clothes appropriate for an audience with the Five Kings. Loose fitting trousers, a leather vest and ankle high Ven boots were his favourite. It was to be enough, he believed, until his mother clasped a long black cloak over his shoulders.

'Here,' she whispered in his ear whilst handing him a leather belt. 'Place this around your waist and attach your swords. Keep them close to your body. Wrap your cloak about you to hide them.'

He did as she instructed, kept his movements calm. He could sense an enormous amount of tension in the air.

'Breathe, lad,' the voice of the Wise One intruded on his thoughts.

'I am breathing,' he offered, although a tingling sensation was spreading throughout his body that confused him.

The captain of the guards cracked his pole arm on the tiled floor. 'Your time has passed,' he shouted, dividing his Ven into two groups of ten. 'Fall in line.'

The captain moved out into the corridor with his ten Ven, waited for the survivors of Bastion to follow, the remaining Ven brought up the rear.

'I've no wish to see the Five Kings,' Rastan explained to the Wise One. *'If we are to be free, I believe now is the time to act.'*

'We have not received any sign from Kian.'

'I don't even know Kian,' Rastan snapped, *'I was a babe when he left. If I am the leader everyone says I am, then I make the decisions. I say we act now.'*

'Are you certain you can do this? What can we do to help?'

'Nothing,' he replied. And it was true. Never had he felt so in control of his own destiny. Everything was clear. The path he walked was now one of his choosing.

He looked over his shoulder at the Ven guards walking beneath the doorway. They tilted their heads forward slightly so their conical helmets wouldn't crack into the doorframe. It was all he needed.

Without a second thought he broke ranks with the column and raced to his left down an empty corridor. A shout came swiftly, curses chased him before the sound of swift footfalls echoed after his own.

He ran with purpose, recalling the corridors he must traverse from his first venture outside the palace proper, almost five years ago to the day. Shouts mimicked his footsteps; the clatter of steel harassed him. But he continued to run, his desire to reach the entry hall leading to the palace grounds his only option. He pushed open the first set of bronze doors, swerved to avoid a Ven standing guard, then raced across the patterned marble floor to reach the next set of doors. They were already open. Several Ven in gaudy clothing, both male and female, were passing through. He twisted his body, slipped past as startled faces traced his flight. Sunlight fell across his body as he stepped outside the palace for only the second time in his life.

'What is your plan now?' asked the Wise One.

'This is it. I provide a distraction. If my family are clever, they'll make their own way out.'

'Not if they're still guarded, they won't.'

'The guards followed me,' Rastan replied, and he was right. The blue-feathered captain and his twenty guards were spilling past the grand doors as he conversed. They fanned to either side, pole arms clenched and lowered, steel blades shining.

It was as he hoped.

He spun about to face them, his eyes baleful, his own hands clenched at his side.

'Halt this madness!' bellowed the captain, taking a single step forward. 'The Five Kings will not tolerate such brazen behaviour. You have been summoned!'

He remained silent, as he had his entire life.

A moment passed. He took a breath, felt the sun on his face. There was no breeze, few birds fluttered in the midday heat. But he could sense them. He could sense the birds and the insects, could sense the lizards and the crawlies. He could sense the *serrin* hiding amongst the trees.

A collection of Ven, visitors to the palace on this fine day, began to form a circle behind him, mirroring the one formed by the guards on the marble steps.

Another deep breath. He could hear the Core babbling inside his head. They were nervous, curious, somewhat perplexed by his behaviour.

It wasn't as long as he hoped for, but the excited voices of Ven onlookers became silent as the Five Kings appeared, stepping lightly past the twin sentinel trees and onto the grass before him.

'*Is this what you wished for?*' the Wise One made his voice heard from within.

'*It is. I am ready.*'

Ik'omi led his brothers to a position twenty feet away. They wore white leather that shone beneath the sun, carried silver blades at their hip. Their feet were bare.

'Where are you headed, Rastan Va?' Ik'omi smiled, looked beyond, towards the gate two thousand feet away. 'The path appears straight, child, but the *serrin* are many. They'll not let you past without our permission.'

Rastan shrugged, saw Ruvin and Donal sneak past the doors to hide behind the growing number of Ven now watching. His mother and old Neema were not to be seen, however. He prayed they were safe.

'You were fearful of them once,' continued the first-born king. 'Now you have grown. Would you like to see them again?'

'*I don't like the smirk on Ik'omi's face. Nor the look in his eyes, Rastan. They know who you are. What have you done?*'

Shien stepped forward, sent a shrill whistle to cut through the unmoving air. A moment passed before gasps could be heard amongst the crowd.

Rastan knelt, placed his hand atop the grass. A subtle vibration tingled against his palm. The *serrin* were coming, powerful legs launching heavy bodies past dense foliage and tall trees. He saw the first to arrive on his left. It was massive, corded muscles rippling beneath sparkling red skin. A matted blue-green mane blanketed its shoulders and head, swept down its spine.

Five more joined the first.

Silver claws twinkled in the sun.

'No soul has ever walked away from our palace before, Rastan Va, at least not without our consent,' Ik'omi took another step forward, his right hand caressing the hilt of his sword. 'You may believe you are special, so we've been told, but you'll not go far. We rule here, boy. Nothing happens on this world without us knowing.'

Shien and Vega joined him on the right, Ky'elk and Solaii stepped to his left. Their eyes appeared to reflect the sunlight; their movements became graceful. Every fibre of Rastan's being screamed for him to run.

He lifted his right foot, placed it forward and spun as he touched the ground. His arms reached out wide, collapsed inward, then went high. He twirled, began to dance as he and Nae-oki danced throughout the morning.

'Nice of you to dance for us, boy,' Ik'omi again, mocking his every movement with searching eyes. 'But we've seen you dance in the past. It will avail you not at all. Come, it is time you returned to your chamber.'

Ik'omi motioned for his brothers to step forward. They were close, merely ten feet away, seeking to crowd him. He continued to spin and leap, to move his hips and sway his shoulders. He recalled the lilting music he so often heard, danced like one of the greatest Ven dancers. He was one with the spirit, consumed by the force of nature.

The Five Kings drew their blades, threatening him to comply.

Rastan's arms folded in, across his chest, down to his waist. His hands snaked beneath the cloak he wore so tight.

He grasped the hilts of his twin swords. Drew the Jaguar Blades so they could sing.

A flash of light proceeded a ring of steel.

Ik'omi was the first to see the danger. Nimble on his feet, he backed away to level his own sword with Shien and Ky'elk. Solaii was not so quick to react. He stood in shock as a line of crimson stained his throat, bulging a second later to release a torrent of blood.

The snap of whipping blades drowned a chorus of screams. Vega pressed close, his two swords clashing with Rastan's, furiously beating like a hammer on an anvil. But the dance wasn't finished. Rastan found his rhythm, used his own strength to push back and slash his weapons into soft flesh. His speed was blinding, the audacity of his moves uncanny. By the time Vega fell lifeless behind him, he was already engaged with Ik'omi, Ky'elk and Shien.

A smile began to tease the corner of his lips as he continued to move. His eyes sparkled like the emerald stones embedded in the hilt of his blades. It felt as though his swords clashed a thousand times against those of the immortal kings, singing a song never heard before. Every lesson he'd ever endured led to this moment. The jumping and running, the climbing of trees and diving in the pond. The swordplay with duelling sticks when Ruvin was not so old. And the internal lessons taught by his myriad masters. Lessons with the Mercenary, the Swordsman, the Instructor and the Fighter, all fused with lessons from the Dancer.

He ducked a vicious cut from Ik'omi, kicked a foot into the knee of Shien. A second later he spun to avoid Ky'elk's thrust.

Rastan's smile grew wider. Shien whistled for his *serrin* to intervene, aware of the danger they faced. Only the enormous wild cats sat in silence, their muscular legs unmoving.

Rastan knew they'd remain seated; he could sense their mood. Likewise, he knew they sensed his own. A bond to be shared amongst caged animals. A bond greater than the threat of death.

Another swipe from Ky'elk, this one wide as fatigue began to seep into over-exerted muscles. Rastan took a chance, thrust a sword high, then pulled it low to slice across Ky'elk's thigh. The king fell with a whimper, raised his eyes in time to see a steel blade smash into his skull.

Ik'omi and Shien circled, a flicker of uncertainty in their movements. Three of their brothers lay dead. Their people watched in fright. They pressed with renewed vigour, sought to overpower the young man with strength and cunning. Hatred and frustration surged in their veins.

Yet the Jaguar Blades continued their music beneath the shining sun. Rastan's chest felt as though it would burst, his arms were on fire. A scream began to manifest inside his head.

He swayed to his left, lunged, then twisted in the air to knock a blade to the earth.

Blood arced as he spun once more. He became a summer tempest roaring in anger.

Shien caught one of his swords in his shoulder, Ik'omi clutched his stomach as the other sliced true. Sweat beaded on Rastan's brow. The sky called to him.

Rastan leapt into the air, his head thrown back, his long black hair flying wildly behind him. Both hands still held tight to his gleaming blades, dripping immortal blood.

Then he screamed.

It was the first sound he'd ever voiced. A sound of anguish after years of suppression, hidden beneath thousands of souls. It was a sound to be released, a clarion call.

A challenge, perhaps.

An awakening.

*

The pain gripping his body was relentless, yet the smile he shared with the sky was the widest it had ever been.

Ruvin lay on the grass outside the palace, Donal by his side with an arm wedged beneath his shoulder. A tightening in Ruvin's chest caused his vision to swim and his breathing was sporadic. It felt as though enormous, invisible hands were about to crush him.

Yet he continued to lift his gaze towards the sight of Rastan Va, the boy he raised, hovering twenty feet in the air as he screamed at the heavens.

It was a miracle, as incredible as the battle he just witnessed.

'Go,' he managed to grab a fistful of Donal's jacket, 'go and find Kayla.' He motioned towards the palace doors. Rastan was screaming still, a relentless barrage, a screech of torment causing Ven to flee as they covered their ears. He had no idea how long it would last. Prayed it would end soon.

Donal jumped to his feet and ran in the direction he pointed. Amongst all the confusion earlier they'd lost sight of

Kayla and Neema. If they were lucky, Donal would find them in quick fashion.

Wild hair and bloodied swords caught Ruvin's eye. What was Rastan doing? How was he levitating so high in the air? What could he do to make him stop?

A movement from beyond channelled his focus. The six *serrin* decided to move closer to the young man, loping with easy strides to rest beneath him whilst he hovered. Golden eyes fixed on Rastan, watched as he began to drift gently towards the ground.

His screaming ceased as his feet touched the grass.

It felt as though the world itself sighed in conclusion.

A spasm caused Ruvin's head to twitch. The pain in his chest intensified. He wished Rastan could reach him, but he had no strength to call him over. Instead, he watched him take three steps to the slumped body of Ik'omi.

The first king shifted his hips, propped himself on one arm. His other hand was pressed tight over his stomach, blood bubbling through his fingers. 'We heard you were Star-Born,' he managed to say, 'but we did not believe it.' A cough raked his body. Ruby droplets sprayed from this mouth, slid across his chin.

'I am many things, Ik'omi,' Ruvin heard Rastan speak his first words. His voice was powerful, like a deep rumbling shaken free from the earth.

A spasm gripped Ik'omi's face, but his eyes were curious, still seeking to know the one thing he couldn't comprehend. 'You've killed us all,' he spat a wad of speckled phlegm. 'How could you do such a thing?'

Ruvin could see Rastan's eyes burning with anger at Ik'omi's words. 'It was my only choice,' he replied. 'You and your brothers were tyrants, nothing more. The Ven here have no freedom. My family had no freedom. Nothing should be placed in a cage. Ending you and your brothers ends your ridiculous tyranny.'

Rastan placed the tip of one sword against the last king's chest. He lent his weight against it, pushed it deep. As the light began to fade from Ik'omi's eyes, Rastan spoke once more. 'Ven legend says there will come a time when the Fallen shall fall again. That time is now. Once you were something. Now you are nothing.

'You'll be remembered as the Gods who Fell.'

Ruvin fell backwards onto the grass. It was soft, cool on the side of his face. Footsteps approached.

Rastan's wild eyes and blood-spattered form appeared above. Ruvin looked to the boy who was now a man. Looked to the son he called his own.

'I'd like to believe we taught you everything we could, my boy,' Ruvin's voice was raspy, lacked volume.

'Can I help you?' Rastan knelt, dropped his swords. His hands were drenched in blood.

'No, lad. It's my heart. It's run its course,' he coughed, felt needles stabbing in a hundred places. 'I've lived long enough. I've seen you become a man. That is my reward.'

Tears welled; he could hardly see him. A hand clasped his own, held it tight. Ruvin tried desperately to take another breath, but his chest refused to expand.

'Thank you, old man,' the deep voice forced its way into his ears. Another hand cupped the back of his head. 'You'll always be my father. I love you, Ruvin Ciricello.'

A black mantle spread across his vision, sprinkled with a million stars.

He'd already taken his final breath.

LATER

The chambers of the Five King's Palace were vast.

Numerous rooms and halls could be found within, entire levels dedicated to showcasing Ven artifacts stolen centuries ago. They were mostly totems and statues from a different time, weapons claimed from those who fought against the Five Kings and lost. Glass cabinets contained rare stones found beneath the earth, interspersed with animal trophies and pressed flora. And then there were the sprawling kitchens, bathing rooms and halls designed for frivolities. Chambers for trading exotic goods and sampling unique foods weren't far away. It truly was a city within a city, except the denizens were chosen by the Five Kings. No beggars lined the pathways, prophets and naysayers were expelled. Everyone had their place, fulfilled a role.

It was true for every soul within the palace.

Even for Reefe O'Bannon.

For years he'd been free to do as he pleased, a directive handed to him by Ik'omi himself. In return he provided knowledge. Knowledge of his people, his home, knowledge of everything he could remember.

He could recall countless nights regaling the kings with stories of Bastion. He spoke of his adventures, his cunning, those he loved and those he fought.

He spoke of the pyramid, Aston's Tear, and the dark day that followed its awakening. And when he felt he had nothing more to share, they asked him to reveal everything he knew about those he travelled with. Especially about the boy known as Rastan Va.

As a reward, they allowed him to wander the palace and engage with the Ven, to experience the wonders they provided.

The years passed, blurred by the toxins flowing in his veins. For a time, he forgot who he even was or where he came from. He believed his life was perfect. Charmed because the kings told him it was so.

The last year was different, though. His habits declined; his mind became less clouded. Thoughts of Kayla Tolsten resurfaced. Instead of spending his days indoors, he began to wander the palace grounds, communicating with those guarding the gates and tending the gardens, learning what he could from a race he barely knew.

Everything he learnt led to now.

He bent low, placed his hands beneath Kayla's arms and lifted her to his shoulder. She was slender yet incredibly muscled, weighed more than he cared for. But once he passed under the northern gate, his passage would become easier.

He couldn't believe he'd come this far.

The morning routine of eating and lounging was well advanced when shouts in a neighbouring hall shattered the silence. Armed guards raced throughout the palace, calling to each other, issuing commands. Screams sounded moments later.

Somehow, Reefe found the will to seek out the cause of the disturbance.

Confusion and awe confounded his senses as he entered a hallway. Guards were being thrown against the walls, swept by an invisible hand. A screeching wind whipped clothes and the long hair of the Ven. He raised a hand to shield his eyes, saw old Neema standing amongst a dozen guards with clutching hands. They pressed close, sought to drag her down. Kayla stood behind her, fearful and alone.

Reefe stepped away from the hallway, raced through an adjoining room. He appeared moments later, ten feet behind Kayla via another passage. A small leather pouch containing a stimulant known as *farasti* found its way into his hands. He cupped a hand, filled his palm with azure powder. Then he took three quiet steps towards Kayla, pressed his powdered hand over her mouth from behind. She gagged, but he forced the powder into her mouth, made her swallow. For a non-user, it was enough to knock her out within seconds.

Thankfully, Neema was too preoccupied with her battle against the guards to witness his transgression. Kayla's brief struggle dissipated; his hands were quick to slide her out of the hallway.

Now he was at the northern gate, exhausted, it must be said, but relieved. News from the palace had already travelled outside. There were no guards to watch him pass, for they had been called inside. It was quiet here, peaceful.

He shifted Kayla higher on his shoulder, walked under the towering gate that resembled a twinning tree, looked down the street. A shadow detached itself from a laneway. A dark hood covered the face, but Reefe knew who it was.

'There you are,' Reefe spoke softly. 'Waiting, as you said you would be. I told you one day I would bring her to you.'

Quick steps saw the stranger standing before him. Dirty, clawed hands reached for the hood, pushed it back. The face of the man was primal, half covered by a mattered beard, his head was bald.

Reefe did well to hide his disgust. 'Here,' he passed the comatose Kayla to the stronger man, 'it's your turn to carry that which you seek.'

He was rough, but the easing of his burden was welcome.

'The Dark Lord will be pleased,' Jed Ironmonger spoke with a heavy voice. 'As requested, I will lead you to him and the portal you seek. I know the way. Come, it is best we do not loiter. We have a long road ahead of us.'

Reefe gave a solitary nod, wondered if he'd made the right choice. Like everyone else, he wished to return to Bastion. When he first stumbled across the crazed hunter prowling the streets outside the palace, he was promised a way home if he provided Kayla Tolsten. How could he refuse? The hunter had survived fifteen years living in the wild awaiting his prey. It was a small price, really. A price he was willing to offer for his freedom.

And who knew what might befall the hunter when the portal was found?

Who might be the hero to rescue Kayla from evil?

Reefe repositioned the pack he'd slung over his left shoulder. It carried necessities for the long road ahead. Ironmonger said the journey would take months, but they would arrive before the winter cold set in.

'Lead on, then,' Reefe's words carried to Ironmonger, already steps ahead of him. 'Do as you promised and lead me home.'

*

He had a choice to make.

Jarred, still wearing his Vulpan mask, stood inside Aston's Tear, shimmering golden-silver light from the rotating sphere bathing him. The hundred-foot corridor to the outside world lay behind him, the spanning bridge began where his feet now rested. For ten heartbeats he'd stood with mouth agape, the realization and enormity of his mission now dawning on him.

Irongate seemed so long ago.

It hadn't been, though.

He left the old watchtower earlier in the day, progressed towards Aston's Tear via the sewers until he reached a crumbled monastery bordering the pyramid. He wormed his way to the surface through a shaft designed to catch water, squirmed into fading sunlight and climbed the tallest brick wall he could find. There he sat perched like a decorative gargoyle, his eyes scanning the streets for a path inside.

Hope dispersed with the setting sun.

The streets were awash with hunters and fighters. Feathered Aquilan, scaled Deios and the enormously tall bull-headed Taur roamed close by. Wolf-like Lupen and the smaller fox-headed Vulpen skittered over debris to his left, the Ophidae and Murden to his right. Blaring horns signalled the battle, answering calls confirmed the carnage to come. Within moments blood-curdling shouts and roars of aggression mingled with the screams of the dying. He could smell spilt blood on the streets, saw the dark stains spread.

Then he saw him, the Dark Man never far from his dreams. The one he feared most. He saw him, marked him, felt the blood in his veins turn to ice. Those within sight of the Dark

Man became crazed, raced in all directions seeking blood and death.

Jarred watched him, mesmerized, caught in his hypnotic power. Then watched as the Dark Man shifted from Aquilan to Deiosian, from Deiosian to Lupan. Every street he roamed, every corner he stepped beyond. A sudden shimmer, a merging of flesh, scale and fur. Another commanding creature. A god to the race he now claimed as his own.

Night fell, and with it fled the spell. Free at last from Ahriman's alure, Jarred made his way to the paved stones below. With numb fingers now cracked and bleeding, he moved to an area of scattered dead, sought a path amongst the corpses. He kept low to the ground, kept alert to the prospect of approaching feet. Shadows became his friend, inviting and safe, kept him from the prying eyes of savage beasts.

The sun had set an hour past when he found his feet climbing red-granite steps. He moved in silence, careful, his breathing minimal. Bodies sprawled everywhere he looked, visible beneath morbid starlight and a gibbous moon. As he crested the final step the silver-blue glow of Aston's Tear took his breath away.

He tip-toed past broken bodies towards the darkened entrance. He could still hear the fighting, hear the curses and the screams. Horns continued to call, shrill whistles were accompanied by pounding feet and the clash of steel.

But he was a shadow of the night, all alone, silent as an elder contemplating his last moment of life. He was a fox-man, cunning and swift.

He found his way into the pyramid, sprinted the last hundred feet through the dark hallway. He'd been here before, felt comfortable with his surrounds.

Now he was standing before the spanning bridge, the portal spinning with raw power, his heart racing. The *Nepharii Uranometria* was close, sitting in its recess on the elegantly carved lectern.

Yet he stalled, for the fighting outside was replicated within. Large warriors with heavy cleavers clashed and growled before the glowing sphere. He could not move between them for fear of being struck. He was too small to stand against them, too frightened to even try.

The noise of stomping feet echoed down the hundred-foot corridor behind him. Reinforcements were arriving. Or enemies. Or another race altogether. Jarred had nowhere to go.

On a whim he squatted to the floor and swung his feet over the edge of the bridge. Then he lowered himself until only his fingers held his weight. He could sense the vast void beneath him, see the myriad stars shining along the outer curved wall. He could not see the floor. There was only darkness at the greatest depth.

Footfalls came close, passed swiftly. The fighting before the sphere continued. He thought to pull himself up and onto the bridge, but months of hiding at Irongate had weakened him, his strength was gone. He felt exhausted and frail, had nothing more to give. Thoughts of failure swam in his mind. He was so close.

His fingers, already bloodied, slipped an inch.

The sigh of one defeated came next.

He let go . . . and fell without a sound.

*

The faint screams of the dying still reached their ears.

Tarsin Va, king of Dervae, walked a path well-trod as he contemplated their next move. For an entire night he and his men listened as battle was waged for Aston's Tear. The prospect of engaging lay heavy on their minds. Without reinforcements from the Southern Field, the venture was seen to be folly. Cale Griffith agreed. So did the Panthians, Tahu and Zai. There was little they could achieve with so few. When the requested aid arrived, decisions could be made. Until then, it was a matter of waiting out the night.

He never knew a night could be so long.

And yet as dawn crested those buildings still standing in Bastion, a sense of urgency began to infuse every fibre of Tarsin's being. The city was teetering on the cusp of being lost. He could feel it. He needed soldiers.

And yet hours later, as the sun reached its zenith, the soldiers he yearned for had yet to arrive.

'Still no sign of Will and his men,' Griffith stomped from the direction of the tower. Three men were positioned at the highest level, eyes searching for activity.

'And Aston's Tear?' Tarsin asked in return. 'Do they continue to fight?'

Griffith stretched his broad shoulders, lifted his face to the warming sun. 'Aye, they still fight. Skirmishes, mostly, but there are too many to handle if you're thinking of heading in with just our thirty men.'

He thought as much, knew a venture into the city would be a risk.

'Sometimes,' Griffith moved closer, 'you need to take a step back before you can go forward. Perhaps now is such a time. We need to know what is happening in the Southern Fields. We need to know where our councillors are, where Will Tolsten has ended up. We could do with John Rhys, Lloyd Henrickson and Inesco by our side.'

Tarsin nodded at his friend's wise words. Nen said his path would cross the Dark One's at some point. There was no need to rush on his behalf. It would happen.

'You're right,' he slapped the big man on the shoulder. 'I feel as though I've been pushing our path forward through will alone, because Aston's Tear is my goal. Maybe the fork in our path is suggesting otherwise.'

'So, what are your plans now?'

'As you said, we need men, experienced ones at that. I believe it's time to discover what's keeping Will from returning to us. I have an inkling as to what it may be.'

'The Southern Lords,' Griffith almost snarled the words.

'The very same. We've been absent for months. A shift in power has most likely occurred. There will be a new leader amongst the ranks.'

'So, we march to the Southern Gate instead, find out who is pulling the strings.'

'Aye, I don't believe we have a choice.'

'It could be dangerous. The Southern Lords will not relinquish their newly won power. If you stride into their camp demanding they bend the knee, they'll most likely behead you for treason.'

'It's a possibility,' Tarsin shared a smile, knew such an outcome was likely, 'but we've men and women of our own who will fight for our cause. In the end, we have a single task. We must find the Dark One and kill him. Everything else will fall into place once we've accomplished such a deed. It's time we had a little faith.'

'I have faith,' Griffith's grin split his red beard. 'I have faith in whatever decision you make. You are my king, Tarsin Va. I'll follow you into Hell's Domain if I must.'

'Remember that, big man, when blood stains the streets and the dead begin to fester, for Hell is never far away.'

A gut-wrenching scream sounded to the east, no more than two streets away. Griffith clapped his arm over Tarsin's shoulder and pulled him close. 'I think it's already here, my friend.

'And like you, I am ready.'